Jess Haines ° PO Box 7634 ° Clearwater, FL 33758

www.JessHaines.com ° jh@jesshaines.com

SMOKE and Mirrors

BLACKHOLLOW ACADEMY: BOOK ONE

BY

JESS HAINES

www.JessHaines.com

To the man who makes me smile. I love you, baby.

Chapter One

"Someone saw you."

For an instant, Kimberly's breath caught, thinking her teacher meant someone spotted her stealing more than her share of food in the school lunch line again and reported her thievery. Then her heart constricted in terror as the real meaning behind Professor Reed's words sunk in.

She had to swallow several times before she could choke out a few words around the lump that had formed in her throat. "I thought you weren't going to tell anyone until after the finals?"

"It couldn't wait," the professor said. "I overheard Professor Lim in the teacher's lounge mention what he saw as cheating during your last couple of practical assignments. You know you're not supposed to use illusions for that."

So it was true. She was out of time. The other students and teachers—the *real* magi—would soon know she wasn't truly one of them.

"I had no choice. How else can I pass the class?"

Kimberly's sputtered protest echoing in the vast, empty lecture hall was met with a flat stare. The professor set one hand on her desk, fingers splayed like a scorpion preparing to leap upon prey as she tapped an impatient rhythm with one finger. Her familiar, a sleek hawk on a standing perch set a few feet behind the desk, cracked one dark eye to focus on the source of the sound before fluffing its feathers and resuming a state of rest.

"If you had come to me to discuss it first," Professor Reed said after a long, thoughtful pause that did an excellent job of further fraying her student's nerves, "we might have found some alternative. Regardless, it's too late now. We knew this had to happen eventually. The good news is that the dean and faculty accepted my vouching for you and they will not strip you of your magic out of hand. The bad news is that they will be alerting the parents and local covens that there is a sorcerer attending Blackhollow Academy and the dean will be keeping very close tabs on you for the remainder of the school year."

"How bad is it? How much danger am I in?"

"Bad enough. You have a rough road ahead of you. You need to watch your back, more than ever, and I won't always be there to keep you safe."

Clinging tightly to either side of the flat wooden stool she sat upon, Kimberly fought against the urge to sink to the floor and pray for it to swallow her up. Her mouth moved, but no sound emerged. Dreams of clawing her way out of poverty through graduating from Blackhollow as an accepted member of mage society and finding a place in a coven were vanishing before her eyes.

The tightness around the professor's eyes grew into deep furrows as she frowned at her student, spidery digits tensing as she leaned over the desk. "Don't give up hope yet, Miss Wells. As I said, they are not stripping you of your magic outright, which is more than could be said for any other sorcerer discovered in the five boroughs since the 1800s. If—*if*—you graduate without incident, you will be granted the legitimacy no sorcerer has had claim to since the Dark Ages. It's too much to hope that the other students will not figure out that it is you. They will test your patience and your resolve. However, as I chose to sponsor you, I expect you to live up to my expectations and not retaliate to any teasing or bullying. You *will* graduate, and you will do so without incident. Yes?"

Kimberly hadn't even considered what the other students would think of her once they knew she wasn't a true mage. Not like the rest of them. She'd been too busy worrying about having what little power she had stripped from her to even consider that aspect of her "condition" until that moment.

Her voice was little more than a whisper once she managed to find it again. "I... Professor, I can't—"

"You can."

"They'll hate me. They'll try to—"

"Their like or dislike has no bearing on your own conscience, abilities, or competence. The only one who can prove you would never use your powers for ill is you. You made it this far without doing so, did you not?"

"I did, but I can't summon. Professor Lim must have seen through the fakes I conjured. You said weeks ago you had a solution to that for me, right? I need a familiar, don't I? If I can't summon one, I can't pass the finals."

"That's correct, you need a familiar to graduate."

"So... am I pretending some other way? If he can see through the illusions, I don't see what else I can do."

"No, absolutely not. Now that the other teachers know there is a sorcerer in the student body, they'll be on the lookout for the signs and use any excuse they can to discredit you. You realize that cheating is grounds for expulsion?"

Twitching fingers went still. Then tugged so hard that the loose string on the hem of her shirt Kimberly had been toying with broke, her voice coming out as no more than a strained whisper. "Expulsion?"

"Yes. There's no room for games anymore. You may not be a mage, but you are still my student. Time is running out, and I don't want to see a repeat of that incident from your second year."

Kimberly flinched at the reminder of her failure, and how the professor had unearthed her dark secret. She had missed three days of work and had sported sickly pinkish scars on her arms for weeks after. It was one of the few times she had been thankful for being so different from the other magi; her illusions made it possible to hide her wounds from her mother and her coworkers.

Before she could open her mouth to protest, Professor Reed continued.

"I shouldn't have to remind you that cheating by using illusions to make it *look* as if you have mastered a skill is dangerous. Not only for you, but for your classmates and teachers. I shouldn't need to point out that you won't be able to fool the senior staff at exams."

"Professor, please, I didn't mean—"

"Stop that, now. Excuses won't help. Something needs to change."

Kimberly reddened, heat blossoming in her cheeks. "I've been trying my best to master summoning, but nothing I do is working. It's not as easy for me to find a workaround for it as it was for the other arts."

"I know. That's why I called you in to see me."

Kimberly bowed her head, waiting for the inevitable. She expected to be forced into private lessons which she couldn't possibly fit into her schedule or afford. Having a bit of supernatural power at her fingertips didn't mean she could magically make money appear in her bank account. Unlike the magi she was pretending to be, she didn't have the ability to alter the nature of physical objects to create food or shelter. She could fool someone else to make cardboard look and taste like pizza or vice versa, but true transmutation was beyond her.

There were still nights where the thought of using her skills to pass a few scraps of paper for dollar bills didn't seem like such a bad idea. Nights she went hungry when tips weren't so good. With all her time spent studying magical arts, she didn't even have a G.E.D. yet. This meeting was already making her late for work, and she prayed her boss would cut her some slack. She couldn't afford to lose any more hours—or her job.

"You're a gifted illusionist, Kimberly. I won't deny it. But if you can't summon a familiar, you'll need to find something with fae blood already on this plane to bind to you."

That was not what she was expecting. "I thought both you and Professor Lim said we're not supposed to bind Others. Isn't that against the rules?"

A grim smile briefly quirked Professor Reeds' thin lips with a ghost of approval. "I'm glad you've been paying attention in class. However, seeing as you aren't like the other students, I think your situation merits special circumstances. If you can find an earthbound supernatural creature powerful enough to offer a measure of protection and convince it to consent to a binding—*convince*, mind, not coerce with your skills—then you should take advantage of the opportunity."

"Wait, this is... So you're telling me I should ignore the cardinal rule of Other etiquette? How am I supposed to convince—

what am I supposed to convince? I'm guessing other magi and elves and vampires are right out—"

The professor held up a hand, nipping off the full-fledged ramble Kimberly was building up in the bud.

"Fae blood, Kimberly. Of course vampires don't fit that mold. And no elf or mage would ever agree to such a request, or any other humanoid, for that matter. Review your planar studies textbook again. The rule is never to bind *against the will* of the potential familiar. If you can get one to agree to work with you rather than taking it by force, there would be no breech in the Accords and no reason for you to worry about retribution. That aside, you should be on the hunt for a creature that will be powerful enough to deter your fellow students—or any of their parents, for that matter—from attempting to corner you, which also means you would want its full cooperation."

The professor turned away for a moment, leafing through a stack of papers on her desk. The rustle of shifting papers was extraordinarily loud in the cavernous classroom. Kimberly's foot twitched nervously in the interim, though she forced herself back to stillness once the professor tugged a single sheet near the bottom free and slid it across the desk.

It took a long moment for Kimberly's glassy stare to focus on what was on the paper. Her eyebrows slowly crept toward her hairline as she took in the neatly penned list of Others known to live in the area. A few made sense to her. She had seen gargoyles guarding numerous buildings throughout the city, and was very familiar with the names of the local werewolf packs and influential vampires. She had even had drinks in one of the vampire clubs once, on a very ill-advised date that she'd sooner forget.

Frowning, she skimmed down to the less obviously humanistic creatures on the list. Some were as foreign to her as another language, but there were many recognizable types she hadn't expected to see inhabiting New York City.

"Faeries? We have faeries in Central Park? I didn't realize... Oh, man. There's no way a unicorn would give me the time of day. A gryphon, maybe? No, I don't even know how to talk to one... Wait. A *dragon?* There's a *dragon* in New York?"

"Several, actually. Your choice is ambitious, but I believe you've made the correct one." The professor tugged the paper out of Kimberly's grip and returned it to its place in the stack before her student had a chance to spit out the 'you've-gotta-be-kidding-me' on the tip of her tongue, then folded her hands and leaned across the desk. "Now, let's be honest here. I am aware of your monetary troubles, which means you can't afford the special tutoring you require, or the bribes it would normally take to seek an audience with the local draconic representatives—"

"But I don't know any—"

"—so I'm going to recommend you speak to Cormac Hunter. He can direct you where to find what you need and tell you how to get it."

Kimberly wasn't sure herself what she needed. Dazed, she took the thick, cream-colored business card her professor slid across the desk and into her numb hands. Aside from the hours of work she'd miss going on a ridiculous hunt like this, the thought of asking a dragon to be her familiar filled her with dread. Not only did she have little to nothing to offer a creature so powerful and influential, they were cunning, crafty, and had been known to eat magi. Not for a few hundred years, of course, but there were documented cases.

Then it occurred to her that her professor was reminding her in a roundabout way that dragons had hoards. And a dragon as a familiar had to be considered a golden ticket into a coven. No one would want to turn her away with a dragon at her command, even if she could barely summon enough spark to light a campfire.

Even if she wasn't *really* a mage. Even if they normally killed her kind on sight.

Maybe she wouldn't even need a coven to support herself if she had a dragon familiar. At the very least, she'd never have to count on stale pastries to tide her over until payday again.

"Cormac is expecting you this evening."

That pronouncement brought Kimberly crashing back to reality. "But I have to go to work!"

"Yes, yes, I know. I made you an appointment for 10:30PM. His office is only a few blocks from that coffee shop of yours. If you bring him an extra hot latte, heavy on the cream and hazelnut syrup, that should offset any hard feelings he will have about your request."

Kimberly gave a reluctant nod, staring down at her hands, not really seeing the text on the business card, only briefly registering that the letters were printed in silver foil. She couldn't help but worry about what the next school day would bring—and why the professor was so intent on helping her survive it.

"Kimberly."

Dazed, she looked up, meeting the fierce green glow of her professor's gaze and doing her best not to flinch from the sparks of power that danced in the depths of her teacher's pupils.

"You can do this. Now get moving. Stay alert. And good luck."

Grabbing her backpack and stuffing the card into her jeans pocket, she ran out of the classroom, not looking back.

Chapter Two

As Kimberly rushed down the hall, she kept glancing from side to side, and then behind her. The multihued globes of light suspended at intervals between now-empty classrooms allowed no shadows, but the skin between her shoulder blades itched, as though she was being watched.

In the morning and early afternoon, this place would be bustling with activity and she'd be lucky to sprint more than a few steps at a time. This late in the day, the squeak of her sneakers on the marble tiles was the only sound echoing in the hallway, which opened into a cavernous room ringed with columns of pale rose stone. The skeleton of a rearing unicorn faced those of a plunging dragon in the center; a nod to the *Barosaurus* and *Allosaurus* in the Theodore Roosevelt Rotunda in the Museum of Natural History several stories above.

Aside from the architecture and arrangement of the bones, there was little about the room that bore any resemblance to the museum. Caged juvenile salamanders—summoned planar beings made of fire, not the amphibious sort—hung from decorative golden cages scattered throughout the room and cast enough warmth to dispel the sensation of being underground. Illusory daylight shone through the arched windows high above. Between most of the columns, separated by their own queues of velvet-roped stanchions to form orderly lines, were gigantic mirrors surrounded by stone frames etched with numerous arcane symbols on the sides. Each mirror had a huge imprinted metal label on top advertising one of several convenient locations—Central Park, Grand Central Station, both JFK and La Guardia airports, to name a few—all in multiple languages.

Kimberly looked around one last time, verifying there were no small familiars, such as insects or mice or the like, following her. Then she hitched her backpack higher on her left shoulder and stepped into the "77th and Columbus" mirror.

The tingle of the Gateway's magic whispered against her skin like unseen cobwebs. The brisk April wind did not.

Shivering and tugging her jacket closed, she rushed away from the gate that was disguised as a conjured deep shadow beneath one of the trees lining the street. She fell into pace beside a man about her height who was headed in the same direction. With a brief extension of her will, she made it appear to any prying eyes as though she continued on at his side, using him as an "anchor" for her illusory self while she stayed where she was, making her true self disappear. She couldn't manage full invisibility, but by bending the light around herself—she'd seen an alien do that in a movie once—spotting her without the aid of tracking magic would be nigh impossible.

Some of the tension in her shoulders eased as the sense of being watched faded with the growing distance between herself and the man trailed by her illusory doppelganger. Once they turned a corner, she dropped her makeshift camouflage and picked up her pace to beat the blinking red hand at the crosswalk. She had no watch or cell phone to check the time, but judging by the angle of the sun, she was going to be at least twenty minutes late for her shift.

Buildings with chrome and marble facades flew by, soon replaced by brick and glass. She bolted down the street, dodging pedestrians, trees, hot dog carts, and even the occasional cab as she rocketed through crosswalks. The scents of the city drowned out the spring growth, sporadic patches of trees, bushes and flowers barely noticeable under the coffee and pizza and hot pastries and alcohol and urine and smog all vying for dominance.

Breathing hard, she slid to a halt in front of Allegretto's Café, just a few blocks north of the theater district and a little too far from Times Square to attract many tourists on foot. It was more a bakery than a café. The mouth-watering scent of fresh vanilla custard, chocolate cannoli and anisette biscotti that wafted out as she pulled the glass door open attested to that. Don Allegretto insisted they were a family establishment first, a coffee house second, a bakery third, and anything else dead last.

She thought Don's priorities were hilarious considering the flyer for the latest Mothers Against Others neighborhood meeting taped to the glass inside, right next to the café's hours of operation. The agenda for the latest meeting included "how to talk to your kids about saying no to vampires" and "spotting the signs of glamour in your loved ones." Don or his wife must have posted the flyer that morning, seeing as it hadn't been there when Kimberly locked up the night before. Most of the time Don was a nice guy, but he didn't have a clue what Kimberly was and had said a few unkind things about Others in front of her that had set her teeth on edge.

Shaking her head over the flyer, she slipped inside. A couple were browsing the displays of pastries, affably arguing over whether to split a few biscotti or rainbow cookies along with their coffee, and old Mister Grimaldi was checking out the racks of fresh-baked bread. Kimberly nodded and waved to Annabelle, the clerk she should have relieved 18 minutes earlier. The clock behind the register ticked forward another minute, the hands moving like an accusation. A moment's concentration made Kimberly's simple T-shirt under her jacket look like her work shirt, and dispelled any signs of sweat or B.O. from her mad dash across town.

Her stomach growled as the warm, mouth-watering scent of pastries and coffee washed over her. Despite the anxiety twisting her stomach into knots, hunger was rearing its ugly head. She had a fleeting wish that she could cast an illusion on herself to make either the scents or the hunger disappear, but while she could fool anyone else's senses with her magic, she was immune to her own phantasms.

Ignoring her stomach growling, she moved behind the counter. Annabelle turned from the cappuccino she was making, pointed to the clock and mouthed, 'I gotta go. You got this?'

Kimberly nodded. She tossed her bag under the register counter and shrugged out of her jacket before taking over for Annabelle. The tall, willowy blonde shot her a weary smile and blew a few errant tendrils of hair out of her face as she got out of the way. A few quick hand signals later and Kimberly had all the info she needed about who had ordered what and who still needed to pay, and Annabelle was bolting out the door.

In a few moments, Kimberly handed the couple two cappuccinos, two rainbow cookies, and one fig-walnut biscotti to share, and Mister Grimaldi was settled with two loaves of his favorite sesame bread and a rosette. She breathed a sigh of relief into the quiet once the last customer shuffled out, giving her a moment of peace to sag against the back counter with the espresso machine and coffee maker and relax.

"Kimberly! Get your ass in my office," rumbled a deep, male voice.

Cringing, she twisted around to meet her boss's glare, hoping the heat on her cheeks from her guilty blush wasn't too obvious. "Sure, Don. Just give me a minute to finish cleaning."

Don stood by the kitchen door, currently propped open by his steel-toed boot. His thinning hair was hidden under a bandana and his long-sleeved Rolling Stones T-shirt was rolled up past his elbows. He watched her rinse off the mixer and finish wiping the counters, his flour-covered hands clasping his thick, hairy forearms. As soon as she was done, he stepped aside, still holding the swinging door open for her.

She headed straight to his office, a tiny closet of a space made even more claustrophobic by the addition of a filing cabinet, chipped Ikea desk, and single rolling chair. There was a security monitor perched on the desk that he used to keep an eye on the front. The camera was angled down to catch anyone entering or leaving, as well as view the contents of the register.

Don waited until she was inside. The office door banged shut behind his bulk and he moved around his desk to place his knuckles on it, leaning forward. The fiberboard creaked alarmingly under his weight. "What time does your shift start?"

Miserable, Kimberly stared down at her shoes. "Four. Sir."

"And what time was it when you arrived?"

"4:18, sir."

Don heaved a deep sigh, his tone mellowing as he eased into his chair. The leather squealed almost as much as the rusted wheels as he settled back. "Kimberly, I like you. You're a good kid, but I need you here *on time*. At least give me the courtesy of a call if you're running late. I can't keep paying the others overtime when you don't show. This is the last warning I'm going to give, kiddo."

She nodded, dragging her gaze up from her shoes to focus on the curling laminate that was peeling off of the fiberboard on the edge of his desk instead. "I'm sorry. I would have called, but I don't have a phone. One of my teachers wanted to talk to me after class and I couldn't say no."

"You're the only kid I know who doesn't have their own cell phone. Hell, my six-year-old daughter has an iPad."

Your kid doesn't depend on a single parent who works minimum wage part time jobs, she carefully didn't say. Instead, she mumbled, "I'm really sorry, Don. I'm almost done with school. As soon as the first week of May rolls around, I'm out."

Out of this job. Out of this life. Into a coven with people who understood and valued what she could do. Even if she had to carve a position out herself, prove to them she wasn't dangerous. She had to make it work, otherwise she'd never make more than the pittance she did as a barista and sometime-baker for Don. That, or she might spend the rest of her life on the run from angry magi who wanted nothing more than to get rid of her.

Don's eyes narrowed, lines appearing around his mouth. She wished she'd thought to say something else, something that wouldn't make him suspect she planned on walking out of this place the moment she had something better lined up, but movement on the monitor drew his eye off her.

"Customer. Go take care of it."

With a relieved nod, she headed back to man the register, plastering on a smile she didn't feel as she greeted another one of their regulars.

For the rest of the evening, business was brisk. The moment one order was filled, another customer took the last one's place. It got busier as the evening wore on, people strolling in looking for dessert or an after-dinner coffee. Don emerged from his office around 8PM to prep the bread, croissants, muffins, scones, danishes and rolls for the morning shift, as well as popping in to check on Kimberly and lend a hand now and then when things got too busy. He even laughed when she teased him about the dabs of flour on his face.

A couple hours after sunset, midway into Kimberly's shift, a vampire and her human companion came into the shop together. The two weren't doing a thing to hide what they were, and were practically joined at the hip with each others' hands in the other's back jean pockets. Her eyes glimmered with a touch of red from some strong emotion—maybe hunger, or maybe she was turned on by the guy's touch—and every time she laughed or smiled her fangs peeked out behind lips painted a slick, shiny red. The guy had fresh bite marks on his neck, along with a patchwork of similar scars that he hadn't bothered to cover with so much as a band-aid. His free hand was constantly roving, brushing against her cheek, twining with her hair, and his smile was deep, genuine, and infectious.

The pair got in line, and the man gestured to a couple of things in the display the vampire didn't see since she was so focused on leaving a few lipstick imprints as she got on tiptoe to pepper his cheek and jaw with kisses. Kimberly grinned. The two made a cute pair.

Once they reached the counter, Don not-so-surreptitiously interposed himself between Kimberly and the couple, and he called over the woman bundled in a thick wool duster behind them.

The vampire frowned, and the guy looked over his shoulder as the lady stepped around him to take their spot in line. When the vampire opened her mouth to protest, her companion shook his head and pulled her aside. The lady in the duster edged around them with a furtive, guilty look, then ordered a cappuccino and a couple of pastries.

"Don, scoot over, I'll take care of those two."

He shook his head, gesturing for Kimberly to get the woman's drink. Casting a helpless look at the vampire and her beau, she did what she was ordered. She focused on the hiss of the espresso machine and breathing in the sweet, heavenly-scented steam as she silently counted to ten so she wouldn't say something she'd regret later. It wasn't fair, but she had already screwed up once tonight and couldn't afford to risk alerting Don to what she really was. She thought it was unfortunate the two hadn't taken notice of the flyer in the window; they might have realized sooner that Others weren't welcome here.

As soon as the woman in the duster was served, Don leaned over to see around the vampire and her donor as they stepped up to the counter so he could wave the next couple in line forward. The vampire growled softly, sending everyone but the guy at her side skittering back a step or two. Kimberly tensed, her stomach knotting as she prepared to summon what little elemental energy she could if things got ugly.

The vampire's voice was sweet and melodious, commanding attention. "Pardon me, but I do believe we were in line first."

"Go ahead," the guy behind her said, his jerky wave at the counter speaking of his nervousness. "I'm not in a rush."

"Forget it. It's my shop, and I'll serve people in whatever order I want," Don said.

The vampire set her hand on top of the glass display, leaning forward. "What is the problem here? Why won't you serve us?"

"We don't serve your kind here," Don snapped.

Save for the vampire and Don matching glares, and Kimberly's horrified focus on Don's stubborn expression, every eye in the room was roving to find anything else to look at.

Kimberly could have told Don that meeting the vampire's eyes was a terrible idea, but she couldn't risk blowing her cover and losing her job. He wasn't in much danger anyway. The vampire would be hunted down and killed if she did something so blatant as to mess with Don's thoughts in front of so many witnesses, even for something as relatively insignificant as making him change his mind about serving them some pastries. Black enchants like that were illegal for good reason.

Don's discrimination against serving Others was also illegal, but no one—including the only other Other in the place—was up to meeting the vampire's shocked gaze as she scanned for anyone who might support her and call Don out on his bigotry. Even her companion wasn't up to it, tugging her arm to get her to follow him out.

"Babe, come on. They obviously don't want our business. We'll give 'em a shitty Yelp review and hit Starbucks instead."

The vampire gave one more half-hearted growl before giving in to her lover's urging, stalking out of the café with him.

For a few moments, everyone stayed right where they were, unmoving, not speaking. Then Don shook his head and waved at the next couple in line, who were both still staring out the window. Everybody jerked into movement simultaneously, busying themselves with forgetting what they had just witnessed, chattering nervously to each other or focusing too intently on the cookies and pastries behind the glass bakery display case.

Kimberly kept her head down and immersed herself in her work, silently repeating her mantra: *You need the money. Stick with it until you graduate. Just a few more weeks to go. You can do this.*

She prayed the sweet scents of coffee, sugar, and buttery pastries wouldn't provoke nausea everywhere she went after she left this job behind.

Things were strained between Kimberly and Don for the remainder of the night, but the shop closed on time at 10PM. Kimberly finished tying off the last of the bags of leftover cookies and other sweets. The day old bags always sold out within hours of opening the next morning. There were no croissants or loaves, but there were three rosettes. Don had finished reconciling the register a few minutes prior and handed over her share of $14.27 in cash from the tip jar after she put the last bag of cookies in the discount basket on top of the glass display case. She did her best to hide her disappointment at the paltry sum, stuffing the money in her pocket, where the brush of the parchment-like business card against the back of her hand reminded her she had somewhere to be in half an hour.

As she shrugged on her jacket, Don nudged her arm on his way back into the kitchen.

"Take some of the day olds," he said. "On the house."

Don handed her a bag full of the leftover sweets, then a second one for some rosettes. Kimberly flushed and stammered out thanks that he waved off before the door swung shut behind him. She stuffed the puffy sandwich loaves into a second bag, then buried the food in her backpack. Then remembered she was supposed to bring a coffee, too.

Yanking two singles out of her pocket along with the card, she slapped the money on the counter for the drink, knowing Don would find it later.

Soon, she had the address to some place called the Wild Hunt memorized, an extra hot café latte (heavy on the cream with two shots of hazelnut) in hand, and braced herself to face a total stranger to ask him to help her do the impossible. Wrapped in her threadbare jacket and armed with sweets, she huddled against the chill night wind and tried not to be too nervous about the coming meeting, praying her professor was right.

If Cormac Hunter couldn't help her find a familiar, she had no clue where else to turn.

Chapter Three

The building housing the Wild Hunt was an eclectic mix of a walk-up and a studio in a trendier part of town, flirting with the edges of Chelsea and Hell's Kitchen. It was too far north to be sandwiched in with the art galleries. Instead, it was just far enough east to crouch stubbornly between the Garment District and Midtown Manhattan's serious-minded commercial buildings, as if daring either to encroach. Even the sign hung on the overhang above the door had a bit of brazen challenge to it, Kimberly thought. Full of loops and whorls, a metal contraption depicted golden words that spelled out the name of the business in hard, no-nonsense letters couched by a nest of bronze vines and thorns and ivy leaves speckled with pale green spots of oxidation from the weather.

There were no windows at street level, which she thought exceptionally odd. There was no heavy thump of music or sound of chatter from inside, so it wasn't a club or restaurant. Curious, she double-checked the business card.

Right business name. Right address. No other info, save for the name of the proprietor. That, and the thick, creamy paper put her in mind of supple leather. Expensive.

Carefully cradling the drink, she took the stairs two at a time and tried the oversized front door. It swung open on well-oiled hinges, and light spilled out, momentarily blinding her.

As she stepped inside, the hard, heavy pulse of a ward stopped her in her tracks, crackling over her skin like a smothering blanket of static electricity. Her fingers tightened and some of the coffee spilled through the top of the cup, staining the cuff of her shirt. This was nothing like the wards she was used to, which usually stretched like cellophane in warning instead of hammering down like an invisible door slamming shut in your face.

"Do you have an appointment?"

The deep, disapproving voice drifting out of the shadows from somewhere beyond the labyrinthine stacks of furniture inside sounded far too much like Don for her peace of mind.

"Yes, I do. I'm Kimberly Wells, a student at Blackhollow Academy. Professor Reed sent me to meet with Mr. Hunter." When the deep voice didn't respond right away, she added a little more force to her tone. "He's expecting me."

A low harrumph was the only response the unseen source of that voice gave her. That, and the unexpected lack of invisible wall to prop her up as the ward disappeared, making her stumble and spill a bit more coffee on herself.

Cursing under her breath, she licked the sweet liquid off her hand and dropped the current illusion—her work shirt—then summoned a bit of power to make her school shirt appear spotless. The fabric was still wet and sticky against her skin, but she ignored it and stalked inside.

Intense magic tingled and bit at her skin. It was *everywhere*, and made all the tiny hairs on the back of her neck and her arms stand at rigid attention. Incense, furniture polish and dust drowned out the scent of everything else, though she passed a series of bookshelves with rack upon rack of herbs and common spell components. Even the dried garlic didn't make an impression against the eye-watering combination of burning cedarwood, ginger, lotus, and a splash of myrrh. Curious, she picked up a bundle of sage, examining the tag as she navigated the furniture maze.

Once she rounded a corner created by a crushed velvet couch set on its arm and a larger than life oil painting of some lady in a too-tight corset and fancy Victorian dress, the labyrinth was left behind. The opening spilled her out into a sprawling smorgasbord of trinkets, treasures and trash of every variety, both magical and mundane. There was little rhyme or reason to the layout that Kimberly could see; hip-high bookshelves full of atlases, memoirs and occult texts flanked a case full of jewelry, rare stones, cut crystals, bones, and scraps of various furs. Carvings and paintings leaned against end tables, and stone idols sat in otherwise empty chairs. There was such a heavy aura of magic on the place that she couldn't pinpoint which items were enchanted, which added a touch of disorientation to her already considerable trepidation.

A tall, slender man in a fitted waistcoat stood behind the antique register atop a counter that ran half the length of the display floor. *Nice body under those weird clothes. Very nice,* she thought, noting how the coat somehow managed to both make him look like a gentleman while emphasizing his trim waist and the impressive span of his shoulders. The first thing that struck her once she got past the strange clothes were his eyes. An intriguing shade of icy blue set in a hawkish face, focused with the keen intent of a raptor upon his visitor.

Everything about the man, from his anachronistic dress to the way he slicked back his dark hair in messy spikes, hinted at something feral hiding behind a thin veneer of culture. A culture from another time, maybe, but it didn't seem to matter—she couldn't tear her gaze away from those mesmerizing eyes.

That is, until he spoke. His voice was low and husky, like whisky and smoke, warm with a hint of sting underneath.

"Come closer, Kim. I don't bite."

Kimberly jerked into motion at his words as it hit her that she'd been standing there, staring like a fool. She skirted around a stack of plaster Green Man wall hangings and set the cup on the counter, praying the heat in her cheeks wasn't broadcasting her embarrassment and ignoring the little furrows that appeared between his brows at the streak of liquid left behind on the polished mahogany surface as she nudged it toward him.

Get it together, she admonished herself. *Keep it professional. Think about school. Graduating. The future. A cold shower. Oh, man...*

She took a deep breath to compose herself, then spoke in a rush. "It's Kimberly, sir. Here's your extra hot café latte, lots of cream, and a splash of hazelnut. Professor Reed said you'd like that."

He nodded, but didn't touch the drink. "You're late. Let me see your school ID, if you please."

"Story of my life," she muttered, extending her left wrist so he could see the stamped coin on the silver wire bracelet. The school symbol on the coin was a combination of simple and complex; a trio of Nordic runes inset around the triple looping spirals of a Celtic triskelion, which was in turn surrounded by a snake eating its own tail. Like every other student of Blackhollow Academy, hers was keyed specifically to her, acting as her hall pass to give her safe passage through the school's gates. At his nod, with a bit more grace, she withdrew and added, "I'm sorry. I came directly from work as fast as I could."

His icy gaze did not reflect any amusement. "Lack of punctuality has been likened to a lack of respect. I do not appreciate my time being wasted."

Kimberly paused. The guy was already ticked at her and she hadn't even been there five minutes yet. This did not bode well if she was going to ask him for help. She closed her eyes, clasping the sage bundle closer to hide how her hands were shaking, and then bowed her head in what she hoped was a good show of contrition.

"Mr. Hunter, sir, I am very sorry for being late. It wasn't my intention to waste your time."

"It may not have been your intent, but you certainly succeeded."

Why wouldn't he just drop it? She gritted her teeth against letting something unforgivable slip. "It won't happen again."

No, it certainly wouldn't. After tonight, forget how handsome he was—she hoped she never had to lay eyes on Cormac Hunter ever again. The last thing she needed was one more person in her life looking down on her and thinking she was just a waste of space. Once she got what she needed from him, she never wanted to see—or smell—the Wild Hunt again.

For a long moment, he stood there staring at her, impassive. Then one corner of his lips twitched upward, betraying the cool exterior. That little slip softened his features, making him look more human, less predatory, to her eyes.

"I'll let it slide this once," he said, his smile widening just a fraction. "Well, Kim, I thi—"

"It's Kimberly. Not Kim. Not Kimbellina. Not Kamehameha. *Just* Kimberly."

The moment the sharp words left her runaway mouth, she slapped a hand over the traitor, eyes wide with horror at her own slip. The last thing she wanted to do was alienate Cormac before she even had a chance to ask for his help, but much to her relief, he chuckled instead of taking offense.

"I suppose I deserved that," he said once the laughter tapered off. His tone went wry. "Well, *just* Kimberly, perhaps you'd like to tell me what you're doing to my merchandise?"

She looked down at the bundle of sage crumpled in her fist, and gasped in horror. He cocked his head and leaned forward as she frantically pawed through the twine and broken bits of twigs in her hands.

"What are you looking for?"

"The price tag. I'm so sorry, I didn't mean—I'll pay—"

* * *

Cormac found himself amused with this young woman though he wasn't sure yet what it was about her that made him so tolerant toward her snippiness or manhandling of his stock. Maybe how she'd been so noticeably attracted to him from the moment she set eyes on him. He had tried to stay neutral but a very male part of him preened under that admiration in her gaze. Not to mention how she was so flustered in his presence that he couldn't quite bring himself to be angry with her.

At her stricken look and obvious panic, his smile faded. Her reaction was disproportionate considering it was a common, cheap spell component, but upon closer observation he noted the frayed edges of her shirt sleeves peeking out from under her school jacket. That, and the wear on her far too sensible, low-heeled shoes.

Though he would normally have demanded immediate payment for the damaged goods, a pang of sympathy and an uncharacteristic desire to set her at ease made him hold his tongue. Instead, he held out his hand.

"Nonsense. Give it here. I'll find a use for it."

"You don't have to do that. I'll pay for it."

His eyes narrowed, lips pressing into a thin white slash. When she didn't back down, he took a sterner tone. "Unless you're practicing hedgewitchery in addition to the finer arts, you have no need of it. I'll take it."

"No," she said, to his utter bafflement, tilting her chin up and meeting his gaze with a fierce look of her own. He couldn't remember the last time someone had denied him, let alone been so bold when facing his... well, if not wrath, his irritation, at the very least. "I can find a use for it, too. And I broke it, so I'll buy it."

"Very well, Kimberly. Perhaps you'd like to tell me what you came in search of aside from some crushed sage."

Spots of color appeared on her cheeks, but she didn't back down. "My professor told me that this was the place to come if I wanted to find a dragon. I was hoping you could point me in the right direction."

He burst out in laughter again, though when she flinched, he coughed into his hand to cover it. Then cleared his throat and rolled his shoulders to rid himself of the unwanted tightness building in his chest at the sight of her drooping shoulders. The way she bit her lip and avoided his gaze made it clear that mirth was not the reaction she'd been expecting from him.

Eleanor hadn't specified why this student simply had to speak to *him*. The sheer, ludicrous gall of this request explained why his old friend had hedged about the details. The old bat must have thought sending this desperate mageling to him was a pretty good jest, but the hurt in the girl's eyes cut right through his mirth.

"I may have many fine items in my catalogue, my lady, but I'm afraid I have no dragons to sell you."

He wiped the smirk off his face and beat back the urge to offer an apology in response to the moisture building in those hollow, vacant eyes that would no longer meet his gaze. That tightness in his chest returned when she withdrew. Subtly, maybe, but his keen eyes didn't miss the way her shoulders hunched or the way her fingers knotted in the hem of her shirt until her knuckles went white.

"Fine," she said, voice gone thick. "But maybe you can tell me where I can find one? Or sell me a map? A book? Something to help me search?"

Fun was fun, but this was going a bit too far. "Young lady, I would strongly advise you against this search. Dragons are dangerous beasts."

A flicker of life returned, her jaw clenching briefly before she responded. "If you can't help me, just tell me how much I owe you for the herbs and I'll get out of your hair."

"I didn't say I can't help you," he replied, wondering what in the name of the gods possessed him to say so, "and I'll be damned if I'll take your money for that blasted bit of leaves and sticks."

Her eyes had gone so wide he could see the whites all the way around. The desperation digging tiny crinkles around her eyes and mouth vanished in a cloud of excitement and the sharp scent of herbs. "You can?" He suppressed a smile at how she clung to his words like a limpet, latching on and seeking answers. "How? Please, I'll do anything."

"Don't make promises you can't keep," he chided, not really meaning it.

She placed her hand flat on the counter, leaning forward as she met and held his gaze. Her voice was pitched low and deadly calm. "I don't."

He believed her.

Chapter Four

Cormac was deeply troubled by Kimberly's request. Had she been sent by anyone other than Eleanor Reed, it would have been a suicide mission. The moment she left his shop, he was going to call his old friend to find out what in blazes she thought she was doing by dropping this load of baggage in his lap.

What bothered him most was that she bought his implication that he *could* help as a promise that he *would*. A part of him wanted to help her. Something about her expressiveness—and perhaps a bit more than that, her stubbornness—intrigued him, but he wasn't about to give anything away for free. Particularly when he knew so little about why she had come to him.

"If I'm going to be able to do anything to assist you, I think I need a bit more information," Cormac said.

He gave her a pointed look as he picked up the now lukewarm coffee and cradled it in both hands, resting his elbows on the counter.

Her brows knotted before she spoke. He wasn't certain if it was in reaction to the flicker of magic and sudden temperature change in the air around his hands or due to his request for her to elaborate. Hot steam began drifting up from the hole in his cup lid, and he kept his gaze and metaphysical senses riveted on her as he took a sip. The drink was smooth, rich, and with just enough hazelnut syrup to soothe his sweet tooth. Perfect.

"Well," Kimberly said, "I don't know what Professor Reed told you, but I'm in trouble. School ends in less than a month, and I still can't summon a planar familiar."

"You look a bit young for college."

She frowned at him. "I'm not a child, and Blackhollow doesn't base admissions on age. They take you on as a student as soon as you start showing signs of magical talent. Usually puberty."

"Oh? And how old were you when you found out you could cast?"

Kimberly reddened. "I was thirteen, but didn't enroll in Blackhollow until I was seventeen. I kept a lid on it since I thought maybe I was imagining things. I didn't want to tell my mom and end up locked up for being crazy, you know? Seeing stuff that wasn't there."

"Understandable. That makes you... twenty-one, yes? Oldest in your class, I imagine?"

She shook her head. "There are a few others who enrolled late. Ones like me who didn't know right away."

Cormac took another sip, then flicked his fingers in the direction of one of the bookshelves.

"I see. Well, there's a book over there, *Familiars For Dummies,* that I've been told despite its title is rather useful for shoring up any educational gaps that may be giving you difficulties on the subject."

She huffed, fingers tightening on the already mangled remains of sage again, sending a puff of herb-scented dust into the air.

"I know the theory behind how summoning works, and I can create and close a circle as well as anyone else in my class," she said, and in a tone that conveyed the unspoken *'How stupid do you think I am?'* loud and clear. "It's the *power.* I'm an illusionist—all elemental spells give me trouble."

He tilted his head in question, forehead wrinkling. In answer, she held his gaze as she lifted her hand with the sage. It burst into flames.

Cormac straightened, eyes widening. Everything, from the flickering fire, to the crackle of charring sticks, to the pungent, earthy scent added to the already considerable miasma of aromas in the store, gave the impression that it was quickly burning to nothing more than a tiny pile of ash.

Then she blew on the ash, and a cloud of miniature, flaming butterflies launched from her palm. Their wings brushed against his cheeks as they flew by, stirring his hair, then winked out of existence. As each butterfly disappeared, the sage came back into view like a picture coming into focus, appearing to turn solid in her palm again once the last one was gone.

He shut his mouth, realizing it had gone slack.

"Fair enough," he said, giving her a stiff nod.

A spell so finely woven, one that seamlessly blended olfactory, visual, audio and tactile impressions on a target, took considerable skill. He hadn't seen illusions that fooled his finely tuned senses so thoroughly in more years than he wanted to think about, and that it had come so easily to her made it clear that she had mastered the art. Such power was dangerous in the wrong hands.

He eyed her intently over the rim of his cup, leaning closer to her. A surreptitious sniff told him that the fire and butterflies were not the only illusions she had cast. She smelled of coffee—*his* coffee—and nothing else. No soap, nor sweat, nor skin, or any of the thousand microscopic particles of the city she should have picked up on her way to his shop. Was that the only thing she was obfuscating? He couldn't help but wonder whether she had done something to alter her appearance as well as her scent.

Next time she came to his shop, he would be more prepared to deal with her prestidigitation.

"If you can't conjure, that's one thing. You obviously have the talent to secure yourself a decent position in a coven, so what are you worried about?"

"No one will hire me without a diploma from Blackhollow. And I can't graduate without a familiar."

Cormac shook his head, frowning. That wasn't how he recalled things being done back when he bothered himself with the affairs of magi. Granted, that had been decades earlier, so he supposed it was possible their requirements for entry into a coven had changed with the times, much like the rest of the world. Instead of interviews by senior members of the coven and making the potential cast a few things to show a measure of skill, now they required background checks, drug screening, and diplomas (oh my).

"That still doesn't explain why you're set on finding yourself a dragon. Why not something a little less dangerous? At the very least, one less likely to eat you."

Her voice wavered, but she lifted her chin and didn't flinch from giving him the answer he was looking for. "Because I'm broke and I'm desperate. I'm a sorcerer, not a mage, which means I need a familiar who can protect me until I get accepted into a coven."

Cormac went still. Kimberly either didn't notice or chose to ignore the sudden surge in ley line energy that swirled to life around them. She continued on as if he wasn't activating protective glyphs, one after the other. It was all that held him back from directing them at her.

"Before you ask, my teachers already know what I am. It's the other students and their parents I'm worried about. If I had a choice, I'd take anything, even a brownie or a wood sprite, just to pass my final exams. The problem is that I need a strong familiar to show them I'm not a pushover. If I can bind a dragon, there's no way I'd be turned down when I apply for a place in a coven. And even if I was, I wouldn't have to worry about supporting myself or how to keep my mom safe from the others anymore. She's a mundane—she doesn't have any magic, and I can't be with her at all times to keep her safe. I need help, Mr. Hunter. Please."

His eyes widened. Her candor was almost as striking as her admission, leaving him reaching for her unthinking—then catching himself and pulling away.

Dangerous, he reminded himself. *More dangerous than she looks. Hands off—for now.*

Clearly Eleanor Reed had recognized that a sorcerer could be useful, but if she didn't have the power to pull the strings necessary to get Kimberly a place in her coven, then her reasoning for involving him and sending her on this fool's errand began to make sense.

Terrifically small-minded creatures, magi, he thought. Illusion had many uses in clever hands, and a sorcerer willing to play by the rules of a mage coven was nigh unheard of in this day and age. Not since the sorcerer bloodlines had been nearly wiped out to extinction by magi in the 1920s. He was intrigued and curious, but needed to know more before he made any commitments.

"I see," Cormac said. "I'll have to do some research on the matter."

She opened her mouth, maybe to argue. He held up a hand, forestalling whatever she was about to say.

"Seeing as your professor was not so forthcoming as yourself, you've caught me unprepared to deal with your request."

Kimberly closed her eyes for a brief moment as though to pray, and then opened them. She pressed her lips together and let a slow breath out through her nose in a quiet sigh before she nodded, resigned.

"Come back tomorrow evening. Same time. Bring me another coffee."

He had to remind himself that he was buying time for himself, not granting her wish yet. The spark of barely suppressed joy that lit her from within at those simple words of his shouldn't have meant a thing. Yet, a chill that had long settled over his heart melted just a little to bask in the sunny smile she turned on him; so much warmer than the fog of fear and despair she'd been carrying like a cloak.

Tomorrow. That should be enough time for him to prepare counter-spells to negate her illusions, fascinating though they were. He wanted to question her again when she had no way of hiding her emotions from him or altering his perceptions. Without scent cues and with the possibility that she was only projecting what she wanted him to see, he couldn't be sure she was telling the complete truth. He wasn't about to ask her what she expected to give the dragon in return for its services or how long she intended to keep it bound without knowing with certainty that she meant what she said.

He also needed to speak to Eleanor to confirm whether his theory about what had possessed her to send Kimberly to him was correct. And, more importantly, find out what was in it for him.

"Thank you so much, Mr. Hunter," Kimberly said.

"Don't thank me yet."

He hadn't yet decided if she had bought herself a golden ticket out of all her troubles or a ringside seat to her own downfall.

Chapter Five

Kimberly declined the cab Cormac offered to call, lying through her teeth when she said it wasn't much of a walk back to her apartment. Judging by his snort and narrowed eyes, she didn't think he believed her, but there was no way she could afford a cab ride back to her rent regulated apartment. The slip with the sage was bad enough. Figuring out how to pay for another drink for him tomorrow was making her stomach roll, so she focused on putting one foot in front of the other and making her way home.

Once Cormac saw her out, she waited until she was about half a block away to bend the light and shadows in her vicinity to make herself nearly invisible to any other passersby on the street. A two mile trek home through the heart of New York City in the middle of the night wasn't safe for anyone. Unlike most, she had the ability to keep herself hidden from the eyes of predators lurking in the dark, human or Other. Exhaustion made her concentration slip now and again, her wavering image appearing in puddles or reflected on windows, but her twist on an invisibility spell kept her safe from most of the denizens of the night prowling for an easy mark.

Head down and hands pocketed, she spent a good portion of the walk thinking about Cormac Hunter.

She wasn't sure what to make of the guy. There were times when she was positive those strange blue eyes had seen right through her illusions, cutting through the image she portrayed of a polished, if ordinary, student to see the coffee-stained, ragged, rumpled ragamuffin underneath. Whatever he saw, he didn't make her feel like she was being judged. More like coveted, though she couldn't put her finger on why.

Not to mention how her heart did a funny little leap in her chest at the memory of his smile.

What help he might be able to give still eluded her, but for the first time in weeks, some of the panic and pressure of the looming end to her time at Blackhollow was lifting. She wrapped her arms around herself and took a deep breath, inhaling the lingering scents of incense on her skin and smog-tainted city air. A weight she hadn't realized was dragging her down had faded, making the world around her a little brighter, somehow.

Not to mention making enough room in her chest for a butterfly flutter of excitement at seeing Cormac take residence where the ever present knots of stress used to be.

By the time she reached her apartment building, it was nearing midnight, and she was dead on her feet. Swaying with exhaustion, she stumbled up the uneven steps to punch in the security code. Then entered the code a second time when one of the buttons got stuck.

Down came the illusion. Up three flights of stairs she went. Then five doors down on the left. The hall still smelled like dog pee. Her next door neighbors on the right, Charlie and Zack, must not have finished cleaning up that morning after their daschund, Schlong, and his latest "accident" in front of the apartment of his nemesis, Princess the not-exactly-purebred Persian.

Taking shallow breaths through her mouth, as soon as she got past the third lock on the door, she lurched inside.

"Mom? Are you home?"

Nobody answered. She tossed her backpack into the hall and then shut the door behind her, closed her eyes, and leaned her back against it as she slowly sank down to sit on the floor.

A TV's constant, distant mumble filtered through the walls. Somewhere, a kid was crying that it was *not* bedtime. And a surly growl had her eyes popping open, searching the dark hall and what she could see of the living room until she spotted the eerie yellow-green luminescent eyes glaring at her from the shadows between the milk crates that made up their coffee table.

"Can't I have five minutes without someone getting pissed at me? Just five. That's all I'm asking," Kimberly said to no one in particular, then groaned as she heaved herself back to her feet. At the cat's insistent meow, she hushed him. "I know you're hungry, I'm coming. Hold your horses."

Kicking off her sneakers, she locked the door, dragged her backpack behind her, and flicked on the kitchen lights. After a brief delay, the fluorescent track lighting flickered to life.

There was a note from her mom on the counter.

> *Working late tonight. Food for Monster on the counter. Don't stay up too late. Rent due in four days.*

Aside from the note, nothing. A niggle of panic for her mother's safety was beaten back by closing her eyes, taking a series of deep, gulping breaths, and reminding herself that it was too soon for anyone to take a shot at her family. She hoped.

Kimberly couldn't be everywhere at once. Logic dictated any attacks would be directed at her, and they would more than likely happen at school between classes. Maybe after school let out, when she was on her own and away from the watchful eyes of the dean and teachers.

In between everything else on her plate, she'd have to find the time to cook up some protective spells in some form that her mother could carry around.

Trying not to think about all the horrible things that could happen to her mom without her around to keep her safe, she put her backpack on the counter and then checked the refrigerator, which was just as empty as it had been when she left that morning. Nothing in the fridge but a few condiments in the door. The freezer had a bag of spinach and an empty box of Lean Cuisine. With a deep sigh, she tossed the box, got herself a glass of water, then poured the Ziploc baggie of cat food into a dish for Monster as he complained at her slow pace so loudly that the upstairs neighbor thumped something heavy a few times.

"Sorry!" she shouted, then shushed the cat again as she put his food on the floor.

The big Maine Coon arched his back and butted up against her legs, nearly knocking her off her feet on his way to his dish. Then he took a swipe at her when she dared give his back a little pat.

"Asshole cat," she muttered, leaving him to his meal.

While pouring the cat's food, she had noticed her hands were still shaking. The weakness in her limbs wasn't just exhaustion. Digging through her backpack, she pulled out the bag of sweets, the rosettes, and the orange she'd swiped from school. Aside from the banana scarfed down during a break at Allegretto's, she hadn't eaten since lunch. Her stomach growled so loud when she caught whiff of the pastries that the cat stopped eating long enough to give her a surly stare.

Sipping her water, she leaned against the counter and half-heartedly picked the skin off the orange, eating a slice at a time despite her gnawing hunger. As soon as the last slice was gone, she took apart the rosette with a bit more gusto. The bread practically melted in her mouth, the flavors of thyme and butter exploding over her tongue. Don might have been a thoughtless prick sometimes, but damn, the man knew how to cook.

Though she was sorely tempted to polish off a second rosette, she took one out for her mom and left it on the counter, then knotted the bag and tucked the last one into her backpack. She had no such compunction about leaving all the sesame and rainbow cookies, which she didn't care for, while pulling out the remaining biscotti, chocolate-dipped wafers, and the lone cannoli for herself.

Fruit, bread and cookies. The dinner of champions.

She headed to the lone bedroom, dragging her backpack with her, pausing along the way to pick up the shredded remains of a scarf that had previously hidden the cigarette burn in the left arm of the couch and re-drape it as best she could.

Both beds were still unmade from that morning. She collapsed facedown into her own, groaning into the pillow at the relief to be off her aching feet. It would have been wonderful to simply lie there, but when she dropped the illusion on her clothing, she got a good whiff of herself. *Parfum de* sour coffee and sweat made her nose wrinkle.

With another heartfelt groan, she rolled out of bed, undressed, took a quick shower, then brushed her teeth and threw on an old T-shirt and pair of gym shorts. It was nearing 1AM, and the other bed was still empty.

It had to be a late shift. Nothing more serious than that.

Had to be.

Sinking back onto the bed with a low squeal of bedsprings, she stared at the bedside clock blankly. Then reached out a hand to touch a phantom image of her mother she'd conjured.

Unlike those she summoned illusions to fool, she could always see through her own creations, no matter how much effort she put into them. The ghost of a touch from the slender fingers twining with hers lingered, but it was more a tingle of her own magic prickling over her skin to tell her she'd made contact with her construct than like anything solid and real.

"I'm proud of you," a whisper in a familiar voice told her, and she almost believed the illusory smile.

"I wish that was true."

The phantom said nothing.

Jerking her hand away, Kimberly dismissed the illusion, turned off the lights, and drew the covers up to her chin, using them to wipe away the dampness on her cheeks.

Chapter Six

Cormac hardly waited for Kimberly to set foot beyond his threshold before he had snapped his wards back up to full power and strode with purpose to his office above the store.

He had purchased the building decades earlier, entrenching himself in the heart of the city, much to the irritation of the local powers-that-be. The master vampire of New York, Alec Royce, had once attempted to bribe him to move on to greener pastures. Since that meeting, not a single Other in the city—and perhaps quite a distance beyond that—had made any effort to oust or accost him.

Knowing his reputation, the magi usually kept a healthy distance. Perhaps it had been too long since the last example had been set, he thought. Eleanor should have known better than to meddle in his affairs.

Taking the stairs two and three at a time, he slashed a hand through the air as he reached the top of the stairwell, cutting a path through another layer of unseen protective spells and wards. The previously invisible glyphs etched into the thick wood burst into a fierce red glow, casting strange, dancing shadows against his pale skin and on the walls. Once he passed through, the wards sealed behind him with an audible crack of expanding, superheated air.

Candles set on candelabras of all sizes lit themselves as he passed, illuminating the massive, open chamber. A pair of heavy leather chairs flanked a large couch facing the plasma TV hung over the fireplace. Oak tables in a variety of sizes dotted the room. At the opposite end, floor-to-ceiling casement windows gave a view of the street below.

There were no bookshelves. No magazines. No DVD racks, artwork, or other distractions to be found, greatly at odds with the clutter downstairs.

He went straight to the kitchen. He'd had it redone recently. The bulk of the electronic gadgets baffled him, but he rarely used the space for more than storing food in the fridge. The phone on the island in the center had a short list of phone numbers written on a pad next to it. The paper was yellowing and curling, but the writing was still legible.

He dialed the fourth phone number on the list, fingers tapping out an impatient rhythm on the limestone countertop.

Within a few rings, there was a click, followed by a familiar voice. "I was wondering when you would call."

"You know very well," he ground out, "how much I detest games like this. Why did you send her to me?"

"She deserves help."

"You've never been known for your charitable contributions to the less fortunate. What's in it for you?"

"Maybe I have a soft spot for the girl. She reminds me a great deal of myself when I was her age."

He waited, knowing there had to be more to it than that.

Eleanor didn't disappoint him. The moment the silence bordered on uncomfortable, she told him the real reason. "She also needs someone who can guide her, both morally and magically, once she realizes just how much power she has. Her skill set is valuable if she can learn to work with others and keep her pride in check."

"She's in a bloody school full of magi brought up to hate everything she is, all learning the same spellcraft she doesn't have a prayer of mastering. They'll never learn how to work with her and most likely more than a few of your own coven want to see her dead. Don't insult my intelligence."

"I don't think you understand, Cor. She lives with her *human* mother in the projects. Won't leave her side. And the other kids avoided her until now since they assumed she's nothing more than a half-blood. I've heard the things they call her in the halls and when they think the teachers aren't paying attention. She needs someone to lean on who won't put up with her attempts to sidestep protocol, and someone who can keep her and her mother safe until I can convince the rest of the coven she's worth having."

He harrumphed, the immediate edge of his anger taken off by the admission. The projects? Most magi would conjure up a fortune or the appearance of one for themselves if they didn't find a way to earn money on their own. Living with the human half of her parentage explained the ratty shoes she hadn't thought to disguise and why she kept fiddling with loose threads on her clothes. That, and the brief look of panic that flit over her features when he suggested she take a cab home.

And if the young magi gave her grief for being half-blooded in the halls where teachers could overhear, he could only imagine what might befall her once word got out what she truly was.

"You're the only one I trust to do that effectively," Eleanor continued, taking his silence for belligerence rather than contemplation. "You remember what it was like, I'm sure."

Ha. He knew he was right. He still pretended he hadn't guessed exactly what Eleanor was up to, adding an edge of disgust to his tone that wasn't much of a stretch considering what he thought of her coven.

"You've tagged her for The Circle?"

"Don't sound so surprised. Or put off. They won't take her without knowing she's stable. I've laid the groundwork. I need your help to do the rest."

Once more, Cormac didn't respond immediately. Like most Others, he was well aware of how easy it was to put your foot in your mouth and sign away a promise or a service without intending to when dealing with those versed in magic arts. He'd already done as much for Kimberly, though he thought she might be a bit too green to understand yet just what he had committed himself to doing for her by promising his aid. One's word being one's bond wasn't just a saying to magi and their ilk—it was law.

When she wasn't busy doing her civic duty as a professor, Eleanor Reed was a high-ranking member of The Circle—the premier chantry of magi on the East Coast, and the largest and most influential in the United States. The last thing he wanted to do was agree to anything more than he'd already offered without knowing more about Eleanor's intentions. If she wanted Kimberly in her coven, there was good reason for it.

He thought about telling the girl to run while she could, but he had a taste of her tenacity down in his shop. Taking a step out of poverty and the human world to rub elbows with the elite of the supernatural community had to be one hell of a carrot to have dangling just out of her reach. Particularly with her no doubt in a perpetual state of worry that either her own or her mother's life was in constant danger. No wonder she had told him she was desperate.

"You know what you're asking," he stated quietly, resigned.

"I do."

"Are you officially calling in the favor I owe you?"

"I am."

"Fuck you, Eleanor."

She laughed and hung up on him. He slammed the phone down, hard enough for the plastic to give a decided *crunch* it wasn't intended to make.

While he might have willingly made the choice to help the girl, if only to sate his curiosity about her, being cornered into working for anyone else didn't suit him one bit. Eleanor obviously wanted him back under her thumb, which led him to wonder if Kimberly was in on it. Perhaps she had played him from the start. Any other magi in her shoes would have been salivating at the offer of a walk-on position into The Circle, let alone having a dragon at their beck and call. He assumed she was no exception.

Stomping to the center of the iron circle etched into the kitchen tile, he suppressed a growl. He would know the truth soon enough. If the magi wanted to play hardball, he could play, too. With a harshly uttered Word, the circle blazed to life, and he rolled up his metaphorical sleeves as the real work began.

Chapter Seven

Kimberly tried very hard to concentrate on the illustrations in her textbook, but her heart was pounding so hard she could barely focus. She kept rubbing her sweaty palms against her ill-fitting skinny jeans, but it didn't help much.

Professor Reed had made some special arrangements for her students to practice practical application of what they had learned in her Other Etiquette: Know Your Others, Know Your Place class thus far. Though she never said anything to that effect, Kimberly suspected by the way the professor's tone had grown shorter and sharper over the course of the school year that she didn't think they were making the kind of progress the professor was hoping for. Not that Kimberly thought many—if any—of the magi in this class would deal with any Others outside class aside from ordering a drink from a vampire bartender in the city or maybe taking a cab with a werewolf for a driver. As interesting as some of the inter-Other politicking might have been, she also had her doubts that much of what they were being taught had any practical application outside the classroom. Aside from being shoved in the direction of a dragon, Kimberly herself had never dealt with anything more magically exotic than another mage's familiar.

For the day's class, Professor Reed had invited a mage with an earthbound familiar to visit, and she was currently pacing on the stage at the front of the auditorium going over the rules one last time. If one of the students "accidentally" provoked the creature, the mage it was bound to was supposed to keep it in check. As a last resort, in the unlikely event it lashed out, they were to rely heavily on fire-based defensive spells.

Kimberly had figured it would be a cinch to pass the test since it shouldn't involve casting anything. It was considered inconceivably rude by the bulk of supernatural society to use one's powers on another Other without invitation, save in times of war. Aside from which, the whole point of the class was to teach the young magi the arts of supernatural diplomacy.

What had her worried were the whispers by some of the students behind her, easier to hear than usual since attendance was sparse after the announcement had been made that there was a sorcerer attending Blackhollow. She wasn't sure who said it, but someone had said her name and then someone else muttered something about "heating things up," followed by snickers.

Her inability to grasp elemental magic meant that, when it came down to it, she couldn't defend herself in the same ways as everyone else in the class. After four years of studies with them, they knew her weaknesses just as well as Professor Reed. Maybe more so now that rumors were circulating about the sorcerer in their midst.

Going to the professor would only delay the inevitable. If the person who whispered her name was who she thought and she went to the professor to ruin their plans, they'd only corner her after school to do something worse. She knew from experience that she had to handle it herself.

Whatever prank they intended to pull, she had to think of something quick, or she might end up badly hurt.

A brisk rapping on the doorframe cut the professor's safety lecture short. Her severe expression softened with a welcoming smile as she gestured the two men to step inside.

They were both dressed in jeans and button-down shirts, but which was the mage and which the familiar was obvious. The sandy haired mage was grinning and giving the apprentice magi a friendly wave, striding over to the stage at the center of the auditorium-style classroom to join Professor Reed. His surfer's tan was not as dark as that of his taller, swarthy companion lingering near the door. The other man's black eyes were wide, scanning the rows of several dozen student magi before him.

"Oh my God," the familiar said, loud enough to be heard by the whole class. "You breed?"

Titters sounded from all around the classroom. The mage reddened. "Sam, shut up."

The professor stepped in, her sharp *ahem* doing an excellent job of silencing the laughter. "Class, this is James Gardner of the Commune of the Everglades, and his familiar, a naga."

The taller man stared around at all the magi, most of whom were staring back. "So many. I thought you were like natural disasters, not locusts."

"*Sam.*"

The naga had spoken like he hadn't heard a word from his master or the professor, and Kimberly couldn't help but feel a measure of dismay at the genuine horror in his tone. He obviously didn't want to be there. The stiff way he shuffled to James's side spoke volumes for his reluctance to play along.

"All right, everyone," the professor said, "that's enough. Aidan, you're up first. Come down here."

One of the students near the back got up. Kimberly had recognized his voice in the whispers behind her. Judging by the flat stare he was getting from their teacher, maybe the professor wasn't entirely oblivious to what had been going on.

He had his hands shoved in the pockets of his slacks and a smarmy grin plastered on his face as he slunk down the stairs. His interest in the familiar was palpable, as was that of most of the other students in the room.

A mage always had the option to bind a native supernatural creature instead of summoning an ethereal planar being to be their familiar. The trouble was that most earthbound Others worth the effort of making into familiars were well aware of what it meant to be bound to a mage, so it was rare for one to consent. Due to the inherent difficulty in convincing any intelligent earthbound supernatural like the naga to submit to a bond, they were coveted status symbols.

There was no way for Aidan to take control of the naga, but that wouldn't stop him from drooling over it like someone else's brand new Mercedes.

Once Aidan reached the last step, James made an idle "get on with it" gesture at Sam. The naga shot his master an annoyed look before sidling another few steps along the stage to meet Aiden halfway and shifting into his native form.

The students gave a collective gasp as his body darkened and stretched, growing well beyond the natural bounds of any typical shapeshifter. It only took moments for the tall, nondescript man to be replaced by a thirty-foot snake, wide as a tree trunk and with the broad, muscled chest and arms of a man. From his lower jaw to the tip of his tail, his underbelly was covered with wide, yellow-white plates. The rest of him was covered in jewel-toned scales varying in shades from blue to green to a dark bronze. There were wide, burnished copper cuffs on his wrists and a matching collar circled his throat. The blunt snout lifted and lidless, golden eyes scanned the room as his forked tongue flickered out, tasting the air.

Aidan scrambled back, knocking over one of the other students in his haste to get away from the naga. He flushed at the laughter from James, but more so at the sharp reprimand from Professor Reed.

"*Aidan.* You've been incalculably rude to our guest. Apologize at once."

Aidan's normally borderline pallid features had taken on a ruddy hue by the time he managed to regain his feet and sketch a formal bow to the naga—from a healthy distance away, of course.

"My apologies, great one," he said. "I greet you as a representative of Blackhollow Academy and humbly beg... beg... umm..."

"Your blessing," Professor Reed said, her tone flat.

"Your blessing," he finished.

The naga cocked his head to one side, then the other.

"What now?" James demanded.

"I see no gifts. Where is my tribute in return for the blessing?"

The voice of the snake was deep, and strangely musical despite the hissing sibilants. Aidan turned a panicked look on his teacher, whose pitiless gaze showed no sympathy.

"Professor, I—"

"Don't tell me. Tell him," she said, waving her hand at the giant snake coiled and waiting before him.

Aidan's color gradually paled. "I... umm. I'm terribly sorry if I may cause offense, but I forgot my homework—your gift—oh, great one."

The naga bowed his head and voiced a low hiss that sounded very much like a sigh. The snake turned to its master and spread its hands.

James shook his head, and the naga turned its back on Aidan in dismissal. Crestfallen, he turned to Professor Reed, who gestured for him to return to his seat. Trudging back up the stairs, he shot a venomous look at one of the younger magi who dared snigger at him as he passed.

Professor Reed made a note on a clipboard. "Would anyone else like to cop to 'forgetting' their homework?" A few tentative hands raised. She made more notes on her clipboard, then scanned the remaining students. "Kimberly. Why don't you show us what you've got?"

Kimberly swallowed hard, then nodded and turned to dig in her backpack for the last remaining rosette from yesterday. She was glad she'd saved it so she wouldn't flunk this exam. It wasn't much of a tribute—nothing like the gold and jewels she had read about naga traditionally being showered with in return for a blessing—but hopefully he wouldn't spurn it outright since she didn't have any fancy jewelry or money to offer him.

Her shoulders hunched self-consciously at the laughter and whispers that started up as soon as she pulled the bread in its clear plastic bag free of her backpack. Keeping her eyes focused firmly on the ground at her feet, she stalked to the stairwell at the end of the aisle and didn't stop until she reached the edge of the stage.

When she looked up, golden eyes the size of tennis balls were focused on her. She took a deep breath to steady herself, then went down on one knee and bowed her head as she extended the hunk of bread.

"Forgive my meager offering, wise one. I greet you as a representative of Blackhollow Academy and humbly beg your blessing."

Kimberly held her breath, silently praying that he wouldn't spurn her gift. She could still hear the whispered chatter in the background and did her very best to ignore it.

Lame. Cheapskate. Loser. Stupid freeloader.

Dirty sorcerer.

Monster.

"Receive your blessing, representative of Blackhollow Academy."

Surprised, she looked up, eyes wide. The naga bowed his snake head over the offering as she placed it into his large, scaled hands, though she suspected his gaze was still focused on her.

Just as he reached out to grant his blessing, the rosette in his palm burst into white-hot flames.

Chapter Eight

The naga's cobra-like hood flared as he shrieked and flung the burning bread away from himself. The flaming missile hit a girl in the shoulder near the last row at the back of the room and bounced away, disappearing under a desk. As the great snake flailed and howled in pain, Professor Reed shouted instructions, trying to be heard over the overturning desks and the panicked screams of her students.

James stepped in, laying his hands on the whipping tail of the naga—which was far less dangerous than the curved, needle-like fangs as long and thick as his index finger bared at the younger magi.

An arm as thickly muscled as a body-builder's passed through Kimberly as Sam swung around to face his master. The illusion fragmented and disappeared. Sam's cries of pain tapered off as James used his grip on the naga to channel magic into him and heal the burn. Sam was panting, his hood flaring in and out, but no longer on the verge of attack.

Despite that he had calmed, many of the students were still screaming and fighting to hide behind one another at the back of the room. They were clustered so tightly together that they were shoving some of the rows of school desks off the edge of their platforms and onto the lower rows.

"*Silence!*" thundered Professor Reed.

Stalking down the stage, she gestured sharply at the burning bread—now charred to a blackened husk, and starting to catch a nearby sweatshirt on fire—and the mess dissipated into steam and ash. The scent of burning bread, fabric, and a pungent charred meat smell from the Naga's injuries that was more fishy than reptilian.

"Who did this?"

No one responded. All of the students were wide-eyed with fear—first of the naga, but now of their teacher—and were huddled together in the back rows of the auditorium. All save for Kimberly, who had ducked away behind a veil of illusion as soon as the bread was out of her hands and was at that moment hiding behind the professor's desk.

"Who cast that spell?"

The naga, who had slithered behind his master and was holding the wrist of his injured hand, tipped his nose toward a cluster of students in the corner farthest from himself. "The boy. The one who brought no gift."

"I did not!" Aidan shouted.

The professor turned to the naga, placing a fist over her heart as she bowed low. "My deepest apologies, honored one. I am so terribly sorry. I will see that the boy is suitably punished. Is there any penance I can offer you?"

The naga opened its mouth, but James cut him off. "Relax, Eleanor. He'll be fine."

Sam hissed. "I will *not*. No one would have *dared* back in India—"

"Oh, don't start that again!"

"—where I was *worshipped*—"

"You're not in Kansas anymore."

"—and treated like a *god*—"

"Yawn."

"—and—"

"*Sam.* Shut up. No one cares."

The naga did shut his mouth with a clack of fangs, fists clenched tightly at his sides. James turned back to the professor.

"Look, I think we've hit his limit for the day. We can try this again in a few days, once he calms down."

The professor nodded, but Sam hissed again. "No. I won't come back here. I'll give the girl the blessing since I already said I would, but you can't make me do it for anyone else."

James made a protesting sound, but Professor Reed placed a restraining hand on his shoulder. She ducked her head and briefly used her free hand to rub the bridge of her nose just above her glasses before turning her attention back to the students inching their way back to their seats.

"Class, you are dismissed to the library. For the remainder of the module, you are to study proper comportment when dealing with nagas. Aidan, Kimberly, you two remain."

The rest of the students shuffled out of the theater, all of them giving the naga a wide berth. The stares and whispers made Kimberly's skin crawl with discomfort. She hoped she didn't have to stick around for more than the blessing. Aidan would make her pay for it later if she was around to witness whatever it was the professor was planning on dishing out.

It didn't take long for the room to empty. Professor Reed gave Aidan a pointed look, and he sullenly shuffled into one of the seats at the front row.

"You don't have to do your thing if you don't want to," James said to Sam.

"I'm not going back on my word."

James shrugged, then waved Kimberly over. She hesitated, but did as directed, though she stayed a healthy distance away from the giant snake whose tail was still twitching with obvious irritation. James gave her a playful punch on the shoulder and a wink as he headed over to join Professor Reed and Aidan.

"Quick thinking with that illusion, kid. Nice work."

She nodded thanks, but kept her eyes glued to the naga. Sam inclined his head, those unblinking gold eyes focusing with unnerving intensity on Kimberly's face. His voice was low, quiet, not intended to carry to the ears of the other magi.

"You knew he would do it. You're not one of them."

It wasn't a question, but Kimberly gave him a mute nod anyway.

"I wondered why you used an illusion... I am sorry if I frightened you."

That startled a short, high laugh out of her. "It wasn't your fault. *I'm* sorry you were hurt. We're not all like... like that." She gave a vague wave in Aidan and James's direction.

Sam briefly dipped his head. She couldn't read his face; the snake-head didn't have the musculature to give her any hint of an expression aside from the glitter in his eye. Yet she was sure he was seeing something more than what was on the surface. The sense of being studied right down to the fae power running in her half-blood veins was unnerving, but she kept her mouth shut and waited patiently for his response. He didn't take long to bob his head again.

"Yes, I know. Being Other does not exempt us from making foolish choices." He rubbed his hands together, then held one out to her. "Kimberly, yes? I am Samudra. Or Sam, if you prefer."

Though she hesitated, she soon reached out to shake his offered hand. She had thought his skin might be rough or maybe even slimy, but his palm was cool and smooth against her own, and his grip surprisingly gentle during the brief handshake.

"What's your preference?" she asked.

Kimberly could have sworn he was smiling, though nothing about his expression changed. "Sam will do. May I touch you? It will work better that way."

Mouth dry, she nodded again and stepped closer. His forked tongue flickered out, probably sensing her nervousness. Once she was within arm's reach, he placed his right hand on her forehead, his claws lightly trailing through her hair until the very tips brushed her scalp. It didn't hurt, but she still shivered at the touch.

A light tingle of some kind of foreign magic crept over her skin. If she hadn't been hyped up from fear and so focused on what he was doing, she might not have noticed it.

Sam withdrew, and the tingle faded. He bowed his head, lightly touching the fingers of his right hand to his own brow.

"You have a kind heart. I do wish you luck."

Kimberly mirrored his gesture, though she wished she could ask exactly what he had done. She didn't remember reading about anything quite like this in her school books. By his formal tone, she thought the words might carry more significance than simple well-wishes, so she responded in kind.

"Thank you, wise one. I will honor the gift you have given me."

She couldn't be sure, but she thought by the tilt of his shoulders and the way he tipped up his chin that he might be pleased with her response. She *had* studied the chapter on proper comportment around dragons and their ilk before—and again that morning before class, brushing up her knowledge since she expected Cormac might introduce her to one soon.

"I thought he was resistant to fire! Look at him. He looks like one of the *Draconis* family!"

Aidan's rising voice echoing in the auditorium cut through the pleasant buzz of the naga's blessing. Kimberly and Sam exchanged a look before turning to the others. While she couldn't be sure what Sam was thinking, Kimberly was mortified.

"Right family, wrong genus," James said.

The professor wasn't close to finished laying into Aidan. "He is a water-based elemental, you foolish child! Why do you think I instructed to use fire-based shields instead of projectiles if you needed to defend yourself? You could have killed him."

"It was just a little prank. I'm sorry!"

"Not sorry enough. Get your things and report to the dean's office. *Now.*"

Aidan shot Kimberly a venomous look before grabbing his backpack from between his feet and then stalking out of the classroom. Professor Reed snapped her fingers, and her hawk familiar roused itself from slumber, spreading its dark brown wings to follow Aidan and ensure he did as he was told. Once the boy was gone, the professor turned to James.

"Again, I am terribly sorry about this. If there is anything—"

"—you can do, I'll call you. Don't worry. Sam, let's go."

The naga took a deep breath, then appeared to shrink into himself. James didn't wait for him to finish shifting, heading toward the exit. In the space of a few heartbeats, the dark-haired, dark-skinned man stood in the giant snake's place. A muscle tic in his cheek jumped as he stared after James, jaw clenched.

He inclined his head in a brief nod to Professor Reed, then a deeper one to Kimberly before following at James's heels.

The professor didn't speak until she and Kimberly were alone.

"Did you receive your blessing?"

"Yes, professor."

Though her posture remained ramrod straight, some of the tension in the professor's shoulders eased. "Good. Do you remember what the school symbol stands for?"

Kimberly paused, her fingers involuntarily drifting to the bracelet she'd been wearing for the last four years. She had no clue what that had to do with what she'd just witnessed. "Um. Safe passage?"

"That is part of it, yes." The professor's gaze slid upward, eyes going distant. "The triskelion represents personal growth, development of power, and spiritual expansion. You know your runes. I'm sure you know that those three stand for travel, protection, and social order. And, of course, the ouroboros, which represents both wholeness and infinity."

Kimberly nodded, her eyes wide. While she had known what the individual symbols meant, she had never put together the significance of their combined meaning before. She suspected the professor was trying to tell her something in a roundabout way, but whatever the lesson might be escaped her.

With a sharp exhalation, the professor turned to face Kimberly, giving her a piercing stare over the rims of her glasses. "While things didn't go as I expected today, I hope you learned something from the experience."

A test. All that mess, and the professor was still testing her knowledge.

Setting her jaw and meeting Professor Reed's gaze, Kimberly took a deep breath through her nose, let it out, then launched into the impromptu dissertation she thought her teacher wanted.

"The naga was only here because Mr. Gardner made him come. He didn't enjoy being on display, but I don't think he was given a choice. He responded well to courtesy and I believe he was put at ease by ceremony."

Professor Reed's lips drew back in a thin smile. "Yes, but not what I'm looking for. I need to get to the dean's office, so I'm going to be frank. Work with Cormac to get yourself a familiar, but don't be another James. Once you seal a bond with a familiar, never forget that the creature who consented is a living, thinking being."

Kimberly bit her lip, then nodded. "Mr. Gardner doesn't respect his familiar."

"Correct. Some day, I expect it may be his downfall. However, that's neither here nor there—and I need to get going. Go join the other students in the library. And think long and hard about what you've seen today."

Kimberly scooped up her bag and took off at a run, more than ready to escape the classroom—and to take some time to plan how to convince a dragon she would never treat it so cavalierly as James treated Sam.

Chapter Nine

Kimberly arrived at the Wild Hunt right on time. Cormac's wards didn't stop her when she opened the door and reached a tentative hand out to check for a barrier, so she wended her way through the maze of furniture until she reached the main portion of the floor.

As she made her way between the last pair of bookshelves that spat her out by the sales counter, her skin crawled with a strange sensation, like tiny insect feet marching in a steady wave all over her body. A brisk shiver dispelled the feeling.

Cormac sat on a thickly cushioned footstool and watched her progress toward him with interest. He snapped the book in his lap shut and set it aside as he eyed her, head to toe, his gaze coming to rest on her shirt. He was a bit surprised to note that while she did use her illusions to improve the apparent quality of her clothing, as he'd suspected, she had done nothing to alter her own appearance.

Oh, maybe smoothed her hair a bit and put a touch of color on her lips and cheeks, but she was the same green-eyed, russet-haired girl who had stood before him the night before. If anything, she was too thin, her bones a little too prominent under her smooth, pale skin.

Though he was finding himself surprisingly put out at the scent of some Other on her. Something draconic in nature, though not a true dragon. A male. If he had not been so intent on getting his questions answered, he might have growled his displeasure.

After seeing his expression, Kimberly wondered if she'd managed to spill coffee on herself again. She stopped in her tracks to peek down at her shirt and pants—and couldn't hold back a sound of dismay.

She'd walked right through a dispelling glyph and hadn't even noticed. Though her clothing was clean save for a small smear of powdered sugar by her hip, the frayed cuffs, faded material and poor fit previously hidden by illusion were now all too obvious. Not to mention that she'd barely bothered to run a brush through her hair after work, knowing it would be windblown after the walk to Cormac's. She'd even added illusory makeup for once—not totally sure why—and now it was all gone.

Reddening with embarrassment, she rapidly backed into the shadows between the bookshelves, coffee spilling over her hand and dribbling on the floor.

"Stop. Kimberly, please, come here."

She didn't move. Cormac's voice was a lot gentler than she remembered it, but she couldn't seem to find her own to say anything in reply.

"I'm sorry. I hadn't realized..."

"Realized what?" she asked, her voice breaking. "That I might not want to know if you were planning on cutting me off from my magic so you could interrogate me? Christ, I could have at least worn a better shirt for this. Brushed my hair. *Something*. Oh, my God."

He sighed deeply, rising from the stool. As he took a step closer, she took a few steps back. Sensing she was on the verge of bolting, he paused, then extended a hand instead.

"It was not my intention to upset you. I'm a very private man, Kimberly. I don't have much occasion to have anyone, let alone someone who uses trickery as the foundation of their magic, ask me for favors. I didn't do this with the intent to embarrass you."

"Yeah, well, I'm not exactly dressed for an interview. I'll come back later."

"Don't go," he said, cursing himself for only thinking about getting what he wanted rather than considering her potential reaction or any other reasons for her to dress herself in illusion aside from making herself look more attractive. She didn't know him well enough yet to realize just how much it had cost him to apologize or just how much he hated being wrong. "We both know once you walk out that door you won't come back."

He could hear the click in her too dry throat as she swallowed. Her low voice didn't hide the waver. "Maybe that's for the best."

"You doubt I can help you?"

"No."

"Why, then?"

She put the coffee cup down on the bookshelf and backed away. If he didn't move fast, she'd have one foot out the door in moments. "What can I offer a dragon? Look at me. I'm a mess. I couldn't even tell when you used a dispelling glyph. And after what I saw today, I can't help but think it'll hate me on sight. How am I ever going to do this?"

He wasn't sure what to tell her. It was bothersome that he thought she had implied with her refusal that he didn't have the power or connections to give her what she was looking for, only to find that he was—again—wrong in his assumptions. What was worse was the foreign sensation of... was that regret? Something he didn't like, whatever it was.

The depth of his error was obvious. She was ready to give up what might be the only road she saw out of her problems all because he managed to yank off her mask. The deepening scent of her shame, like some sour fruit, was clinging to her even stronger than lingering scents from her job—sugar, coffee, and bread—and the cheap lavender detergent she used on her clothes. He was used to people fearing and sometimes even loathing him, but he had never so carelessly shredded someone's pride before. It didn't sit well with him.

"Please, don't leave," he said, thinking fast to come up with some excuse to make her stay. Why, why did he want her to stay? "Your company—and your honesty—is more important to me than the clothes you wear. And I still have questions for you."

He took a slow, measured step closer. She stayed where she was instead of inching her way toward the exit. Progress.

Taking care not to startle her into flight, he tugged his neatly folded cream-colored handkerchief out of his breast pocket and held out his other hand. He waved off her weak protests about the inevitable stains, and she didn't pull away as he dabbed at the mess. The Swiss cotton soaked up the coffee like a sponge. Once he sopped up as much of the spilled coffee as he could, he took her arm and led her back into his store.

Blood still running close to the surface of her skin from her blushing was hot against his fingertips, and that teasing scent of some Other leaving its mark on her was distracting him. Then she jerked and shivered as they moved back into range of the glyph he had installed late the night before. Her muscles tensed like she was getting ready to bolt again, so he slid his hand down to the small of her back to keep her moving, then urged her to take a seat on the footstool so he could settle into a crouch before her.

It took a little time before she stopped looking anywhere but at him, her wandering gaze eventually settling on her shoes. Her fingers kept fiddling with a loose string on one of her shirt cuffs.

"I'm sorry," she whispered.

"Sorry? Why are you sorry? I'm the one who should be apologizing."

She shook her head. "I overreacted. I'm never like this. I've just been so nervous all day. That spell—the naga—"

Cormac clenched his fists so tightly his knuckles cracked. That explained the Other scent. "What naga?"

She pulled back, just a little. He took a breath and let the tension ease out of his shoulders and arms, then another to ensure his tone stayed even. He repeated his question, this time without the possessive growl.

"What naga, Kimberly? Tell me what happened."

"Professor Reed invited another mage to class today. We were supposed to practice comportment with his familiar—the naga—but one of my classmates hurt it during my turn and it would have killed me if I didn't see it coming and use a simulacrum." Cormac opened his mouth, but she held up a hand to forestall him. She bit her lip, then took a hitching breath and continued. "After what I saw today... After I saw how the mage treated Sam, I've been wracking my brains all day trying to think of any reason for a dragon to ever agree to let me put it in that position. You know what I came up with?"

Cormac took one of her shaking hands in both of his, stilling her nervous fidgeting. "Not a damned thing. Am I right? Because I was intending to ask you about that very thing from the moment you told me what you were looking for. That's what the glyph was for."

"I can't do this," she said, voice gone dull. "I need to, but I can't. I can't think of anything I could offer a rational, thinking being to convince them I would never treat them like I saw James treat Sam today."

Chapter Ten

"I don't think things are quite as dire as you believe," Cormac said. "Though I certainly won't lie. Dragons are proud, fickle beasts. A mountain of jewels would never be enough to buy their servitude. Though some may be more inclined to help a person in need than you might think."

She gave a weary nod, but it was clear by her slumped shoulders and dull, reddened gaze that it was all she could do to keep from further disgracing herself in front of him by bursting into tears.

Cormac had been out of the loop for some time, but even he had heard about the young naga tricked into servitude by some upstart mage looking for a way to fast track himself to the top of a major coven. The mage's single-minded greed was too much of a turn-off to the magi who might have helped him realize his ambitions. Thus far, even the good luck granted him by the serpent hadn't led James beyond his own small slice of land bordering the Everglades. Though he had done exceptionally well at the casinos.

Sam, the naga, was naïve and too sheltered in his temple to know how cutthroat some magi had become in their efforts to secure a powerful, intelligent Other as their familiar. Considering his background and his kind's proclivity toward setting themselves up as minor deities in their remote riverside and jungle temples, it was no wonder he had fallen for the offerings and praise. Sequestered from the world as he was, any Other raised in a tradition of being worshipped as that naga had been would have found the mage's flattery disarming. His folly had become something of a cautionary tale to the rest of the Other community; a reminder that letting yourself be shackled into servitude to a mage wasn't a guarantee of mutual respect, admiration, and assistance like it had been in the past.

Cormac still thought both Kimberly and Eleanor were a few beers short of a six-pack if they thought he was going to do anything other than keep the girl off the scent of any true dragons.

Yet her despair was genuine, as was her distress about what she had seen the other mage do to the naga. He tasted no deception whatsoever in her scent or words thus far. The shimmer of the luck charm the naga had bestowed on her didn't have the power to alter his perceptions, but he could readily tell that it was making him more inclined to be helpful. Had he minded or thought she was deliberately using the charm to get what she wanted, he could have twisted that aura of good luck into its polar opposite.

As it was, he didn't think she had grasped what kind of gift Sam had given her or how to use it. Most magi he knew would have wielded the luck like a weapon, aimed straight at their heart's desire. Kimberly gave no sign of being aware of the subtle shifts it was causing in the ley lines around her, tiny gold threads twining through the natural blue, white and green streams of power only visible to those with Sight to see it. It was something like moving chess pieces in place to improve her chances of success. He also considered the naga might have had the right idea and used his grip on her hand to buffer the charm with some of his own magic, strengthening the spell.

He was starting to rethink his original plan, too. Rather than keeping her off the trail of *any* Other who might be persuaded to accept her, perhaps a pseudo-dragon like a wyrm, wyvern, or maybe even another naga (if he could find one as foolish and naïve as Sam) might suit her. If only he didn't dislike the idea of letting someone else do something so intimate as bond with her. His possessive streak was the damnedest thing; he couldn't put his finger on what was drawing him to her, but his instincts rarely lied.

Regardless, he still had questions that needed answers. First and foremost, he wanted to know more about her and the path that had brought her to him. His efforts to delve into the magical side of her parentage through skrying and divination had turned up nothing, and he wasn't about to ask Eleanor. Distasteful as he found it to be so blunt, he supposed if she could be brave enough to sit here and bear his scrutiny despite her discomfort, he could do her the courtesy of being as direct as his nature allowed.

"I would like to help you, but I need to ask you a few personal questions. As much as I trust Eleanor's judgment, not every Other in town thinks the same, and I need to be prepared with ready answers if I'm going to convince anyone else to meet with you." Not exactly the truth, but it was close enough to it that she probably wouldn't detect his little deception. The only convincing he would have to do would be to demand it be so, and most any Other in town would bend to his wishes—but he didn't think she knew that. "That is, if you want to continue to pursue this quest of yours."

She didn't answer right away, staring down at his hands wrapped around her own. Then she took a breath and straightened her spine, using her free hand to swipe a palm under her eyes and then sweep her hair back before focusing on his face instead. He was pleased to see the flicker of resolve returning, bolstered by the threads of luck reweaving her destiny.

"Okay. Yes. If you think there's a chance, maybe I can do this."

He did his best to ignore the pang of guilt that statement caused him. He just had to keep telling himself that keeping her off the scent of any true dragons was more important than his desire to help the less fortunate.

Maybe if he repeated it to himself enough, he'd eventually believe it.

"First, I would like to know about your family. I understand you live with your mother. She's human, yes?"

Kimberly's eyes widened, and she pulled away just a bit in surprise. "How did you know that? Have you been checking up on me?"

He gave her a smile with a few too many teeth showing. "You asked for a shot at wooing one of the rarest and most powerful Others to walk this world. They don't usually accept an audience without knowing beforehand that the intentions of their visitors are pure."

She didn't flinch from his posturing, giving him a wry look. "Melodrama suits you. You could have done things the easy way and just asked me. But to answer your question, yes."

That startled him into dropping the fierce look in favor of a bit of laughter. "I suppose I do tend to the overly dramatic now and then, don't I? Yes, I'd like to know a bit more. Who your father is, for starters. Any magical connections in your bloodline you're aware of. What can you tell me about yourself and your family?"

"I don't know who my father is. My mom said she had a one night stand back in her clubbing days and the guy must have been a mage. Her parents kicked her out when she got pregnant, so she's raised me by herself. I've been helping her pay the rent doing odd-jobs and babysitting since I was eleven. We didn't even know I could cast until I was sixteen and started summoning illusions every time I got stressed." She coughed and blushed, giving him a sheepish smile. "She didn't believe it until we had a screaming match about a guy I was seeing and it looked like I turned her into a giant shrew. As soon as it wore off, we looked into how I could get some formal training to get it under control. That's how I got into Blackhollow."

He gave a snort, amusement curving his lips. "I see. Well, your lineage isn't quite as important as your circumstances or your intentions. Tell me a bit more about what you're doing now and your plans for yourself and your familiar."

She pulled her hand out of his grip, grasping the hem of her shirt to pull it out and brush at the patch of powdered sugar against the dark green button-down. He couldn't help but notice that the third button from the bottom was missing. To keep from staring at that enticing hint of flesh visible between the gap in her shirt, he focused his gaze on her face instead. That's when he noted the dark circles under her eyes for the first time and just how prominent her cheekbones were.

Exhausted and probably hungry, it was no wonder she'd had such a difficult time finding her composure. He would get his answers, then send her home—and think of some way to help her. He didn't want to keep her too late waiting for takeout and wasn't prepared to feed her, which bothered him far more than it should have. He would remedy that tomorrow.

"Well, I was really hoping to get a job in the entertainment unit at The Circle after I graduate, but I'll take anything I can find as long as it pays better than what I'm doing now and I actually get to use my skill set. I'm working at a café—"

"Which one?"

"Allegretto's. Anyway, I take as many hours as I can to help Mom pay the rent. I go every day after school, and I usually work a shift on Saturday and most Sundays, too. The rest of the time I'm in school or studying."

That explained the smear of sugar on her shirt. He waited to see if she had anything to add. Maybe discuss spending time with friends or greater ambitions than a job designing themed illusions for parties hosted by those rich enough to afford such extravagance. Which still didn't explain what she wanted the dragon for. He would have assumed a walk-on position in management, or maybe doing some flashy sub-contracting work for the Department of Defense. Considering Eleanor's involvement, it was the most logical assumption.

As the silence stretched between them, he frowned and tilted his head as he studied her, taking a surreptitious sniff to see if he might have missed a scent cue.

Nothing.

"Are you honestly telling me you want a dragon familiar, but have no intention of using its power?"

She swept a hand through her hair and gave an impatient huff before answering him. "Of course not. I need to graduate, don't I?"

"Yes, yes," he replied, impatient, "but once that's done and you have your dream job—then what?"

She shrugged. "I guess I'd let it go. I don't need a familiar to cast my illusions, and I wouldn't be any use to anybody anywhere else in the coven. It would be nice if I could borrow from its hoard to get a nicer place—maybe some new clothes, too—but I'd pay it back as soon as I could."

She believed every word that came out of her mouth. There was not the slightest hint of a lie in her scent, no taste of deception from her. He was utterly baffled by her lack of greed and ambition. What she'd said was true—all she wanted was to improve her lot. After seeing her wardrobe, he supposed he could understand why.

That sent the very last of his doubts and assumptions about her out the window. The situation was not what he had assumed at all—though Eleanor had a hand in it, which meant he still had reason to be wary.

"Very well. I can see you're tired. Why don't you go home and get some rest. Tomorrow night, I'll meet you at your café and we can get started."

His heart gave a lurch at the surge of hope shining in her eyes. "You'll introduce me to a dragon?"

"Not yet. But," he hastened to add, hoping to alieve that crushing disappointment killing the hope in her eyes before it had chance to take root, "you'll be taking a big step in the right direction."

Now if only he could find a way to give her what she needed without destroying her—or her building trust in him—in the process.

Chapter Eleven

The next day, Kimberly breezed through her classes, for once looking forward to heading to work. Having learned her lesson about relying on her illusions, she had picked her best clothes out of her closet and talked her mom into helping her put her hair into a neat French braid before they both rushed out the door that morning.

Most of the other students gave her a wide berth throughout the day. There was new graffiti on her locker, and a wooden coin on a string which had a repel evil glyph etched into it, which was insulting but harmless. Compared to Aiden's prank with the fire, Kimberly counted herself lucky there wasn't something dangerous or obnoxious waiting for her in the halls beyond some dirty looks and dispel glyphs being air drawn in her direction. She ignored the spattered insults on the industrial gray paint, untied the charm from the latch, and tucked it away in her locker. They weren't cheap, after all. Maybe she could pawn or reuse it.

In both her Understanding and Applying Counterspells and her Advanced Casting Circles: Group Circles and Related Spells classes, no one wanted her as a lab partner. She overheard a few of them whispering about Aidan and the naga a few times. Aidan wasn't around and no one knew if Dean Morrell had expelled or just suspended him.

The only student brave enough to ask her about what had happened the day before was a boy named Xander. Though she'd seen him around—he was a 4th year like her, and they had a few of the same classes—they had never spoken before until they were assigned as lab partners in the counterspell class. He was a lot more popular than she was and, truth be told, she'd had something of a crush on him from afar. He had a kind, charmingly crooked smile that always made the corners crinkle up around his eyes, but considering the company he usually kept, she had never felt comfortable approaching him.

They worked together to draw the intricate runic circle designed to dispel electrical energy. He kept sneaking looks at her from across the table until she got sick of it and asked him what was on his mind. They both kept their voices low so as not to draw the Professor's attention.

"Do you know what happened to Aidan? Yesterday, I mean?"

Her charcoal smudged as her hand jerked, and she cursed quietly under her breath before answering him. "Professor Reed took him to see the dean after he hurt Sam."

"Sam?"

"The naga."

"I didn't know it had a name."

At her incredulous look, he reddened and turned his attention back to filling in the thicker portion of the spiral he was working on with his charcoal. Neither of them said anything for a few minutes.

"It—Sam—he gave you luck, didn't he?"

Kimberly kept her eyes glued to the newsprint, though her hand went still on the paper. Considering how things had gone for her the night before, she wasn't so sure about that. She shook her head, then resumed sketching out an oval with a line through the center.

"Maybe. I don't know. The way things have been going for me the past few days, I'll be lucky to make it through the rest of the school year intact."

He gave her a smile that soon had her smiling back.

"I wouldn't worry about it," he said. "You've got skills the rest of us don't. I always wanted to ask you about those illusions you did in our first conjuration class. Professor Harrington, right?"

Their laughter got them a visit from Professor Cohen, who stood over them tapping his foot while they put their noses back to the shared table and diligently applied charcoal to paper. When he moved on a few minutes later, they continued a whispered conversation and agreed to meet over the weekend to do homework together. For the first time in a long time, Kimberly thought she might have made a friend.

So she was in good spirits when Cormac arrived at the café a little after 9:30 that night, a half hour before her shift was supposed to end. After serving a late night dessert of ladyfingers and an espresso to the man ahead of him in line, who was giving him a strange look, she leaned over the counter to give Cormac a sunny grin and take his order.

He had been taking in the rest of the store—every visible inch, not just the selection of sweets, muffins, and specialty loaves of bread—and in return was being ogled by the few customers hoping to get a late night discount. Their blatant stares might have had something to do with the severe wool peacoat and neatly pinned cravat he was wearing. Or maybe it was the chiseled cheekbones and intense eyes, combined with just enough scruff to make him look like a rake in duke's clothing. No doubt, the getup was odd and anachronistic, even for New York City and its legions of hipsters.

"What can I get you while you wait?"

He shook his head and turned those icy blue eyes on Kimberly, his look so intense it momentarily stole her breath away. She could have sworn something in that look said *you.*

"What would you recommend?" he asked.

A little flustered, she turned away, bustling over behind the display case with the cookies. "Um, our biscotti is out of this world. You like hazelnut coffee, so you'd probably like the chocolate-dipped cinnamon hazelnut. Or maybe the anise? Oh, or the banana-rum—"

"The first one sounds fine," he said, the quirk of his lips slipping from sultry to amused. "Choose something for yourself, too. My treat."

She got him his coffee and biscotti—then a second biscotti for herself when he insisted—and rang him up. After she slid his change across the counter, he tugged a bill out of his wallet that made her eyes bug and stuffed it in the tip jar, along with the change. Ignoring the look she gave him, he picked up his treats and headed to one of the three circular tables over by the windows.

For the next half hour, Kimberly did what she could to ignore how he watched her every move over the rim of his cup. Staying industrious helped, but her hands were shaking with nervous energy and she fumbled a few times, spilling coffees and dropping pastry crumbles on the floor and counters.

It wasn't very busy, but Don eventually came out to help her clean up behind the counter. He gave his best *shouldn't you be moving along* look to Cormac, but it didn't do a thing to stir him.

"This guy bothering you?" Don asked, not bothering to lower his voice.

Kimberly set down the rag she was using to wipe down the counter and put her hands on her hips as she gave Cormac a pointed look while answering Don. "He's being a bit of a weirdo tonight, but no. He's waiting for me."

Don looked back and forth between the two, frowning. He radiated disapproval for the remaining five minutes Kimberly had on the clock, and didn't say a thing when Cormac offered her his arm. She tilted her head, staring up at him with a puzzled expression as he led her outside. She waited until they were half a block away from the café before she opened her mouth.

"What is up with you tonight? You're acting so strange."

He glanced down at her, a hint of that rakish smile returning. "I'm finding I'm enjoying this excuse to get away from my responsibilities for a night."

That, and he thought he might be able to upstage that naga that had left its mark on her with what he had planned. His actions tonight would set in motion the first steps of his strategy to scare up a decent familiar for Kimberly. The stir his involvement would cause in the local fae community would be delicious and was guaranteed to pique the interest of any number of powerful elemental creatures. Never mind that the thought of someone else bonding with her made him grit his teeth. He relished the *challenge* of it.

So they walked, arm in arm, urged along by the brisk April wind.

Kimberly kept sneaking looks up at Cormac, hardly noticing where they were going. He was such a puzzle to her. Handsome and severe, and maybe kind in a quirky way, but she wouldn't have pegged him as adventurous. Plus she was starting to wonder if he might be attracted to her. Nothing else made sense of him doing his best impression of Colin Firth, with his Darcy-esque staring in the café, or why he was going out of his way to be so nice to someone who was basically a stranger to him.

Being an adult about it, she decided to ignore that for now.

"Where are we going?"

"Not far. I'm taking you to meet an old friend of mine who runs a café of her own."

"If you wanted to do dinner, we could have stayed. Don makes a mean chef's salad."

"Delightful as that sounds, I'm afraid I have an ulterior motive for asking you to dinner. This place is something of a congregation spot for Others looking for a safe place to meet and relax. I'm taking you along to... well, let's just say we're showing you off."

She nudged his ribs with her elbow, prompting him to glance down at her. "What's that supposed to mean? Showing me off... to whom? Or what?"

Cormac lightly bumped her shoulder in return, giving her a smile brimming with anticipation as they passed under a street lamp. "The local network of elementals. All the creatures that want to hide from your kind. Remember to play nice."

Eyes wide and so firmly focused on him that she didn't notice a crack in the sidewalk, she didn't get a chance to respond as she tripped. Her jaw snapped shut as she stumbled, tightening her grip on him to stay on her feet. He stopped, moving inhumanly fast to catch her before she could fall.

He held her that way a long moment, one arm around her waist and the two almost nose-to-nose, both of them breathing a bit too hard. She slowly straightened, and he pulled back once she was steady again, fingertips lingering on her arms.

When she cleared her throat, he stepped back and offered her his arm again. They resumed walking, a bit slower this time.

"Thank you," she said. At his nod, she chuckled and scuffed her shoe on the sidewalk. "Some big, bad, scary monster of the night I turn out to be. Can't even watch where I'm walking."

"There is nothing scary or monstrous about you. There are plenty of Others who might disagree, a few of which will be at the café tonight, but this will lay the groundwork for us to find what you need."

She laughed again, not quite so strained this time.

"You say the sweetest things. So, back on track. You're telling me there are a bunch of different kinds of Others a mage might want to make into their familiar in the city, and they're all hiding in plain sight? I mean, Professor Reed did show me a list of some Others that supposedly live here in town, but I was having a tough time believing it."

"Of course. Like many other cities, some breeds native to this part of New York are extinct, or nearly so, thanks to the encroachment of humanity and interference from spellcasters of all kinds. The bulk of those still alive keep their heads down and live on the outskirts of civilization, avoiding magi for the most part. Many of them hide behind a human guise most of the time. Those who do live in cities mostly live in a constant state of fear of being discovered, and only congregate in safe havens like the one I'm taking you to tonight. Which, for their safety and yours, I ask you not to visit without me."

Kimberly shook her head, her smile slipping. "They really do hate us, don't they?"

Cormac didn't respond right away. When they paused at a crosswalk, he tilted his head up, squinting at the few stars visible in the sky. Even with his keen vision, the light pollution from the city made them hard to spot from his current vantage point.

"Centuries ago, it used to be an honor to serve with a mage. There were contracts, agreements, mutual benefits... but times have changed. It's more like slavery now. There's no guarantee they'll be given their freedom back. Can you blame them for being afraid?"

"No. Of course not."

"Don't worry about convincing anyone about anything tonight. For now, we're just stirring the pot to see what comes to the surface. My contact won't fear you. She knows almost every Other in the Tri-State Area and hates magi with a burning passion."

Kimberly jerked to a halt, her hand slipping from his arm. He paused, looking back to her in question.

"Hates magi? Why the hell are you taking me to meet someone who will hate me on sight?"

He grinned. "Because as soon as she hears what you're looking for, she'll get in touch with everyone she knows and tell them to go into hiding. The ones strong enough to be worth your while will be struck with insatiable curiosity and stir themselves to investigate. Some may even come to you with an offer."

She frowned at him. He just held out one hand for her own, sweeping the other out to gesture in the direction he'd been leading her.

"Trust me, Kimberly. If there's one thing I know, it's how a dragon thinks."

Chapter Twelve

Kimberly wasn't too familiar with the area on this side of Central Park despite that her school was right across the street from it and Allegretto's was only a few blocks away. What little time she'd spent at the park had been in the sprawling, open field known as Sheep's Meadow and had always been during the day.

It wasn't that she had avoided Central Park because of its lingering reputation for being a haven of depravity, where one was as likely to be mugged or shot as looked at. Quite to the contrary, this part of New York was in no way the crime-ridden cesspool it had once been. Developers had been buying up the property around the park, building condos and lofts that sold for tens of millions of dollars. Between the gentrification and the combined efforts to discourage crime in the area courtesy of the NYPD and the Moonwalkers, a local werewolf pack that claimed Central Park as its territory, it was a great deal safer than it had been in the 80s and 90s.

It was also a given that Others would be crossing through the park at any hour of the day. The Moonwalkers didn't do a thing to police the foot traffic during the day, but they were a constant presence after the sun went down. There was an unspoken agreement that any Other who wasn't a Moonwalker didn't linger in their territory at night. Kimberly sensed the werewolves nearby, following her and Cormac under the cover of darkness on the other side of the street, pacing their movements. She wasn't too worried, but she did keep glancing at the greenery in the midst of all the towering buildings around them for any visible signs of their shadows. She'd yet to meet a Were and wasn't sure if these were the circumstances under which she would want to be introduced.

Nearing Central Park North, Cormac steered her into a dark, narrow alleyway between two towering apartment buildings. She hadn't been paying much mind to the buildings they were passing since she was more interested at the prospect of spotting a werewolf across the street, but the abrupt change of scenery and encroaching shadows thick as molasses had her digging her heels in.

Cormac paused when she did, giving her a wry smile that seemed totally incongruous given the menacing dark of that alley.

"The fear is setting in, isn't it?" he asked. "I feel your heartbeat accelerating."

She swallowed hard and nodded, then pulled back as she thought she spotted movement in the dark at the far end of the alley. Something shifting behind a Dumpster. Was that a flicker of red eyes?

"That's one of the wards kicking in, trying to drive you off. It's nothing but smoke and mirrors—something like your own illusions. You're safe."

She shook her head. "There's something back there."

"Yes. Where we need to go. Close your eyes and take my arm again. Nothing will happen to you. I promise."

Though a bit dubious, she did as he said, clinging to his arm and closing her eyes tight. She had to believe that he wouldn't have taken her this far only to let some boogeyman snatch her and drag her into that soul-sucking darkness at the end of the alley. Even though she kept repeating that silently to herself, every hair on her body was standing at stiff attention, and her muscles kept trying to seize on her before she could take another step.

With her instincts screaming at her to flee, she barely heard the Word Cormac uttered. Some kind of key to let him past another ward, though she was too frazzled to note what he'd said or what sort of obstacle he'd removed from their path.

What felt like an eternity later, the formless terror in her gut dissipated so abruptly that she was left gasping for air. Eyes popping open, she stared up at the bright blue and white neon sign for the Black Star Café above the awning of what looked like a perfectly ordinary coffee and pastry shop. Then glanced back over her shoulder. The park was still in view, a pool of light from a street lamp illuminating the opening onto Central Park West just a few yards away.

They hadn't gone more than a handful of steps, but she would have sworn they had crossed the length of a football field.

Shivering from more than the spring chill in the air, she hitched her backpack up higher on her shoulders and then tugged her jacket closed with one hand as Cormac led her inside. She went in first as he held the door for her, and she once again found herself struck immobile with fear. There was a short, pale slip of a girl behind the register who was an absolute *powerhouse* of elemental energy. So much so that Kimberly didn't have to rely on her inner sight to see the threads of power gathering around her, and that steady glow was building as she pointed in Kimberly's direction.

"*Mage!* Get out of my store!"

Every eye in the place turned on Kimberly. Before she could move a muscle, the tiny woman flung her hand in her direction. Kimberly flinched back, but between one blink and the next, Cormac had stepped in front of her and snatched the projectile out of the air. He passed the shiny silver dagger to her, and she fumbled and dropped it in her nervousness. It fell to the floor with a bell-toned clang.

"She's with me," Cormac said, his voice a low, dangerous purr. He was not very broad in the shoulders, but something about the way he held himself made him seem so much bigger than before. An immovable mountain rather than a whipcord blade. "Attack her again and it's your hide, changeling."

The woman slammed her hand down on the counter, and the register gave a metallic *bing*. "You will *not* disrespect my wishes, you filthy betrayer. Get out, and take that... that *thing* with you!"

"Are you voluntarily revoking your territory's status as neutral ground?"

There was a collective intake of breaths as the other patrons in the restaurant focused on the woman. Their shared fear ratcheted up the tension in the room by several notches. Kimberly only managed to catch a glimpse of the mostly human faces before Cormac turned to pull her to stand before him, his hands resting in what she thought was an uncomfortably obvious show of possession on her shoulders. She preferred hiding behind him considering the woman had thrown a dagger at her heart mere seconds earlier.

The woman came out from around the counter, fists clenched at her sides. Kimberly didn't mean to stare, but it was obvious that whatever flavor of Other she might be, in her human form she was afflicted with albinism. Her skin and hair—even her eyebrows and eyelashes—were parchment white. Her pallor was made all the more striking by a seamless silver collar around her throat and her white silk clothing. Even her heavy boots were a solid white, polished until they gleamed. She flicked a wrist, and another silver dagger appeared in her hand. She stared at Kimberly with murder in her crystalline blue eyes.

"Don't push me, you son of a bitch. The moment that monster makes a move toward me or any of my customers, you can kiss your ass goodbye. I'll kill you both myself."

Kimberly glanced at Cormac over her shoulder, her voice wavering in a shaky stage whisper. "I thought you said this woman was your friend?"

The lady answered before Cormac could. "If he's playing with magi, he's no friend of mine. What the hell are you doing in my café?"

"She's in the market for a familiar, Rieva. A dragon."

There were a few muted gasps and whispers around the room. The albino, Rieva, stared at the two for a very long moment before slowly, deliberately setting her other dagger on the counter beside her.

"You're not known for your sense of humor, Hunter. I really hope you're joking."

Cormac bared his teeth in a semblance of a grin. "It's no joke. Relax, she's not going to bind anyone on your turf."

"Ha-fucking-ha. Order something or get out."

"Two coffees. And bring my friend a dinner menu."

Though she continued to glare for a long, tense moment, Rieva soon spun on her heel and busied herself behind the counter. Cormac led Kimberly to an empty table near a rickety-looking stage by the back of the room. As soon as they moved away from the door, half a dozen people got up and fled, disappearing into the shadows of the alley.

Once they were seated, Kimberly let her breath out in a whoosh, and returned some of the wide-eyed stares she was receiving from the patrons who remained. While she had some trouble with elemental spells, she had no difficulties seeing through the illusions a number of the Others in the room were cloaking themselves with.

Some were true shapeshifters. When they were masquerading as human, she had no way of knowing what they really were, since they were for all intents and purposes in a flesh-and-blood body sculpted and shaped in ways to let them fit in with mundane society. Aside from the glimmer of unnatural energy in their auras, they could have been mistaken for human or low-grade magi. Others already resembled humans enough in form that all they needed was an illusion to cover up the growths, scales, fur, feathers, or other signs of their supernatural nature. The pair of elves by the door, for example, who used illusion to roughen their facial features, hide the tips of their pointed ears, and dim the glamour that might make those susceptible become entranced by their beauty.

She also spotted a water nymph, a satyr, and even a minotaur. No vampires. No magi. Much to her surprise, she also realized that a couple of the people sitting closest to her and Cormac were mundanes. Normal humans with no hint of magic in their blood. They were staring at her and whispering behind their hands, making notes on a pile of papers they had between them and gesturing excitedly.

That was when she realized just how eclectic the rest of the place was. Just like the myriad patrons, the furniture was all strange and mismatched, but fit together in a way that bespoke safety and comfort. Easy chairs, rocking chairs, wicker chairs—an odd collection that flanked tables of all heights and sizes, and scattered bookshelves filled with everything from history books to chapbooks of poetry to romance novels. Most everyone was nursing cups of coffee or tea and had books or magazines in their hands instead of tablets, cell phones or laptops.

The Black Star Café really was a haven.

Chapter Thirteen

"You're bleeding."

Cormac lifted his palm, examining the shallow slice the dagger had made when he caught it. The wound was already closing.

"So I am. It will be gone in a moment. Nothing to worry about."

"Yeah, right," Rieva said, slapping a couple of menus down on the table, making Kimberly jump. The proprietress then set a small tray with mismatched coffee mugs, a carafe, and a tiny pitcher of fresh cream down between them. The scent of hazelnut wafted from the cup she set down in front of Cormac; despite her attitude, she clearly knew what her customers liked. "Sorry I'm not sorry about the hand. If you're not going to do me the favor of fucking off, then tell me what kind of cosmic joke made you darken my doorstep."

"Rieva, as always, your establishment remains a bastion of civilization and grace in these troubled times."

"Spare me, you insensitive prick."

"And as eloquent as ever, I see."

"I'm only vulgar to short-sighted, obtuse ingrates who clearly don't know how to take a hint."

Kimberly cleared her throat, drawing the irate gaze of Rieva. "Ma'am, I am terribly sorry for my intrusion into your territory.

Had I known it would distress you like this, I would never have come."

Rieva's harsh look might have been intimidating, but Kimberly didn't flinch away. The changeling ran her tongue over her teeth, glanced at Cormac, then let some of the tension ease out of her shoulders. She eyed the bracelet on Kimberly's wrist before speaking again, her tone gone flat.

"Nice to see you're more polite than the company you keep. Honey, you can do much better than this asshole."

Cormac watched their exchange like a hawk. His look of warning to Rieva went completely ignored.

"She isn't here for you," he said, making a shooing motion with one hand as he reached for a menu. "Give us a few minutes, will you?"

Raising her hands in defeat, Rieva turned on her heel and stalked away, leaving them alone.

Kimberly shook her head and grabbed the other menu, hiding behind the thick tri-fold. She ground out a few words between her teeth, doing her best to focus on the neat script under the dinner section of the menu so she wouldn't start glaring daggers at Cormac.

"You might have warned me when you said she hated magi that you meant she hated us with a homicidal passion."

"It's inconsequential. You're under my protection. It's all bluster; she won't try to hurt you again."

Unable to concentrate on anything but price tags that made her stomach plunge, she set the menu down with a sigh and reached for one of the mugs of coffee, dumping in a bit of cream and sugar. Even the drink was an extravagance she couldn't afford, but she wasn't about to offend Rieva by sending it back, so she figured she might as well enjoy it.

"I'm not sure if I'm more angry with you or myself right now." She took a sip of her coffee, and her eyes went wide, pupils dilating. "Whoa, what's in this?"

"Rieva brews her drinks with water infused with concentrated ley line energy," Cormac answered absently, still perusing the menu. "There's no need to be angry. We've done what we set out to do tonight. You were seen with me and your intentions were announced publicly. Now we wait to see who takes the bait. You really should try the American wagyu. It's out of this world."

The description of the specialty steak had sounded amazing, but she'd also seen the triple digit price tag.

"Thanks, but the coffee is fine."

He lowered the menu, his icy blue eyes colder and more implacable than Rieva's judgmental glare. "You need to eat something." He paused, then softened his command with a wry smile. "The least you can do to get me back for putting you through this dog and pony show tonight is hit me in the wallet. Go on, get whatever you like. They only recently added the dinner menu here. It would make Rieva feel better if we gave her the business."

Though she didn't have much appetite considering how much adrenaline was still rushing through her veins, she had to agree that she should eat. The coffee—or, more specifically, the power it was infused with—was making her head spin. As off balance as the situation and most of the price tags on the menu made her, she shrugged it off and told Cormac she'd have whatever he was having.

Rieva soon returned to take their orders. Cormac ordered the steak for himself and Kimberly, along with a slice of the chocolate decadence cake for dessert.

"You realize I'm doubling your tab with the pain-in-my-ass tax, right?"

"Whatever makes you happy," Cormac replied.

Rieva returned his smile with a sly, toothy grin of her own. "I can't wait to see how you screw this up, Hunter." She then turned a slightly more cordial look on Kimberly, taking the menu out of her nerveless fingers. "If you know what's good for you, the minute you leave here, start running and never look back."

Kimberly gave her a wan smile of her own. "I would, but I'm already in this mess up to my neck."

"Hey," Cormac said, frowning.

Rieva started to turn away, then paused. She slapped the menus against her leg a couple of times before turning back, hands on her hips.

"I get it when a mage wants a familiar, but why a dragon?" Rieva asked.

Kimberly scrubbed a hand down her face, then gestured vaguely in what she thought might be the direction of her school. "It's a long story, but I'm a student at Blackhollow. I can't graduate or get a job without a familiar, and I don't have the skillset to summon one. If I can find an earthbound elemental to help me out for a week or two, that's all I need. My teacher suggested a dragon would solve a lot of problems for me, and she's the one who thought Cormac could lend me a hand. So here I am, trying not to make an ass out of myself."

A snort was startled out of Rieva. She shook her head and then laughed in what sounded like genuine amusement. For the first time, Kimberly noted how lovely the tiny woman's voice was. Her laughter was like the chiming of silver bells; clear, ringing, and utterly mesmerizing. That sound would haunt her dreams later, she was sure, and had probably lured more than its fair share of mortals to their doom.

Once the laughter died out, Rieva placed a fingertip on Kimberly's chin, tilting her head up to peer into her eyes. Kimberly tried not to blink, figuring the woman was reading her aura and wouldn't appreciate having the contact cut, even though she hadn't asked permission. Considering how high-strung the Other was, Kimberly wasn't about to risk doing anything else that might piss her off.

Rieva broke eye contact moments later, turning a speculative look in Cormac's direction even though her words were directed at Kimberly.

"You're not half bad for a spark," Rieva said. "Try not to invest too much of yourself into this hunt. I'm afraid you won't like the outcome."

"No one is going to hurt her. I won't let them," Cormac said.

Rieva's only response was to level the full force of her stony expression on him before shaking her head in disappointment and gliding away with the menus.

Once she disappeared behind the swinging door into the kitchen, Cormac added some cream and sugar to his own coffee before taking a deep pull, giving no sign of discomfort at Rieva's warning. Kimberly braced for the jolt of energy as she sipped her own drink, and tried not to worry too much.

She was starting to suspect that Cormac knew more than he was telling her, and something about this "hunt" of his wasn't ringing true. Time would tell, she was sure, but that wasn't a commodity she had in great supply.

Studying him over the rim of her coffee cup, she reminded herself that he had promised to help her. Though in the back of her mind a part of her whispered that he hadn't yet put a price tag on his aid or told her what was in it for him.

She set down her cup, fingertips toying with the rim as she stared at the vibrations on the surface rather than at her dinner partner. "I wish you'd warn me next time you put me in mortal danger. Am I going to have to worry about monsters following me home tonight? Is my mom in danger? Will someone be waiting to shiv me in the hallways at school tomorrow?"

Cormac reached across the table, his warm fingers pressed lightly over her own, stilling them. "Stop worrying. Like I said, I won't let anyone hurt you."

She nodded, though fine lines of strain remained around her eyes. "My mom doesn't have the spark. I've got school and work—I can't always be there to keep her safe—"

"Kimberly."

She looked up, her haunted gaze meeting his.

"No Other in their right mind who plans on keeping their freedom will approach you directly. Even if one of them is foolish enough to try something, I'll be watching out for you. And your mother, if you wish."

He sat back as Rieva approached with their dinners. She took one look at Kimberly's stricken face, set the plates down, then reached over to a nearby table to grab a napkin wrapped around silverware. Shaking the square of cloth out, she pressed it into Kimberly's hands, shot an accusatory look at Cormac, then flounced off back to the kitchen.

Cormac watched the changeling go, his eyes narrowed to dangerous slivers. Then he turned back, gesturing to the steaming plates of steak and lightly grilled vegetables. The scent wafting up was divine, but he ignored his hunger, waiting for Kimberly to take the first bite.

She didn't touch the food. He knew she had to be hungry, but she was just looking at him with the strangest expression, wringing the napkin so hard her knuckles were going white.

"What is it?" he asked.

"What are you?"

There were a couple of choked-off sounds and whispers nearby. Though it wasn't a question one normally asked of an Other—speciesism was frowned upon—he didn't take offense.

"A friend. Come on, eat up."

She continued to stare, though she went through the motions of cutting up her food. It didn't escape her notice that Cormac didn't touch his own food until she took her first bite.

She could have sworn for a second that she had seen beyond his skin and that, like Rieva, he was a veritable wellspring of power. Not that she doubted it, but she usually had to concentrate to see elemental magic. Her Sight tended to be limited and hazy, and it was doubly odd that she had seen something without having to put effort into it first.

That coffee must have been tweaking her perceptions. The other creatures who were shifted into a human form rather than using illusions to hide their nature gave off a similar aura, but nothing near the level of power she had detected from the changeling or from Cormac.

Obviously, he wasn't interested in giving her any straight answers. She turned her attention to her food—not very difficult, considering the steak was some of the best she'd ever tasted, and the thick slice of rum-infused chocolate cake they shared for dessert was melt-in-your-mouth delicious—but throughout the meal, the question remained in the back of her mind.

The aura of magi "sparked" with their unconscious influence on their environment as they absorbed power, often in a miasma of colors unless they were gifted in the use of a particular element. Elemental Others were more like bubbling springs or fountains, a constant flow of power shaded with the colors of the elements that formed their essence.

Though he was doing something to mask the strength of his nature, she had seen his brand of power, and it was like nothing she had ever encountered before. While she had never seen her own aura, or that of another sorcerer, somehow she didn't think he was like her.

He was no mage. Nothing remotely human.

Seeing as he wasn't about to come clean on his own, and she was beginning to suspect Professor Reed would remain similarly close-lipped if she asked, she had to figure out what kind of mess she had walked into. Everything about him and his motives was now suspect. After the night's fiasco, she couldn't afford to wait for him to get around to telling her what he was or why he was helping her on his own time. Time was running out and even with Professor Reed's recommendation, she couldn't be sure his offer of protection was genuine. She would need to do some research of her own into Cormac Hunter.

It might be the only way she could survive this hunt intact.

Chapter Fourteen

Despite Cormac's reassurances, Kimberly couldn't stop worrying about her mother's safety. If she had any skill whatsoever with elements, she could have fashioned a protective spell to shield her. Instead, she would have to rely on enchanting a few runic stones and hope her mother wouldn't forget to keep them close enough to be effective.

Kimberly's ability to infuse an enchantment into an item was greater than that of most of the other students at her school, but she didn't have all of the necessary ingredients or any idea what she should be protecting her mother against. The only protective runes she could make at home were basic, and she'd have to use some of her school supplies to do it, but it was better than sending her mother out entirely unprotected.

Dragons and their ilk came in as many flavors as there were elements. They didn't have to breathe fire or use their great strength to be dangerous. Not to mention there was no way to guess what the specialty of any attacking magi might be.

While the major elements—fire, wind, water and earth—were easy enough, there were hundreds of sub-specialties and cross-element spells that could be used. No runic glyph existed that could stop them all. If some enemy turned her mother's heart to stone, filled her lungs with water, froze her insides, cut off her oxygen, poisoned her food—there was no single catch-all shielding spell Kimberly could concoct to protect against all of those things. As a mage, she had some innate sense of when such spells were being cast and could counter them herself without relying on components or charmed objects. Her stonework counterspells still needed some work, but otherwise she was just as proficient as the next student in personal shielding.

Her mother had no spark. She wouldn't even know what was happening, and had no way to sense a magical attack coming. She could be dead before she even knew something was wrong.

When she got home, Kimberly tore through her third year *Semi-Permanent to Permanent Enchantment* and fourth year *Counterspells & You* and *Intermediate Redirection, Countermagic and Sheilding* textbooks. She knew the counterspell and defensive spell books were all geared toward teaching personal protection cast on the fly, but she was hoping she could find some way of applying them to what she knew about wards to set a myriad of protective enchantments on the apartment.

Her mother came home just after midnight, still wearing her black slacks and stained long-sleeved shirt from her latest stint at the diner down the street.

Like Kimberly, she was skinny and a bit hollow-eyed from constant stress. They shared similar bone structure and the same skin tone, but Kimberly had gotten her reddish-brown hair and fae green eyes from her father. Her mom's hair was much lighter, almost blonde, and chopped short in a pixie cut. Her brown eyes were heavy with exhaustion, and her lips twisted with displeasure the moment she walked in the door and saw the candles, mortar and pestle, and baggies of various herbs, shells and stones spread out around Kimberly in the middle of the hallway.

"I wish you'd do your homework in the living room, kiddo."

Kimberly flushed and scrambled to her feet, making some room for her mom to slip by.

"Sorry, Mom. This isn't homework."

At the thundercloud passing over her mother's face, she ran back to her supplies and grabbed a handful of runic stones, like small, round river stones, freshly etched with glowing symbols. Her mother shook her head and moved into the living room, tossing her purse on the couch as Kimberly held out the stones for her mom to see. She didn't touch them.

"Don't be mad! This is important. Please, keep these on you at work, okay? Put them in your purse or your pocket."

Her mother didn't object as she put the stones in the faux leather purse, watching with a weary expression. She didn't say anything at all until Kimberly stopped bustling around and turned to face her again.

"You know how I feel about this stuff. I really need some help this month. If you've got this much free time, I need you to use it putting in more hours at the café, not messing around with this voodoo junk. We're short on the rent and I can't get any more hours at the diner."

Kimberly tried to ignore the constriction around her heart, but she was still having a hard time speaking around the lump in her throat. "Mom, please—"

"Don't get started. I'm going to shower and get some sleep. Finish your homework, clean up this mess, and get to bed. Let me know what Don says about your hours tomorrow."

Kimberly stood there as her mother headed into the bedroom. A few minutes later, the shower was running.

Clenching her fists in frustration, she glared a burning hole in the floor where she'd left her spelling ingredients—then dismissed the illusion before her fury might freak out any neighbors smelling the fake smoke. Angry and frustrated beyond measure, she thought about throwing everything out, just out of spite—but then common sense kicked back in.

Even if her mother didn't want to have anything to do with this side of her, Kimberly still had a responsibility to do everything she could to protect her.

Though she'd probably get grounded for sending their security deposit on the apartment down the drain, she used her spelling chalk and etched a series of protection glyphs around the door frame. The pale blue chalk wasn't so visible in the dark against the cream-colored paint. Maybe she'd get lucky and her mom wouldn't even notice the marks until the danger was past. Even if she did spot it and tried to clean the chalk, it wouldn't come off. Kimberly set the glyphs; a fae light briefly glimmered in the shadows of the hall, then faded. Now her power, or that of a stronger magic user than herself, was the only thing that could remove them.

Her mom might not like it, but at least they would be safe from most basic elemental attacks or intrusions. Someone could still set the building on fire or destroy it with a bomb, but no one of a supernatural nature would be sneaking into the apartment or lobbing any magical grenades inside anytime soon.

She spent the rest of a mostly sleepless night tossing and turning, unsure if she'd thought of every possible type of protection rune to stick in her mom's purse. Also trying and failing to come up with a decent plan to keep herself safe, too.

As soon as the sun rose, a little after 6AM, Kimberly was up and at her books again. This time she was searching her textbooks for any clue how to decipher what an Other was when they were hiding in a conjured body instead of using illusion to blend with their environment. There was plenty of information about tactics for seeing through the illusions an Other might use and how certain turns of phrase in their speech might give some general clues, but no specifics, and nothing about how to read their auras.

When her mother woke up, she found Kimberly sitting cross-legged on her bed surrounded by books. She was staring at the one in her lap like she could glare the answers she wanted out of it with the force of her will alone.

She grimaced, but rolled out of bed and started getting ready for work without doing anything to interrupt her daughter's concentration.

Kimberly lost track of time and didn't notice until she overheard her mother's dismayed shout—looked like she found the glyphs—and voiced a curse of her own when she spotted the time on the clock on the bedside table. Flying off the bed, she threw on her clothes, ran ragged fingers through her hair to get it out of her face, and scrambled to find the books she needed for class.

"What did I tell you? This mess better not still be here when I get home tonight, young lady!"

"Yes, Mom!" Kimberly shouted in reply, hopping on one foot as she fought to tug on one of her sneakers.

"I mean it!"

"I *know*, I'm *sorry*! I'll get it tonight! Go to work, you're gonna be late!"

Minutes later, Kimberly was following her mother out the door, sprinting down the hall and taking the stairwell instead of the ancient, rickety elevator. Bursting out into the street, she took off full-tilt for school, huffing like a bellows as she clutched her backpack straps tight.

She was glad it was still cool out in the mornings. It made her straining lungs not ache quite so much as she ran two and a half miles through the city streets. The buildings around her gradually—and in a few places, not so gradually—shifted from old brick and granite, some with boarded up windows, to shining marble and gleaming chrome.

It didn't take as long as she had feared it would to get to the Museum of Natural History. She still had almost half an hour before her first class started. Breathing deep, she started circling the block to walk off the stitch in her side.

When she rounded the corner on Central Park West, Xander was on the other side of the street waiting at the crosswalk. She returned his wave and paused when he shouted for her to wait up. She leaned against the short stone pillar holding up the museum's fencing at the corner. She surreptitiously weaved a bit of magic to hide just how sweaty she was, then reached up to tie her hair in a ponytail to get it off her neck.

Moments later, Xander trotted up to her side. He nudged up his sunglasses with his thumb, giving her a cheerful smile. "Hey, you're here early. Want to grab a coffee before class?"

"Nah, but I'll go with you if you want one."

They headed to a Starbucks only a half a block away. It was packed with people in suits and a few early bird tourists, but the service was quick, and Xander was soon sipping a caffè americano.

"I don't know how you can drink that bog water," Kimberly teased.

"Hey, it's expensive, so it must be good," he replied, grinning.

They headed to the deep shadows under one of the trees in front of the museum. Just as Kimberly was about to step into the hidden Gate disguised as a natural alcove in a tree that would take her directly to one of school common rooms, a leather-clad arm shot out to block her way.

She jerked back, looking up into eyes an unnatural yellow hue, arrestingly luminous in an otherwise unremarkable face. Aside from his height and strangely colored eyes, there was nothing obviously out of the ordinary about him. He grinned down at her, his teeth gleaming white and sharp.

"So this is the fierce and ferocious dragon hunter. You're shorter than I expected."

Xander stepped closer, his gaze flitting back and forth between the two. "Kimberly, what's going on?"

The strange man cut Kimberly off before she could stammer out an answer. "Get out of here, boy. This doesn't concern you."

Kimberly skittered back, and the man straightened, never taking his eyes off her. She held up her hands to ward him off before he could take another step closer. Nearby pedestrians were giving them a wide berth. One of the security guards by a driveway in front of the museum was muttering into a walkie-talkie, his eyes glued to the three.

This went against everything the two magi had been taught. The first rule of being Other was, above all else, *blend with humanity to survive*. The obfuscation spell on the Gate was limited; it only worked if you weren't doing anything to call notice to yourself. Anyone making a point to stare at the spot, like that security guard, would see the people disappearing into thin air as they stepped into a patch of shadow beside a particular tree. Even if they got rid of this newcomer, Kimberly, Xander, and any other Blackhollow students who were planning on using the Gate on 77th and Columbus would have to find an alternate route inside this morning thanks to the attention they had drawn.

"Look, I don't know what you want, but I've got to get to class."

"Not today, you don't. I've got a proposition for you. Come with me and we'll talk about it."

Xander stepped between them. To anyone without a drop of spark in their blood, the power gathering around his upraised palm would be invisible. The passerby might assume he was doing an impression of The Supremes, telling the stranger to stop in the name of love, or something very much like it. Whereas to Kimberly and the Other who had accosted her, to their Sight, the threads of red and white energy were building a formidable fire-based shield that shimmered into life between them.

The Other finally broke his unblinking stare, switching that cold, calculating gaze to Xander. The mage held his stance, unflinching.

A slow, wicked smile revealed too many fangs behind the Other's lips. "Your white knight can't keep you safe forever. Watch your back, dragon hunter."

A hand appeared on his shoulder, spinning him around. As Cormac leaned in, the stranger scrambled back and out of his reach. Neither Kimberly nor Xander had seen Cormac approach; it was like he'd appeared out of nowhere.

"You watch yours, Viper. Slither back to your hole and don't let me catch you anywhere near the girl again."

The man he'd called Viper snarled something Kimberly didn't catch, then turned on his heel and fled. He melted into the pedestrian traffic so rapidly that both magi quickly lost sight of him.

Xander lowered his hand, clenching his fist around the glittering threads of energy he'd summoned. The (mostly) invisible shield winked out of existence, giving an audible *pop* that made a few people walking nearby jump in surprise and look around for the source. He took a sip of his americano, looking around with mild curiosity as if he, too, were searching for the source of the sound.

Cormac didn't look at either of them or make any attempt to blend with the crowd, his gaze focused in the direction Viper had disappeared. When he spoke, his voice was a low, husky growl that sent shivers up Kimberly's spine.

"Use the entrance off of 81st. Use the Gate to Grand Central when school lets out and I'll escort you to work."

"Are you serious? I'll be late for work. If I'm late again, I'll lose my job!"

"I wasn't counting on someone like Viper taking an interest in you. I'd rather you be safe than risk another encounter with him."

"Hey, would one of you like to clue me in on what's happening here?" Xander asked. "What did I just step into?"

Cormac turned, eyeing Xander with a decided lack of enthusiasm. "He wasn't after you. Thank you for your attempt at heroics. I'll be taking it from here."

Kimberly frowned at Cormac before answering Xander. "Thanks for your help. Let's get moving, class is starting soon. I'll fill you in on the details at lunch." She started walking backwards, waving at Cormac. "And thank you, too! But I can't go to Grand Central, that'll take me way too long to get to work. Meet me on 81st?"

He nodded, so she gave him a thumbs up. Xander followed a bit more slowly, his mystified expression deepening as Cormac disappeared in the foot traffic behind them.

Chapter Fifteen

The two magi didn't have any classes together for the first half of the day. Kimberly did her best to keep away from Xander during the lunch hour, but she couldn't avoid him when they continued their lab project in Professor Cohen's *Advanced Circles* class. Xander waited until they both had their heads bent over the paper spread out on the table between them to start whispering his questions.

"What the heck was that about this morning? Who were those guys? *What* are they?"

The tip of Kimberly's charcoal snapped off. Her gaze flicked up at him, then back down to focus on filling in the thick lines of the rune she was working on.

"You know as much as I do about Viper. Cormac is a friend, I think. Professor Reed has him helping me with some stuff after school."

"Dragon hunting?"

Either some people were listening in, or he'd spoken louder than intended. Kimberly was positive half the eyes of the classroom were now focused on them. Her own whispered reply came out harsher than she intended.

"*No.*" She paused. "Okay, yes, sort of. It's a long story."

Xander's palpable excitement was drawing the eye of Professor Cohen again. He was eyeing them over the horned rims of his glasses and leaning in their direction. Kimberly spoke up a little louder.

"What page had the picture of the transference rune again?"

Xander didn't miss a beat. He used the back of his thumb to turn the pages of his copy so he wouldn't smudge charcoal all over his textbook. "58. See, I knew that angle should have been like this."

The professor lost interest, moving on to check on the progress of some other students. Kimberly let out the breath she'd been holding and pretended to be busy reading the fine print under the picture in the book.

"If you want to help me," she muttered under her breath, "maybe you can do some research and see if you can figure out what Cormac is. He's *something* magical, I just can't figure out what. And I'm pretty sure he has ties to dragons."

"That is *so cool*. Have you seen any yet?"

"No. Just some elves, a minotaur, and a couple other things last night."

Xander's jaw dropped, his eyes going wide as saucers. Then he realized he was drawing attention to himself again and quickly got back to etching one of the major elements into its place around the larger protection rune Kimberly was filling in.

The project they were working on was practice for their final exams. It was the basic binding pattern for the inner workings of the summoning circle they were supposed to use to call their familiars. This was their last practice run doing the pattern on paper. Next, they would etch it in spelling chalk on the specially built platforms in what was dubbed the summoning room; a chamber built specifically to keep out any outside interference and allow the student magi to safely summon their first familiars. The room was designed to keep any planar escapees trapped should the summoning circle or binding spell fail.

When the time came, Kimberly would need to use something similar, sans the calling symbols and items like clay and water for a planar creature to form a body to use. Whatever manner of familiar she convinced to step into her circle, it would be earthbound. She lacked the ability to call anything ephemeral to do her bidding. No, she would be convincing a living, breathing, flesh-and-blood elemental monster to step into her circle of its own free will—and to put that will in her hands.

One thing was certain. If she couldn't find a dragon, Cormac was some flavor of earthbound Other. She wasn't sure what, but he knew what kind of trouble she'd be in if she couldn't find and convince a dragon in time. He was willing to help her search, and said he would protect her, so if things got down to the wire, maybe he'd be okay with becoming her familiar for a few days. Obviously he was *something* powerful, and that was all she needed to prove to the mage community that she was capable of protecting herself.

Even if she couldn't find a dragon, as long as she had some kind of familiar, she could walk away with a diploma and maybe get her foot in the door of a decent coven with an internship if there were any openings. It wouldn't be the same as walking into her dream job, of course. There was a chance she might have to suck it up and work for Don longer than she'd planned just to make ends meet until she met the requirements for a better position somewhere. She might even have to settle for a place in a smaller coven, or one out of state that needed someone with her skills. That would still be better than failing out of the academy at the end of the school year and seeing all her hopes and dreams slip through her fingers.

She only had one shot. There were no do overs when it came to final exams. You either passed, earning the diploma you needed in order to qualify for a license, or you didn't, earning nothing but enough of an education to know better than to attempt to cast or sell your services as a mage without the proper licensing and paperwork. Her original plans to use illusion on her tests had all gone out the window, making it frightfully easy to fall into panic mode every time she thought about how little time she had left to meet the one major requirement she had no workaround for—finding a suitable familiar to bind.

Xander flicked a small hunk of charcoal at her hand, drawing her out of her momentary funk.

"You okay? Where'd you go just now?"

She gave him a thin smile. "Thinking about the future. We better get this right."

They concentrated on their sketches. Near the end of the period, the professor swung by their table and checked their work.

"Good job. Looks like you're almost done. You can both get started on your circles in the summoning room on Monday."

"Thanks, professor," Xander said.

"Have a good weekend, you two. Stay out of trouble."

They managed to finish the drawing just in time, putting their charcoal down just as the bell rang.

Xander helped Kimberly put away her materials and hefted up her backpack for her, walking with her out of the classroom. "We still on for our study date tomorrow?"

She shrugged. "I'm not sure. Things are a little up in the air with this hunt."

"Hey, don't sweat it. What's your cell number? I'll call tonight, we can figure something out."

That prompted a grimace. Things like cell phones and computers were luxuries she couldn't afford. They didn't even have a phone at the apartment. If she needed to do mundane research or type reports, she did it on the computers at the library.

She took her backpack back as they reached her last class for the day, not meeting his eyes.

Xander wouldn't be following her inside; she was taking the optional high school equivalency and college admissions prep course. The student magi who didn't need the class were either heading home for the day or heading to the library to check out whatever references they needed to cram over the weekend for their upcoming finals. Most didn't bother; it was the "failsafe" course to ensure that any mage who couldn't qualify for a job in a coven could still apply to mundane college to make something of themselves in the human world.

He chewed on his inner cheek, realizing too late what an awkward position he'd put Kimberly in and not sure how to pry his foot out of his mouth.

She gestured vaguely. "Maybe you can swing by my job for lunch tomorrow? I work at this café not far from here, Allegretto's. I should know more then."

"Oh, yeah, I know the place," he said. "That's perfect. I've got a family thing tonight, but tomorrow morning I can hit the books and see if I can find out something about that guy. I can also ask my parents. My dad works at the Great Neck Commune and my mom is a cop. If they don't know anything, I'll bet they can find out."

"Hey, it's not that urgent," Kimberly protested. "Cormac hasn't done anything wrong—"

"No, no, I just mean they might know what he is. I won't have Mom bust down his door." Xander grinned.

Kimberly gave him a wry grin in response, then a light punch on the shoulder. "Don't scare me like that. The last thing I need is to freak him out and drive off my best lead for a familiar. Oh, and ask them if they know about an Other named Rieva, too. Or a Black Star Café."

The first bell for the last period rang. Students were filing past Kimberly and Xander in a rush to get to their seats. Xander grabbed Kimberly's arm as she turned away, holding her back.

"Before you go, it's driving me crazy. Why are you looking for a dragon?"

"I can't summon," Kimberly admitted, pulling away as his grip loosened in surprise. "I'll tell you all about it tomorrow, I promise. I'll see you later!"

Kimberly headed into the classroom, taking one of the last empty seats near the back row.

"All right, everybody. Butts in the chairs, eyes on me. That means you, Tony. Let's do a quick refresher on Social Studies, and then we're hitting the science chapter again."

Kimberly pulled out her book, groaning along with half the rest of the class. Arnold Moore was a high ranking mage on loan from The Circle to meet the coven's tithing requirements for Blackhollow. He was a good teacher, but tough. Despite that, she liked him far better than the guy who had been running the class last semester.

Blackhollow was one of five magic academies in the U.S. While some magi might take on apprentices, there was no guarantee for the apprentice to find a place in a coven once they completed their training. Most major covens would not accept magi without formal training and a letter of recommendation from one of the established academies as too many apprenticed magi relied on dark arts and black enchants to get results. All covens for the areas falling under the purview of their academy paid tithes to guarantee the service of tenured professors, and housing and materials for students like Kimberly who couldn't otherwise afford tuition.

In addition to paying tithes in terms of materials, the covens were also expected to send a representative or two for each semester to assist with tutoring, seminars in advanced classes, and prep for non-magical subjects like taking the tests for the high school equivalency. It helped offset the burden on the local covens from supplying all of the training and tenured professors, and gave every coven in the academy's territory an equal shot at wooing potential future blood infusions into their ranks.

Arnold was something of an anomaly in the mage community. He had multiple college degrees, but worked in security for The Circle. Having spent a great deal of time in the mundane school system, he was uniquely suited to preparing the next generation of magi not only to take the tests for their high school equivalency, but how to blend with mundanes should they choose to pursue higher education. That experience combined with his job in security added to his eye for good potential prospects, and led to him being a natural choice for teaching the closing class for the last semester for that school year.

It had only been a little over a decade since the Twin Towers fell and Others announced their presence to the world. It might have started with the Moonwalker werewolf pack offering to help dig survivors out of the rubble of the Towers, but magi didn't take long to follow in their footsteps. Some covens, such as The Circle, took advantage of the instant fame and global interest in their kind, selling magical services to anyone who could pay their fees. Many smaller ones might offer simple services to locals—charms and the like—but those magi had a tendency to do those services on the side while working "normal" jobs to blend and pay their bills.

Kimberly had high hopes, but she had known before the end of her first year that she would need to take the extra classes and to be prepared to fill out a plethora of paperwork for student loans. If things went the way she hoped, filing that paperwork would be unnecessary. If The Circle turned her down, or all she could get was an internship, she would still pursue a college degree. No matter what happened, she refused to be stuck working in diners and cafes, struggling to make ends meet, for the rest of her life.

She refused to follow in her mother's footsteps.

Chapter Sixteen

Cormac was waiting for her on a bench near the Gate on 81st when she got out of class. This time he wore dark sunglasses and was dressed in a high-collared woolen frock coat, one leg slung casually over the other. She was just a teensy bit surprised to see he had foregone the usual cravat for a slightly less conspicuous white formal shirt with a point collar and dark tie threaded with gold. Despite how enormously frumpy she felt next to him in her jeans and plain T-shirt, she had to admit he cut a striking figure, with or without the odd suits.

He held out a coffee cup for her when she reached him, taking a sip from his own. She lifted it to check out the midnight blue logo, curious since it wasn't instantly recognizable. Then suppressed a shiver when she spotted the text under the silhouette of a coffee cup with an eight-pointed star above it. Just like the neon sign she'd seen the other night.

The Black Star Café.

"I hope I put in the right amount of cream and sugar," Cormac said.

"I'm sure it's fine," she responded faintly. She could swear power was radiating through the thin paper cup, sending a strange tingle up her arm. "Is this stuff safe? It made my vision funny last time and I barely slept a wink last night."

He rose from his seat, falling into step beside her as they headed toward Allegretto's. The sly smile he gave her was all too pleased. "Did it? Excellent, that means it's working."

She shot him a look, but he didn't elaborate. They continued for a little over a block before Kimberly blew out a frustrated breath and turned her gaze heavenward.

"You're driving me crazy."

That drew a surprised glance from Cormac. "Am I?"

"Can you let me in? Just a little bit? Seriously, what is this stuff doing to me?"

He tapped the cup lid lightly with a fingertip, the hollow tap sending ripples of stronger tingles crawling up her arm.

"You said you had trouble with elemental magic. You're drinking it in a distilled form. Since you're not used to it, I'm sure it might feel a bit strange at first, but it should be helping wake up any dormant senses or abilities you might have."

She pursed her lips, considering that. Then sighed again before taking a long pull from the coffee cup. If only she had heard about this stuff four years ago, back when she was first starting out as a Blackhollow student, she might have saved herself a great deal of grief and difficulty. Using her magic during most practical assignments in class had been like trying to force a square peg through a round hole. The only way around the endless frustration had been to make it *look* like she'd achieved the results of the spells using her illusions, leading to her little teacher-student conference with Professor Reed the other night.

As the strange, warm tingle seeped into her limbs, she examined the cup again, focusing on using her second sight. It was so full of fae water-based energy, ranging from robin's egg around the edges, deepening to indigo and then midnight blue in the center, it was like holding a tiny, pulsing star in her hand.

Cute. The café name made a bit more sense.

"I guess I owe you another thank you," Kimberly said, tipping the cup at him in salute.

He nodded in reply. If she hadn't been so close, she might not have noticed that his gaze kept flicking around behind those sunglasses, searching for something. Or that his own aura was sparking today, so bright and hazy with power that it was too blinding to look at directly. Different from last night. It looked more like that of a mage this time. Albeit, one who outclassed every mage in terms of raw power that Kimberly had ever encountered.

She looked away, and was immediately overwhelmed by a bewildering array of magical auras on the street around them. Oh, they were still outnumbered by mundanes. But there were nearly a dozen magical creatures on the street around them, more hazy outlines visible through the walls of the surrounding buildings, and even one strange, big shape on the rooftop of a brownstone across the street.

She shook her head and dispelled the Sight, not wanting to see every passing Other for what they were. Not to mention lingering enchantments and the swirling, multi-hued ley lines all around them. In the middle of a major city like this, the Sight was as dizzying as a kaleidoscope when one was standing perfectly still. Trying to See while walking was giving her a headache.

That stuff in the coffee seemed to be making her Sight stronger than she remembered, too. Better to focus on something a little less likely to give her a raging case of vertigo.

"Any chance I can get you to spill what you are yet? You know I'm going to find out eventually."

That sly smile of his faded. "Someone who went through a rough patch, somewhat like you. I admire your talent, your bravery, and your perseverance. If you believe nothing else, trust that I am doing what I can to help you."

"I don't doubt that," she said. "What I'm worried about are how all the things I don't know might come back to bite me on the ass. Like this morning. Who was that guy? Viper?"

Cormac tossed his empty coffee cup into a trash can as they passed, then put a hand on her arm to stop her. He tugged her body flush against his as he leaned against the brick façade of the brownstone on their left, leaving her gasping and dropping her drink to grip the lapels of his coat to steady herself. This close, she couldn't help but notice how warm he was, and some kind of exotic, spicy scent on his skin. It wasn't the incense from his shop, though there was some hint of it clinging to his clothes. Whatever it might be, like his aura, Kimberly had never encountered anything quite like it before.

He leaned down until they were cheek to cheek, whispering in her ear.

"Don't speak his name again. He's too close."

She shivered, tightening her grip on his coat as she whispered back. "Is he dangerous?"

"Until you find someone to bind, yes. He's the only Other I've ever heard of who successfully made a mage his familiar. If you don't have one of your own, you're fair game, and he's been looking for another to take the last one's place for decades."

Shocked immobile, Kimberly stiffened against him as a wave of terror jolted through her. Cormac lightly tugged a lock of her hair, his voice lowering to a throaty growl.

"He'll never touch you. Not while I'm here."

After the initial shock wore off, she pulled back, searching his face. With the sunglasses, it was a little hard to figure out what he was thinking, and his closeness was terribly distracting. The moment she realized just how tightly pressed she was against him, she pulled back, flushing.

"There's nothing he can do to me. The binding spell won't work without my consent. I'd never agree to that. Ever."

"We can't be sure of that. There's no guarantee he would play fair, and your teachers have left a deliberate gap in your education if you believe that rubbish," Cormac said. "It's my fault he's after you. Until we get you what you need, I'll be shadowing you to keep you safe."

Kimberly voiced a half-hearted curse under her breath, then gestured in the direction they'd been headed. She couldn't quite bring herself to completely break their body contact.

"We should keep moving. I can't be late."

He slid an arm around her waist, keeping her close as they resumed their trek to the café. Though she felt silly doing it, she leaned into him, enjoying the warmth of his touch.

She knew she should have been angry with him for his cagey responses and for making her problems worse, but his calm reassurances and closeness made her feel better. Not totally safe—but better.

"You said he's close," she said, keeping her voice low. "How close?"

He flicked his fingers to indicate the rooftop where she'd seen the odd shape. The scarily large, very inhuman shape.

Staring up at that rooftop as they passed, she tightened her grip on Cormac just a bit. Then scanned the street with her Sight again, using her hold on Cormac to keep herself steady. Once she found what she was looking for, she couldn't help the spread of a triumphant smile.

"Let me lead," she told him.

Mystified, he shifted his grip so she could direct them across the street. At the crosswalk, he couldn't help but notice that they came so close they nearly brushed shoulders with a couple of the Others he had peripherally spotted trailing them. The minotaur and one of the elves that had been in the café the night before, and it appeared they were both more interested in Kimberly than Cormac. The two both had matching guilty expressions when they saw the sharp look he gave them.

Then he blinked as their forms shifted and wavered in his vision. He was soon looking at a mirror image of himself and one of Kimberly, and a couple of nearby pedestrians were doing double-takes. His hackles raised when he thought he scented another of his kind—but then he realized that the scent originated from what had been the minotaur, along with heavy notes of incense that came very close to matching the mix he used in his store.

He no longer smelled like himself. Or anything, in fact. He couldn't even see his own hand when he lifted it in front of his face, even with his Sight.

Illusion. Kimberly intended to throw Viper off their scent with duplicates.

And it was working perfectly. Now that they'd been made and their targets looked to have disappeared into thin air, the minotaur and elf made it a point to rush off in opposite directions, not yet realizing their appearances had been altered.

He sensed Viper's presence moving with grace and speed, leaping from rooftop to rooftop, fading in the distance as he followed the elf who had been made to look like Kimberly. Then a light pressure on the small of his back propelled him forward. It was surreal not to see or smell her but to still feel Kimberly's fingers sliding around to take his arm.

"That was very clever," he said.

"Thank you," came her disembodied voice in reply. "I'll drop it in a couple minutes. We're almost there."

"I wonder what other clever things you can do with this talent of yours."

He grinned as her heartrate sped up under his fingertips, her body temperature rising. Kimberly gave him a light jab with her elbow, a hint of breathless laughter in her voice.

"Are you coming on to me, Mr. Hunter?"

"Come to think of it, yes. I like you. Very much."

It was difficult to say who was more surprised by the admission. They continued on in relative silence, only their footfalls and the occasional ripple in a puddle giving away their presence.

When they were just around the corner from Allegretto's, Kimberly waited until she was sure no one on the street was looking to drop the illusion. Her sober expression as she regarded him cut right through his good mood.

"Are you sure about that?"

He frowned down at her, covering her hand on his arm with his own. "Of course. Why wouldn't I be?"

She pulled away, speeding up to head into Allegretto's first. He lengthened his stride to catch up, holding the door for her. She didn't answer his question, hurrying behind the counter. Annabelle scooted over to make some room, her eyes widening when she spotted Cormac stalking inside behind her.

As Kimberly shed her jacket and tossed her backpack under the counter, Annabelle sidled over to the display to stop before Cormac.

"What can I get you, handsome?"

He dragged his gaze off of Kimberly, not returning the flirtatious smile Annabelle gave him. He studied her briefly before returning his attention to Kimberly, speaking a bit louder than necessary.

"If you can get her to answer me, that's all I require at the moment."

Annabelle and Cormac both stared at Kimberly. She glanced over her shoulder, then threw her hands up. "Not now! I'm working. We'll talk about it later."

Don stuck his head out of the kitchen door, mopping sweat off his face with a bandana before turning the full force of his frown on Cormac. He looked back and forth between him and Kimberly, then eased his way out to take a casual lean against the counter. The thick muscles of his arms bunched impressively as he leaned forward.

"This isn't a public park, son. No loitering unless you're buying something."

Though a muscle twitched under Cormac's left eye, he gave a cursory look at the selection of sweets before pointing out a chocolate croissant. He kept his eye on Kimberly the entire time Annabelle prepared and rang up his order. When he turned to look, there were no free seats, and Don was still giving his "move along" glare.

Voicing a low growl of frustration, he turned to the door, glancing at Kimberly over his shoulder. "I'll see you when you finish your shift."

She nodded, not meeting his gaze. He'd get a piece of her mind soon enough.

Chapter Seventeen

Cormac took a deep breath once he was outside, tucking the bag with the croissant into an inner pocket of his jacket, then made a beeline for a dark alley between buildings just down the street.

Once under the cover of late afternoon shadow, he melted into the darkness between the buildings. It swallowed him up, letting him slide between the bars meant to keep passing pedestrians out. Within a few yards, he reached a fire escape about sixteen feet above the ground, with the ladder extending only a bit below that.

He leapt. Aside from the faint clang from his shoes hitting the platform and his hands grasping the rusting metal rail tight enough to make it squeal, he made no sound as he worked his way up to the roof.

He pulled himself over the edge and stalked over to the section overlooking the café, crouching down and settling himself in to wait. His fingertips bit into the granite cornice and his gaze went distant as he focused on other senses to remain aware of any potential threats approaching.

The sun continued its trek across the sky, sliding past the horizon. Stars winked into view, visible at that height even with the haze of smog and light pollution lingering over the city.

Cormac remained still, unmoving save for the occasional gust of wind stirring his hair or clothes.

While he was aware of his surrounds, a great deal of his attention was turned inward. He was starting to see why Kimberly was driven so crazy by his tendency to sidestep her direct questions.

He could not imagine why she was so spooked by his admittance of fondness, nor could he figure out why she was so hesitant to tell him why she thought he didn't mean it when he told her so. She'd returned his physical advances, initiated touch on her own a couple of times, and was trusting enough to take him at his word. So why the hell did she think he didn't really want her?

He was positively *burning* with curiosity, and even found himself tempted to stomp back into Allegretto's to make an offer for the café to Don just to free her up to talk to him. It wasn't like he didn't have the money to burn—but even as he had the thought, and though he wasn't any flavor of human, he knew that would be pushing her boundaries a bit too far.

He wanted her talking to him because *she* wanted to. He wanted her close. He wanted her *happy,* damn it.

The worst part of it all was that he was beginning to think it had been a mistake to keep his nature from her. She deserved to know. He knew that. Now that he knew her better, it was clear she wouldn't have posed a threat to him had she known from the start. The trouble was that he was sure she would shut him out the minute he came clean.

He didn't think he had erred in being direct about his feelings, but he was almost certain that she was turning skittish because she had picked up on his failure to be completely honest with her.

It was a dilemma, and he had no ready answer for how to fix it. In all his years, with all his experience and power, he had never had the urge to spend time with a female the way he did with Kimberly. He might let off steam with a willing partner now and then, but he didn't form attachments—let alone relationships. She wasn't greedy or grasping for his money or power. She wasn't put off by his bristling or attempts to brush her off. More than that, he liked speaking with her. He liked showing her new things, seeing the wonder in her expression, and her admiration when she found something he did or showed her impressive.

He needed to make things right before he dug himself a deeper hole. Even if he was helping with her hunt, she already suspected he was more than he appeared.

Or maybe she had caught a glimpse of the real him when she drank the special brew from the Black Star.

After a time, the hairs on his arms rose, and a silent snarl twisted his lips. A small chunk of the cornice crumbled to sand as he clenched his hand, then he rose and swung around to face Viper standing on the opposite side of the roof behind him.

"I never thought I'd see you protecting a mage. A sorcerer, no less."

"And I never thought you'd be foolish enough to challenge me a second time. She's *mine*."

Viper's yellow eyes flared in the dark, his razorblade smile prompting another growl out of Cormac. The newcomer stepped off the edge of the roof, his trench coat flaring out around him, coming to a halt when there were only a few meager yards separating the two men.

"The bird's not yours. You haven't marked her. You haven't taken her. You haven't given in to her not inconsiderable charms." Viper licked his lips. "That smells a great deal like fair game to me, Hunter. She doesn't even know what you are yet, does she?"

Cormac's own eyes glowed a fierce white-blue, fallen stars flashing in the night.

"Oh, hit a sore spot, I see."

"I may not have marked her—yet—but she's mine, all the same."

"Rieva doesn't think so. She thinks you're bad for the girl." Viper laughed. "Worse than me, if you can believe it."

Cormac hissed and took a step closer. Viper stood his ground.

"If you touch this one," Cormac said, "I'll kill you. No warnings. No second chances."

Viper cocked his head to one side, his eyes flaring brighter. "I don't think such theatrics are necessary. I think she'll come to me of her own will. As soon as I tell her whose company she's been keeping, she'll be the one begging *me* for help in her little quest."

Cormac darted forward, hands outstretched into claws, but Viper was already on the move. His form was expanding, wings darker than the night spreading to catch the wind and carry him up and back, away from the rooftop and far out of reach.

Cormac stood there, fists clenched at his sides, staring after the fleeing form winging away into the dark. He was tempted to give chase, but there would be little point. If he gave in to his urge to hunt, that would leave Kimberly alone and unprotected.

Viper wasn't the only interested party out there. After seeing how many Others had been following them on the street, he was on edge, ready to lash out at the next unlucky creature to make a move on Kimberly.

The litany in his head was growing louder.

His. She was his.

He didn't stop growling until he realized his fingernails had bitten into his flesh, blood dribbling from his fists to patter on the tarred roof. He flexed his fingers, letting the wounds close. With a thought, the tiny droplets of blood that had fallen burned away into steam and rust-colored flakes, flitting away on the wind.

He resumed his place overlooking the café, not really seeing what was happening below.

He couldn't be around Kimberly every moment of the day, and couldn't be certain that those he'd assigned to guard her mother were capable of dealing with a threat as significant as Viper. He had to figure out how to tell Kimberly the truth, and do it quick, before Viper could slither in and do it for him. He had to find some way of convincing her that he hadn't deliberately set out to hurt or deceive her.

If he couldn't manage that much, he had to make sure she understood that Viper would never help her, and that he'd only be looking out for his own interests. Not hers.

Gradually, he got control over his temper. No matter how therapeutic he thought it might be on the short term, shifting and rampaging through the city wouldn't help his case.

Taking a steadying breath, he kept an eye on the comings and goings on the street below. There were a few Others who came by, probably sniffing Kimberly out, but they were soon making haste elsewhere when they caught his scent.

Rieva was living up to expectations, spreading the word. Cormac had never guessed she would have mentioned anything to Viper. Not this soon. Of all the possible outcomes, of all the many creatures he had thought might have been curious and tried their hand for winning Kimberly's interest, Viper was one of the last he had wanted or expected.

He might have been able to convince someone else to let Kimberly bind them for a few days or weeks. Just long enough to get her foot in the door at The Circle. Buying himself more time to figure out how to come clean.

He couldn't risk waiting much longer. Viper hadn't been lying; the snake was right. If Viper told her before Cormac did, she'd run from him and never look back. Right into the arms of the very creature that would use her until every last spark of her power was gone.

Chapter Eighteen

Kimberly went through the motions, making coffees and serving pastries, ringing up customers. Don snapped at her a couple of times to get her head out of the clouds. She'd jump to whatever task needed doing, but she was soon right back where she started, the hamster wheel in her head spinning in circles around the questions and suspicions she had about Cormac and his motives.

She liked him. A lot. He had been kinder to her over the course of a few days than people she'd known for years.

But she was certain he was hiding things from her.

She didn't want to think it, but she suspected he might have been avoiding her questions because he was some kind of draconic elemental. Not a naga like Sam, but something similar. He had to have ties to the draconic community or Professor Reed never would have sent her to talk to him.

Instead of giving her a chance to sink or swim on her own, he had done nothing to put her in front of a dragon yet. He had warned them about her, and now she had some kind of monster following her that might try binding her instead of the other way around. And she had sat there, trusting Cormac all the while, as he sold her out in the worst way imaginable to the very creatures she was hoping to convince to help her.

Nothing about his behavior added up unless she took into consideration that Cormac might be leading her around by the nose to keep her off the scent of any true dragons. If he was lying about helping her on her search, did that mean he was lying about liking her, too?

Added to the glimpse she'd seen of his power and the effort he was putting into obscuring his true nature, the only thing that made sense was that he was keeping her busy to prevent her from finding what she was looking for. If that duplicity extended to his feelings about her, considering the way she was starting to feel about him, she wasn't going to let him use her growing infatuation as a weapon against her.

Despite that he might have been trying to keep her off the trail of any dragons, she had other options open to her. She could believe that Viper was dangerous, but she'd seen how many other creatures had come out of the woodwork in search of her. They may have been keeping their distance when she and Cormac were on the street, but she was willing to bet if she made herself approachable—leaving Cormac out of the equation—a suitable Other might come forward to talk to her.

At this point, she was beyond caring if she wooed a dragon to be her familiar or not. A dragon may have solved a great many of her problems, but that dream went up in smoke when she saw just how dangerous it was to announce her intentions. The bad juju vibes she was picking up from Viper and Cormac's warnings meant she'd just stepped into a big pile of trouble. If Rieva's reaction and that of the patrons of her café were anything to go by, she'd made a grievous error in etiquette and put herself in a position that gave Cormac the excuse he needed to watch her every move.

If he cared about her, then he would understand why she needed to avoid him until after she graduated. She wanted to believe he liked her, but she had no way of trusting that he meant it until whatever reason he had for hiding his nature from her was moot.

She could grit her teeth and plow through her final exams in a few short weeks. She'd take some time after work tomorrow to go somewhere open and public, neutral ground for those Others who had been sniffing around to come talk to her. With the kind of interest Cormac had helped her generate, there had to be at least one who wasn't a danger to her that she could convince to help her for a day or two. Whatever Professor Reed might have thought, Kimberly now believed it would be far safer to select a familiar who couldn't turn her into magic flambé.

Once she had her exams behind her, then she might have the time to go on an actual date with Cormac and get to know the *real* him.

Assuming he still wanted her.

While relieved to have a plan, she was still terribly nervous that some Other with an axe to grind—Viper, perhaps—might come into the café to harass her. That, or do something to her mother. The sooner she convinced an Other to be her familiar so she could slip back under the radar, the better. She was beginning to think the fast-paced life of the Other community outside the school was better left out of her reach. Schoolyard pranks and a few bad luck charms on her locker were nothing in comparison to the nightmarish threat of becoming a familiar herself. Maybe she wasn't cut out for The Circle if this was the kind of pressure that came with the job.

As the evening wound down and Don started preparations for closing up for the night, she realized Cormac would be waiting outside to escort her home. He would find out where she lived. She wasn't ready for him to know that much about her yet. Whatever was going on between them was going far too fast in the wrong direction for her peace of mind.

"Hey, Don? Can I ask a favor?"

He looked up from the register.

"If that guy who came in with me shows up—"

"Dude with the funny clothes?"

She laughed and nodded. "That's the one. If he shows up looking for me, let him know I'll be back on shift tomorrow?" At the beginnings of an angry gleam coming to light in his eye, she was quick to continue. "He's not a bad guy. He's just being overprotective and wants to walk me home."

Don shook his head. "You barely know that jamoke and he's already trying to find out where you live? Trust your gut, doll. I knew he was bad news from the minute I first saw him."

"It's not what you think."

"They got specials about girls like you on those cop shows and Law & Order marathons. What do they call it? Special Victims Unit? Don't fall for his tricks."

"He's not that kind of guy," Kimberly said, exasperated. "Trust me, he's trouble, but in a totally different way."

"Yeah, that's what all those girls say. I've seen enough TV. You watch yourself. Need me to drop you home tonight?"

"*Don.* I'm fine. I just don't want him finding out where I live until I've known him a bit longer, that's all."

He snorted, shoving the register drawer closed and folding his arms as he turned to regard her. "When the police come canvassing for suspects, I'll know just who to point them to. You need someone to kick his ass for you, you tell me first."

She couldn't help but roll her eyes, but smiled anyway. "You got it. Thank you for your concern."

"No worries, kiddo. I've got your back."

They got back to business; Don counting out the register and Kimberly doing clean-up. When it was time for her to go home, she waited until Don had his back turned, doing something behind the counter, to wrap herself in illusion and rush out the door.

Cormac, five stories above, was instantly alerted by the disappearance of her aura.

Kimberly did not hear his snarl or see the great, dark beast that exploded out of the form of the man who had been crouched in his place.

She used the full of her concentration to move unnoticed. At least the illusion kept her safe from being seen or tracked by anyone. Every time a smidge of doubt or worry wormed its way into her consciousness, she compartmented it away for later. Never mind that Cormac would be ticked at her for ditching him. She'd have plenty of time to think of a convincing reason to tell him why she'd split and continue worrying and planning after she got home.

Despite how draining it was to maintain the illusion for so long, the brisk walk did her good. By the time she got to her building, she was breathing easier, even though a pang of guilt for leaving Cormac in the lurch made her shoulders hunch. Then, as the realization hit that she had also forgotten to do as her mom had asked and see about extending her hours, her eyes burned with unshed tears and stomach twisted with guilt. Work was the last thing she wanted to think about when she had to worry about crazy Others following her trail, possibly discovering where she lived, and harming her mom or her neighbors.

She could always check with Don during her next shift, though she would put off taking any extra shifts for the week until after her study date with Xander. She didn't want to be studying or taking tests while completely exhausted from working her tail off, then staying up late to cram in last minute review and memorization anyway.

Once she was inside the foyer, she dropped the illusion. As she dashed up the stairs, in the process of pulling out her keys, a wave of elemental energy slammed into her.

Her keys flew out of her hands and she barked her shins on the stairwell. Crying out, she breathed deep, forcing herself to focus so she could figure out what the hell that was and where it had come from.

Her Sight showed the next pulse of the radar-like combined tracking and stun spell coming her way, homing in on her location. Bracing herself, she flung up a hand and closed her eyes tight, putting all her will into creating a curved mirror to bounce the beacon back at the caster.

See how the asshole liked being knocked on their own ass by an unexpected curveball.

Panting, she scrambled to find her keys and pull her version of illusory invisibility back into place. Once the illusion hid her aura, the tracking spell would pass through her, not seeing anything to report back to the caster. She hadn't noticed someone was trying to find her until she'd dropped her own spell. The next pulse of power was delayed, but whoever was looking for her had to know that they were onto something. As soon as they recovered, they would know the area to aim the next strike even if they hadn't quite caught on to her specific location yet. If she could maintain her concentration long enough to get to her apartment, the wards would prevent anyone from pulling a stunt like that again.

Until she left for her Saturday morning shift tomorrow, but she'd burn that bridge when she crossed it.

As another jolt of power knocked the air out of her lungs, she stopped hunting for the keys, going still, and put every ounce of concentration into making herself invisible again.

Now that she was on the alert for it and had the invisibility spell locked into place, she noticed the whisper of magic that brushed over and passed through her altered "not-there" aura. She stayed where she was for a long moment, not moving, catching her breath and making sure her spell was holding.

Seeing as the caster wasn't teleporting into the stairwell or sending some other nastiness her way, she had to hope the bastard hadn't gotten enough information to pinpoint her location. Whoever it was had a tremendous amount of power and was spreading it out over a wide area. Chances were good that the most the caster had gleaned about her position was the general neighborhood. Maybe to within a few block radius. Worst case scenario, they might know which building she was in.

Deflecting whatever that spell had been with the mirror-like reflective aura had been pure instinct. She'd called on that part of her that relied on something other than elemental power and it had *worked*. Professor Winter never taught her anything about that kind of counterspell in his class on defensive magic.

She had never counted herself so lucky to be versed in illusion before.

Once she had her breath back, she resumed her search for her keys. They had slid down to the landing below her. Though she limped a bit, wincing with every step, she retrieved them and headed back up, this time maintaining her invisibility until she was inside her apartment and well past the wards.

She dropped her backpack in the hallway and went back to bolt every single lock on the door. Monster was growling at her— nothing new there—but she ignored the grumpy cat and marched straight into her bedroom. She then kicked off her shoes, climbed into bed, wrapped a blanket around herself, and hugged a pillow tight to her chest as she set her back against the wall.

If that spell had been Cormac's doing, maybe Don was right about him.

Chapter Nineteen

Exhaustion set in long before Kimberly's mother got home. She found her daughter like that, head tilted back against the wall, snoring away. She eased her down and tucked her in. That done, she set the alarm for Kimberly's morning shift and then went to sleep on the couch in the living room since she didn't have to work until the afternoon on Saturday.

When the alarm went off, Kimberly jerked awake with a short-lived scream. Slapping the clock to turn it off, she groaned and thumped the back of her head against the wall.

She'd meant to take some time to plan, but the lack of sleep from the night before combined with maintaining the invisibility spell for so long had wiped her out. There was a touch of a headache pulsing behind her eyes, and she had less than an hour to get ready for work and figure out what the heck she was going to do to go unnoticed until she got there.

Whoever was looking for her would likely figure out where she worked. That is, if they didn't know already. They wouldn't make a scene in front of mundanes—no Other in their right mind would—so as long as she could keep up the invisibility spell for a few blocks to keep the location of her home a secret, she could deal with a confrontation on the street.

She didn't have to hide when she wasn't worried about anyone's safety but her own. Illusion could be just as dangerous as a true elemental spell in the right hands.

Once she was ready, she took one last glimpse of her reflection in the mirror to remind herself that she could deal with this. Setting her shoulders, she grabbed her purse, cloaked herself with invisibility, and tiptoed out of the apartment, locking it quietly behind her so she wouldn't wake her mother.

Though fatigue set in before she even made it all the way down the stairs, she clung to the spell like a lifeline.

She'd barely made it a block before her muscles burned with strain. The headache pulsing behind her eyes gained in tempo and strength, her vision wavering a bit more with each stabbing pain. She blindly trudged forward, focusing on nothing but maintaining the spell to keep herself out of sight for as long as possible.

She wasn't sure how far she'd gone when someone cried out and flailed when she brushed too close. A random blow connected with her temple, knocking her aside. Her invisibility spell fell.

And she was hit seconds later with the tracking spell, sending her stumbling to a knee and clutching for a nearby stairwell railing for balance.

"Holy shit! Did you see that?"

"Dude, that chick just bamfed like Nightcrawler!"

Kimberly didn't wait around to see how many witnesses caught sight of her. Sure, Others may have made their presence known to mundanes, but she'd committed a tremendous faux pas by letting herself be seen actively casting in public without a permit.

On the bright side, without the overstrain of pulling too much magic again too soon blinding her, she could now see that she'd gone about six blocks, nearly seven, from her apartment before the spell fell. Far enough away that the caster was unlikely to have figured out where she lived. It was also a great deal easier to bat back the stunning aspect of the spell when she didn't have to pour so much concentration into making herself match the environment, chameleon-like, constantly shifting her image.

It took three more pulses of energy before the source of the spell stopped hurling it at her. They either knew where she was, or were getting tired of being bitch-slapped with their own stun being thrown right back at them.

Pleased with herself, she kept on the alert and maintained her Sight, and never mind that it was making her dizzy. There were Others on the street. A few that glanced her way as she passed, but she didn't see any sparking with recent signs of casting elemental magic. Her tormentor couldn't be too close—or perhaps she was looking in the wrong places.

The notion that the *thing* she'd seen on the rooftop last night wouldn't be found at street-level skittered through her thoughts, and she glanced up.

All she caught was a glimpse. A monster easily the size of a two-seater plane, but with an unmistakably serpentine form. Wide, sickle-like wings were limned with sunlight and lightning-like flickers of energy that traveled over the outline of the massive beast in the air above her.

Dragon, her mind gibbered.

It flew against the sun, and she had to look away, blinded.

With a sound very much like a sob, she made a mad dash for the café. Though she had no way of knowing for sure, she thought she felt its gaze on her, and that it might dive down and destroy her by flame or claw if she dared look at it directly again. It might have been her imagination, but she could swear the pressure of the wind whipped up by its passing brushed against her skin with every steady wingbeat.

The temerity—the sheer *gall* of her—to think she could tame a force of nature like that. She'd had no idea it would be so large. Such a perfect, primal predator. Panic beat in her breast and drove her to run, to be anywhere but caught in its shadow like a mouse being hunted by a hawk.

Don was putting out the first round of freshly baked loaves of bread and a tray of cinnamon rolls when she staggered against the door, thumping against it so hard she nearly cracked the glass. He straightened, putting the trays down and hurrying to unlock it and let her inside.

"What the hell's wrong, kid? Somebody chasing you?" He was already pushing past her, trying to peer outside.

"N-n-no," she stammered, grabbing his arm so tight he winced as she urged him to go back inside. It did stop him from stepping foot beyond the threshold of the store. "It's gone. It's—never mind. I'm okay."

A thundercloud of rage started building behind his eyes. He tugged up his sleeve on the arm she wasn't holding, baring a thick, tattoo-covered forearm. "It's that fancy-pants guy, isn't it? I need to go kick some wholesale ass for you?"

"No! Don, don't. I... I thought a mugger was following me. They're probably gone now."

He frowned at her. She met his gaze unflinching, feeling about two inches tall for lying to him so blatantly.

Still, being chased by a mugger sounded a heck of a lot more believable than saying she thought she had a dragon tailing her to work.

Even now, with vampires owning night clubs in all the major cities in the U.S. and werewolves volunteering with rescue teams and magi putting on shows at Vegas to rival Siegfried and Roy, some types of magical creatures were just a little *too* extraordinary to believe. Aside from that, Don and the rest of the staff at the café didn't know she was a mage or that she had any involvement in supernatural business, and she planned on keeping it that way. She had to if she wanted to keep her job, equal rights measures or no.

Swiping sweat off her brow with her forearm, she ducked past Don and headed behind the counter. He still peered out the door, checking both ways, probably looking for Cormac. If only she knew for sure he wouldn't find him.

As he locked up behind her, she hid the shaking of her hands by pretending to busy herself with hunting for something in her purse before putting it down in the storage spot below the register. She held her breath until her lungs were on the verge of bursting, then let it out slow. Some of the involuntary trembles eased.

Don watched her closely, but didn't ask her anything more about the supposed mugger who had been following her. He must have known she was full of it, because he didn't bother asking for a description or suggest she call the cops. Awkward as it was, they still finished opening preparations in good time. Most of it went without a hitch, save for the first batch of morning buns coming out with burnt bottoms, filling the kitchen with the acrid scent of charred bread and sugar. She frantically worked the espresso machine to make a couple batches of their most pungent dark roast, and then mixed cloves and cinnamon into one of the coffee pots they always kept filled with hot water for tea to cover up the smell. Don propped open the back door and ran the industrial fans they usually only used in the summer to blow the worst of it outside and into the alley behind the shop. Once it smelled more like a bakery than leavings from Powdered Toast Man's old underwear, he didn't let her open for the first customers of the day who were lined up outside, insisting on doing it himself.

Cormac wasn't among the people gathered out front waiting to get in—but Viper was.

He strolled inside like he owned the place, his broad shoulders back and chin up as he breathed in the scents of the café. His dark brown hair was slicked back from the sharp, angular planes of his face. Her Sight showed his black leather trench coat was still trailing elemental sparks in his wake, bright sparkles of color that shimmered like the scales she'd glimpsed outside, but otherwise he'd clamped down tight on his aura until it was difficult to tell him apart from the mundanes around him.

Kimberly's back thumped against the counter behind her as he zeroed in on her. His eyes weren't glowing this time, instead a pale whiskey brown, looking her up and down with obvious interest.

Don straightened and looked back and forth between them, then tilted his head at Viper in question. Silently asking Kimberly if he was the creep, and if he needed to put his past experience as a bouncer to good use. She gave an almost imperceptible shake of her head, trying to breathe around a throat constricted with fear.

If Don tried anything, Viper would kill him. She could see it in the set of the Other's shoulders, the slight curl of his fingers, hooked like they were customarily clawed. It was in the glint in his eye, hopeful for a challenge, searching for something to toy with until it became too tiresome and was put out of its misery.

Breathing shallow, she moved in a dazed haze behind the register, taking orders. Viper had, in what might have appeared to be an act of politeness, stepped aside and gestured for the other people who had been waiting to go first. Biding his time for his chance to speak with her uninterrupted, she was sure. She got the coffees and pastries and breakfast sandwiches other people ordered, dreading the moment the Other would take his turn in line. On alert to her discomfort, Don stayed up front as much as he could, but a few of the orders required him to go back to the grill in the kitchen.

Viper must have noticed. When it was his turn to order, he put one arm on the glass display beside the register, leaning in to close the distance between them and giving her a whiff of a woodsy scent tainted with a hint of carrion. His thin, sly smile widened as she jerked back.

"Good morning, love. I'll have a coffee and one of those breakfast sandwiches. Extra sausage, hmm?"

Don muttered something under his breath, but went into the back to cook the order. Kimberly punched the numbers into the register, keeping her voice low as she stared down at the key pad.

"I'm not looking—I don't want—"

He set an empty paper cup from the Black Star down on the counter. Nudged it closer with one finger. "This says you do want. Very much."

She gasped and made a grab for it. It must have been the cup Cormac had given her last night. Something she'd owned, however briefly. Something that left a trace of her behind. Viper didn't bother trying to stop her as she crumpled it in her fist and hid it behind her back, like it would stop him from casting the tracking spell all over again.

His low voice was pleasant, calm, and completely at odds with the way his fingernail traced a shallow line in the countertop. "You should be more mindful where you discard things someone might use to track you."

"What do you want from me?"

"A chance to talk. Not here," he said, his gaze briefly alighting on the kitchen door before refocusing on Kimberly's pale features. "I'm sure your friend has been telling you I'm the worst kind of monster and to avoid me at all costs."

She didn't bother to deny it.

"Give me a chance to tell you my side of things. Perhaps it will clear a few things up for you. Like what he is, which will go a long way toward explaining why he doesn't care for me. That is, if he hasn't already told you..."

Kimberly couldn't help but make a small sound deep in her throat. A mix of confusion and fear.

He could tell her about Cormac? Finally clear up the mystery about what he was? If that were true, then Viper was being more open with her straight out of the gate than Cormac had ever been, and she couldn't for the life of her fathom why. It smacked of manipulation, but that didn't make his offer any less intriguing.

Had Cormac lied to her? Was Viper really as dangerous to her as he had said?

The addition of the stunning aspect to his tracking spell that had been intended to keep her from bolting said he was—but the thought of learning more about Cormac's nature was too tempting a prospect to ignore.

She gave a quick look over her shoulder to make sure Don wasn't listening in before meeting Viper's bright, avid gaze. "Fine. This afternoon. Say around 3? You already know how to find me."

"As long as you don't pull the same trick you did last night. Bugger and blast, but I'd love to pick your brain about that."

Swallowing hard, she nodded. "As long as *you* promise not to try to pin me like a bug again while you're at it, I won't."

"Cross my heart," he said, making an exaggerated "*X*" over his heart with the same finger he'd used to cut into the counter. "Ah, that smells delightful. Don, is it?"

Don leaned around her to pass the wax paper wrapped sandwich over the counter, giving the Other the hairy eyeball. Viper accepted the food without further comment, leaving a twenty on the counter. He also waited patiently as Kimberly got him the coffee she'd been too flustered to remember he'd ordered.

He then dipped his head in a slight nod to Don and gave her one last, wicked smile before he slipped out into the sun, hiding those strange eyes behind a pair of reflective shades.

Kimberly wished she had some way of knowing whether she'd just signed a deal with the devil or if she'd found the answer to all of her prayers.

Chapter Twenty

Kimberly kept her head down for most of her shift. She was both concerned and relieved that Cormac didn't come by to check on her. When she'd found the courage to ask Don if he'd swung by after she left the night before, he shrugged and said he hadn't seen him.

She would probably end up having to go to his shop to apologize, but she wouldn't do it until after meeting with Viper.

She also wasn't sure what it said about her that she was more excited about the prospect of uncovering some of Cormac's secrets than she was about meeting with an honest-to-goodness dragon.

Xander showed up promptly at noon, grabbing one of the tables when Kimberly gestured for him to get one before anyone else in the growing line could. She wasn't able to join him until Annabelle showed up a few minutes later and took over manning the register so Kimberly could take her lunch break.

Annabelle managed to snag her for a moment before she took off.

"Are you playing the field?" she asked with a grin and a nod in Xander's direction. "What happened to your guy in the fancy suit?"

Kimberly flushed and pulled away to grab a couple of sandwiches she'd had Don make for her and Xander before the lunch rush started. She gave Annabelle a "drop it" look before answering her.

"It's nothing like that. We go to school together. We're helping each other with homework."

Annabelle gave her a knowing glance before hustling over to the register. Kimberly huffed and stomped over to join Xander, bringing the sandwiches over and settling into a seat across from her schoolmate. She had a hard time staying annoyed at Annabelle's interest in her love life when she got close enough to see just how wound up he looked.

He was practically vibrating with excitement, brown eyes alight. His sandy-colored hair was a bit tousled, and his shirt was clinging to him with sweat, like he'd run a long way to get to the café on time. Leaning forward, he stage whispered across the table, not yet touching his food.

"You are not going to *believe* what I found out!"

Wide-eyed, Kimberly paused with her roast beef on sourdough halfway to her mouth. "What? Something about Cormac?"

"Sort of. Nothing you probably don't already know. You heard he's a dealer in arcane objects, right? Owns a weird store not too far from the school?"

She nodded, then took a bite out of her sandwich, rolling her other hand in a motion for him to continue.

"He's no one you want to mess with. He's got some powerful friends. Dragons, gryphons, unicorns, gargoyles—all kinds of strange creatures. Apparently he acts as a liaison between magi and earthbound elementals they want to contact for spell components. Phoenix feathers, dragon scales, unicorn hair—whatever you need, he can hook you up. So there's that."

Kimberly mulled that over as she chewed. While not unexpected, it did make more sense why Professor Reed had sent her to him in the first place. If he was supposed to be some kind of middle man between magi and the rest of the Other community for requests of such a sensitive nature, it was no wonder he took such care not to take her straight to a dragon. Announcing what she was looking for in the Black Star instead of going directly to one of his friends made a bit more sense. No Other would ever trust him again if he had taken her straight to some unsuspecting dragon's lair.

By letting them come to her instead of the other way around, it kept him safe from retaliation or sullying his reputation and scaring off his sources of income. It didn't tell her everything she needed to know about Cormac or his motives, but it did make a lot of sense why he had taken such care not to put her directly in the path of a dragon.

She swallowed her food, then nodded. "Okay. That puts a few pieces of the puzzle in place for me. What about the Black Star? Or Rieva? Find out anything about them?"

His eyes lit up, and he was practically laid out on the table in his efforts to go unheard as he leaned in to excitedly whisper his findings.

"That's where things get weird. Check this out—when I asked my parents about the Black Star Café, they both flipped out. Told me to stay away from it and pretend I never heard about it. It took me a while, but I managed to get the story out of them.

"Rieva is some kind of draconic shifter, and she used to be a familiar. She killed her master. Can you believe it? Not let him die, not arranging for someone else to do it—she managed to resist the bond and used her own two hands. Claws. Magic. Whatever."

Kimberly's eyes were wide as saucers. She'd never heard of an Other having the power to break a familiar bond. By its very nature, the bond should have made it impossible for Rieva to do harm, directly or indirectly, to her master.

The bond filled the Other with a strong urge to protect their master, and was designed to prevent a familiar from doing any knowing or active harm to the mage who controlled them. Passively? They could sit back and watch as a car mowed down their mage—but they were supposed to be driven by an impulse to help or heal him if he survived.

If the bond was strained and the familiar was powerful enough, as Kimberly had noted when James brought Sam the naga to her classroom, it was in the realm of possibility the familiar might *think* murderous thoughts really hard. Even say them, and spit out threats. He just wouldn't be able to act on them, except indirectly. Even if something had hurt James, Kimberly was sure Sam would have been driven to do something to help him, no matter how much he hated the guy's guts.

While her first reaction was to dismiss the story as some kind of exaggeration or urban legend, she paused upon recalling how powerful and deadly accurate with her throwing knife Rieva had been. The changeling had been ready to kill her for stepping foot over her threshold. Hell, she'd *tried* to kill her. The only reason Kimberly was still alive was due to Cormac's intervention.

"I'd ask if you were kidding, but after what I saw, I can believe she's capable of it. Whoever bound her must have been horrible to her. She's not overly fond of us."

Xander gaped at her, then snapped his mouth shut when he remembered he had just taken a huge bite of his sandwich. He got it down and choked out a few words.

"You *met* Rieva? And lived to tell about it?"

Kimberly arched a brow. "Yeah. So?"

"So? *So?* She's like our personal bogeyman! She keeps that café of hers as a safe place from magi and vampires for—get this—*mundanes* and Others. She kills any of us who cross into her territory, and there are rumors she hunts vampires for sport. Mom would barely whisper her name when she told me the story."

It was a little late for it now, but Kimberly thought that would have been good to know before she'd gone traipsing into the woman's lair.

"No freaking wonder she hated me on sight," Kimberly whispered. "I'm going to throttle Cormac for taking me in there. Cripes."

"Whoa, hold the phone. You've been inside the Black Star Café?"

"At the risk of sounding redundant—yeah, so?"

Xander slumped back into his seat, agape as he stared at her. She flushed and dropped her eyes, picking at her sandwich and rolling tiny balls of dough between her fingers from the pieces she broke off the bread.

"It's not like I would have gotten in without Cormac," she said, not sure if she was making the excuse for him or herself.

"Mom said finding that place is like stumbling on the lost treasure of Cortés. Rumor says it's full of powerful unbound supernaturals at any hour of the day or night, and there isn't a mage alive who knows where it is. Well, except for you now, I guess."

She frowned at him. "There's no way I'm the only one who knows. Cormac does, so it can't be that big a secret."

"Are you kidding? I bet The Circle or one of those other big covens would pay out the nose to know where it is. It's not like any

124

of us would know who to ask, or like any of the elementals would give up their safe house. I doubt even a familiar bond could make one of them tell. I mean, that's the point of the place, isn't it? To keep them safe from us."

Kimberly brushed the crumbs off her fingers and shoved her paper plate to the middle of the table. She'd completely lost her appetite, and was feeling more and more like she'd been railroaded into a position far above and beyond her capability to handle. Cormac hadn't said a word about any of this to her. Hadn't warned her or breathed a word about the importance of staying quiet about what she had seen.

More important than that, he hadn't told her what he was. The first time she'd glimpsed his aura, she would have sworn he was some flavor of earthbound elemental. Yet the second time she'd seen it, the sparks had led her to believe he was some kind of powerful mage. If that was the case, why would Rieva let him anywhere near her café?

She needed answers. If even a fraction of Xander's story was true, it was in her best interest to keep everything she had learned about the Black Star Café and its owner very much to herself. Something told her that her knowledge of its location might be dangerous, but that sharing that information could have deadly consequences.

It was either terrifically flattering or horrifying that Cormac trusted her enough to show her the way. She wasn't sure which yet, but she hoped the meeting with Viper in a few hours would clear up some of her questions.

Xander took advantage of her momentary brooding to polish off what was left of his sandwich. With a shiver, she answered his questioning look at what was left of her lunch with a flick of her fingers for him to go ahead. She would have to work out something else for her dinner. He scarfed what was left down in just a couple of bites, licking a smudge of mustard off his thumb.

"Listen," he said, "I know you're a little freaked out right now, but try not to worry. I didn't tell my parents about you, I just asked a few questions. Your secret is safe with me."

Kimberly's lips curving in a tremulous smile. "Thanks. I never doubted you—I was having one of those 'look at your life, look at your choices' moments."

He chuckled. "I doubt you've got anything to worry about. You walked in and out of the Black Star Café and met Rieva Ke'rin and survived. I know you had a rough time with some classes, but you've got a unique talent. All that has to count for something."

"Maybe. I could really use some help with some of the basics, though. Some of the conjuration stuff and a couple of the charms are still giving me trouble."

"Sure, no prob. I'll help you with that if you'll lend me a hand with enchantments. You always ace those. Maybe you can tell me what I'm doing wrong. And show me some of those illusions, too."

"You got it." Her smile eased into something a little less strained, a little more natural. "I've got to meet with someone later this afternoon and run an errand. Are you free tonight?"

"Not tonight, but I'm free all day tomorrow. My place? I'll take care of lunch this time around."

He wrote down his address for her on a clean scrap of napkin, and she tucked it away in her jeans pocket. As they got up to clear the table so she could finish her shift and make room for a waiting customer, he patted her shoulder on his way to the door.

"Don't worry," he told her, tipping her a wink and a nod. "You've got this."

She hoped he was right.

Chapter Twenty-one

Kimberly wrapped up her shift at work, leaving Annabelle and Don to handle the rest of the heavy weekend traffic. Fridays and Saturdays were always the busiest, though Sunday afternoons tended to leave Don and whoever was on shift swamped. Kimberly, Annabelle and Thomas, one of the other two clerks who worked days, usually switched off on Sundays. Kimberly needed the paycheck, but she had promised her hours to Thomas when he begged for it last week to make the extra cash he needed to pay for some concert tickets.

That was before she heard about the issue with paying the rent from her mother. She didn't want to disappoint Thomas, but her mom had not left a note, and she had no idea if the rent was paid on time or not. The last time they had received a pay-or-quit notice had been early last year, and the two of them had to work around the clock picking up every shift and odd job they could to pay it off before they could be evicted. Kimberly had ended up missing two days of school, and would have had a third if not for the advance Don had given her when he noticed how ragged and stressed she was.

He wasn't always a bad guy. He had a protective streak a mile wide, but that only extended to those he thought were mundane like him and his wife and kids. Considering how he was on his last rope with her and how she was counting down the days until she could quit, she didn't feel right asking him to extend her the same kindness this time around. It might save her and her mother from a few premature gray hairs, but she still had her pride, and she wouldn't go begging for a handout unless she had no option left open to her.

Mulling over the issue, she chewed on her inner cheek in thought as she slowly made her way to Central Park. The Moonwalkers wouldn't care very much for her presence, she was sure, but Sheep's Meadow was a wide open space with plenty of people around at this time of day. It was considered neutral ground for Others during the day, so the pack of territorial werewolves wouldn't accost her unless she stayed past sunset.

With the cloudless sky a lovely robin's egg blue and the chill edge of winter fading into the warmth of spring, there would be tons of tourists out in force and locals out for picnics and a little sun. Not only would the profusion of mundanes make it unlikely Viper might try anything untoward, she also thought it might be a good place to leave herself open and approachable to any Others who had been scared off by Cormac's proximity. She wasn't hiding anymore, and she'd noted how a few of them had been following her and Cormac around after that incident at the Black Star.

As she'd suspected, every time she scanned with her Sight, a pair of Others were following her path from across the street. A man and a woman, they looked like unremarkable twenty-somethings until the Sight betrayed their flowing, green-tinted auras.

They kept shooting her curious looks when they thought she wasn't paying attention. She might have been preoccupied with her monetary woes, but not so much so that she'd let her guard drop and miss such an obvious tail.

Rather than pull a disappearing act, at the next crosswalk, she turned and waved at the two to come to her side of the street. They both gave her matching deer-in-headlights stares, pausing in their tracks. After a long moment, they turned to each other and exchanged a few heated whispers before the woman crossed the street to join Kimberly.

Once she was closer, Kimberly realized she had seen her at the Black Star the other night. She had straight, dark brown hair that had a few sun-bleached streaks and fell to her waist, some of it spilling forward to obscure her features as she stared at Kimberly through her bangs. Her clothing was very nondescript; a simple sandy-colored top over russet khakis tucked into mud-stained hiking boots. No jewelry. She looked like she was ready to hit the hiking trails in the Catskills, not like she was wandering the streets of one of the busiest cities in the world.

As soon as she was close enough, Kimberly gave her what she hoped was a reassuring smile. The woman held herself a little too rigidly, like she was wary or afraid.

"I saw you two following me. Did you want to talk to me?"

The lady cleared her throat and shot a look back at the man waiting across the street. He, too, looked like every muscle was wound up tight as he stared intently in their direction. She waited until they were alone on the corner to speak, save for the occasional passing pedestrian, keeping her voice low.

"I'm sorry if we're bothering you," she said, her voice throatier and deeper than Kimberly expected, "but I saw you at the café with the Hunter. Were you telling the truth? That you just want a familiar for a few days?"

"Yeah, that's right. I mean, it might be more than a few days—probably two or three weeks. Why? You know a dragon?"

Her cheeks pinkened. "No, I'm afraid not. I was hoping you might consider one of my herd. If you'll have it, one of us will agree to be bound temporarily if you'll provide us a service in return."

Kimberly blinked, then tried her Sight one more time to see if she could get a clue what this woman and her companion might be. The pair both had comparable levels of power. Steady, strong natural defenses, but nothing powerful along the lines of Viper or even the naga, Sam. It wasn't like she would need to cast much, but whatever they were appeared to be depressingly mundane and poor conductors of elemental magic. No wonder they wanted a mage to help them; they probably didn't have the ability to cast much of anything on their own.

A little disappointed, Kimberly bit her lip, trying to think of a good way to explain that she didn't think they would fit the bill for what she needed.

The woman took her hesitation the wrong way, quick to jump in with reassurances. "Please, it's nothing extraordinary. I know you're still just a student. All we want are some basic wards to protect our range, but we can't afford the fee to hire one of the local covens. A pack of werewolves has been pushing into our territory and we need to keep our colts safe. None of us have the gift and Eddie can't be everywhere at once..."

She trailed off, gesturing helplessly at the man watching them so closely across the street.

Clearing her throat a few times, Kimberly shifted her weight from foot to foot, considering. The two needed help and they were stuck in the same position as she was. Needing something desperately but not having the money, power or influence to get it without help. For the lady to have to come to her this way, hat in hand, must have chafed, and helped Kimberly make a snap decision to help no matter how things turned out.

Considering the talk of herds and ranges, she had a suspicion what the pair might be. They weren't ideal material for familiars, and certainly wouldn't be a sterling example of her skills when she applied at The Circle, but they would get her through her exams. If things with Viper didn't pan out or Cormac didn't deliver, she could keep these two in mind for what she needed.

"Okay, here's the thing," Kimberly said, "I'm actually on my way to meet with someone else about this very thing. Wait, don't worry—I think I might be able to help you either way. If things go sideways with this other guy, I'll take you up on your offer. If not, maybe you guys can owe me a favor. Like give me a spell component or something if I need it at some point. Does that work for you?"

The woman's breath hitched, and she nodded. It made Kimberly feel even more awkward over performing what she thought was at best a minor favor.

She knew exactly how painful and humiliating it was to be stuck without any way to pay somebody back for a favor or kindness, and to be treated like a charity case. By adding in the alternative of giving her spell components (which might be anything from a few strands of hair to a flower or plant they might find on their farm) if she didn't need a familiar, Kimberly had just saved the face of the woman and her herd while still giving them what they needed. She thought the poor girl was on the verge of crying with relief.

Kimberly gave her a minute to collect herself before saying anything else.

"What's your name? I can't stick around—I have that meeting—so how can I get in touch with you?"

Sniffling, the woman put her hand over her eyes. "Oh, my gosh. Where are my manners? I'm so sorry, I was so worried you would say no—"

Kimberly cut her off with a laugh. "Really, don't worry about it. I'm happy to help."

"I'm Damaris. That's Eddie across the street. He's a little nervous about meeting you. Here, let me give you my card..." She dug around in her pockets and handed over a slightly crumpled business card. Kimberly was unsurprised to see that it was for a farm feed and supply store on Long Island. "When can you come by? I'll ask the others to be ready to meet you."

"I'm not sure."

The woman's face fell. Kimberly ran a hand over her face, not wanting to have to keep reassuring Damaris that she wasn't going to back out on the deal or get into detail about just how broke she was. Getting a cab across town was completely out of her price range. Taking one to Long Island and back would be insane.

"Transportation might be a bit of an issue. Can one of your people give me a lift? There and back?"

"Oh," Damaris said, obviously relieved, "oh, of course."

Kimberly made the arrangements to be picked up after her shift at Allegretto's the following Saturday afternoon. That would be cutting things close. Her finals were the week after. If she didn't have arrangements for a familiar made by the Monday after next, she would be totally screwed.

Though it was a load off her shoulders having a sure thing lined up, Damaris, Eddie, and the rest of their herd only had enough magic to do basic, ingrained defensive spells. Shifting into a human form, probably a few simple camouflage or misdirection spells, that sort of thing. Nowhere near the level of power Kimberly needed her familiar to have in order to impress The Circle.

For that reason, she hoped that Viper was not as dangerous as Cormac had made him out to be. As far as she was concerned, Viper was still on the table as an option for a familiar, though she wouldn't be so foolish as to trust the man without getting to know him first. There wasn't much time, but she felt she was a decent judge of character.

If he turned out to be a creep, even if he was exactly what she was looking for, she would take the safe road and take up Damaris's offer. She was a bit worried considering how heavy-handed Viper's attempt at tracking her down had been, and taking into account what Cormac had told her. However, she wasn't going to write him off without hearing what he had to say first.

She exchanged goodbyes with Damaris, waved to Eddie across the street, then continued on her way to Central Park.

Chapter Twenty-two

Sheep's Meadow, so named because it used to house a herd of sheep until the 1930's, was a sprawling, 15 acre open field near the southern end of Central Park. It was surrounded on all sides by trees, some turning bright with fresh, pale green spring leaves. Skyscrapers hemmed in the park, visible beyond the tree line. The scent of lilacs drifted over the grassland from the white, pink and purple flowers by the northern end. Surrounding it all was the hustle and bustle of a busy city, the sound of not-so-distant traffic punctuated by the hum of conversation and trills of birdsong.

Just as she'd suspected, now that it was warming up and since the day was clear, the wide open field was jam packed with people. There was a group in tights, yoga pants, tanks, and sports bras doing lunges and half moons on the grass. Single people and couples lounged on blankets, getting sun or having late picnics. A few painters had their easels and art supplies. A group of teenagers were flinging a Frisbee around, people were exercising with their dogs, and children ran, laughing and playing.

It was a sea of green tranquility in the midst of a concrete jungle, and it looked like a good portion of the population was out to make the most of it.

Kimberly headed to an empty patch of grass and lay back, using her purse as a pillow as she folded her hands behind her head. She closed her eyes against the sun and enjoyed the warmth of it on her skin.

She let her senses drift on the neat, orderly ley lines that composed the park's nature magic. It was an oddity in the midst of a city like this to have such a strong well of elemental energy to draw from. Considering the park was manmade, it added to the mystery of why in the midst of a city that represented man's mastery over nature so much natural magic thrived. There were rumors that The Circle had a hand in it since the lay of the lines conformed to the various sections of the park, like the Pond, the Reservoir, Sheep's Meadow, the Great Lawn, and so on.

She couldn't tap into and use that power until she had a familiar to help filter it—but she could ride along the streams to feel any disturbances in the web of elemental energy in the area.

At precisely that moment, there were 6,529 mundanes enjoying the charms of the meadow. At the far northern end, near the lilac walk, she detected the power signatures of a group of werewolves. Out to keep an eye on things, she was sure. There was another mage making a small, reverse whirlpool-like indentation in the western line as he or she sucked up some of its power through a familiar. A few other elemental beings were soaking up the sun, minor power sources that swirled and eddied in mutual exchanges with the lines of energy, scattered all across the meadow.

No sign yet of Cormac or Viper. The two were such powerhouses that they would have disrupted the flow far more spectacularly than the mage even if they weren't casting a thing.

Little by little, her muscles lost their tension. It was hard not to let the serenity of the park seep into her bones, soothing her troubled mind.

Then the pings of a tracking spell rippled over the web-work of energy, making nearly undetectable waves that brushed over her skin before bouncing back. Not hammering into her this time, though it still sent her heart into her throat as the first ripple bounced back off her aura.

She followed the wave as far as she could, trying to pinpoint which direction it was coming from so she wouldn't be caught flat-footed when the source of the spell appeared. Northwest. The general vicinity of the museum.

Rubbing her eyes, she sat up and cut her link to the ley lines. Wrapping her arms around her knees, she took a few deep breaths, holding them as long as she could before expelling them and taking the next in an effort to calm her racing heart.

Answers were finally forthcoming.

She didn't have to be tapped into the lines to feel the surge of energy as Viper drifted out from behind the tree line. Even the mundanes were looking around, some tugging cardigans and light jackets on or packing up and getting ready to leave as shivers of foreboding chilled their enjoyment of the afternoon sun. Aware of the carnivore in their midst, even if they didn't know what to look for.

He took his time picking his way around the people stretched out on blankets or sprawled in the grass. Utterly nonchalant in his unconcern for the reactions he was causing in the people around him, he strolled across the green, head lowered and hands pocketed in acid wash jeans. Most looked up as he passed, eyeing him warily, some edging away.

Kimberly stayed frozen where she was, muscles locked as she watched him approach. Her heart had crept up in the region of her throat again. When he reached her side, he paused, scanning the sky briefly before hunkering down on the balls of his feet beside her, knees bent and arms resting on top of his legs.

"A lovely day for a walk in the park. I can't fault your choice of meeting places."

Kimberly wasn't sure if that was meant as a compliment, so she just nodded. He grinned, teeth gleaming very white and sharp in that brief show of amusement.

"Go on, ducks. I know you must have any number of questions for me. Let's hear it."

She swallowed hard. This was the moment she'd been waiting for. It looked like Viper was ready and willing to answer all her questions.

So why was she still so nervous?

"Well," she said, slow and drawn out. It took a couple of tries before her voice stopped wavering in her throat. "I guess my first question is what kind of dragon are you?"

That stirred a low chuckle out of him. "Oh, I'm not a dragon. Not exactly, though my kind has often been mistaken for one. I am a wyvern. From a very noble line, considered a symbol of royalty for any number of European countries and fiefdoms, I might add."

Wide-eyed, Kimberly stared for a very long moment before she remembered her manners and scrambled to get to one knee, her hand over her heart as she bowed her head. "I am honored by your presence, wi—"

"No, no—none of that, now," he said, interrupting the impromptu formal speech of greeting she was about to launch into. "Not that I'm usually one to say no to a bit of ceremony, but this is not the time or place."

She gave him a jerky nod, fingers tangling in the hem of her shirt in nervousness. Now that she was faced with the next best thing to a dragon, she wasn't quite sure what to do with herself. Viper was perfectly capable of squishing her into a fine paste. If she said the wrong thing, he could very well decide she was too much trouble to bother with and destroy her.

Plus it was more than a bit intimidating to be faced by an honest-to-goodness wyvern. They were fierce hunters, intelligent winged serpents very similar to dragons in appearance, and often used as symbols of power, prestige and royalty. Unlike their larger counterparts, in addition to their wings, wyverns only had two hind legs, no forelegs. They used the claws attached to the wrist joint on their wings, similar to the thumbs on a bat, to make their way on the ground.

He may not have been a dragon, but he was close enough as to make no difference to her. Now she needed to figure out why Cormac had been so dead set about warning her away from him—and why he was so interested in her. If she wasn't so intent on getting answers, she'd have been immeasurably pissed off at Cormac for trying to lead her away from Viper. It was beginning to look like he was exactly what she needed.

"I'm flattered—*very* flattered—that you've chosen to speak with me about this. I guess Rieva already told you what I'm looking for?"

"Yes. A temporary draconic familiar to ensure you find a place in the coven of your choice, if I'm not mistaken."

She nodded. "Right. It shouldn't be for more than two or three weeks, I don't think. I'm afraid I don't have much to offer in return. If you need an illusion, I'm your girl, but I'm not sure if you heard that I'm not good at elemental spells..."

She trailed off, a little uneasy by the way his eyes took on that subtle golden glow as his smile widened. Even in the sunlight it was noticeable.

"Not to worry, ducks. That's just the sort of skill set I need. I'll tell you what. You let me bind you—temporarily, of course—and I'll return the favor."

Kimberly jerked back with a gasp. Cormac hadn't been lying. She'd never heard of a mage agreeing to such a thing. She'd honestly thought it was some bad joke or exaggeration since that sort of thing wasn't supposed to be possible.

The thought of having the tables turned on her filled her with dread, but she wasn't sure if there was an alternative that would handle all her problems so neatly as this.

"H-h-how long do you...?" she stuttered out.

"Give me the rest of today and tomorrow. Then we can do your little school project when you return to class on Monday."

He leaned in, extending one hand in offering for her to seal the deal. She stared at it like it might bite, panic rising.

She had no idea what it meant to agree to his offer, and was frightened half to death of the potential consequences. Familiars could not control what power was ripped from them by their masters. If Viper intended to use her for that, she could spend days knocked out from exhaustion. She'd also heard the stories of what happened when an incorrectly summoned planar being managed to turn the tables on their summoner. The mage was often burned from the inside out once they were bound as the planar being took revenge by filtering too much energy for them to handle. Some magi had even lost their spark entirely, too fried by the influx of raw elemental energy to control or cast anymore.

It was nightmare fuel for a mage, and for good reason.

Seeing her hesitation, Viper let his hand drop, his eyes narrowing. "You feel my offer is inadequate?"

"No, it's not that. It's just I... I didn't think..."

"Didn't think you'd have to return the favor," he said, unamused.

She bit her lip.

"I wouldn't hurt you, if that's what has you worried. I'm quite skilled at finding the threshold of my partner and modulating the energy tap. It can be... quite pleasant."

Judging by the heated way he was looking at her, he didn't mean for him. Flushing all the way to her toes, she averted her gaze and held up a staying hand.

"This is a bit much for me. Cormac warned me you'd want something like this. I feel a little stupid saying this, but I didn't believe him, and I just wasn't prepared to make this kind of snap decision. Can I have a minute to think about it?"

Viper made a soft hissing sound of irritation between his teeth, pulling back from her. "Cormac has no vision. I know what I want and I'm prepared to offer anything to get it. You have but to ask."

Well. There was one thing. Her cheeks flared crimson and she squirmed a bit before stuttering out another question, swallowing back her embarrassment.

"You keep a hoard like a dragon, right? I don't suppose you would consider loaning me a little? I swear I'd pay it back."

His head tipped to one side, and he looked her up and down anew. She suspected he was just noticing her frayed cuffs and cheap shoes. He'd been so intent on getting whatever it was he wanted out of her that he hadn't paid attention to the package it came in until now. When she caught the very slight curl of his lip, there and gone in a flash, embarrassed heat filled her cheeks.

Feeling both dirty and humiliated, she ducked her head. "Never mind. I shouldn't have asked. I'm sorry, I don't think I can do this."

"Come now, I'm sure it's not that hard. All it takes is a yes."

"No," she said, this time with a bit more vehemence. Cormac was right. There was something off about Viper, and never mind what a perfect ass she'd just made of herself. Worst of all, that flash of disgust showed he obviously had no respect for her. At least Cormac never made her feel *tolerated*. "Thank you for the offer, but I'll find some other way of getting what I need."

He slowly rose to stand, heaving a sigh as he settled back on his heels.

"That's unfortunate. This would have been much easier if you had agreed."

Kimberly would have asked what he meant by that, but the look in his eyes froze her in place.

His eyes burned a molten gold as he spread his arms, which were expanding and shifting at an alarming rate. Faster than she might have thought possible, he was growing, his clothing melting and skin disappearing under a layer of metallic scales. Nearby, people were noticing, shouting and screaming in fear as they stampeded in every direction to escape the shapechanging Other in their midst.

When he ceased growing, from the tip of his nose to the end of his tail, he was over thirty feet long, with a wingspan half again that size.

Kimberly sat immobile, unable to so much as squeak in terror as the beast before her lurched back to arch its neck and spread its wings, barbed tail lashing as it growled at her. One thick, talon-tipped paw lashed out, flattening her on the grass and squeezing the air out of her lungs. It gave an awkward, one-legged hop forward to catch its balance before clenching its claws to dig deep furrows in the grass and close around her waist and legs, pinning her.

Then those wide, ribbed wings began to flap, the sun playing off the tones of brass and copper and gold. The ground fell away, people scattering before the airborne monster.

And Kimberly could do nothing but pray, staring up at this great beast that had her in its claws.

She'd gotten what she'd asked for. Now she would have to pay the price.

Chapter Twenty-three

Cormac was beside himself with a combination of worry and frustration. When Kimberly had disappeared the night before, he had been ready to tear apart the city to find her.

Then realized what a terrific ass he would make of himself by exposing his nature to her that way.

As damnably frustrating as it was, he thought he should give her the space she so obviously wanted. He had been too heavy handed and cagey with her. It was in his nature to be so, after all, but it appeared it was necessary for him to back off for a little while.

The time apart would be good for both of them, he told himself. It would give him time to think of a way to tell her what he was without sending her fleeing straight into the arms of that snake-in-the-grass, Viper.

Yet his instincts were urging him to hunt her down and *make* her talk to him, to *make* her understand.

It took a great deal of effort, but he beat down that animal urge. That was no way to treat her. Not if he wanted her to continue to look at him like she had when he had first offered to help her. With that sparkle in her eye, all hope and warmth and gratefulness. To sink into him like she had when he had pinned her against that wall, melting against him like they were made to fit together. Sneaking those coy, curious looks at him under her lashes, leaning into his touch, laughing and talking with him like he was a person instead of a monster.

He wanted that back. He wanted it so badly he thought he might even agree to let her bind him if only to keep her from experiencing that intimacy with anyone else.

But he didn't want to see the inevitable look of betrayal on her face when he told her the truth.

It was maddening. He stayed in his shop, pacing the labyrinth of furniture, fists clenching and unclenching at his sides as he fought the urge to leave and find her. What if she came to the shop to tell him why she had fled his protection? What if she called? He shouldn't leave, just in case.

He had neither the need nor the desire to sleep that night, so he attempted to focus on polishing the furniture. Then reorganizing his books. Then rearranging his herbs, spices and incense.

None of it was working. All he could think about was how he needed to find a way to fix things with Kimberly before he could make it worse. His many mistakes in how he had dealt with her from the beginning were a constant litany in the back of his mind, worried over again and again like a sore tooth he just couldn't leave alone. If only he had told her what he was, if only he had asked one of his contacts directly instead of making that foolish announcement at the Black Star...

One day, he promised himself. He would give her one day to have some time from him, and he would leave her to her own devices for the time being so he could think of the words to make things right.

Sometime after midnight he had flown out over the Long Island Sound for a couple of hours to clear his head, then returned to his shop to see if she might come to him there. He had never been moved by such a primal urge to keep a woman close, safe, and—strangest of all—*happy*. Not knowing where she was or being certain that she was safe and well was turning into a constant worry, a pebble in his shoe, always present in his thoughts.

Come the first light of morning, he had sent a couple of his allies to check Allegretto's throughout the day for him, advising them to call him with urgent updates. To bring him back some of that excellent hazelnut coffee and biscotti, too. He would give

Kimberly the space from him she desired, but he had no intention of leaving her open to attack or danger.

When she finished her shift, he knew about it within minutes. One of his informants trailed her from a discreet distance, reporting when she stopped to speak with a couple of the local centaurs. Not dangerous. Nothing for him to concern himself about.

When she arrived at Sheep's Meadow, he relaxed a measure. No one would be so foolish as to accost her there. He went so far as to head up to the roof to get some air, hunkering like a gargoyle on the ledge overlooking the street above the entrance to his shop. Watching over his territory like that was usually one of his favorite ways of spending his time when he needed a little space.

This time, it was nothing more than a distraction. He kept breathing in the potent bouquet of the city, taking in the mixture of humanity, cats, dogs, vermin and birds, an assortment of foods, smog, oils, hot asphalt, refuse—a variety of aromas that usually soothed him with their familiarity.

Now, he found low growls escaping him when he failed to capture anything more than a ghost of her scent lingering near his doorstep. Kimberly was beyond the range of his natural senses, and he did not want to alarm her with the type of casting he might have to do to pinpoint her location.

And then he received the phone call.

When his cell phone rang, he almost didn't answer it. Just before it went to voicemail, he shook his head and plucked the tiny piece of plastic out of his pocket. Seeing it was one of the young earthbound elementals he had employed to run his errands, including keeping tabs on Kimberly for him, he tapped the answer button. Then hissed when it didn't work, sliding his finger along the touch screen, picking up the call. He still wasn't quite used to using the technology.

"Boss, it's me. You're not going to believe this. Viper just took off with Kimberly. He has the girl."

He very nearly exploded out of his skin in a blind rage when he heard the words "Viper" and "Kimberly" in the same sentence. Then the rest of the news broke through his haze.

Gone. Taken.

By that cowardly snake.

His roar of outrage shook the heavens. Up and down the street, windows shattered, and people cried out in shock and fear. No sound like that should have been able to escape a human throat. The plastic shattered in his grip as he clenched his fingers, then fell with a clatter on the rooftop.

Then he was gone, a snarled Word teleporting him to the center of the node where the ley lines in that part of Central Park converged. More cries of surprise from human throats rose around him as he appeared in their midst, pigeons scattering as a dark apparition that radiated deep fury perched upon the shoulders of the bronze angel statue atop the center of the Bethesda Fountain. In moments, he was leaping from the statue, landing far from the surrounding pool and speeding toward Sheep's Meadow in a blur.

There were a number of police, media, and quite a few Others in the fringe of onlookers pointing, staring, and taking pictures of the deep divots in the grass. Footprints. Claw marks. He'd recognize the tracks anywhere, as if the bitter, acrid scent of Viper in his true form weren't hint enough.

Where most would have had to elbow their way in, Cormac had no trouble finding a spot that gave him a clear view of the scene. He cut through the crowd like a shark ghosting through a school of fish, making his way to the leading edge so he could get an unobstructed view. People instinctively parted before him, rushing out of his path even if they weren't sure why, sensing the beast under the veneer.

His contact, a young changeling like Rieva, was one of those onlookers near the front staring at the growing media circus. As soon as the boy noticed him, he bowed his head deep in subservience to Cormac, then struggled to elbow his way through the crowd to get closer. As he was disguised in the form of a preteen boy, he had to weave and duck around the adults milling around him chattering about the "monster" that had taken off with the girl.

It wasn't hard to imagine why so many people had turned out to investigate. Vampires and werewolves and magi may have captured the imagination of the general public, but many other varieties of Others had chosen to keep their existence secret. Not only for the fear and panic they might cause, as Viper had done, but because it was unwise to alert the local magi to their presence.

It took a few minutes before the boy reached the empty space the humans had left around Cormac at the front of the police barricade. He ducked his head and shoulders a few times in an attempt at the acceptable bow to use when in the presence of mundanes, keeping his eyes on Cormac's face for any clues as to how he should proceed. He kept his voice low, leaning in as much as he dared to relay what he knew.

"My lord, I am so sorry, I had no way of stopping it. The wyvern shifted right here in the meadow and took off with her to the east. I lost sight of them once they cleared the trees."

If Viper managed to bind Kimberly before Cormac could stop him, he would rip the blasted serpent's wings off and feed them to him, piece by piece. He voiced a soft hiss between clenched teeth before speaking.

"Go to Rieva. Tell her what has happened. And get word about this to Eleanor Reed at The Circle."

The boy's eyes widened, but he nodded and took off, having a great deal more difficulty finding a way through the crowd than Cormac had. He wasn't gifted with the aura of a predator yet; that would come when he was older.

Once the young changeling was gone, Cormac scanned the area with every sense, magical and mundane. He noted the placement of the three-clawed footprints and the slighter indentation where one had obviously pressed Kimberly to the ground before clenching about her. The ley lines showed signs of a deep pull on their energy where the wyvern must have shifted. It left behind an incorporeal trail, only visible by using his Sight, showing him a ghostly afterimage of the change and where it had taken off.

Underlying the damage to the line was a faint glimmer of something bearing the taint of magework. A tiny runic stone, still active and glowing like a tiny white star in the sea of roiling earth and wind magic stirred up by Viper's presence. The stone was meant to protect the bearer against basic magical attacks.

He focused sharply on the location of the rune, dropping his Sight so he could see beyond the heavy shimmer of tempestuous energy overlaying the entire area. One of the cops was pawing through a purse on the ground, searching for ID, no doubt. The frayed straps and faded material had to be Kimberly's. The stone with the rune would be inside.

Ducking around the police barricades, Cormac stalked forward. The policewoman looked up, her budding anger and harsh command to get back behind the line dying on her lips the moment she got a good look at him. Some of the other nearby cops swung around, but they, too, were struck with a sudden unexplainable terror that rooted them in place and sent a few scrambling away from the scene. People around the edges of the barricades were edging back, pushing into the people behind them, setting off a new wave of fear.

Ignoring the frantic mortals all around him, Cormac knelt by the purse, placing a hand on it as the policewoman crab-walked away as fast as she could, never taking her eyes off him. He drew on the power of the ley lines surrounding him, calling on wind and earth and spirit to tell him where the owner was now. As Kimberly's possession, it was an extension of her—something he could use to focus his spell on a particular target. An intangible connection that he committed to memory for future use, even as he flung his power outward to do what he did best. Hunt.

The first wave searched, a formless circle that would echo back her location if she was anywhere within a hundred mile radius.

As he set his anger aside to concentrate on finding his target, the predatory aura he'd been exuding was also reined in. The police began edging closer. One of them tried to get his attention.

"Sir? Sir, you need to get back behind the barricade."

He ignored them.

A solitary *ping* in his consciousness turned his focus to the east, and slightly north. Somewhere across the Sound. He sent a more concentrated wave, seeking an exact location.

"*Sir*. Get back. I'm not going to ask again."

Cormac growled, low, soft, and sent a great many of those nearest to him stumbling backwards in efforts to escape the formless dread growing root in the pits of their stomachs.

Another *ping*. She was over water, skimming the coast of Long Island. Viper had to be taking her to his lair in the Pine Barrens.

Cormac's growl deepened, the tone going from barely audible to bone-rattling in seconds as his form shifted and grew. People surged away as his great bulk appeared, his own talons digging far deeper furrows in the earth than Viper's. A tremor pulsed through the ground as he settled onto four legs. Though he retained enough presence of mind to keep from stepping on any of the tiny creatures frantically moving around his feet, he only took enough time to orient himself before trumpeting a challenge to his adversary.

The force of his roar sent people to the ground, many of them mid-stride in their mad dashes to escape him, falling to their knees and clutching their ears. The earth trembled. Trees shivered. Distantly, car alarms rang and glass shattered.

Once the sound died down, a fresh wave of panic sent the crowd of onlookers and many of the cops fleeing. Only a couple of the reporters rushed off, most of them screaming into their mics and pointing cameras his way.

He didn't care. In moments, he was spreading wings nearly triple the span of Viper's, powerful hind legs launching his serpentine frame into the air. Trees bent, cameras and police equipment scattered, and people fell, flattened on the ground in the wake of his flapping wings, trenches deep enough to lay bodies left behind by his curved talons.

All the while, his focus was on nothing but the sense of Kimberly's presence, growing closer with every beat of his wings. He was not a creature given to put much stock in faith or prayer, but he silently prayed that he was not too late, that Viper would not succeed in binding her before he could reach them. That she was safe.

I'm coming, Kimberly. Hold on.

Chapter Twenty-four

Kimberly had spent the first ten or fifteen minutes of her first flight terrified to the core of her being, too scared to move. Viper had her clutched close to his chest, legs tucked tight to his body for flight. What parts of her weren't pressed to his hot, scaly body were freezing and her eyes kept watering from the wind stream. When she managed to turn her head enough to look over her shoulder, all she caught behind whipping strands of her hair was a body of water that must have been the Long Island Sound and a slice of the western coast of the island far below them.

There was no comfortable position in the wyvern's claws. Held prone, she had nothing to support her head or neck, and bony ridges around his claws dug into her back, legs, and sides. Cold and terror made her body quake with spasmodic tremors, her blood an icy sludge in her veins. Her arms weren't pinned, but her fingers had long since gone numb locked around the curve of one of his talons. While the razor points weren't slicing into her clothes or skin, she could barely breathe for how tightly he held her.

That might have been a good thing considering they were flying at a height and speed that would leave her nothing but a red smear on the ground should he drop her.

It took less than an hour, but to her, time crawled like a snail hurtling headlong through frozen molasses. When he made an abrupt shift in course, tilting at a sickening angle as he turned inland, she nearly spilled her lunch. They cut over a slice of beach and then a harbor. She spotted what looked like hundreds of boats out for a day on the water, white hulls winking in the sun, and some of the tiny figures far below pointing up at them. Then they flew beyond it and over a great deal of greenery spotted with houses. Some of the properties even had pools, which was an extravagance she had heard of but never seen before. Her whole apartment probably could have fit in some of those houses several times over. Any wonder she might have felt at seeing homes that looked like things she'd only seen in magazines and movies before was brutally dampened by the icy wind and her cramped muscles.

Soon there were no more buildings. Just acre upon acre of trees, dotted by the occasional clear patches of fields and ponds.

She'd never seen this part of Long Island before and was totally lost as to where they might be. She'd never ventured any farther than Queens or Brooklyn and hadn't realized that there was this much untamed wilderness so close to home. Even if she managed to escape once they landed, she had no idea how to get back to the city from wherever it was he was taking her.

Then she noticed he was losing altitude. *Fast.*

She could have sworn some of those treetops were skimming her dangling feet as he took her over a heavily forested area. Heart lodged in her throat, blocking the building scream straining to escape her lungs, she closed her eyes tight, not wanting to see what came next. Moments later, every bone in her body rattled and she gave a breathless yelp as the wyvern jolted to a hopping, one-legged stop, stirring up great gouts of leaves, pollen, and dandelion fluff in his wake.

Birdsong halted mid-note. Brush rattled as larger animals fled, smaller ones hunkering down in hopes of going overlooked. The world went quiet and still, holding its collective breath as the great serpent in their midst settled to earth.

Kimberly slowly opened one eye to peek and see where they were, then the other, her jaw going slack.

They were somewhere deep in a wooded area. There were no signs of a trail, buildings, people or cars, visible or audible anywhere through the ring of scrubby trees surrounding the small field Viper had chosen for his landing. Not even a whisper of distant cars honking or voices. It was obvious "scream all you want, no one will hear you" territory.

Using the hooked fingers on the wrist joint of his wings, Viper pulled himself forward, keeping his back arched and Kimberly clutched tight to his underbelly with one clawed paw. She could have reached down to brush her fingers over the waist-high huckleberry, catbrier and brambles, and the scent of pitch pine was chokingly thick, even with the wyvern's musky scent clogging her nostrils.

She sneezed. Then again. Viper paused, lifting his right wing to peer back at her. She tilted her head to stare back at him with watering eyes.

Giving a disgusted snort, he pressed on, slipping between the trees with surprising grace despite his great size and encumbrance.

It wasn't long before he arrived at a point of ley line convergence so strong, it started her muscles involuntarily twitching and made every hair on her body rise. The trees had grown in strangely here, arching unnaturally to provide cover from any watchers from above. There were deliberately placed stones, stacks of containers of spelling ingredients, and a deep, wyvern-shaped depression off to one side. He dropped her near the outer edge of this strange haven, his claws flexing open so suddenly that she couldn't catch herself. Her numbed fingers slipped and she came to a painful landing on her ass onto a thin cushion of dead leaves and pine needles over hard-packed, sandy soil.

He slithered around, watching her with narrowed golden eyes as she scrambled back, crab-walking on her hands and feet to get as far from him as she could. Then brained herself on the wall of the circle he had summoned to trap her.

A fresh wave of panic surged through her as she looked down. At her feet was a point of a large pentagram drawn in ashes over a patch of sand that had been cleared of dead leaves, along with several symbols that were all too familiar. The same symbols she had been working on in class with Xander in preparation for drawing her own binding circle. All this one had needed was familiar material to be set in the center. Her.

When he had closed the circle around her, she was effectively trapped until he banished it. She had no way of breaking it from inside. Even if she smudged the carefully drawn symbols, he'd already activated their power. Though she knew some planar beings succeeded at turning the tables on their summoner, she had no clue how they did it and no idea how to reverse the process Viper had set into motion. At this point, the only question was how long she could hold out before his will overtook her own, binding her to him.

Viper must have planned to bring her here from the moment he heard she was in the market for an earthbound familiar.

Hyperventilating in panic, she sneezed again, then gasped for air. She knew it was useless, but she rolled to her feet and placed her palms against the wall of the circle, ignoring the burn and ripples of energy as she cast out her Sight in search of any cracks in her prison she might use to escape. Or at the very least slow down the inevitable.

The reality of what she had planned to subject a dragon to was now all too real.

"This will be much easier on you if you simply submit," purred the deep but familiar voice. He sounded strangely human despite that the words came from the mouth of a giant reptile. "There will only be pain if you resist, ducks."

"Please, don't do this! Let me out of here!"

"You may come out when I am done. Be a love and don't fight it. We've a great many things that need doing, and I can't get them done with you in that circle."

Kimberly increased her efforts, pressing harder against the wall of energy, hunting for the tiniest chink in its armor that she could pry open. It was like a giant, rock-solid soap bubble, the surface oily and slick with a thousand iridescent colors and stronger than any circle she had ever drawn.

Panting in terror, she yanked her burning hands back and hugged herself, staring at the wyvern curled around the outer edge of her prison. He wasn't speaking the words of binding aloud, but their power coiled around her will like a snake, constricting her thoughts.

Frantic to save herself, she did the only thing she could think of. She yanked her invisibility spell around her like a shield, praying it would work to hide her from the binding spell the way it had shrugged off his tracking and stunning spells before. She couldn't be sure since she had never tried to cast inside someone else's circle.

It took longer than she was used to, and it was harder to maintain than usual, but the invisibility spell snapped into place. The pressure of the binding spell lifted from her thoughts.

Viper hissed in displeasure, the sound making her quiver. His rear talons flexed, digging deep furrows in the dirt as he reared up, wings cupping the circle as though he feared she might somehow escape his trap.

"Stop this foolishness," he said, his voice deeper than before. "Do you think this little trick of yours will keep you safe? You can't maintain it forever."

He was right. But as long as she wasn't moving, she could cling to it a lot longer than if she was running.

His growl might have made her bones rattle, and the spell might have been taxing, but she stayed where she was, clinging to the thought that this was the only thing keeping her from becoming his puppet. Though she did test a theory by reaching for the edge of the circle. It still singed her fingers and kept her trapped, but at least she could hold him off for a little while.

He slid around to where her fingers had caused a ripple in the surface, head cocked to one side as he peered down with one glowing eye. She sneezed again, then slapped her hand over her mouth and nose. As if things weren't dire enough already, there must have been something in the air she was allergic to.

Satisfied that she had not slid beyond his circle, the wyvern settled to the ground once more. He folded his wings and sprawled comfortably in the mulch, watching with cold, unblinking eyes. Biding his time with the patience of a skilled carnivore knowing it has only to out-wait its prey for her strength to flag and spell to fail.

"I do not understand," he said, "why you choose to make this much harder than it has to be. No one knows you are here. No one will come to your aid. You must know the outcome is inevitable."

Kimberly swiped a hand under her nose and turned her back on the monster, even though he couldn't see her tears. She knew that as well as he did, but that didn't mean she was ready to sit back and let him have her without a fight.

With every passing moment, the magic of the circle pried away bits and pieces of her power, slipping past her defenses. Even with her aura disguised, he'd be inside her head again before long. If she wasn't so stressed and tired, she might have been able to maintain the illusion for hours. Now, between her fear and exhaustion, and the power of the binding spell, she was afraid she only had a matter of minutes before she lost her grip on her invisibility.

She closed her eyes and cleared her head of everything but the need to remain unseen.

Until the ground shuddered under her feet, causing her concentration to fail. Viper reared up, his head whipping to one side even as a gigantic, shadowy blur cut through the trees, smashing them aside with all the power of a freight train. Whatever it was, it was *huge* and coming right at them.

The wyvern roared and leapt straight up, exploding through the canopy of leaves overhead, his wings snapping out to drive him into the sky as rapidly as possible. The monstrous *thing* charging toward them with ground-shaking strides—so much bigger than Viper that it was snapping fully grown pitch pines like twigs—darted into the air after the wyvern like a hawk chasing a sparrow.

And Kimberly cried out as her fear overcame her ability to cling to her own senses, the wyvern's will washing over her in a wave of fierce possession.

The binding snapped into place before she had a chance to muster any defenses against it.

Chapter Twenty-five

Cormac gave chase to the wyvern, his scaly lips peeled back from his clenched fangs so far that they were visible all the way to the gums. As he burst beyond the canopy in a flurry of broken twigs and leaves, the sun shone on his deep blue hide. The base of his scales ranged from a vibrant indigo to a midnight color so dark in places it was nearly black, each scale limned with shining silver. His wing membranes were a paler steel blue, casting heavy shadows on the treetops. Ivory talons, horns and spines were threaded through with the same silver that lined his scales, as if some master metalworker had taken the time to dip each individual scale and claw to ensure some part of him would shine even in the darkest shadows.

A living, breathing jewel, he was both terrifying and magnificent in his raw, primal beauty, arching across the sky in pursuit of the wyvern like a shooting star.

The only reason he had not laid waste to the area with a swath of fire was because of Kimberly. Even in the deepest throes of bestial rage, he knew better than to risk her life like that.

Now that they were clear of the trees, he had free rein. The wyvern may have been a large and formidable foe to anyone else, but Viper was dwarfed by the massive dragon on every physical and magical level.

Pulling on the nearby ley line, he hurled a ball of compressed white-hot energy as big as the wyvern's head straight at the golden serpent's torso. With a dip of his wings, Viper narrowly avoided the magic missile, swirling into an aerial spin to throw a similar projectile, his threaded with and trailing black sparks, back at his assailant.

Almost contemptuously, Cormac snapped it out of the air with his jaws, ignoring the sting to his throat and forked tongue.

And then Viper disappeared.

One moment he was there, dead ahead and as panicked as Cormac had ever seen him, and the next—gone. Even to his Sight.

His wing beats faltered. That could only mean one thing. He had failed. Kimberly was bound, and now Viper was using her powers to augment his own abilities.

Claws scraped along his back in an attempt to tear the base of his wing membranes or disable the thick shoulder muscles that controlled his flight. He twisted and snapped at the golden claws before they could dig in too deep, but Viper blinked out of sight before he could land a blow and latch on.

He slowed down, struggling to maintain a glide to listen or detect the slightest change in air pressure that might give him a hint as to where his adversary had gone. Though his senses were acute, he couldn't hear or feel or smell a damned thing to tell him where Viper was hiding.

Then a powerful blow struck his side, the illusion hiding Viper from his senses faltering as the smaller Other used fang and claw to rip at his throat and belly scales. Cormac's thick hide protected him from the worst of the attack, but red-hot blood was spilling down his long, thick neck from where several fangs had pierced his scales, and the poisonous bite was so painful he couldn't help but voice a thunderous roar of protest.

Before he could reach out a claw to snag Viper and return the favor, the smaller serpent was gone.

Whirling with a snarl, he opened his jaw wide and breathed a swath of flame that singed nearby treetops, head whipping in every direction in hopes of catching the little coward before he could slip too far away. He maintained just enough presence of mind to aim the flames no higher than the treetops, wanting to avoid starting a forest fire or catching Kimberly in the conflagration. Though he was momentarily satisfied at the shriek of pain and locked onto the hint of the wyvern's outline in the smoke and fire, diving forward, he was distracted by the very human cry of pain and terror coming from the trees below him.

Kimberly. Viper must have been drawing from the ley line through her to heal himself. Of course she'd be in pain, seeing as she had no experience in using that kind of power. If he didn't end this quick, Viper could burn out her spark, destroying her ability to use magic forever.

Viper took advantage of his momentary hesitation to swing around and latch onto his throat again, his smaller wings beating furiously to keep himself out of range of the flailing claws of the dragon.

He wasn't counting on Cormac twisting his entire body, snake-like, to coil around him, wings clapping inward to trap the wyvern and yank him close. He sank every one of the five splayed talons tipping each of his four paws deep into Viper's ribs, stomach and thighs. They tumbled together toward the ground, the wyvern shrieking in high counterpoint to Cormac's earth-shattering roar.

At the last possible moment, Cormac shoved Viper away from him, adding momentum to his fall into the trees below. Though the dragon's wing beats staggered from a deep tear one of the wyvern's spines had made in the membrane between his third and fourth finger, he was able to gain a little height, hovering above long enough to ensure that Viper would remain where he had fallen.

His scales had given him a modicum of protection, but Viper's wings had been shredded in the fall and by Cormac's claws. A few boughs had punctured his hide, golden scales splashed with crimson, and several bones had been broken. He lay gasping on the ground, hind legs weakly clawing for purchase in the dirt and broken branches.

Cormac spread his wings wide and tilted them back to let the air spill free so he could control his landing, extending his hind legs to settle lightly in the underbrush. He took such care that the ground barely shuddered under his weight as he came to rest upon it.

He set his forepaws on either side of the fallen wyvern, looming over him. Though Viper made an attempt to arch his neck up to snap at Cormac, the dragon voiced a deep, threatening growl that set small stones and shattered trees to shiver in response. The defeated wyvern subsided.

"Release her," Cormac rumbled, "and live. Do it *now* or I *will* kill you."

"Tired words, old friend," wheezed the wyvern.

It struggled to lift its head; failed. Golden eyes drifted shut.

Cormac growled again, his head dipping down to sink his fangs into the scruff of the wyvern's neck, lifting the much smaller Other like a mother cat transporting a kitten. Viper hissed a soft protest, but he was too hurt and weak to fight back.

Cormac dragged him like that nearly half a mile, returning to the place where they had originally taken off. It didn't take very long, but every precious moment counted. Every time Viper resumed his struggles, a slight shake was enough to make him stop. Once they reached the small clearing, the dragon couldn't fit his great bulk between the trees without risking sending several of them toppling down onto Kimberly's prone form.

With a snarl, he flung the wyvern across the clearing, far from Kimberly.

"Fix it," he hissed.

Viper didn't move—but Kimberly did. His raptor's gaze was sharply drawn to the scuttling form withdrawing from him.

A sound of displeasure rumbled in his throat, the spines around his head and neck flaring. She cried out and flung her hands up over her head, curled into a shivering ball in a nest of pine needles at the base of a tree.

Cursing himself a thousand times over for frightening her, he concentrated on forcing his scales and spines to settle back into place. He inched forward, dipping his head to sniff for any clues to how much damage Viper had done to her.

Under the stink of the wyvern, she reeked of fear. Unsurprising, given the circumstances. Worse, under that, the ozone of heavy casting. Her pulse was rapid and weak, breathing sharp and short. Her skin was too cold when he lightly nosed her. The pained, terrified sound she made at the touch made his heart ache for her—and curse himself once more for being the cause.

Then she slapped at his jaw, the blow carrying with it an extra *oomph* of illusory pain to drive him back. As badly as he wanted to hiss and bare his teeth, he managed to clamp down on the urge, instead pulling back just enough to give her some breathing room. She had been frightened badly enough already.

She wasn't physically injured, but some of Viper's pain leaked through the familiar bond, twisting her already frightened features with agony. Until the link was severed, as long as Viper was hurt, he would be offloading some of that pain on her to improve his chances at survival.

That would have to be remedied.

He tilted his head to one side, examining the fallen wyvern. Drawing on the nearby ley line, his forked tongue flickered out as he tasted the bitter, burnt-chalk remnants of the binding spell still drifting up from the circle.

Standard, simple, and brutally efficient. It had probably hurt like hell if Kimberly had fought it for any length of time.

Though he was tempted to rip the spell to shreds, he had to tread with delicacy lest he hurt her in the process of destroying the link. If Viper died without her energy to draw upon, so be it. Within hours, the elements summoned by the circle would solidify into a solid, permanent binding that could only be removed by Viper's consent. Once that happened, he wouldn't just be able to use her power. He'd know her thoughts, be able to summon her to his side at any time without her consent, and be able to force her to cast spells on his behalf. The longer Cormac waited, the stronger their bond would grow.

As it was, this was going to hurt both of them a great deal since he would have to rip portions of their power from them. It was considered a black enchant. Taboo, dark magic that was normally forbidden. Long before the laws had been laid regarding use of such magic, he had mastered the art. He hadn't lied when he had told her that Viper was the only Other who had successfully bound a mage as a familiar. The theory behind the spell was simple. Had he desired it, he could have done it himself.

The type of filth it left on one's psyche was a permanent stain, a constant craving for power above and beyond that which they were already blessed with.

He would use the same method some planar beings did to banish the binding. It took a different form of energy—the same type Kimberly used to cast her illusions. She may have known she was no true mage, but he was sure she did not understand the source of her power. She couldn't cast elemental magic because she had no command over the elements. Her power was rooted in manipulating the life energy and minds of others.

Sorcery. Not magecraft.

He would have to use his own brand of sorcery to burn out the bindings, using their own energy against them.

Cormac didn't relish causing her any more pain than she had already suffered, but it was necessary if he was going to free her from the constraints of the bond. He inched forward, extending a clawed paw to rest in the center of the circle. Hints of power pulsed upward, throbbing in time with his heartbeat. He focused on the tether that stretched between the two, using the circle as his focus.

One by one, he unwound and then snapped the elemental threads that bound them together. The matching runes in the circle for each element flared briefly under his claws, then faded to nothing. Little by little, her breathing eased and heartbeat strengthened.

Viper lifted his head a fraction, a snarl of protest rattling in his throat, but it died off into a choked wheeze before long.

As her strength returned, Kimberly struggled to rise. Most likely to hide from him. Her legs wouldn't hold her, so she didn't keep it up long. He tuned out her thrashing, knowing what was coming next was going to hurt her. Ancient and experienced as he was, he couldn't bear to watch, knowing what he was going to do to her.

As the last of the intangible threads tying her to Viper broke, he thrust his will into them both. It didn't take much effort to locate the link in their minds that left her vulnerable to Viper's manipulations. It was a hot, pulsing thing, dark as pitch and alive with the transfer of energy between them as Viper sucked on her fading life essence to sustain himself and heal his injuries. Without the addition of the elemental threads to support the bond between them, he was killing her, leeching away the golden spark of her magic and spirit instead of using her as a filter to draw from other sources of energy in the vicinity.

Expending an effort of will was all it took to fry the growing threads between them, but it was far more delicate work reaching in to scoop out the ingrained commands and desires inherent in the bond. It was the most dangerous part of his task, because there was a good chance he could rip out vital parts of her spark in the process. If he didn't, all Viper would need to do to reinstate the full bond would be to get some focus object and make another circle to reestablish the elemental threads between them. She wouldn't even have to be present for it to work.

She clutched her temples, her screams sending ripples of dread through him that made his scales rise and fall in pattering waves. Doing his best to ignore her distress, he concentrated on his task, putting every ounce of focus into his Sight as he used his will to nip and yank at the mental claws Viper had dug so deeply into the source of her power.

The moment the shadows in her mind dissipated, with a thought, he seared the connection of the spirit to cauterize the psychic wounds he had made. The two cried out simultaneously, both in a great deal of pain, before they slumped unconscious into the mulch.

Cormac strongly considered killing the wyvern out of spite, but he was far more concerned with Kimberly's wellbeing to bother. He wouldn't know for hours—maybe days—if he had saved her spark as well as her life. Viper had learned his lesson and would not be showing his scaly hide anywhere near the city for a good long while, he was sure. He could wait. Kimberly could not. He needed to get her as far from that thrice-damned circle as possible and somewhere she could recuperate in peace and safety.

He surged forward, lightly resting his jaw on Kimberly to protect her from the falling trees as he slid forward so he could reach her with both forepaws. Heavy branches and even one trunk struck his thick skull with muted thumps, barely registering beyond the minor annoyance. It was likely for the best that she was not awake to see the cage of talons descend upon her, clasping her to him with all the delicacy he could muster.

He clutched her limp frame in his forepaws, moving slowly so as not to crush her or nick her with his talons. She dangled like a broken marionette in his claws. He arched back to cradle her to his chest, tail coiling and snapping with his agitation, uprooting and slicing through several tree trunks in the process.

Without a backward look spared to the fallen wyvern, he used his hind legs to thrust himself into the air, flinging out his wings to catch the wind. He barely noticed the pain of his injured wing, the blood still flowing from multiple wounds ranging over his body. All he cared about was getting her out of the pine barrens and taking her to his lair where he could properly stand guard and fortify his defenses against anything else that might consider accosting her.

It was all his fault she had been hurt. If he had done things differently, if he had told her what he was, if he had just agreed to be her gods-be-damned familiar, none of this would have happened.

When he was searching for her, he had prayed that she would be unbound and unhurt. It hadn't done much good the last time he had done so, but this time he prayed that she still had her spark and that she would accept his offer to be her familiar once she woke up and he had a chance to explain himself. It was the only way he could be sure she would be safe.

It was the only way to make sure he never lost her again.

Chapter Twenty-six

Kimberly woke up in someone else's bed.

She couldn't remember how she got there. Or what had happened before she blacked out. Every muscle ached, each movement torture as the soft cotton sheets rubbed against the cuts and bruises littering her skin.

Barely able to move, she squinted her eyes open and peered around herself, stilling when turning her head prompted another wave of pain. There were a few fat, white candles placed on the candelabras around the room that kept the darkness at bay. The diffused light still made her eyes sting. The scent of some kind of incense lingered, as did some kind of musky, spicy smell that seemed familiar but she just couldn't place.

The room was sparsely furnished. Aside from the huge bed she was currently lost in the middle of, there were a pair of end tables, an armoire, and a few standing candelabras. No artwork or mirrors. Her Sight phased in and out, visions of what looked like hundreds of runes magically etched into the walls all aglow with power playing havoc with her already burning eyes.

The combined weakness, pain and disorientation was the only reason she wasn't luxuriating in the Egyptian cotton sheets, cool and silky against her damaged skin, believing all of this was some kind of surreal dream. There were no clocks anywhere to be seen and blackout curtains on the windows, so she didn't know if it was day or night.

Then it hit her just how odd it was that she was in someone else's bedroom. A man's, if the plain, heavy furniture and lack of interior decorating was anything to go by. Tucked in and wearing an oversized shirt that didn't belong to her.

Her first thought was *vampire*. Terror made her go rigid.

Then Cormac strolled in from the open door across the room toward the armoire. Shirtless. As distracting as that was, it took a second for it to register that he was only wearing loose, dark blue pajama pants. The getup was so casual and unlike what she'd seen of him thus far that she couldn't help but stare.

If she hadn't felt like she'd been hit by a truck, she might have been intrigued by his current state of undress. His taste in strange, concealing, Victorianesque clothing had hid a lean but deliciously toned body, and a few tattoos that pulsed with dark, arcane energy against his pale skin. Runic symbols, though she was too tired and rattled to place them beyond the obvious one for concealment etched over his heart. A weird place for it, she thought.

His steps faltered briefly when she tilted her head to look at him, his gaze flicking in her direction as he caught the movement out of the corner of his eye.

"You're awake," he said, changing his course to take a seat beside her on the bed, twisting around to lightly brush the back of his fingers over her cheek. "You slept for so long I was starting to worry you wouldn't wake up."

She closed her eyes and leaned into his touch, her initial panic and worry subsiding into a drowsy contentment. He was the source of that warm, woodsy scent she hadn't been able to place. Funny, she hadn't noticed it on him before.

"Tired," she mumbled. Then summoned a bit more energy, forcing her eyes back open as fragments of memories resurfaced and some of the worry returned. "How did I get here?"

"Shh. Relax. You're safe. Viper can't touch you here."

Her features twisted, first in confusion, then deepening into horror as it all came back to her. His hand shot out to press her back into the bed as she struggled to sit up.

"He *took* me, he *bound* me—"

Cormac leaned into her, using his torso to keep her pressed into the bed while his hands cupped her cheeks, urging her to look up at him. She clawed at his arms briefly, then stilled, chest heaving and moisture building in her eyes. Once the futility of fighting against his strength sank in, she focused on him.

"Listen to me. The binding is broken. You're safe now but you need to rest. I've taken care of everything."

"He was in my head! Cormac, he took my magic, I couldn't stop it..."

Her voice was starting to rise, wavering with horror. The memory of having her powers being sucked out of her, slipping like sand through her metaphorical fingers no matter how hard she had tried to hold onto them, were all too fresh in her mind. The only thing keeping her from dissolving into a total wreck was his steady warmth, holding her tight, keeping her anchored in the present.

"It's over now. I promise you that. You're safe with me."

"Dragon," she whispered, the tears spilling down her cheeks as she stared up at him, pupils dilated with fear and panic. "There was a dragon. A real one."

"Yes. And he brought you back here after he broke the familiar bond. Kimberly, this is important. Do you still have the Sight? Can you feel your spark?"

Cormac held his breath as she blinked a few times, then focused her watery eyes on him. The import of what he was asking didn't sink in immediately. Then she frowned at him.

"Of course I can. Why wouldn't I?"

His breath left him in a rush, and he lowered his head to rest his brow on hers as he sagged against her in what she thought might be relief. She squirmed a little bit, and he pulled back to give her some breathing room. His worry over something that seemed so insignificant in light of what she had faced was bordering on comical to her, and did a better job of jolting her out of her own anxious state than anything else he had done thus far.

Lifting a hand that had been clinging to his arm a bit too tightly, she mirrored his touch, resting her hand on his cheek. He tilted his head into the soothing stroke of her fingers, making a deep sound of contentment that rumbled straight down to her bones.

"I'm the one who should be comforting you," he said.

That may have been the case, but he wasn't pulling away. She returned his wry smile with a tentative one of her own, her fingers stilling. He placed his hand over hers, then turned his head to lightly kiss her palm.

Her cheeks grew hot at the brush of his lips, then hotter still when she recalled she was wearing one of his shirts and was tucked into his bed.

"Did you... umm..."

She trailed off, too embarrassed to finish the thought. He arched one brow in question, then chuckled as her blush deepened.

"Undress you? No, though I admit I considered doing it myself after I saw how badly Viper roughed you up. I'm afraid your clothing was ruined in the scuffle. Rieva stopped by to check in and helped me get you settled. She'll be by later tonight with some food and supplies for you."

"Oh," Kimberly said, not sure if she was more embarrassed by that or relieved. It was strange to think of the angry changeling who hated her kind so much being the motherly type and helping Cormac nurse her back to health. Then worry set back in. "Wait a sec—what time is it? My mom is going to be so mad at me if I'm out too late. I have to get home."

He voiced a soft growl, then brushed her hair back out of her face. She might have fallen right back asleep with him running his fingers through her hair like that, except there was a minor tremor in his fingers and his expression was such a mix of guilt and remorse that she wasn't sure what was going on. When he did speak, the resignation in his tone was clear even through his muttered response.

"I was going to wait to tell you this," he said, "but it's Tuesday night. You were so badly drained, it took much longer than expected for you to recover. You still need to rest."

Kimberly stared up at him in shock, her hand slipping from his cheek. She had met with Viper in the park on Saturday afternoon. She'd been out for days.

Fresh panic over what that meant bubbled in her chest. Her mother had no idea where she was, she'd missed school and work, and who knew what kind of damage had been done to her to knock her unconscious for so long. Cormac placed his hand over hers again, squeezing fingers gone cold.

"Don't worry. I had Eleanor—Professor Reed—explain to your mother that a school project has been keeping you intensely occupied. She might appreciate it if you check in with a phone call, but she was understanding enough when she was told it had to do with your preparations for graduation. I believe Eleanor may also have made some sort of arrangement with your job. If you need it, she is prepared to grant you an extension on your finals, too."

"You did all that?"

"I did. Like I said, I've taken care of everything. All you need to do now is lie back and rest. Get your strength back."

Astounded, she barely managed a whispered "thank you" around the lump in her throat. She couldn't imagine what she had done to merit him doing so much to take care of her, but she was grateful for it, nonetheless.

He gave her a wide, warm smile, leaning in to brush his lips against her forehead again. "You're welcome. Remember, you're safe here. Anything you need, just call for me. I want you to stay until you're fully recovered."

She nodded. Hesitated. "Why did that dragon save me? Where did it go?"

Cormac's gaze flicked away, his smile faltering. "It wants to be your familiar. It will return once you've recovered."

She closed her eyes against the fierce sparking of his aura, settling into the pillows again with a groan.

A real dragon. It may have scared her to pieces, but it *had* saved her. Even if it wanted something from her in return, Cormac's plan had worked. It might take her a little time to wrap her wits around the idea of working with such a powerful Other again after her latest experience.

"I'm not sure how I feel about that," she admitted. "After what happened with Viper..."

His lips twitched, a ghost of his humor returning. "He's nothing like Viper, and very impressed by your credentials. He's quite anxious to help you. So you have an extra incentive to rebuild your strength and get back on your feet. Dragons don't like to be kept waiting."

She nodded, though she couldn't help how stiff she'd gone at the thought, heartbeat thudding in her ears. Cormac traced a fingertip over her lips, jerking her out of the dark pit of doubt growing in her mind. She was brought very much back to the present at his touch, his voice turning husky as the sly twinkle in his eyes grew brighter.

"Not that I mind having you in my bed... but I think we'll both enjoy it more when you're here because you want to be, not because you have to be."

Another blush heated her cheeks. She was all too aware of his warmth, his strength, the comfortable way he had settled and molded his body along hers. It would have been nice to share that intimacy with him, but she was so exhausted and achy that he was right. It wasn't the time. It would be—that decision was surprisingly easy to make—but not until she was better and they were both ready.

Tired and stressed as she was, she hesitated before whispering one last request.

"Will you stay with me? Until I fall asleep? I'm scared to be alone."

His expression turned grave as he pulled back, eyes searching her face. She bit her lip, feeling stupid for asking until he sat up and scooted under the covers with her. His arms slid around her to hold her close, tucking her head under his chin. She almost lost it again, squeezing her eyes tightly closed to keep any more tears from spilling all over his naked chest, even if they were from gratitude this time.

"I'm here," he murmured, fingertips lightly stroking her back. "For as long as you want me, I'll always be here."

Chapter Twenty-seven

After that first night awake, it didn't take Kimberly long to recover her strength. Cormac had briefly woken her up a second time to get some food in her, helping her sit up to eat the soup and drink the fae-infused water Rieva had delivered. She devoured every bite, promptly fell back asleep, and slept the rest of the night through and a good chunk of the following day.

She woke up alone in the bed, refreshed, charged with energy, and ready to take on the world.

Her legs didn't agree, wobbling the moment she put her weight on them. Cormac found her a few minutes later, spitting curses as she fought to get herself out of her indignant sprawl she'd fallen into.

A bark of laughter was surprised out of him at the sight. He set aside the tray he'd been carrying, kneeling down to scoop her up in his arms. She grumbled under her breath about it and yanked at the long shirt she was wearing to keep her bare legs covered, but settled down as he picked her up and took the few steps necessary to deposit her back on the bed.

"What part of *rest* was unclear?" he asked.

His scolding might have been more effective if his shoulders weren't still shaking from suppressed laughter, his eyes glittering with mirth. She stuck her tongue out at him and fell back into the pillows with a huff.

"I'm fine. I feel great."

"That's the water from the Black Star talking." He lightly ran a fingertip from the inside of her elbow all the way down to her wrist, making a parade of goose bumps march down her arm. "Your spark is running hot, but the rest of you needs time to catch up."

She made a low sound of frustration, folding her arms. "I hate this. I need to *move.*"

"Eat something, then I'll help you wander around all you like."

He got up to retrieve the tray, setting it down in her lap. She was only slightly alarmed to see that the surface was still aglow with some kind of power from the faded runes etched in the tarnished metal surface. They were all ancient, of a brand she wasn't familiar with. This tray had been used for spells and perhaps as an altar in the past. Not to mention it was a relic, probably worth more than the entire combined contents of her apartment. She was a tad nonplussed that Cormac thought it made an appropriate breakfast tray.

The plate in the center had eggs, bacon, and toast. A smaller dish held an arrangement of sliced fruit. There was a steaming cup of coffee and a glass bottle of water stoppered with a cork. A quick peek with her Sight showed the by now familiar elemental energy from the Black Star swirling in the drinks. A hint of it in the food as well.

Cormac was clearly determined to have her wired on elemental energy. Never mind that she had no idea how to use it. It had to be doing some good, considering how much better she was feeling and how much her Sight had been improving since she first started drinking the potent stuff.

He stayed beside her, watching intently as she picked at the food. Despite her embarrassment at being watched and waited on, hunger got the better of her. Within a couple of bites, she was devouring the meal with gusto. When there was nothing left but crumbs, she reached for the coffee, eyeing him over the rim of the mug.

"Are you sure I'm not being a bother?"

He grinned. "Believe me, if I thought you were a bother, you would know it. I'm finding I'm enjoying having someone to take care of."

She avoided his gaze, sipping the coffee. He slid the tray from her lap, placing it on the bedside table, then held out his hand for the mug as soon as she lowered it from her lips. With a sigh, she relinquished it, and he set that aside on the table as well. That done, he rose, offering his arm to her for support.

"Rieva will be here any minute," he said. "If you're feeling up to it, you can come down to speak with her."

Kimberly gave him a dubious look before taking his hand, rising shakily back to her feet. He helped her steady herself, but she wasn't quite so wobbly this time around, standing under her own power before long.

"I'm not exactly dressed for it."

"Neither am I," he said, shrugging. Considering he was only wearing a pair of jeans, no shirt, she couldn't help but agree. "She won't care. And if she does, she can always come back some other time. Besides, I thought you might like to choose a book or two, or find some other things to occupy yourself while you're recuperating."

Kimberly fidgeted in place, considering. She wasn't used to lying around doing nothing. It would get boring before long if she didn't have some form of entertainment to distract herself. Rieva had already seen her disheveled state, anyway. There was no reason to cling to her squeamishness and embarrassment if Cormac wasn't worried about it either. Though Kimberly did have some reservations about the woman, Rieva had helped her. She couldn't be all bad.

"I'll take any excuse to get out of this room for a while, but I'm not sure why you think she'd want to talk to me. Doesn't she hate me?"

"Of course not. She wanted to apologize for siccing Viper on you."

No effort was made to disguise her doubt. Rather than continue to worry about what the changeling might do to her in her current condition, she focused on keeping her balance and staying upright on the long trek across the room. Cormac stayed close, ready to catch her should she stumble, but she did a fair job of maintaining her footing.

The extraordinarily complex series of glyphs etched into the door frame blazed to life when she got within a yard of them. Flinching back with a startled gasp, he had to catch her before she could fall.

"Cripes," she said, voice shaking. "Were you planning to use this place as a bomb shelter during the next World War?"

He chuckled. "Something like that. There's no safer place in the city for you to recover. I thought you might appreciate the security."

The glyphs snapped with energy that rippled and fizzed against her skin as they passed through the doorway. All her hair was standing on end as if she'd been scooting around on a carpet in wool socks. When she glanced up, she couldn't help giggling when she saw his own hair was doing the same, like he'd just stuck his finger in an electric socket.

His puzzled frown when he looked at her had her laughing harder. Then he noted how her hair was floating around her head in a messy halo. With a snort, he ran a hand raggedly through his own hair, smoothing the crackling spikes.

"Perhaps they are a bit overcharged," he admitted.

"Just a teensy bit."

With a snort of amusement, he took her arm and led her across his apartment above the Wild Hunt. She peered around with interest, though there wasn't much to see. Like his bedroom, the place didn't look very lived in. It was tremendous and spotlessly clean, but there were no signs of habitation beyond a sparse scattering of furniture and candles providing illumination in addition to the dim, watery sunlight filtering through the rain-spattered windows. Not even a stray sock on the floor to make the place look like somebody lived there.

She nudged his ribs with her elbow. "Are you sure this is your apartment?"

"Of course. Why?"

She waved at all the empty space with her free hand. "It doesn't look anything like your store. I wouldn't have pegged you for a Spartan."

"Ah. No, I would never call myself that. This is just a place for me to rest my head when I'm in the city and don't feel up to making the trip home to the Catskills."

She pursed her lips, looking around again. If he lived all the way in the Catskills, at least a hundred miles away, it was no wonder he kept an apartment in the city. Then again, a trip back and forth like that had to be a bit much to take every few days. Even if he only came in for a couple of days a week to tend his shop, she would think he might have left a few personal items in his apartment here. A couple of pictures, or a book or two. *Something* to give a hint about the interests and personality of the man behind the incredible clutter of the shop.

There were more glyphs on the door frame leading out of the apartment. They glimmered an angry, harsh red with the heat burning inside them, ready to toast any unwanted visitors to a crisp. She stared over her shoulder at them as he led her out and into a dim stairwell.

He took her down a couple of flights, then held the door for her leading into his store. Rieva was already waiting, sitting beside the register, her heels drumming against the counter as she stared up at the ceiling. The moment they stepped inside, she hopped down, her pallor somehow more pronounced by the dark circles under her eyes and crackle to her voice as she rushed forward.

"Oh, Kimberly, I am *so* sorry. I never intended—"

Shocked by the woman's obvious remorse, Kimberly stopped her tracks, going stiff as the girl grabbed her cheeks and yanked her down to eye level. She hadn't realized just how short the albino was until she was standing next to her. Kimberly was only average in height, but the top of Rieva's head barely came up to her shoulder. With all the danger and power she exuded, until that moment Kimberly had thought she was much taller.

Rieva stared deeply into her eyes. The piercing, icy blue so like Cormac's glimmered with some kind of power. Cormac didn't make any move to prevent it, either. He kept a steadying hand on Kimberly's back, but otherwise did nothing to interfere.

There was a bit of pressure near the back of her skull, nothing more. It was the only hint she had that the changeling was digging around in her head. By the time she realized it, the woman was done, her shoulders sagging as she puffed out a breath of relief.

"Good, no permanent damage. You should have full use of your spark again in a day or so."

Hair prickling with unease, though it was a little late for it, Kimberly scooted closer to Cormac, one hand clutching at him in alarm. He slid his arm around her shoulder.

Rieva pulled back and her eyes widened in surprise. Her sharp look became calculating as she looked back and forth between them.

"Well," she said, "I won't keep you long. Truly, I am very sorry for involving Viper. I was hoping it might prompt someone else to act sooner..." Her gaze flicked to Cormac, then away. He made a soft sound between his teeth, almost a hiss, and she took a quick step back. "Never mind that. Let's just say things didn't turn out as I intended."

Kimberly bit her lip before replying, leaning away and fighting the urge to hide behind Cormac. Rieva had the power to see into her thoughts and memories. That was no minor gift. No wonder her power shone like her café's namesake.

"I'm sure you didn't," Kimberly replied, extending a shaking hand. The last thing she wanted to do was offend this woman by spurning her apology. "Everybody makes mistakes. Don't worry about it."

Rieva clasped her fingers in both hands, her relieved smile transforming her whole face. It was terrifying how quickly she went from scary to angelic.

"You really are sweet. Continue to be the exception, Kimberly. It will serve you well in the trials ahead."

Cormac made another low sound in his throat which Rieva took as her cue to change the subject.

"Listen, I brought you some fresh clothes and a few other necessities. If you need a hand and don't want this big galoot to see you naked, I'll help you out with a shower and change of clothes."

He shifted, tightening his grip on Kimberly as he turned a fearsome glare on Rieva that would have sent anyone else cowering under the furniture. The changeling didn't bat a lash.

"No one's going to see her naked but me."

Kimberly huffed, her cheeks flaming with embarrassment. "Oh my *God, no one* is going to see me naked! I can shower myself!"

Cormac frowned, peering down at her with a wistful expression. "Are you sure? I certainly wouldn't mind."

"Sure you wouldn't," Rieva said, grinning as Kimberly ducked her face so neither of them could see how her cheeks burned crimson. "She's the one who minds, you silly oaf. Go count your money for a few minutes, the girls need to talk."

Fear threaded through Kimberly at that. What on earth could the changeling have to say to her that she couldn't talk about in front of Cormac?

Chapter-Twenty-eight

Cormac's fierce expression returned. Rieva returned his stare, not giving an inch. After a long, tense moment, he bared his teeth at her in a semblance of a grin, the warning in it crystal clear.

"Fine," he ground out. "A few minutes."

He helped Kimberly over to one of the chairs by the bookshelves, ignoring the impatient tapping of Rieva's foot as she waited for him to go away. He took his time ensuring Kimberly was settled comfortably, crouching before her as he lightly touched her cheek, giving her a reassuring smile before he rose to head over to the register. He poked through the things Rieva had brought, sniffing at the coffee and making every effort to appear as if he had no interest in their conversation and wasn't hanging on their every word.

As soon as he was gone, Rieva settled on a nearby footstool, somehow managing to look elegant in her silk and silver and combat boots as she crossed her legs and primly folded her hands over one knee. Her white-blond hair fell in artfully arranged spikes as she leaned forward to stage whisper, knowing full well Cormac was listening in.

"Things may not have turned out as I intended, but I think you'll get what you were looking for. If not, I just wanted to let you know that I've got a laundry list of local Others and even a few out-of-towners who would love to take you up on your offer. As soon as they heard you were legit and meant what you said about only wanting someone temporarily, they came out of the woodwork."

Kimberly fiddled with the hem of the long shirt, a sudden chill prompting her to roll down the long sleeves over her arms. "I don't know. I'm still a little freaked out about Viper."

Rieva shook her head, her expression turning grave. "He was a mistake. A very bad mistake. I didn't think he was truly stupid enough to try to make a mage his familiar again. If I had checked his intentions, I would have been able to do something about it. It was foolish of me not to, and for that I can't begin to express my regrets. I know you have your doubts about me—no, no, I saw it when I checked on the progress of your recovery, so don't try to deny it. You're right to be afraid. I'm a fucking monster, and I'll act like it when I think someone is a danger to me or my friends."

A faint choking noise was the only response Kimberly could come up with, her eyes going wide with shock and not a little fear.

"You have nothing to fear from me, Kimberly. I know what it must look like after our initial introduction, but believe me, I've seen enough about you to know you're not a threat. I have no intention of doing you harm."

"I'm sorry you don't like me," Kimberly muttered. "If you're just here to apologize, I accept."

Rieva blew out a breath, leaning back. "No, not exactly. That's certainly part of it. I was hoping you might be interested in something of a partnership."

At the look Kimberly gave her, she laughed.

"Hey, I like making money, and I thought you might like to earn a few extra bucks, too. You'd be surprised how many Others jump at the chance to work with a mage they can trust not to trap them in the process. I know enough about you to know you wouldn't hurt a fly, and I have the contacts to bring in the business, so if you like, we could pool our resources and work together."

That was one of the last things Kimberly was expecting. A partnership with the bane of her kind? That would take a great deal of thought before jumping into any kind of decision.

Good thing she had nothing but time on her hands while she recovered.

"Are you sure that's safe?" she ventured.

"You know what I can do and what I'm capable of. I can manage the offers, use my skills to pre-screen and wash out the types like Viper. If I had thought to check beforehand, he never would have heard about you from me. Now that I know what to look for, it will never happen again. Think about it. Could be a lucrative business for you."

So she wouldn't continue to look like a gaping idiot, Kimberly nodded, then cleared her throat. Curiosity was getting the better of her now that she was sure Rieva wasn't going to pull another dagger on her. She wasn't entirely certain it was a safe topic of conversation, but she wanted to know more about this woman than the few scraps of information Cormac had given her and the rumors she'd heard from Xander.

"Is it true? What you did?" she asked.

"What, that I killed the mage who bound me? Abso-fucking-lutely."

The casual reply took Kimberly aback. Rieva tilted her head, waiting patiently for the next question, though being a mind reader she had to know what was coming next.

"Is that why you hate us so much? Because of that mage?"

"Yes." Rieva's hands slid to her shirt, plucking at the buttons to loosen it.

Kimberly blinked in surprise, then gasped when she saw the patchwork of symbols drawn in thick, pale pink scars on Rieva's skin under the white silk. Blood magic. Considered the most twisted and perverse form of the black arts, performed only by the most dangerous of sorcerers, it was strictly forbidden by every coven across every continent.

Whatever that mage had been attempting to accomplish, by using an Other's blood, it must have been extremely powerful and terrifically nasty business. The type that could make hearts stop, bones crumble, plagues start. The type designed to destroy minds, bodies and souls.

There was good reason it was forbidden.

"Oh, Rieva, I'm so sorry," Kimberly whispered.

"Don't be. Like I said, I killed the son of a bitch. And anyone else I come across who even considers walking the same path he did." She smiled as she re-buttoned her shirt, teeth gleaming white and sharp. "I'm not so blinded by my past that I see his face in every mage I meet, though there's good reason I have the reputation I do. It works for me. It also helps me protect those who can't protect themselves."

Understanding dawned. "That's why you have all those protection spells around the Black Star. You keep the weaker Others safe."

"Mmhm."

Kimberly shook her head in a touch of disbelief. It was incredible to think that someone with such a terrifying reputation in her community was really such a kind and caring individual once you got to know her. Fierce and powerful, yes, but not nearly the bloodthirsty monster she was thought to be. There was no great pride in her for it, either. No smugness or tilt of her chin to suggest she enjoyed being feared. More like satisfaction in her accomplishments.

"Listen," Rieva said, leaning forward to put a hand on Kimberly's knee and giving her such an intense stare that it might have frightened her if she hadn't just heard the truth behind the fearsome reputation. "You can call on me if you ever need help. I owe you after my mistake. Just tell Mister Eavesdropper over there when you're ready to call in the favor and he'll get word to me."

"Thank you," Kimberly whispered, overwhelmed. The significance of a fae creature offering an unsolicited favor was not lost on her. Everything she'd learned about the formalities surrounding fae favors in her etiquette class flew out of her head. "I don't know what to say. I don't have any offerings..."

Rieva snorted. "That's the last thing I want. Don't worry about it. You should be thanking your luck dragon for rubbing off on you."

Kimberly had nearly forgotten about the naga. If anything, she would have thought he'd given her the very worst of bad luck after what had happened with Viper.

Then again, Cormac did say a dragon was interested in being her familiar, and Rieva wasn't demanding a sacrifice or tribute in return for her favor, so maybe things had turned out for the best after all.

That blessing he had given her had turned out to be so much more than she could ever have imagined. Bringing her a future with a powerful familiar, owed favors by influential Others, and—

dare she think it—perhaps a *real* relationship with Cormac, too? She would definitely have to find some way to thank Sam.

"I'll do that. Thank you, Rieva."

"Please, call me Rie. All my friends do."

"Rie, then," Kimberly said, not having to force her smile this time. "As soon as I get things sorted out with school and everything, I'll be in touch."

"Excellent. Think things over, and when you're ready, let me know what you think of my idea. You're welcome in my café anytime."

With that, she rose with a stretch and a yawn, arching her back like a cat. The little tag on the silver collar around her throat jingled with the movement. That out of the way, she extended a hand to help Kimberly back to her feet.

The two women moved over to join Cormac, who wasn't even bothering to pretend he was interested in the packages on the counter anymore. As soon as they were close enough, he put an arm around Kimberly again, tugging her against his side so possessively that Rieva smirked.

"Are you going to need a hand with that shower or anything else? I meant it. If you don't want grabby-hands here pawing you and you're not up to it yourself, I'm happy to stick around a bit longer."

Kimberly's breath was squeezed out of her when his grip tightened around her ribs. She poked Cormac in the side when he voiced a threatening growl at the much shorter woman, and he eased his grip a smidgen.

"No, I think I can handle myself."

Rieva's smile widened, eyes sparkling with mirth as she gave them both a sarcastic salute. "In that case, I'll leave you two lovebirds be. Come see me anytime."

Cormac's eyes stayed locked on Rieva as she turned away, sauntering toward the labyrinth of furniture that led out to the street. Though Kimberly was listening for it, she didn't hear the jingle of the bell over the door or the snap of the wards letting someone pass through, only the light, steady patter of rain.

He didn't appear to be worried they might have a lingering audience. After a moment passed, the tension in his body eased away, and his grip shifted from possessive to supportive in the blink of an eye. Burying his nose in her hair, he breathed deep, then exhaled on a shuddering sigh.

"That woman," he said, "is going to drive me insane."

Sliding her arms around his waist, she leaned into him, closing her eyes as she sank into the protection of his arms. "She's not so bad. Not like I thought before."

"I know. I just don't approve of her trying to take you away from me."

Frowning, she leaned back to peer up at him. "What do you mean? I'm not going anywhere."

He made a deep sound that vibrated in his chest, rumbling over her skin and making her shiver. Lowering his head again, he rubbed his cheek against hers as his grip tightened once more.

"Maybe I'm being foolish," he said, "but I want you all to myself. Let's go get you that shower, hmm? Before I forget that you're still recovering."

She nodded, then gave a little cry of surprise before laughing as he swept her off her feet into his arms. He grinned down at her, then jerked his chin at the things Rieva had brought. "Grab those, will you?"

Sticking her tongue out at him for manhandling her, she did as he asked, grabbing the bags and the two covered cups of coffee, cradling everything in her lap. Balancing the cups on top of everything else with one hand, she slung an arm around his neck, feet dangling as he carried her back up the stairs.

By the time they reached the top of the second flight, he wasn't sweating or even breathing hard to give any hint that he had any difficulty carrying her. She was impressed and maybe even a little turned on by the show of strength. Not to mention his overprotective, albeit sweet, interest in her.

Rieva was right. She *really* needed to thank Sam.

For once in her life, Kimberly had no worries about what the future held.

Chapter Twenty-nine

Kimberly had looked both relieved and a little disappointed that Cormac left her to shower and get dressed by herself. For a long moment, after she set everything down on the kitchen counter and he let her slide down the length of his body until she was steady on her feet, he savored the feel of her against him. That warmth that was just for him.

He was certain the moment he gave in to the urge to kiss her again, he wouldn't be able to stop there. He would take everything she was so willing to give.

That's when he knew he had to bring things to a halt. He pulled away, lowering his head as he led her to the bathroom, leaving her with a mountain of towels and a shower big enough for an army platoon. He'd ignored her confusion and disappointment, making sure she had everything she needed before he left her to shower in peace.

She managed to handle the necessities on her own, though she must have been exhausted by the time she finished drying her hair and shrugging into the set of pajamas Rieva had brought for her.

Despite knowing he should keep his distance, Cormac got concerned when she didn't answer his knock after she'd been in there for a while. He cracked the door open, ready with a cheesy joke about her falling in, when he spotted her slumped on the toilet, snoring away.

With a quiet chuckle, he picked Kimberly up and carried her back to the bed, tucking her in.

While a part of him cursed that she'd stayed awake long enough to dress herself, he was also relieved. He would have been too tempted to peel the clothes off again had she been awake. The green satin material of the pajamas matched her eyes and reflected a lovely luster in her reddish-brown hair, hugging her curves in a way that stoked the already considerable flames in his blood. The changeling had good taste; he'd give her that.

He sat beside her on the bed as she slept, wanting to touch her but not quite daring, waiting for her to wake. As badly as he was crawling out of his skin with the need to clear his head with the thin, cold air above the clouds, the lingering worry that she would wake, alone and afraid, kept him grounded.

He had been ready and eager to take advantage of Kimberly's interest and growing warmth, but as he carried her up those steps to the apartment, sensed the fragility of her slender frame and the way her heart pounded with budding excitement, an attack of conscience nearly paralyzed him. The trusting way she peered up at him when he set her down had been his undoing.

She deserved to know what he was before she gave so much of herself to him. All it took was one look into her bright green eyes, to see how hopeful she was, to cut straight through to his heart and make him feel like the biggest heel in history.

It was that very thought—the he would be taking advantage of her—that led to his decision to let her shower and dress alone. Judging by his own considerable desire, he wasn't sure enough of himself to trust that he could leave her untouched should he join her. Sending Rieva away had been a mistake.

It appeared that he was utterly incapable of rational thought where Kimberly was concerned. The uncertainty of his future with her, the possibility that she might leave him, was playing havoc with his instincts to hunt, to control, and to possess. That wasn't how to go about proving he cared about her. He knew it. Rationally. The irrational part wanted to spread its wings and carry her away, take her to the *real* lair, the place he kept all his precious things.

He hoped and prayed that she would still want him once he told her the truth. There was no way he could put it off any longer. If he did, he risked hurting her so much more than he had already.

Though a part of him trembled at the thought of her reaction—him, the monster who had ruled nations, the fiend to whom kings bent their knees, the behemoth who made lesser beasts tremble in his shadow—he would tell her the moment she woke. He wasn't sure how just yet, but he needed to make things right between them without destroying her sweet innocence. He needed to be worthy of that trust she put in him.

That's when the idea came to him.

Some hours passed, as did the mild spring rain.

She yawned and stretched, her eyelids fluttering open, and all the calm he'd managed to muster as he stood guard over her had flown out the window. Groaning, he took her hand, pulling it to his brow as he bent over her. The inevitable moment had arrived.

It was entirely possible that he could lose her, and there was not a damned thing with all of his knowledge and power that he could do to stop her from leaving.

"What's wrong?" she asked between yawns. "Sorry, I was so tired..."

He had to collect himself. Keep it together. He took a deep breath to steady himself, then another, before he answered her.

"Nothing. Nothing, love. I just have something very important to show you. I've been putting this off too long as it is."

She rolled onto her side, regarding him with heavy-lidded eyes. He brushed some of the hair out of her face, then lightly ran his thumb over her lip. She shivered, her tongue creeping out to slide over where he'd just touched.

Cupping her cheek, he took a measure of courage in the way she looked at him. That desire and trust had to count for something.

"What is it?" she asked.

"The dragon."

That had her bolting upright. "Wait, Cormac, I'm not ready, I need to get dressed—"

He couldn't suppress a smile at her mix of excitement and dread. "Relax, you're fine."

She shook her head, her hair flying about her face and bouncing around her shoulders. It was all he could do not to laugh at her frantic efforts to simultaneously scramble to her feet, grab the pile of neatly folded clothes on the bedside table, and finger-brush her hair. His hands shot out to catch her before she fell off the side of the bed.

"Stop worrying. Take as much time as you need."

Flushing right down to her toes, she paused, putting a hand over her eyes. "Okay. I can do this. I'm fine. I just need a minute."

He was tempted to pull her right back under the covers and distract all the worries right out of her head. With no small measure of regret, he loosened his grip on her. He'd rather not have her fretting about whatever impression she thought she might be making with her appearance. He wanted her as calm as possible, even if it was inevitable even in the best case scenario that she was going to be furious with him.

His gaze followed her as she got up, swaying and a tad unsteady, then grabbed the pile of clothes and rushed into the bathroom.

Folding his hands behind his head, he laid back on the bed, waiting for her to finish getting ready. Laying down didn't help the knots in his stomach or the heaviness in his chest. His usual calm was cracking and he had no idea what to do about it.

When she emerged several minutes later, his heart leapt and a rumbling sound of approval escaped him as he sat up.

"I wasn't sure if I should do makeup or not," she said, pointing to her face as if the change weren't immediately obvious. The slight lengthening of her lashes, dash of color to her eyes, lips, and cheeks, and the shine to her hair made her positively luminous. Added to the dark green silk shirt, black slacks, and kitten heels Rieva had brought her, he could see why she was so off balance. She looked like a completely different person.

He rolled to his feet and prowled closer, dipping his head to breathe in her scent as he wrapped his arms around her. "You were already perfect in my eyes."

Her blush practically singed his skin, she grew so hot. Grinning, he pressed a light kiss to her temple in response to her stammered thanks.

"Don't forget that after this meeting, hmm?"

"How could I?" she asked, smiling.

He shook his head and took her arm, leading her out of the apartment. His own heart was pounding nearly as fast as hers.

Rather than take her down the stairwell to his shop, this time he took her up a flight to the rooftop. She was very nearly vibrating with excitement at his side, her hands tightly clutching his arm. Her nervousness was palpable, a taste on the air, toying with the hungers and instincts simmering under the surface of his skin.

The brisk April air cut through the haze in his thoughts, bringing him out of his single-minded focus and back to the present. He held the door for her, gesturing for her to precede him.

She looked all around, probably wondering where the dragon was hiding. Not that there was anywhere for one to conceal itself on the rooftop. Save for the heating and air conditioning unit and the access door, it was all one big, open space, spotted with a few shrinking puddles. There was a deck near the door with a lone chair set beside a small garden; mostly herbs like what she'd seen in the store downstairs. The rest of the rooftop was covered in some kind of deeply scarred, slate-gray metal set with a few glyphs meant to protect and strengthen the structure of the building.

Fearing her probable reaction, he grabbed the chair and set it down against the side of the gabled structure of the roof access, gesturing for her to take a seat. She shot him a questioning look, but did as he bid.

As soon as she was seated, he knelt before her, clasping her hands in his. She bit her lip, meeting his gaze as he intently stared up at her.

"Kimberly, before I summon the dragon, promise me one thing."

"Anything. You've already done so much..." She trailed off as he shook his head.

"Promise that you'll give me a chance to explain. After."

Her puzzlement grew, tilting her head as little furrows appeared between her brows. Blowing out a breath, he shook his head again and released her hands, moving backward on the rooftop.

A small, niggling pain in his heart burrowed deeper as her puzzlement shifted to panic as he spread his arms and began to change. He shifted slow, the skin of his bare chest darkening and jeans melting away, disappearing under the sprouting scales. Spines sprouted from his forehead, hair and spine, along with great bulges growing between his shoulder blades.

Her green eyes were locked on him, growing wider and wider as he grew bigger and bigger.

She scrambled out of the chair as his forelegs fell forward, talons settling with a series of chiming clacks on the metal and sending a tremble through the rooftop that made the plants and puddles shiver. The glyphs etched into the metal took the bulk of his weight, distributing it, preventing him from collapsing the building beneath his tremendous frame.

Free of that constricting skin-suit, with the use of all his senses and the taste of his city on his forked tongue once more, he squirmed with discomfort. His tail lashed and wings quivered as he spread and stretched them in an attempt to shrug off the lingering sensation of being the lowest, slimiest of salamanders, belly-deep in swamp muck. Even his scales couldn't protect him from the pain slicing deep in his chest at the way she looked at him now.

Afraid. Angry.

Betrayed.

Chapter Thirty

Wings swept outward, twin blue-tinted sails that eclipsed the sun. A flock of pigeons took flight, scattering from the great predator that had disturbed their roosting on the ledge of the cornice. A sound made in that plated chest made the very ground tremble, small stones rattling against pavement and the alarms of cars far below in the street rising in shrieking counter-point to the beast's rumbling.

Kimberly stumbled back out of her chair, one hand reaching behind her to grab for something—anything—to keep herself steady. An involuntary squeak was startled out of her as the enormous wedge-shaped head thrust against her chest, falling just short of crushing her against the wall of the roof access behind her.

Her hands flew out, grabbing a handful of the surprisingly smooth, pebbly skin around his upper lip and one of the wide, ivory plates that ran from the underside of his jaw, all along his belly, and down to a point midway along his tail, to yank him off her. His skin was hotter and much softer than she would have guessed, but she hardly noticed around her need for air.

The overwhelming scent of ash and char mixing with the potent musk of his scent choked her, making it even harder to catch her breath than the pressure of his scaly nose pinning her in place. Nostrils flaring, he withdrew just a fraction, giving her just enough space that she could gasp in a few breaths.

Her hair fluttered, tendrils tickling against the monster's nostrils as it inhaled her scent. Blue, jewel-toned scales along his ribs rose and fell with each deep breath he took, the sound like fat raindrops pattering on a tin roof.

Dragonfear washed over her in a wave, making her body shake with tremors and knees turn to jelly. She couldn't help but notice that a single one of those curved, ivory talons splayed only a few feet away was long and sharp enough to impale a person. Never mind the pearlescent fangs filling that massive maw. Had he opened his jaws, she could have stepped inside that cavernous mouth without ducking her head.

Struggling would get her nowhere. Except maybe eaten. Telling herself that didn't make it any easier to relax, easing up her white-knuckled grip on him and her useless attempts to push him away.

As soon as she stopped squirming, the creature drew back, arching a sinuous neck to regard her with one eye the size of a dinner plate. That single, bright eye glowed with tiny pinpoints of blue-white light, like it contained a universe of stars. If she hadn't been so startled by everything that had happened in the last few moments, she might have noticed he had pinned her to keep her from backing right over the edge of the roof in her haste to get away from him.

She thought she was prepared to face the monster out of legend, knowing it wasn't out to hurt her, that it had saved her from the wyvern, but nothing could have prepared her for the sheer size, the feral grace, or the realization that sent her heart plummeting.

The dragon was *him*.

It was such an obvious, stupid observation to make that the truth of it didn't want to sink in right away. He had been lying to her by omission all along. He *knew* what she had needed, *knew* how important it was to her, and had acted like he was leading her to what she needed. Hell, he had even let her rush around, worrying about what the dragon would think of her, fussing with her clothes and hair like a fool.

Had he meant to keep her from her goal all this time? Had he been leading her by the nose so he could secretly laugh at her foolish attempts to do the impossible?

Had he just been pretending to care about her?

Her mind skittered around that thought. Whatever game he had been playing, it was over now.

He sidled back, arching his back like a cat as he stretched his wings out again before giving a couple lazy flaps that whipped her hair into a frenzy of tangles. She slowly sank down against the wall until she was seated on the ground, turning up her ashen face to stare at the living mountain of silver and sapphire before her.

It wasn't fair that something so deadly and deceitful should be so beautiful.

With a toss of his head, sending a ripple down his scales from his throat all the way down to the tip of his barbed tail, he began to shrink in upon himself. Kimberly couldn't bring herself to move as he shrank back into his human form. The shift back was much faster than the change into the beast he was.

In a few ground-eating strides, he was at her side, his blue eyes aglow with the same haunting blue and silver sparks as his scales. His abs and chest muscles were still rippling with reaction, and his jeans moved more like flesh than fabric as he resettled in his human form and halted before her. The tattoos ranging over his body were all flickering with blue sparks of power, dancing over his skin as they eased his transition back into the body he used to walk among mortal men.

He ran his fingers through the dark hair on his head, brushing out the crackles of blue-tinted lightning still arcing between the messy spikes. As he reached for her, she flinched back. He hesitated at her reaction, hand falling just short of touching her.

"I'm sorry I didn't tell you sooner," he muttered.

If she wasn't already so shocked and ill with his duplicity, she might have found the touch of color high on his cheeks endearing. It wasn't every day one saw a dragon blush.

He stayed where he was, crouching on the balls of his feet with one hand outstretched, wanting desperately to close the gap that had formed between them but not quite daring. She had never looked at him like that before, with that mix of hurt and fear and betrayal. Even the way she'd screamed and regarded him with raw terror out in the pine barrens hadn't cut him so deeply as the way she stared at him now.

"I couldn't tell you," he said, trying to fill the awkward silence, to make her understand. "I needed to be sure... If you still want me"—*Please,* he thought, *please say you'll have me.*—"I'm yours."

She didn't answer him. Her lips parted like she was about to speak, but not a sound emerged.

"Please, Kimberly. Say something."

"You lied to me," she said, in such a small voice that he couldn't help but feel all of two inches tall. If he could have fixed this situation with his magic, destroyed it with flame, torn apart that hurt with his claws, he would have done so in an instant. As it was, he had no idea how to repair what he had broken between them.

"I'm sorry. I know you must have questions—"

It was like a dam broke, releasing a flood of shaky prattle and nervous energy. She rolled to her feet and paced back and forth, her hands rubbing her arms, muscles jerking and twitching as the words tumbled forth. He couldn't be sure she even realized what was coming out of her mouth.

"Seriously? All this time and you didn't say anything. You knew—you *knew*—but you didn't tell me. The professor must have known. That's why she sent me to you, isn't it? Why didn't she tell me? Why didn't *you* tell me? You told all those people what I was looking for. A dragon. A *real* dragon. Wait, you're a dragon and your name is *Cormac?*"

He weathered the ranting and borderline hysteria, flinching at the accusations, but he didn't hesitate to answer her question, silly as it might have been. "Yes."

"Are you really a dragon? Or just a person who can turn into one? Cormac the dragon. Doesn't exactly roll off the tongue, does it?" Kimberly was babbling. She knew it, but couldn't get her runaway mouth under control. Though her voice did become very small again as she stuttered out her last question. "You're not really a mage, are you?"

"No, I am not a mage. I am just a dragon who happens to have picked up the skills necessary to blend with humanity. And my name used to be Kormákr until it came to my attention that I needed to go by a more modern moniker." At her blank look, he wryly added, "I was going to go with Drake St. George but I thought that might be a little too obvious."

It was clear his response didn't make her feel any better. Hugging herself, she stared up at the sky, not really seeing it.

"You think I'm stupid, don't you?" she asked. "Were you laughing at me the whole time I was searching for you? Or someone like you?"

He paused, taken aback. While he didn't expect her to take it well, those whispered words stung him with an unfamiliar pang of guilt.

He *had* thought it must have been some kind of cruel joke at first, some twisted form of mockery devised by Eleanor or someone else at The Circle designed to make a fool of him. Certainly not Kimberly. By the time he had realized how much he wanted to help her—how much he wanted *her,* and maybe more than that, wanted her to want *him*—there was no easy way to explain himself.

She took his silence as answer enough. Turning away, she only made it a couple of steps toward the door before his hand fell heavily on her shoulder.

"I didn't know you when you first walked into my shop."

"Oh," she said, "So making fun of me and pretending to help me was okay? Since you didn't know me?"

"You were treading dangerous ground. I thought I might play along with the joke and keep you out of trouble."

He had thought honesty might be the best policy, but judging by the way her lips thinned and the building moisture in her eyes he spotted before she jerked out of his grasp, he had managed to say just the wrong thing.

"So that's all this was to you? All I am? A joke?"

"Yes. *No.* No, it's not like that. Maybe at first, but not now. Please, Kimberly—"

The glare she leveled on him shut him up. Too late, it occurred to him how thoughtless he had been. He hadn't been on the receiving end of a look like that from anyone he cared about in centuries, and it pained him to see how much his own mistakes had hurt her. The vicious beast who had stared down armies come to destroy him flinched at her frosty tones.

"The joke is over. I don't ever want to see you again. Stay away from me."

All he could do was stand there, hand outstretched to empty air as the door slammed shut behind her.

Chapter Thirty-one

Blinded by tears, Kimberly barely noticed where she was going as she rushed out of the Wild Hunt and onto the street. She was aware of the tremors in the ley lines as a great, winged form sprang from the rooftop above, following her as she dashed headlong into the heart of the city.

Cormac paced her like that, following from a safe distance high overhead. He made no effort to disguise his presence. People around her cried out, screaming and shouting and running for cover as a great, raptorial shadow swept over them.

It didn't take long before she was panting with exhaustion, the adrenaline rush sapping what little energy she'd managed to restore. Chest heaving, she slowed down, a hand pressed to her side as she trudged on, ignoring the chaos around her.

She'd been running the wrong way. Pointedly keeping her gaze focused on the ground, she circled the block like she'd meant to all along, heading home. All she wanted was to disappear under the covers of her bed and never, ever come out again.

She'd been a fool. She couldn't believe how idiotic, how utterly insignificant and deluded he must have thought she was, to consider even for a moment that she was worthy of a dragon. No wonder he treated her quest like a joke. That was all she was.

It was no longer surprising that he'd teased and flirted with her but hadn't returned her tentative advances. With just a few touches in the right place and a couple of stolen kisses, he'd turned her mind into mush, blinding her to the games he'd been playing. He must have thought her attraction to him was just another part of the farce. Just another way to make the parody he was turning her into have a bigger payoff for him to laugh at later.

Every hope she'd had shattered like glass, fading like her dreams of a better life.

Arms wrapped tightly around her ribs, head bowed, she couldn't find it in herself to care that he was following her. Whatever he wanted now, it couldn't be any worse than the laughingstock he'd already made of her.

Even Professor Reed had been in on it. All she could think was that her teacher either had planned for her to fail from the start, or hadn't expected Cormac to be such a monster in character as well as body. She didn't want to believe that the professor had set out from the beginning to humiliate her, but there was no way she could ignore how she'd had a hand in Cormac's plan to make her look like the most asinine, half-witted of simpletons to the entire Other community in the city, if not the whole Tri-State Area.

Kimberly couldn't stomach the idea of facing her teacher or classmates again. Not as such a failure.

Maybe she would be better off moving to another state. Or another country.

If only she could afford it.

Visions of working for Don for the next two or more years as she struggled her way through community college sent a pang of horror shivering up her spine. There was nothing else she could do. Even if by some miracle she graduated from Blackhollow, no one would want to work with her now.

No, now she wasn't just going to be an outcast to other magi. She'd be a gods-be-damned pariah. Not to mention the butt of a round of deeper, more painful mockery than anything she'd ever suffered as just that "broke, half-blood illusionist who lived with a human." Any respect she might have garnered from her peers was gone, washed away by one stupid mistake and putting her trust in the wrong people.

Everything she had worked for, everything she had done to change her circumstances and work toward a better life, all gone on the whim of a creature who thought she was a joke.

Anger was slowly boiling through the humiliation. It kept her warm and focused as she shifted from a weak shamble to a stomping rage back home.

If she'd thought it would do her any good losing him, she would have called up an illusion to hide herself from her shadow, but she didn't want to waste a single iota of her energy on him anymore. Aside from that, if he kept even a scrap of her ruined clothing, plucked a single strand of hair she had left behind on a pillow, or even took one of the utensils she'd used on breakfast that morning, he could use that as a focus object to track her down whenever he wanted. Just like Viper had.

To his credit, he didn't do a thing to interrupt her on her way. She'd never seen the streets so empty as they were as she marched her way home. There were a few motorcycle cops mirroring her path, even if they didn't realize she was the one the airborne monster was following. Within a few blocks, there were also a good number of news and police choppers in the air, circling the dragon from what they probably thought was a safe distance.

As soon as she reached her apartment building, she turned on a heel to glare up at the serpentine form lingering above. He stopped when she did, hovering, each flap of those gigantic, bat-like wings stirring a miasma of trash, dead leaves, and paper fluttering into a whirlwind around her. A couple of the motorcycle cops pulled over, looking back and forth between her and the winged serpent staring down with those glowing, star-filled eyes.

"Leave me alone!"

She punctuated the demand with a slash of her hand, sending the illusion of a jagged spear tipped in searing hot metal hurtling toward him. As he dodged aside, moving by instinct, she slipped into the building.

Her guts went watery at the earth-shaking roar that sounded outside, drowning out the steady drone of the helicopters and sirens, but she ignored it and trudged up the stairs to her floor. A few people were huddling together in the hallway, including her mother and her neighbor, Charlie, who was holding the squirming, yapping daschund Schlong in his arms.

The moment she spotted her, her mother ran forward, gathering her up in a tight hug. Kimberly's face crumpled and she clutched at her mom, burying a muffled sob in her hair.

"Where have you *been?* Did you see that thing outside making all that noise?"

"Yeah, we thought Godzilla might be on the rampage," Charlie said.

Kimberly shook her head, not wanting to talk around the lump in her throat. Frowning, her mother leaned back, peering into her face. Realizing that her daughter was in distress, she turned to Charlie and her other neighbors, wrapping an arm around Kimberly's shoulders as she led her to their apartment.

"Let me know if you hear anything on the news. I'll be back in a little bit."

Charlie and the others nodded, resuming their speculative chatter to each other. Once they were inside, Kimberly's mother led her to the living room couch, sitting her down and wrapping the old throw on the back around her shoulders. Clasping her cold hands in one of her own, she tugged her into a tight hug, kissing her temple.

"Tell me what happened. Where have you been?"

Sniffling, Kimberly choked out a few words, doing her best not to burst into tears. "Oh, Mom, I screwed up so bad. I don't think I can fix it. Any of it."

Rocking her and squeezing her hand, her mom didn't reply right away. As angry as she had been at her daughter disappearing for days without a word, it was clear it wasn't the time to be reprimanding her.

"Whatever happened, whatever you may have done, I believe you are strong enough to get through it. You are smarter, stronger and braver than I ever was. I don't say it often enough, my baby girl, but I'm very proud of you."

That was enough to start Kimberly bawling. Her mom held her tight, tucking Kimberly's head under her chin. When the worst of the sobs died into hiccupping whimpers, she ventured a question.

"Do you want to talk about it?"

Kimberly gave a few uncertain snuffles, swiping a hand under her nose before answering. "I messed up everything. I trusted this guy to help me, but now I don't have any of the things I need and won't meet the requirements to graduate even though the professors gave me a few extra days to figure things out. I made a total fool of myself and now none of the other magi will ever respect me. I'll never get the job I wanted. Which means I have to keep working for Don."

Her mom sighed, lightly brushing her fingertips over her temple before running her fingers through her hair in long, soothing strokes. It was no secret in the household that Kimberly hated her job and planned to leave it as soon as she could afford to. If she knew how to make enough to support them both, her mother would have happily told her to quit then and there. The reality was that without that secondary income and occasional extra free food from Don, they would be out on the street, homeless and hungry.

As Kimberly's eyelids fluttered shut, her mom made a thoughtful sound before speaking again.

"I don't always understand what's happening in your life," she said, "but I know you've been doing an incredible job of balancing school and work. Sometimes it takes a long time to fix our mistakes. I know that better than you probably think I do. But you're doing all the right things to build yourself a better future than the one I've been able to make for you. You'll get through this, baby girl. I know it."

"I don't know," Kimberly whispered. "I wish it would all just go away. I don't know if I can handle this anymore."

"Stick with it, you're almost there. Don't make the same mistakes I did. You haven't had much time to experience life's possibilities, kiddo. I never wanted that for you. I know how hard you work, and I'm sorry it had to be this way, but if I can help make it better in the meantime, just tell me what I can do."

Kimberly wasn't about to tell her she'd already done more than she knew. She was right.

There was no real option but to soldier forward. Professor Reed might have been trying to get rid of her, assigning an impossible task to ensure she wouldn't pass her finals, but it occurred to Kimberly that the centaurs had promised to help her. A centaur familiar certainly wouldn't regain her much in the way of respect, but she could deal with the indignity of showing her face at school long enough to get her certificate of graduation.

If she didn't, she would have to go with the previously unthinkable Plan B and live out her life as a mortal, never using her powers in the open again. She wasn't foolish enough to openly practice magic without her graduation papers. Without that certificate, if word got out to any of the local covens that a rogue mage was casting around town, she'd be hunted down and destroyed for the sake of the greater community. Assuming she wasn't on a most wanted list already for being outed as a sorcerer.

Even after she graduated, no magi would work with her now. Her hopes of being picked up by The Circle went down the drain the moment Cormac revealed himself for being the lying snake-in-the-grass he had accused Viper of being.

Chances were also good that a number of the Others in town would shun her. Rieva had thought they might make a tidy sum working together, but Kimberly wasn't sure how long that would last once word spread about what a fool she'd made of herself.

Even so, while Rieva might have been laughing with the rest about how Cormac had fooled her, the changeling had extended an offer. Kimberly might be able to make a living as a freelancer if she played her cards right and didn't make the stupid mistake of being so quick to trust anyone ever again. She would hold Rieva to her word and see how things played out.

They didn't have to like each other to work together. And anything had to be better than working in that café with a man who openly hated and opposed everything she was for the rest of her life.

It wasn't fair, but nothing in her life ever had been. She didn't have any intention of letting anyone use or abuse her again.

Chapter Thirty-two

Kimberly spent another day recuperating, but insisted on going to school and to put in an appearance at work on Friday despite her mother telling her to stay abed and stop worrying about the rent. She didn't want to miss the last day of school before finals week. She had the feeling there would be some late nights spent studying her materials over the weekend. She also didn't want Don to think she'd quit, or to think about how paltry her paycheck would be with all the hours she'd missed. The least she could do would be to give him an apology in person for blowing off work.

Assuming he didn't kick her back out the minute she stepped foot in the door, that was.

She was too tired and beyond caring what anyone thought about her anymore to bother hiding how sallow her complexion had become or the dark smudges under her eyes. She trudged to school on Friday morning, ignoring the whispers and points and stares as she stepped through the Gate on 77th and entered the main hall at Blackhollow.

Even the snickers of Aidan and his cohorts as she passed them in the entrance hall didn't get more than a slight curl of her lip. Where she once would have flinched and hurried on, now she hardly noticed or cared about their mockery. She had faced down dragons and wyverns. Their taunts were nothing compared to that.

A fair number of familiars were racing up and down the halls along with the students, squirrels and cats and birds and mice, all on the run or wing to deliver messages to the professors before the first classes of the day. Despite the high, arched ceiling, Kimberly had to duck a small flock of ravens flying too low on their way to deliver gold sealed pre-acceptance letters to some hoity-toity coven to Professor Reed's classroom. Budding excitement that one of those letters might be for her died a quick, quiet death when it occurred to her that none of her professors—not even Professor Reed—had given her any indication that they had sent letters of recommendation ahead to any of their covens.

The other students kept their distance, save for Xander. He zipped around a group of chattering third years to fall into step beside her, his relief at seeing her quickly fading into concern.

"Hey, what the heck happened? You never showed on Sunday and I haven't seen you in school or at that café all week. Did you get sick?"

She gave him a wan smile. "Sort of. But I survived. Yay, go me?"

He smiled back, though it was still tempered with worry. "Okay, sure. Go you. What the heck did you survive? Are you sure you should be here? You look like hell."

She snorted. "You charmer, you."

"Hey, what can I say? I know how to talk to the ladies."

That got a laugh out of her. She scrubbed a hand down her face, surreptitiously lightening the circles under her eyes as she did it. The move would have been more effective with a mirror handy so she could see what she was doing, but it would have to do for the time being.

"I'll be fine. I'm just exhausted. I don't want to talk about what happened here. Maybe you can walk with me to work after school?"

He nodded, then reached out to grab her backpack. Ignoring her weak protests, he carried it for her to Professor Lim's classroom for her first period of the day; Conjuration.

"I'll see you in Circles after lunch. Professor Cohen gave me the green light to start your circle for you since I already finished prepping mine and so you won't have as much catching up to do."

She gave him a grateful smile, sinking into her seat. "Thanks, Xander. You're the best."

He winked and shot her with a finger gun, heading to the hall as the first bell rang. "You know it. See you in a bit!"

She waved, then settled into concentrating on her class, even though it was one of the ones where she had to fake results on practicals with illusions. She found the theory behind the spellwork fascinating even if she couldn't conjure enough spark to light a candle. The best she had ever learned how to do was make illusions so thorough that they fooled every sense, including touch.

Her fires might not leave a mark on a person, but they would still feel like they were being fried to a crisp until the illusion was dispelled. Illusory food would have taste and consistency, but it would never satisfy anyone's hunger. There were any number of things she could do, but none of it held the substance of elemental magic. Everything she did was designed to fool the senses, not reshape reality.

The hour spent on reviewing planar conjuration stirred a peculiar longing in her for abilities she'd never possessed. It had been years since she'd yearned so deeply for something she couldn't have. Her acceptance of her failings early on had only spurred on her desire to prove she could make it anyway by graduating and clawing out a place for herself in a world where she didn't quite fit in.

That drive to succeed had served her well over the past four years. Despite all the ridicule, all the setbacks, and all the hardships, she had found ways around all the spells she couldn't cast. Where her own innate magic failed, she found alternate sources of power, sometimes relying on arcane hedgemagic found in some of the most ancient of dusty tomes in the back stacks of the library to find glyphs, runes, and circles that netted her the same results as the elemental spells her fellow students cast.

She wouldn't do well on the final practicals involving elemental casting, but if she tested well on the written theory and passed the familiar binding test, she'd graduate. By the skin of her teeth, but she knew she could do it.

Coasting through her next few classes, she made it a point to take more copious notes than usual, keeping herself occupied so she wouldn't spend too much time wishing for things she couldn't have. When she got to her etiquette class, she lingered outside until just before the second bell, not wanting to deal with Professor Reed a moment longer than she had to.

The professor's attention whipped to her briefly during roll call at the beginning of class. She stared just long enough to make it clear she was not expecting Kimberly to be back yet, and that she had a few things to say. Not yet. Later. After class.

Kimberly intended to have one foot out the door the second the bell rang, both after this class and as soon as school let out. Whatever the professor might have to say to her, she didn't want to hear it.

Like the other teachers, Professor Reed was cramming a year's worth of study into a final review. Kimberly wasn't too worried about how she would do on the test for that class, but she still diligently took her notes and paid attention to the bullet points on the chalkboard at the back of the stage. She could crib off someone else's notes for any lessons she may have missed earlier in the week.

When the bell rang, the professor's voice rang out over the excited chatter of the students. "Have a nice weekend! Study hard. Kimberly—Kimberly *Wells*—I need to see you."

Kimberly did her best to pretend she didn't hear anything, grabbing for her bag and ducking out of her seat. She almost plowed right into the professor, who had anticipated her attempt to rush out the door without facing her. The tall, slender woman had somehow materialized right before her desk with her arms folded, staring down at her student over the rims of her glasses.

"Cormac told me about your little run-in with the wyvern. If you need extra time to prepare for your finals, I need to know now so I can make the arrangements."

Kimberly slumped back into her seat with a scowl, though she bit her tongue to keep from saying something caustic at the mere mention of Cormac's name. Then remembered her manners, mumbling a response.

"No, I think I can handle it."

Professor Reed gave a pointed stare to a group of lingering students by the door. They dashed out when they realized she'd noticed their eavesdropping. The word *wyvern* carried back to her before they disappeared, and she flinched. Rumors would start circulating faster than she'd thought.

As soon as they were alone, the professor dropped her rigid stance, one hand settling on her hip as she ran a hand through her short, light brown hair starting to streak with gray and loosed a frustrated sigh.

"Things did not turn out as I intended. I'm very sorry for that, Kimberly."

It felt like a lot of people were saying that to her lately. "It's fine, professor."

"And you're sufficiently recovered to handle next week? You still don't look well. Perhaps you should see the school nurse—"

"*No.* No, I'll be fine. Can I go now? I have to get to my next class."

"A moment before you go. Cormac also told me that you are quite cross with him and have no intention of accepting his offer to be your familiar. Is that true?"

Kimberly's scowl deepened. The professor frowned.

"I see," she said. "Whatever he may have done, I can assure you, he is top notch familiar material."

"Maybe for someone else, he is. Not for me."

The professor's face tightened. Her tone, while reasonable, was just a smidge too loud. "He has expressed regret for whatever he's done to upset you. He wouldn't give me any specifics about what happened between you two, and I don't wish to pry, but I hope you realize what an opportunity you're turning down by refusing him. I wouldn't have recommended you to him if I didn't think you two would work well together."

Kimberly's flat stare was answer enough.

"Do you have an alternative lined up?"

"Yes," Kimberly said, her response far more sharp than she intended. "Look, professor, I appreciate your efforts, but I've had about enough of people *helping* me to last a lifetime. I've got this."

The professor's eyes narrowed to slits of green fire, her lips going thin. She gave her student a curt nod, then turned away in obvious dismissal.

Kimberly gathered her things and dashed for the exit, not wanting to stick around to deal with the consequences of her snippy behavior. Maybe the professor deserved it, maybe she didn't, but Kimberly was beyond caring at that point.

Just as she reached the door, the professor called out. "Oh, Kimberly? One last thing."

Gritting her teeth, she stopped in her tracks, looking back over her shoulder. The fae power glittering in the professor's eyes was apparent enough that she flinched and turned her eyes down so she wouldn't have to meet that judgmental stare.

"You," she said, "have an appointment in the dean's office on Wednesday evening at 7PM. See that you don't miss it."

Wednesday. The last day of *real* school. The fourth year students would be doing tests Monday, Tuesday and Wednesday, and were supposed to spend Thursday and Friday filling out applications and meeting with representatives from every local coven who had the resources to send one. Their final grades would be issued at the end of the day on Friday, and forwarded with the applications to whichever covens they had applied to.

"I'm sorry, professor," Kimberly said, dodging aside as the first group of students for the next period appeared in the doorway. "I've got to work."

"Make other arrangements. This is a mandatory meeting."

"Yes, professor," she muttered.

"You are excused."

Great. Like everyone else around her lately, it seemed the professor was intent on making her life miserable.

She was sure Don would have a fit, assuming she had a job to go back to.

Chapter Thirty-three

The rest of her classes were uneventful. Xander was waiting for her in the main hall after she finished her high school equivalency and college preparation class. Her teacher, Arnold, held her after class for a few minutes to give her a pile of homework to take home with her and study over the weekend to catch up, as well as a list of dates, times, and locations to take the necessary tests and a variety of college applications for mundane schools. She had shoved everything into her backpack to deal with later.

If anything, once she emerged into the hallway, it was busier than it had been that morning. Students, teachers and familiars were rushing to and fro to carry out last minute tasks. The excitement for this particular weekend was a palpable thing, cheerful chatter booming through the halls.

Xander clapped his thick *Intermediate to Advanced Enchantments* textbook shut and shoved it in his bag as he scrambled to his feet to join her. They walked together in companionable silence to the Gateway room and took her usual portal to the street above the museum.

Not a soul noticed their exit, prying eyes conveniently looking elsewhere and minor (quite deliberate) glitches in security cameras making it appear as if they had slipped around from the other side of the tree or light pole or from a doorway. The Gateways acted as combined portals and permanent illusions— ones that barred the mundane or unwanted Others from stumbling into the hidden school. The incredible amount of foot traffic in and around Central Park and the Museum of Natural History acted as a natural infusion of the chaos needed to permanently imbue the area with an obfuscation enchantment of that caliber.

Once they were far enough away from the school and certain no one was following them or paying them any attention, Xander spoke up first.

"You want to tell me why you look like death warmed over?"

She snorted, glancing at him with a wry smile. Her illusion to hide the dark smudges under her eyes clearly wasn't enough to hide how badly drained she was. "That bad, huh?"

"Yup. I heard a rumor in Counterspells that you fought a wyvern. That have anything to do with it?" He paused. "Wait, it wasn't that one that showed up in Central Park, was it? That was all over the news this weekend. They were saying the wyvern, it... uh... flew off with... with..."

"Me."

He waited for her to continue. She didn't, staring straight ahead as she marched toward Allegretto's.

Xander gave her a light nudge with his elbow, speeding up as she did. "So? Spill. What's the deal? What about that dragon that was all over the news? You know, flying over Uptown and shifting right in the middle of the park. The hits on the Youtube videos are already hitting the millions. Was that the same one who saved you?"

She sighed, then gave him a very abbreviated version of her adventure, leaving out any mention of how Cormac had tricked and betrayed her or where she'd spent the initial few days of her recovery. She also left out that Cormac was the dragon who had saved her.

Xander's eyes went round as saucers, suitably impressed by her story. When she was finished, he gave a low whistle.

"I didn't know Others with magic could use magi like familiars. Or anything for familiars, for that matter."

"Neither did I," Kimberly said. "They didn't teach us anything about that in any of our classes and I haven't seen anything about it in our textbooks or the stuff about familiars or binding. I've been trying since last year to find a better way to summon so I've been over everything on it in the school library at least twice. Something tells me this isn't the sort of thing anyone talks about."

"No, probably not. Maybe it isn't an issue if we have a familiar since there's already a bond in place. That might be why the wyvern wanted you." He cleared his throat. "Since you... well, you know."

She thought about it, kicking a stray empty soda can out of her path. "I guess. I always thought dragon-kin were supposed to be these powers unto themselves. All the stuff in the textbooks talks about them being these intellectual and magical heavyweights. I never thought about them as having the same flaws people do. Greedy, grasping, lying, deceitful—"

"Whoa, whoa, slow down," Xander said, cutting into the building rant. Some of the other pedestrians walking by were giving them funny looks. "What about the dragon?"

Kimberly flushed, toning her voice down. "Sorry. What about it?"

"You said it saved you. Did you hear from it after you woke up? Not all Others are horrible, and it sounds like it did you a solid. Didn't you want a dragon for a familiar anyway?"

"Not that one."

Her tone of voice said *drop it*. Xander didn't get the hint.

"Why not?" he persisted.

"Because he tricked me and lied to me, and it turned out he thought this whole thing about me wanting a dragon familiar was a joke. Okay? Can we drop it now?"

Xander quieted, though his eyes had gone wide again and he was staring at her so intently that he ended up shoulder-checking a woman talking on her cell phone. He stammered out an apology as she flipped him off and continued on her way. Kimberly snorted laughter as he flung out his arm in a helpless gesture, red-faced and frustrated.

"Sorry," she said, though her smile said she wasn't really. It was hard to stay angry in the face of his recent embarrassment. "All right, if you have questions, ask them now. I can't promise you'll like the answers."

He ducked his head, shoving his hand in his pockets with a mock-scowl. "I don't know, man. Sounds like you're in pretty deep."

At her incredulous stare, he gave her a lop-sided grin to show he was joking.

"Okay, yeah. I've got about a thousand and one questions for you."

She answered his questions almost as quickly as he fired them off. He wanted to know everything about the dragon and wyvern. How big they were, what they looked like, what kind of magic they used, where they took her, how she managed to keep it together with the two fighting over her. He had dozens of questions for her, and his curiosity was only held in check because they reached Allegretto's. She was glad for the interruption. Being grilled about her experience—never mind how enthusiastic her audience was—unnerved her.

Before heading inside, she held up a hand for Xander to wait. "Listen, my boss doesn't know about what I am, and I want it to stay that way. No talk about dragons or magic inside, okay?"

He shrugged. "Sure, I can keep a lid on it. I can't stick around, though. I promised my girlfriend I'd take her out to dinner tonight. Can we meet on Sunday afternoon like we planned last week? I still need help with enchantments and I can give you a hand with some of the summoning stuff."

"Absolutely," she said.

He gave her a fist bump and a wave as he started off down the street, calling over his shoulder. "If you don't feel safe walking home alone, give me a call."

She nodded thanks and returned his wave, then ducked inside the café. She hadn't given any thought to walking home alone until he'd brought up the subject. For all she knew, Viper was still out there. Maybe other nasty things that wanted a piece of her. As tired as she was, maintaining her invisibility spell for the walk home was out of the question.

There was no way she would stay after dark. She was already exhausted after the day she'd had at school.

Don was at the register when she came in, dealing with a customer. None of the other clerks were in sight. The combined relief and irritation on his face didn't last long; his expression rapidly shifted to concern.

Maybe it wasn't such a bad thing that she was still so pale and drawn. He could see with his own eyes that she'd been through hell and back. She hoped that meant he wouldn't give her such a hard time for being out so long.

He wrapped things up with the customer, passing them their coffee and a small box of cookies, before slipping around the counter to wrap Kimberly in a bear hug.

"Jesus, Mary and Joseph, girl, you scared the life out of me when you didn't call. How are you feeling?"

"Mmph! Can't... breathe...!"

He quickly loosened his grip. She stopped her weak flailing and returned his hug.

"I'm fine," she mumbled against his chest. "Sorry I didn't show up for so long."

Letting her go, he gave her backpack a little shake and took on a gruff, stern tone. "You wore yourself out at school today, didn't you? Back on your feet before the doctor gave you permission, too, I'll bet."

She started to protest, but he waved her objections off, heading back behind the counter to grab a few things. He began packing loaves of bread, pastries, and a few other goodies in a bag, which he shoved into her hands despite her attempts to give it back.

"I need you healthy more than I need you here. Go home. Get more rest. Come back when you're fully recovered. That's an order."

"Are you sure?" she asked. "I really need the hours."

"Positive. I don't want you getting anyone else sick or handling food when you're ill. Besides, no one does their best work when they're exhausted. You can work a little OT when you're better to make up for it."

Both relieved and chagrined, Kimberly clutched the bag of goodies to her chest, doing her best not to tear up. "I'll be better tomorrow. I'll be here in the morning, I promise."

"Not if you still look like an extra on The Walking Dead, you won't. Annabelle already agreed to come in early, so you're covered if you need more time."

"You're the best, Don. Thanks!"

He gave her a grin. "Tell that to my wife. She still thinks I'm too much of a softie where you're concerned. Now get your narrow behind out of my store and back in bed where it belongs. Feel better."

For once, things appeared to be going her way. Shoulders sagging and suppressing a tremendous sigh, she waved her goodbyes to Don and headed for home.

She was very glad that he wasn't angry with her, and secretly relieved that he'd provided her with dinner. Despite her mother's promises to do everything she could to help her, when she had peered in the fridge before leaving for school that morning, there wasn't much left but a few lonely packets of ketchup and a plastic Ziploc bag of cat food. Monster had given her such a look when she'd picked up the bag to give it a speculative once-over, she had quickly put it back.

After being treated to regular meals while in Cormac's care, her hunger pangs—usually so easily managed or ignored—had become like a raging tiger in her midsection, clawing to be satiated. Lunch at school was free, but when it was her only meal of the day, she had a harder time beating back the sharp edge of starvation. The bread certainly wasn't as substantial as what she had been becoming used to, but she wasn't about to turn it down when the other option was cat food and condiments.

While she had sunk that low in the past, after Cormac took her to the Black Star Café, she had hoped she was beyond such things. Coming to rely on someone else to improve her lot had been a mistake, and she was paying for it already. She couldn't wish food on her table or money in the bank any more than she could wish for the elemental magic she needed to fit in with the other magi at school.

No. She set her jaw and promised herself she would eat something and then get right to bed so she could be rested for a full shift of work. Not only would she have to deal with a day at the café, she had also promised to help the centaurs. She needed her rest.

No one was going to hand her the answers to her problems or deliver her from this life but herself. Leaning on someone else to get her out of it had been a terrible mistake.

One she would never make again.

Chapter Thirty-four

The next day, Kimberly woke up over an hour before her alarm went off. She ate a piece of bread and then puttered around, straightening up the apartment and sorting her school supplies. There wasn't much cleaning up to do. Monster had tugged his favorite scarf off the couch again, which she replaced, and there was some dusting to be done on the bookshelf. When she couldn't put it off anymore, she spent some time reviewing the homework Arnold had given her, flipping through the college applications.

He'd included a note she hadn't seen until she opened the folder he'd stuffed all the applications into that he wanted her to bring a couple of samples of her enchantments, runes and glyph work with her to school on Wednesday. That puzzled her. He didn't teach those classes. She couldn't for the life of her imagine why he might be interested in her enchantments, even if she was exceptional at it.

So she wouldn't forget, she stuffed a few pages of her notes, sketches she'd done for class, and a couple of her personal runic stones into her backpack. By the time she was done, the alarm was buzzing, and her mother was rolling out of bed, getting ready for work.

Despite several requests for info about how they were doing on the rent and how many hours she needed to put in to make up for lost time, Kimberly's mother remained cagey and avoided any talk of money. That was worrisome. Usually that meant there was a problem she didn't want to talk about.

There wasn't enough time to grill her; they both had to leave for work.

Doing her best not to give in to the raging case of anxiety brewing in the back of her mind, Kimberly did her best to focus on the present. There were no Others lingering outsider her apartment or Allegretto's. She got to work a few minutes early, beating Annabelle, who she was a little surprised to see before remembering the schedule change in case she hadn't showed up for her shift. Don let them both in and the three prepared for opening. He even made her sit and have a cup of hot tea and a breakfast sandwich before he let the first round of customers come in.

His insistence throughout the day that she take it easy was driving her batty. Annabelle snickered as she whispered about how Don had hired three new people while Kimberly was out.

One had walked out with the contents of the register. Another had taken a smoke break and never returned. The last one was still on board, but she was doing a terrible job. She'd already caused the coffeemaker to overflow on the floor twice, burned several batches of muffins, and didn't notice a customer wander off with the tip jar. She'd flipped out and caused a scene, crying in front of the customers when Don yelled at her for that, and he hadn't had the heart to fire her.

No wonder Don was so desperate to treat Kimberly well. Finding her replacement wasn't turning out to be as easy as he had probably thought. Even if he'd been looking for someone to take her place, Kimberly didn't want to leave him in the lurch. She swore to herself that she'd find some time to come in during one of the new girl's shifts so she could help out and show her the ropes.

Things were busy but fairly uneventful until after lunch. Kimberly only had another hour or so left on the clock before the centaurs were supposed to show up when Cormac entered the café and got in line behind the other patrons.

Kimberly didn't notice him right away, busy as she was mopping up a spill behind the counter. When she turned around and spotted him in line, he tipped her a nod. Annabelle was looking pleased to see him until she noticed the rage turning Kimberly's face a dull shade of brick.

Annabelle took her arm and hauled her into a crouch behind the counter, her whisper low and urgent so the customers wouldn't overhear. "Girl, get it together! You want me to get rid of him?"

Too shaken and upset to speak, she only nodded.

Cormac spoke up, obviously having overheard them. "I won't stay around long, I just want to talk for a minute."

Some of the chatter in the café was dying down, people at the tables craning their necks to see what was going on. A couple of people in line moved over so Cormac could reach the counter. He set his arms on it, leaning forward so he could meet Kimberly's accusatory glare up from her crouch on the floor with a considerable frown of his own.

"We don't serve assholes here," Annabelle said, standing up to put her hands on her hips. "She doesn't want to talk to you. Get out."

Cormac's frown deepened as he focused it on Annabelle instead. She, as well as many of the people in the café, were struck by a sudden wave of formless, gut-wrenching fear as he briefly let some of his true nature slip with a low hiss of displeasure.

Kimberly got to her feet, ignoring the way her stomach dropped to her feet and hands trembled as she stood between Cormac and Annabelle, leveling an accusatory finger at him. "*Stop that*. You... *you*. Get out of here. I told you I never wanted to see you again!"

Cormac lowered his head in the face of her wrath, immediately dropping the dragonfear aura. Terrified people were rushing for the door, forgetting their coffees and sweets. One woman even left her purse behind.

"Kimberly, I'm sorry. I know you're upset with me, but you're running out of time—"

"Don't say it!"

He paused, his gaze briefly flicking to Don as the other man poked his head out of the doorway leading to the kitchen. The proprietor of the café looked less than pleased to see Cormac had returned.

The dragon bowed his head again. "I know you don't have any reason to take me at my word, but I called in a few favors—"

"Oh, spare me," she said, cutting him off. "You get out of here and take your favors with you. If I ever catch you near me again, I'll—"

Cormac's eyes flashed a brilliant white-blue at the interruption and threat, his teeth bared in a silent snarl. She shut up, and Annabelle knocked a glass jar of sugar off the back wall in her hasty attempt to claw through the wall behind her. Don, on the other hand, came out of the kitchen like a raging bull, veins sticking out in his neck as he clenched his fists and stalked out to match Cormac, glare-for-glare, over the counter.

"We don't serve your kind here! Get out!"

Cormac's snarl turned into a twisted grin, the blaze in his eyes growing. "You don't serve them, but you let them work for you? Seems a bit of twisted logic there, *boy*."

That took the wind out of Don's sails. The rage turning his face a dangerous shade of purple gradually shifted to a stunned, chalky pallor as he turned to look at Kimberly. Her features twisted with horror as she shook her head, trying to deny it.

"You. *You*. Lying little monster. I took you in, gave you a job, treated you like one of my own..."

It occurred to Cormac too late that he had made a mistake. Annabelle was scrambling to put some distance between herself and Kimberly as Don's expression turned blank, empty.

"Get out," he told her. "You're fired."

"Don," she tried, her voice high, strangled, "please, not now, just give me one more week—"

"Get. Out."

"—one week, Don, *please*—"

"*Out!* Get out!" he roared.

Her face crumpled with despair, she hunched her shoulders as she scooted around him to grab her purse and run out the door. Cormac reached out to snag her arm as she rushed by, but she ducked around his grasping hand and dashed outside.

Cormac turned to face Don before following her, the glow in his eyes gone dim, simmering in the depths of his pupils.

"You contemptuous, worthless fool. You have no idea what you've just done to her. None."

"I don't deal with her kind—or yours," Don replied with a snarl. "You're banned from my store. Get out of here."

Cormac set a hand on the countertop, the heat of his rage burning its imprint in the surface. "Gladly. But before I go, I want you to know that I will be taking a personal interest in destroying everything you've built here, piece by piece. I curse this place. I curse *you*, Don Allegretto."

Don's eyes went wide as the power of the curse hit him like a blow to the gut, the bad luck charm swirling around him like a flock of vultures, altering his fate. The man staggered back, flailing at the invisible *somethings* pricking at his skin with painful bites as they altered his aura.

"What... what did you do to me?" he gasped.

"Never piss off a dragon, you son of a bitch."

Cormac took a measure of satisfaction in the waver of Annabelle's voice following him out as he turned on his heel and stalked after Kimberly.

"A *dragon?* Don, is that the dragon from Central Park? Oh, my God, I have to find my cell phone, I have to get a picture and tell everybody..."

Shaking his head, he took a few steps outside before pausing. He shaded his eyes against the sun, looking up and down the street both ways. Then rocked back as an invisible fist landed on his jaw.

It didn't hurt, per se, but it did startle him into backing up a step or two. Kimberly's frame flashed into view, her tear-streaked face twisted with hurt and anger.

"You... you... *you*."

That was all she could get out. She couldn't even put into words how angry she was at him. Cormac reached for her, and she skittered back with a cry.

Undeterred, he moved with inhuman speed, capturing her in his arms so she couldn't rush off and avoid this conversation. What he had to say needed to be said, even if she hated his guts.

"Kimberly, listen to me a moment. Just listen—"

"No. *No.* You let me go, *now,* and get out of my life! You ruin *everything!* Let go of me!"

Frustrated, he let out another growl, his grip tightening. "Not until you listen. You can hate me all you like, but I have something to say, and by the gods, you are going to let me speak."

She shut her mouth, staring up at him with such a look on her face that he had the feeling she was wishing she could hate him to death at that moment. He didn't blame her, particularly since his attempt to make things right between them appeared to be a spectacular failure before he even managed to tell her he was sorry. He had to get the words out before something else managed to come between them.

"I'm sorry about your job. I'm sorry about *me*. I've made a terrific number of mistakes when it comes to you, and I'll be damned if I'm not going to do something to make it right."

She opened her mouth to interrupt him, but he pressed a finger to her lips before she could get a word out.

"You hate me, I know," he continued, "but I can't just walk away. I promised to keep you safe, and I will. I can't just stand aside and watch you slave and suffer for the things you want. You deserve far better than to spend your life reaching for the stars, never able to reach them. Let me bring them to you. Let me give you what you need. Please. If you won't have me, there are others. Other dragons."

The anger making her so tense in his arms eased out of her, though tears continued to trickle from her eyes as she stared up at him. He lifted a hand to brush some of that moisture away, flinching as she pulled back from his touch. Her voice, when it came, was low and resigned, so broken that he ached to hear it.

"You just made me lose my job. Did you really curse the place? Other people depend on him for work. Jesus, Cormac—"

"No, no, of course not. He'll have a little string of bad luck, people treating him the way he's treated Others, that's all. Call it a karmic intervention."

"Fine. Whatever. But you made *me* look like an idiot in front of half the Others in New York. You lied to me, Cormac. How can I believe anything you say?"

He lowered his head, closing his eyes as he took a deep, steadying breath. This was turning out to be far harder than he had expected.

"Ask me for anything, Kimberly. Just ask, and I'll give it to you. Money? Jewels? A familiar? I'll buy your way into The Circle if that's what you want."

Stung, she jerked back from him, some of the heat returning to her eyes. "Is that what you think of me? That you can *buy* me back?"

He instinctively tightened his grip on her. Muscles tense, his voice, while steady, lowered in pitch until she could have sworn her bones were vibrating in response. "I'm trying to make this right. Tell me what it is you want from me. Tell me what I can do to fix this. I'm not used to dealing with human feelings like this, Kimberly. I've tried to stay away, but I can't. Help me understand how to make this up to you."

She leaned forward, her head thumping against his chest. It took a moment for him to catch on that her shoulders were shaking from laughter, not tears, though he could tell by the taste of salt on his tongue that she hadn't stopped crying yet.

"You... you idiot," she wheezed. "You can't buy an apology. God, you are an arrogant ass."

He snorted, pulling her into him and burying his nose in her hair. She couldn't hate him that much if she was laughing at him. Relief nearly made him fall to his knees. He might have, if he hadn't been holding her in his arms just then.

"Runs in the bloodline, or so I'm told," he said.

She couldn't respond, she was laughing so hard. For this first time in his terrifically long lifespan, he found he didn't mind being the butt of the joke.

Chapter Thirty-five

The sound of a throat clearing behind her had Kimberly looking over her shoulder.

She swiped under her eyes with a hand as soon as she saw Damaris standing several feet away, looking both frightened and determined. The centaur was dressed much the same as she had been the first time Kimberly had seen her; prepared for a day of hiking rather than a city excursion.

The woman inclined her head, but kept her eyes glued to Cormac with the awareness of a prey animal in the presence of something it knows might choose to attack and eat it. Cormac went very still before letting Kimberly slide from his grasp, his gaze growing avid with hunger as he prowled in her wake.

Kimberly took Damaris's extended hand, accepting the offered shake in greeting.

"How are you and Eddie and the rest of your herd doing? Everything all right?" Kimberly asked.

Damaris kept her eyes glued to Cormac, who was watching her just as closely, though with far different intent. "Very well, thank you, miss. I... I am very sorry if I interrupted, Lord Hunter."

Cormac smiled, his grin full of a few too many fangs. "Your timing leaves something to be desired."

Kimberly frowned, glancing back at him—then doing a double-take once she realized just what had Damaris looking ready to bolt. She stepped between them, folding her arms and glaring up at him with reddened eyes.

"Are you trying to give me another reason to be mad at you? As far as I'm concerned, you're still in the doghouse, mister."

If anything could have jolted him out of his wolfish mien, that was it. In the space of a heartbeat, he became a different person, the coiled tension in his muscles and the hungry glitter to his eyes disappearing. Lowering his head, he sketched a brief bow to the centaur, the thin smile he gave her now close-lipped and lacking any hint of the threat that had been present a moment before.

"My apologies, Lady Archer. You have nothing to fear from me. Not today."

Damaris did not appear to find this very reassuring. The pleading look she turned on Kimberly made that clear.

Putting a hand to the bridge of her nose, Kimberly took a couple of deep breaths to steady her temper. Both of them were driving her around the bend.

"This day is shaping up to be a contender for a spot in the top ten worst days of my life. Cormac, I made a promise that I intend to keep. I'll talk to you later. Let's go, Damaris."

That prompted a low, rumbling growl out of him. The sound stopped as soon as she rounded on him and gave him a sharp look.

"I don't want to leave you. I only just got you back," he protested.

"Yeah, well, you're on thin ice. I'm not done giving you a piece of my mind yet."

The whites were visible all the way around Damaris's irises. Her harsh whisper was loud enough to be heard across the street. "Do you know what you're talking to?"

"She does," Cormac said.

"I do," Kimberly said, giving him a *quiet down now* look.

Damaris gaped at her. Kimberly threw her hands up. "For God's sake, he's not going to eat you. Or me. Or anyone. Let's just go and get this over with. Then I'll take you up on your offer."

Damaris said, "That's fine" at the same time as Cormac asked, "What offer?"

Kimberly turned around, grabbed his collar, and yanked him down to give him a kiss. He was so surprised at her temerity that he didn't do a thing to try to stop her, and was soon leaning into it.

The moment he reached for her, fingertips brushing over her arms, she pulled back and gave him a little push away.

The green fire in her eyes entranced him as thoroughly as her kiss had as she glared up at him.

"You," she told him, "have no right to ask me that. Pack up that possessive streak and take it with you back to your shop and wait for me there. I'll come and see you when I'm done, and then we can talk about how you plan on getting me my job back and making up for this mess you made of my life. Got it?"

"Demanding little thing," he said, not without affection. "If you're going with Damaris, I'm coming with you. Don't argue with me. Her herd runs too close to Viper's territory for my taste, and I'm not about to leave you unprotected."

Kimberly was reaching the end of her rope. As upset as she had been with him, the mere mention of Viper's name was enough to make her pale and shrink into herself. As badly as she wanted to prove that she was capable of handling her own life and keeping her own promises, the thought of seeing Viper again filled her with cold dread.

Seeing how badly he had upset her, Cormac tugged her against him, pressing a kiss to her temple. "Don't worry. I'm not going to let anything bad happen to you."

She took a shuddering breath, then forced a smile. "Don't make promises you can't keep."

"I don't."

Damaris shuffled awkwardly from foot to foot, drawing their attention off each other and onto her. It was clear from the look on the woman's face that she was not thrilled with the way things were turning out, but was uncertain how to tell them so. Her fear of Cormac had not abated in the least, though she was still boggling over how Kimberly ordered him around.

"Should I come back later?" she asked.

"No, of course not," Kimberly told her. "Lead the way. I hope you don't mind that he's coming, too."

The centaur looked ill at the idea of letting the dragon anywhere near her herd, but she didn't say a thing to protest.

Kimberly was not surprised that the centaur had a pickup truck. The tension in the cab was through the roof with Damaris's stiff, jerky movements and Cormac's unwavering gaze focused on the centaur. He wasn't doing anything overtly threatening, but the mere fact of his presence was worrying the centaur to distraction.

It took a little less than an hour to get to the rambling, open park Damaris explained was where her herd usually ran. They weren't too far from the pine barrens, but the sandy beaches and grasslands were more open and provided a better location for them to slip out of their human skins and be themselves for a while.

It also provided excellent cover for the werewolves who hunted the area during the full moon. Considering the centaurs mostly ran at dusk and dawn due to the possibility of being spotted during the day, that left them open to the danger of being hunted by the pack. The full grown centaurs were usually able to hold their own, but the youngest and oldest were always at risk.

Cormac listened as Damaris explained her problem, and noted how Kimberly's features hardened with resolve.

He had never given the centaurs' welfare much thought. Or any thought, for that matter. They had been his prey in ages past, after all. He could still remember the taste, though it had been centuries since the last time he had hunted them. As humanity expanded their empires and elemental Others were driven out of their ancient homelands, he had altered his feeding patterns, choosing prey animals that weren't magical in nature. The depleted numbers of Others had a great deal to do with his choice, as did his changing tastes as he grew older.

He was, like any shark or big cat, almost exclusively a carnivore. He made no apologies for his hungers, but found, as he learned the hard lesson that his kind was not the only intelligent creature worthy of consideration, that he no longer had any desire to feed on the sentient. Unlike many dragon-kin, while his appetite was enormous, he no longer fed to the point of gluttony as he had as a wyrmling.

Of course, Damaris's delicious scent of fear in the enclosed cab of the pickup didn't make it easy for him to remember that resolution.

When they arrived, Cormac waited by the truck, leaning against the front bumper as Kimberly walked across the sand and gravel to get into animated conversation with the other centaurs Damaris introduced her to. The herd was small; no more than twenty adult members, only three young children frolicking in the tall grasses and a lone teenager come to meet their mage savior.

Their numbers had shrunk quite a bit since he had last bothered to interest himself in their affairs.

While the adults all watched him warily out of the corners of their eyes, he was struck by how quick they were to trust that Kimberly was there to help them. More than that, by how she was so intent on living up to their expectations. She nodded along with their explanations, asking questions, examining the lay of the land the centaurs called their territory. If he hadn't been watching her so closely, he wouldn't have seen her dash away a few tears with the back of her hand while ostensibly crouching down to get a feel for the local ley line energy.

Seeing how deeply affected Kimberly was by the plight of the centaurs had him rethinking his own stance.

As she began pacing off the perimeter of the area they liked to run, he moved to follow at a sedate pace behind them. He kept his hands pocketed and his head down, doing his best to appear as harmless as possible, but they were quick to stop and surround their little ones, not budging from the field overlooking the parking lot.

Kimberly fisted her hands on her hips, and pointed imperiously back at the car. He frowned, pausing in his tracks but staying where he was.

After a long, tense moment, the centaurs resumed their tour with Kimberly, this time keeping their children close. He stayed where he was, closing his eyes and extending his other senses to keep tabs on the group. He noted the few centaurs in their native form hiding amid the trees, bows trained on him, and dismissed them. He was more concerned whether Viper had recovered enough to hunt and sate his no doubt enormous appetite. He would be searching for prey such as the centaurs as soon as he was able.

Cormac's senses told him the wyvern was still very much alive, but not close enough to be a threat. There were no other predators in the area significant enough to warrant him following the group with anything more than his Sight, so he leaned his butt against the pickup truck and tilted his face up to the sun, soaking in the warmth as he waited for them to return.

He was very proud to note that Kimberly was pausing every few yards to etch a mix of glyphs similar to the ones he used to guard his apartment above the Wild Hunt in the trees and rocks.

The wards she was building were strong, though she appeared to be using more obfuscation and repelling sigils than he did.

It took several hours even though it appeared that the centaurs' grazing area must have shrunken considerably along with the size of the herd. Her circle was still much larger than those that many skilled magi he knew were capable of drawing and imbuing with power. This was on the order of the magic used to guard monoliths like the academies and larger covens such as The Circle. That she was capable of putting it together with limited materials or time to study the lay of the land meant she had greater power and skill than he or Eleanor Reed or anyone else at Blackhollow may have guessed. He could sense that her strength was flagging by the time they returned, but she looked so pleased and self-satisfied that any worry he might have had faded away at the sight of her radiant smile.

The centaurs all looked quite pleased as well.

"Cormac, will you step back please?"

He did as she asked, returning to his lean against the car, and he watched with interest as she moved to the edge of the parking lot. She crouched down and used a piece of spelling chalk that was down to nothing more than a tiny nub in her fingers, etching a symbol into one of the big stones that bordered the edge of the field. The hair on the back of his neck and on his arms raised as the nearby ley lines chimed with a tremendous shift in power.

"Okay, that's the last one," she said. "Damaris, Eddie, a few others—can you try crossing over the line and coming back?"

The centaurs did, the one called Eddie snorting as he stepped back inside the range of her protective circle. He scrubbed at his arms, as did Damaris and the two other centaurs who did as she asked.

"Good. Can some of you shift now? Someone on the other side tell me what you see."

Cormac tilted his head, watching with narrowed eyes. Some of the centaurs grew hazy in his vision, but when he blinked, they still looked human to him. Curious, he shifted to using his Sight instead—and was surprised to see they were in their native forms.

"They still look the same, my lady," one of the centaurs said. Others chimed in to say the same.

"Come across the line."

The centaur's sound of surprise told Cormac everything he needed to know. The obfuscation sigils she added to the circle were hiding their native forms from prying eyes. It was a particularly thoughtful gesture on her part. Passing humans, Weres, or other hunters of a non-magical nature would never see the herd for what they were as long as they were outside the circle.

"Excellent. One last test. Cormac, will you try to reach me now, please?"

She took a step back deeper beyond the protection of the glyphs and folded her arms, waiting for him to come to her. Tilting his head, he pushed off the truck and stalked closer, eyes glued to hers as he met her challenging gaze.

He expected to meet resistance. He didn't expect the minor jolt of electricity zapping over his skin, driving him back with a startled hiss.

"Sorry," she said, the edge of laughter in her voice saying she wasn't sorry at all. "Come on, we need to know it'll hold. Can you get through?"

Determined to reach her, he put out a hand, testing the strength of the ward. It crackled over his fingers and gave a fraction, but held under the weight of his will seeking any crack or seam to exploit.

Both hands netted him the same result. The damned thing was near impregnable unless he shifted into his native form and expended a great deal more energy than he was prepared to waste.

The centaurs applauded when he stepped back and sketched a brief bow to concede defeat.

She'd designed it to detect carnivorous Others. The consequence of trying to pass wasn't as deadly as someone not keyed attempting to cross his wards, but it would be painful enough to send all but the most determined Others seeking less dangerous prey.

He couldn't have been more proud of her.

Then she forced her shoulders back and sauntered toward him in a way that lit an unexpected spark of desire in his blood. The smug little smile she gave him said without words that she knew very well just how easily he had expected to walk through her wards and that she had planned from the start to show off.

Xander had asked for her help with enchantments for good reason. Illusion wasn't the only formidable skill in her magical repertoire.

Before she could reach him, the centaurs surrounded her to thank her, shaking her hand and singing her praises. Though they looked like people—people running exceptionally fast—he could feel the thunder of hooves as a small group broke off behind the line to race around in a joyful display in the safety of their circle. The kids were quick to join them, prancing around the adults, all of them radiating relief and delight. She tried to brush it off as nothing, but those who stayed behind wouldn't let her, insisting she let them give her some money, food, and other gifts.

Then Cormac went very still as she said something that froze the blood in his veins.

"Thank you for everything! I'm afraid I do need to take up the offer for a familiar though. Can one of you meet me at Blackhollow Academy on Monday morning?"

Chapter Thirty-six

"Kimberly," he said, gritting the words between his teeth, "can I have a word with you?"

She turned a frown on him. "No."

Then she did the unthinkable. She ignored him in favor of the centaurs.

It took everything he had not to burst out of his skin in a jealous rage. They picked up on his displeasure, many of them edging back over the line of the circle, their fear only making his desire to shift and tear something apart with claw and fang grow stronger.

He went back to the car and stared up at the distant horizon, concentrating on calming himself down. There had to be a reason she would spurn his offer to give her everything she wanted. That she would turn him down in favor of a centaur for a familiar was beyond belief, and quite possibly one of the most insulting things that had ever happened to him.

He couldn't grasp her motivations. He couldn't understand why she wouldn't accept his offer. He didn't get why she didn't want *his* money, *his* jewels, *his* power.

He couldn't figure out what in the nine hells a centaur had that he didn't.

It was driving him daft. *She* was driving him daft.

And he didn't care. As long as she let him into her life, he would let her do whatever it was that made her happy.

It was a strangely calming realization. If he had to suffer her having a centaur for a shadow, so be it. It was a small price to pay considering how badly he had wounded her pride.

Pride. That stirred something. He wasn't sure what the connection was to what she was doing yet, but he'd give it some contemplation when he wasn't so riled or had the distraction of her twisting his every thought to what else he could do to please her and make amends for hurting her.

As she wrapped things up with the centaurs, he took note of the one who promised to be her familiar. Eddie, one of the bucks, he was more than a little displeased to see. The boy looked like he belonged on a farm somewhere, with his tan and sun-streaked hair, and more muscular build than the one Cormac had chosen to use for himself. It raised his hackles to see the way she touched the centaur's arm and smiled up at him.

Telling himself that it meant nothing didn't do a thing to quell his desire to shift and snatch her up to fly off with her somewhere nice and private. At some point he would drive home to her that he meant everything he had said. He had never intended to hurt her. He wanted her like he'd never wanted anything. Not all the jewels and gold and precious valuables in his hoard meant a thing if he couldn't have her.

Some of the tension in his muscles eased when she waved her goodbyes and came back to his side, smiling up at him.

"Thank you for helping with the demonstration. That was very nice of you to keep an eye on things."

He nodded, his lips twitching despite his efforts to maintain a stony and aloof expression. He just couldn't do it when she was looking so happy. That happiness was infectious, and ruining his image of being the biggest, baddest monster in town.

Perhaps he should do something about that.

"And thank you for not flipping out about the familiar thing. I know you're not happy about it."

His own smile widened at that. "Oh, I wouldn't thank me yet. Would you say you're finished here?"

"I guess so—oh!"

He barely waited for the words to finish leaving her mouth before grabbing her and throwing her over his shoulder. She gasped at the treatment, smacking his back.

"Put me down!"

"In a minute." He turned to the centaurs clustered together in a group, gaping at the two of them. "Clan Archer, thank you for your hospitality. If there's nothing else, we'll be leaving now."

Damaris was the first to find her voice, though it still sounded a bit high and strangled. "Kimberly, will you be all right?"

"I'm fine," she muttered, giving Cormac another thump with her fist. "See you guys on Mon—"

Cormac didn't wait for her to finish. A shriek was startled out of her and the centaurs were stampeding away in terror as the monster hidden by human skin burst free. Kimberly threw her arms around one of the growing spines on his back, panting in fear as her sneakers fought for purchase against slick scales. His wings spreading impossibly wide to blot out the sun as he shifted into his draconic form, bunching the muscles near where Kimberly was trying to hold on, making it easier for her to find purchase and steady herself.

It only took seconds for him to change, though he took care to ensure he didn't brush up against the walls of Kimberly's circle or do anything to damage the cars in the lot. The obfuscation spells he typically used to hide himself from mortal eyes when in his native form snapped into place, sending a tingle of magic and sheet of blue-white sparks racing over them both.

Once he was settled in his own skin, he arched his long, sinuous neck to peer back at her, the deep blue orbs glinting with what she was certain was amusement at her expense. With a grunt of effort, she heaved one leg up to hook behind the iguana-like spine that towered higher than she was tall, seating herself properly on his back as she clung to him for dear life.

"That was very rude," she told him, voice shaking as much as the rest of her.

Cormac snorted, a little puff of smoke drifting up from his nostrils. "Proper comportment is the least of my concerns at the moment. Hang on tight..."

Her fingers dug deep into the cartilage of the spine she was clinging to as he took to the air in one powerful leap. Muscles and scales heaved under her legs, rising and falling with every flap of his wings.

"Sorry!" she yelled down at the centaurs rushing pell-mell for the trees. She didn't think they could hear her over their own pounding hooves.

Once they were high above the trees, he steadied into a glide as he rode a thermal taking them back over the Sound. The jarring movements tapered off and Kimberly was able to swallow her heart out of her throat.

As badly as Viper had frightened her on the last flight she was conscious for, this time she had a hard time being scared for long. It was an entirely different experience on dragonback. She had to hold tight with her arms and legs, but it wasn't anywhere near as uncomfortable as being carried and near crushed by a set of razor talons. Soaring with the birds had her stomach bouncing between her shoes and the back of her tongue, but the wind rushing through her hair, the panoramic spread of the Sound and distant city before her, the fresh seawater scent, and the sun on her face filled her with exhilaration.

Knowing Cormac wouldn't let her fall made it easier to slip into the moment and enjoy the rush at the occasional dips and dives he took with the shifting air currents.

Kimberly looked all around, trying to take in everything at once as Cormac flew them over the water. She had to shield her eyes and squint against the wind, and it was colder than she was dressed for, but the view took her breath away. When they reached the city, he slowed down and angled his wings to take them in low. He started to bank to one side as if preparing to go sideways between a row of skyscrapers, but he altered his angle to go around them instead when her grip tightened as she went rigid.

He circled the Wild Hunt once, twice, then a third time, before landing on the rooftop with as much care and delicacy as he could muster. When he arched his neck to peer at his passenger, Kimberly was looking radiant with excitement. Her hair was a total bird's nest, windblown and tangled, and her cheeks were red from windburn, but she was smiling and her green eyes were aglow with pleasure.

Taking his time shifting back to his mortal form, he took care not to let her slip and fall, twisting at just the right moment to catch her in his arms so they were eye to eye. Her breath caught in her throat as she wrapped her arms around his neck and twined her legs around his waist. It pleased him enormously that she clung to him so tightly, but more that she met his gaze without any sign of fear or anger.

Though he knew a single flight fell far short of what he needed to do to prove himself to her, he hoped it helped his case to show her he could carry her wherever she wanted to go. Whether that meant across an ocean, to the stars, or to a better life, he would endeavor from that point forward to support her in any way she would let him.

"That was amazing," she said.

He grinned, lifting a hand to smooth some of her hair out of her face. "So were you, in more ways than you know. You never mentioned you had such talent with wards and enchantments."

"I guess we both have our secrets," she replied before huffing in exasperation. She ran a hand raggedly through her hair—hissing as her fingers got caught in the windblown tangles—before tugging them free and pressing her palm against his chest to put some distance between them. "Which I think we need to talk about. Can you give me a little more warning next time you plan on flying me somewhere? You scared those poor centaurs half to death. And Damaris could have driven us back here."

Cormac set her on her feet with a low, satisfied growl, his hands lingering on her hips. "Among other things, yes. As much as you might enjoy the company of those centaurs, Damaris's driving skills left something to be desired and I am running short on patience. Tell me what I can do to keep you to myself."

Kimberly pulled away, folding her arms and regarding him with a mix of amusement and exasperation. "Did you forget that I'm mad at you? A little time on dragonback is not going to blow those memories out of my head, and it's going to take more than a simple apology to make me trust you again. You can start by letting me make my own decisions about my future. Like picking a familiar I know won't get cold feet to get me through my finals."

He ducked his head, baring his teeth in a grimace. It was perhaps a bit more fang-filled than he meant to display, but Kimberly was not in the least bit intimidated. She regarded him steadily, and Cormac sidled closer to cup her cheeks in his hands.

"I will earn back your trust. I swear it. If I have to step aside for now, so be it—but I expect you to let me take that twice-be-damned donkey's place as soon as you graduate. Sooner, if I can talk you into it."

She snorted. "Donkey? Really?"

He bared his teeth in something that might have been a grin. "I would have called him a horse's ass, but I was trying to spare your sensibilities."

That got a laugh out of her. "Oh, Cormac. Eddie's not that bad."

"Maybe not, but I've never been the type to share. Not to mention that I find your choice of a centaur over a dragon to be more than a little peculiar."

"The herd owes me the favor, and all I need is to get my graduation certificate. I don't need a dragon to do that, I just need to prove I can bind a familiar. What's the big deal? You can help me in other ways. Like finding me a new job."

Cormac's eyes flashed with blue-white light, and though his expression was fierce, Kimberly didn't flinch away. With a snarl, he began pacing before her, his hands clenching and unclenching as he fought the animal instinct to change again and carry her far away from the city and all of the competition for her attentions.

"The big deal? The big deal is that I've wanted you as long as I've known you. Longer. Centuries have left me bitter and alone, never knowing a part of me was missing, waiting for you to complete me. All I want is you. All I've ever wanted was you."

Kimberly hugged herself tight, for the first time finding herself unable to meet his gaze. "I don't know how you could feel those things about me."

He slowly reached out, giving her time to pull away if she wanted to. The constriction in his chest eased when she accepted his light touch, leaning into the fingertips brushing over her cheek. He moved closer to fold her into his arms, breathing a sigh of relief into her hair before answering her.

"Because you're a shining star on the inside, burning away the darkness inside of me. You were always kind and gentle and funny, and wouldn't let me be anything less with you. It shattered the heart I didn't know I had when you turned me away." He took a shaky breath, tightening his hold on her. "I'll make up what I did to you. If it takes a thousand years, a thousand lifetimes, I'll become the dragon worthy of calling himself your familiar. You'll never be alone again. I'll be your sword, your shield, and anything else you would have of me. Let me be there to catch you when you fall. Let me be yours."

"You and your melodrama," she mumbled against his chest.

The salt of her tears on the air sent knives of guilt into his heart, piercing him with shame for ever hurting her, filling him with remorse for being the reason for those tears. Frowning, he set his chin on top of her head, savoring the warmth of her as she relaxed against him.

"I mean it, you know. I can never be sorry enough for how I treated you. For letting Viper hurt you. Please, Kimberly. I've never wanted anything—anyone—like I want you. I can wait for you to accept that. Forever if I have to. But I can't stand by and leave you unprotected. Let me be your familiar."

"What if I said no?"

The faint sound he made in his throat was choked off by the lump that appeared there like magic. Then he realized that she wasn't trembling in his arms because she was crying—she was laughing.

Her fingers twined in his shirt as she arched back to look up at him. Her eyes shone, her lips trembling with a shaky smile.

"How about you just try being my friend?"

He growled, his own eyes twinkling as he grinned down at her. "I don't know if I can handle that. I want so much more. To be your guardian, your confidant, and your lover. I want to be yours forever."

Her jaw dropped, cheeks turning pink. He closed his eyes tight and bowed his head in comical contrition, giving a theatric sigh as one hand dipped low on her hip, toying with the waistband of her jeans. That delicious heat she was radiating grew hotter under his touch.

"...but seeing as I managed to screw things up so badly, I suppose I can be patient for a bit longer for you to give me a chance to be more than friends. I've waited lifetimes to find you, after all."

Shoulders shaking with suppressed laughter, she squirmed a bit to give him a good poke in the side. "Stop trying to guilt your way into my bed. I'm supposed to be mad at you."

"You can be mad. Angry sex is always good."

Gasping, she flushed right down to her toes, heart pounding a staccato rhythm. "You really *are* a beast."

His smile turned wicked. "Surely you've heard the tales of how we dragons have voracious... appetites."

"I don't know about that. Greedy, possessive streaks a mile wide..."

"If wanting to keep you all to myself forever makes me greedy and possessive, guilty as charged."

She buried her face against his chest again, groaning. "If you don't stop being so charming, I'm going to forget that I'm supposed to be mad as hell. It's not fair."

"Does that mean my dastardly plan to lure the gentle maiden off to my lair is working? I've heard dragon flights off into the sunset are considered romantic by some..."

"Yes, damn you," she said, laughing. "As long as you don't carry me around in your claws like a sack of potatoes. And give me some warning next time before you try carrying me off."

"As my lady commands."

With that, he leaned in to kiss her, gentle at first. The moment she melted into him, he deepened it into a fierce, possessive assault, chest vibrating with a hungry, animal sound of need. Her hands slid up his chest, tangling in his hair as she kissed him back, her hunger and desperation made all the more satisfying by her sweet tears.

Before he lost his mind, he needed to be sure of one last thing.

Lightly nipping her lower lip, he withdrew just enough to whisper against her cheek, his lips trailing over her skin in a delicious tease that had her shivering with need in his arms.

"Does this mean you'll bond with me?"

A frustrated noise escaped her as she tugged lightly on his hair to pull him back down to her. "Only if you keep kissing me like that. Don't stop."

With a satisfied growl, he obliged her.

Chapter Thirty-seven

Cormac led Kimberly back inside once he realized she was still shivering. He made a mental note to purchase her a set of goggles and warm clothes to fly with him in the future. Once they reached the kitchen, he put on a pot of coffee and leaned against the counter, holding his arms open for her. She leaned against him, gratefully settling into his warm embrace as they waited for the coffee to finish brewing.

"I'm sorry about what happened with your job. I didn't realize your boss didn't know what you were."

Kimberly grimaced, tightening her grip on him. "I was hoping I could keep things under wraps until I finished school. Don wasn't such a bad guy. Just... ignorant, I guess."

"You shouldn't have to hide what you are just to make ends meet."

"No, but I wasn't exactly flooded with job offers, either. Covens don't hire students, and it was Allegretto's or Starbucks—and Starbucks wasn't as flexible with their schedule."

Cormac snorted at that. He could see why a young mage not connected to the Other community would have a hard time finding work, but he was still annoyed on her behalf.

"You deserve better than to work for someone who can't appreciate you for who and what you are," he told her. "Put all of that behind you. I'll take care of you now. Whatever you need, just ask."

Tilting her head up, she frowned at him. "I can take care of myself. I just need a new job to tide me over until I can get a position in a coven."

He met her frown with one of his own. "You don't have to work. How much money do you need?"

"I don't want you *giving* me money, Cormac. That's not the point."

Cormac thought about this, brows furrowing as he stroked the tangles out of her hair with his fingers. She closed her eyes and laid her cheek against his chest with a contented sigh. As bothersome as he found her refusal, he didn't think he'd be doing a thing to endear himself to her by forcing the matter.

Pride. Eleanor had warned him that she had difficulty keeping it in check. Her refusal to take anything he had to offer her was starting to make sense. Though he might not have agreed, he was starting to see why she didn't want him to simply *give* her anything.

He suspected she took the centaur over him not just because she didn't trust him, but because she either thought she hadn't earned access to his power, or didn't deserve it.

The situation with the centaur was a perfect example of what must have been going through her mind. She settled so readily into his arms that he found it impossible to believe her lack of trust in him went so deep as she claimed. She was so adamant about earning her way that it was clear someone had made her feel unworthy in some way.

It hurt something deep in his heart to know that. Whatever pain she might have endured in the past, somehow it had burned a lesson in her that she couldn't shake. Something that told her not to accept that good things could be given freely with no price tag attached.

Knowing that, he chose his next words with care.

"Would you feel better about it if I had you do some work for me? I could use an extra set of hands in the store."

Kimberly shook her head, not opening her eyes. "I wouldn't feel right about it."

"Tell me why. Are you afraid someone will judge you for accepting a helping hand?"

She reddened, ducking her head to hide her blush in the folds of his shirt. "No. Maybe. Oh, Cormac, I don't know. When I asked Viper if he'd loan me a little something from his hoard to help me get by as part of the familiar deal, the way he looked at me made me feel like something he found stuck on the bottom of his shoe.

I'm not a charity case, you know? I told him I'd pay him back, and I meant every word, but the way he *looked* at me..."

She trailed off in a whisper, shame making her voice grow weak. Cormac found his own voice caught on an unexpected lump of emotion in his throat. He lowered his head to rest his chin on her hair, tightening his grip to keep her from pulling away, wishing that somehow he could stop the tremors making her shake in his arms. If only he knew how to undo the humiliation she had suffered.

He should have killed that blasted snake when he had the chance. That Viper had wounded her emotionally as well as physically was nigh intolerable for the beast inside him. His animal nature was clawing to burst out of the cloak of human flesh to seek out and destroy any threats to the wellbeing of his mate.

She must have taken his shocked silence for disbelief or something like it. The defensive tone she took with him made it clear she wasn't so much trying to convince him as herself that there was nothing wrong with her.

"I work hard, you know? I'm poor, not stupid. Just because me and my mom don't make a lot of money doesn't mean we're lazy leeches looking for some easy road out. Do you know what it's like, counting pennies and praying that if I skip more meals than I already do that I'll have enough to make rent? Do you know what it feels like to look at the cat's food dish and wonder if what's in it can tide you over unless your boss takes pity on you and gives you the stale leftovers at the end of your shift? Or you could steal a few pieces of food from the school cafeteria? Have you ever felt what it's like, knowing everyone you meet is judging you, or expecting you to be grateful for their scraps, never knowing how hard you work for what you have? Have you ever known that no matter what you did, it would never be enough to cover everything?"

Cormac cleared his throat, but his voice still came hoarse with sorrow. "I have never been in your position, and can only imagine what that must have been like for you. I never thought you were looking for the easy road or that you were trying to be some sort of freeloader, and I hope you didn't think I am even remotely like Viper in any way. All I want is for you to be happy, Kimberly. I'm not trying to turn you into a charity case—I'm trying to give you a helping hand to get yourself out of the mire you and your mother have found yourselves stuck in. You don't have to struggle through it alone anymore.

"I want you to focus on finishing school since I know how important that is to you. Tell me how much money you need to tide you over until then. If it makes you feel better, you can pay me back after you find another job. I know you are capable of finding one on your own, but it would make *me* feel better if you let me help you in some way to get what you want. It worries me to think you might go hungry or without shelter because of me. Let this be my amends for making you lose your job at the café. Fair enough?"

Kimberly bit her lip and nodded, still not looking at him. Her agreement eased the constriction in his heart. He had the feeling there were other terrible things she may have had to do aside from filch some food from school or her job just to survive. Things she wasn't ready to tell him about. Things she might never be ready to speak of with him, or anyone, at any time. Still, he thought her willingness to accept his offer was a tremendous leap in the right direction.

It was a start on the road that would lead to him finding ways to help her turn her circumstances around. Though it went against his instincts, he could temper his urges and find ways to assist rather than doing it for her. The significance of her agreeing to let him do as much was not lost on him.

As bothersome as he found it to realize that she had carried those burdens alone for so long—well, perhaps with a bit of help from her human mother, who could not begin to understand the fae side of her child—it was a great deal more humbling to him that she now was trusting him with shouldering part of the weight she'd carried. He would do his best to honor that trust and be an arm to lean on when she needed it, rather than a crutch for her to rely on.

With a low sigh, he slid his thumb under her chin, tilting her head up so she would meet his gaze. "Would it be pressing my luck to ask you to stay here with me?"

She gave him a tremulous smile. "As much as I would like to, I can't leave my mom to fend for herself. The two of us together were barely making ends meet."

He nodded, leaning across the counter to pour them both cups of coffee. She took a step back, her heartbeat picking up tempo as she put distance between them. Nervous.

"I have to go home," she said.

"You're worried about her?"

"Sort of. I have to tell her what happened at work. I also have to get cracking on my homework. I'm supposed to meet with Xander tomorrow for a study date. It's my last chance to cram in some study."

Cormac nodded again. "Fine. I'll come with you."

She choked on her coffee, then swiped the back of her hand under her nose to get rid of the splashback, "I hope you're just talking about walking me home. I don't think we've reached the 'meet the parental unit' stage in this relationship yet."

"I'm not making any more mistakes when it comes to your safety. If you prefer, I can stand guard from the air or rooftops, but I don't want to take any chances until you have a familiar bond. Be it with me or..." Cormac paused, his lip curling. "...or the boy."

"Don't get too excited, now," she said, tone wry. "You don't have to do that. I'm just not sure how my mom will react to you. She's not a big fan of the Other mojo I give off, so..."

"You think she'll be afraid of me?"

"Maybe. Can you keep a lid on the 'argh, gonna eat you' vibes? You might have noticed that doesn't go over well with the non-draconic folk."

He laughed. "Yes, I can do that. I'll make a special effort and be on my best behavior."

Kimberly couldn't help giggling at the faux-serious expression he made as he straightened his shoulders and tilted up his chin. The hard set of his jaw was not very intimidating when combined with that mischievous twinkle in his eyes.

Leaning back to grin up at him, she shook her head. Then fiddled with the buttons on his shirt and straightened the wrinkles she'd made in the pale blue cotton as she clutched at him. His roguish look turned hungry as he lightly captured her hands in his, stilling them and drawing her attention back up to meet his gaze.

"We may not have the opportunity to be alone together for a few days. Want to take advantage of it while we can?"

Snickering at his brow waggle, she shook her head again. "You are incorrigible. I hope my mom is ready for you."

"People are rarely ready to meet their first dragon."

"Don't I know it," she muttered.

Chapter Thirty-eight

Cormac managed to convince Kimberly to let him buy dinner to start off on the right foot with her mother. It hadn't taken much to get her to agree. Before long, the two walked together, hand in hand, and picked up dinner to go at the Black Star Café. Rieva rang them up, radiating curiosity but not asking any questions.

When they reached Kimberly's apartment building, she led Cormac inside, doing her best not to flush when one of the keys on the pad for the front door got stuck. He was careful to keep his composure, giving no sign of how distasteful he found the chipped paint and general disrepair of the building, though he couldn't help but wrinkle his nose once she led him up to her floor. The mix of old cigarettes and dog piss underlying the thicker scent of curry from someone's dinner wafting through the hallway was an assault to his acute senses.

Cormac held his breath, eyes narrowed as he waited with as much patience as he could muster for Kimberly to let him in. The tingle of her wards activating in response to his presence was far less of an irritant than the smells making his eyes water.

She went inside but held up a hand for him to wait. She set down the coffees she'd been carrying on the kitchen counter, then returned to the door frame and pressed one palm to it as she concentrated on the power infused into the runes she had drawn there a few days before. Some of them came to life with a dim white glow, pulsing with her intent, growing brighter as she reached out to touch Cormac's hand. A touch of ozone and a brief, blinding flash signaled the adjustment she made, granting him access.

As soon as the crackle of electricity over his skin vanished, he was through the door like a shot, sliding past her with serpentine grace. She grinned at his obvious and deliberate attempt at nonchalance, then shrugged and shut the door behind them, calling out.

"Mom? Are you home?"

"In the living room. Did you talk to Don about extending your hours yet? The electric bill just came in."

Kimberly grimaced, and headed down the hall to the living room, sparing Cormac a glance. He was peering at Monster, who was staring up at him from the end of the hall, back arched and tail fluffed out to twice its normal size. She nudged Cormac with her elbow and gestured for him to follow her. As soon as he started moving, Monster hissed and dashed away to hide in the bedroom.

"Um. Not yet. Can we talk about that later? I have a guest."

Her mother hastily got to her feet as they emerged from the hallway, running a hand through her hair and then over her food-spattered shirt. It was clear she hadn't been home from work very long and hadn't had a chance to freshen up, her eyes a bit red with telling dark circles under them. Her smile was forced, but she made an effort to put on a cheery face.

"Why didn't you say so? Who's this?"

"Mom, this is Cormac Hunter. He's been helping me with my homework. Cormac, this is my mom, Heather Wells."

Cormac set down the bag of food on the tiny, rickety table with a pair of mismatched chairs, and then extended his hand to shake. Kimberly's mother stared at him intently as she took his hand, though she kept her expression cautiously neutral. Kimberly bit her lip and tried to keep a cap on her nervousness about this meeting. She hoped her mom didn't pick up that Cormac was the one who had driven her home in tears. This situation was already awkward enough as it was.

"Nice to meet you," Heather said. "Please excuse me a minute. I wasn't expecting company."

"That's fine. Kimberly and I will get dinner ready. Take your time."

Her lips briefly formed a moue as she turned a sharp look on Kimberly before nodding and hurrying to the bedroom. Cormac pulled the containers out of the bag while Kimberly went to the kitchen to get plates and cutlery.

Since the tiny dining table only had two chairs, he began to set everything up on the coffee table before the couch instead. It would be a tight squeeze, but it was the only place the three of them could sit down to the meal together.

As he was moving some papers from the coffee table, he spotted a notice of eviction tucked in with a few other bills and pay stubs. With a scowl, he covered it up with some of the other papers and envelopes, then set the stack aside and continued unpacking the food, surreptitiously noting his surroundings.

Far too small to shift in should the need call for it. A small collection of secondhand (or perhaps third, or fourth) furniture, with dings and scratches and stains hidden by some colorful but artfully draped scarves, was scattered around the room. No TV. A leaning bookshelf with a collection of battered paperbacks and a scattering of shells and sea glass served as an entertainment center. There was a single picture on the top shelf, framed, of a younger Kimberly with her arms wrapped around her mother's waist as the two smiled at the camera. The rolling, deep blue waves of the Atlantic Ocean was in the background.

He moved about as if he'd been there a thousand times before, setting aside the throw pillows and knitted afghan and retrieving a rag from the kitchen to wipe up the condensation that leaked onto the table from the tops of the containers. Their arms and fingers brushed each other more than once as they transferred the food to the plates, and he could feel her vibrating with nervousness. With a low, muttered Word and a pass of his hand over the food and drinks, they were again steaming hot.

Some of the self-conscious tension knotting Kimberly's shoulders fell away as he took a seat and folded one leg over the other, an arm stretched along the back of the couch. He made an effort to appear more at ease than he was. The cramped quarters and irritating scents still plugging his nose were making him itch to regain his true form and clear his head in the heights of the clouds. Her quick, tight smile and the grateful glint in her eyes made suffering the assault on his senses worth it.

Shortly after they finished preparing everything and Kimberly settled beside Cormac on the couch, her mom came out of the bedroom in a clean pair of jeans and a plain but faded T-shirt. Her face was freshly scrubbed and her short blond hair had been slicked back from her face with water. She paused when she saw the spread on the table, brown eyes gone wide. The steak with caramelized onions, kale salad with tangerine slices and pine nut garnish, and prosciutto wrapped asparagus looked incredible, even on their chipped stoneware plates. The addition of coffee and a slice each of cheesecake, chocolate and apple pie for dessert was the topper on an already overwhelming surprise.

When she managed to peel her gaze off of the feast on the table and pick her jaw off the floor, she waved a hand at the spread. "You—this—Mr. Hunter, this is—"

"Please, Mrs. Wells, have a seat. Enjoy it while it's still hot."

She settled gingerly on the opposite end of the couch from Cormac, Kimberly between them, her jaw still slack with surprise. "It's Miss, but you're going to make me feel like *my* mother if you call me by my last name. It's Heather. And thank you for all this."

"As you wish, Heather. It was my pleasure."

They tucked into the meal with gusto. Once again, Cormac didn't touch his own food until Kimberly took her first bite. When Heather exclaimed over how decadent and tasty everything was, Kimberly shot a grateful look at him. After they finished off the main course and started sipping coffee and sharing the desserts, everyone trying a bite of all the different sweets, conversation turned from the food to more personal matters.

Heather took a bite of cheesecake before setting down her fork, leaning forward to see around Kimberly and turn a piercing, curious look on Cormac. "What is it you do, exactly? I'm curious what brought you here tonight."

"I run a specialty store. Antiques, mostly. I procure rare, arcane objects. I've been looking forward to meeting you, Heather. Kimberly cares about you very much."

"Is that right? Tell me how you met my daughter. She hasn't said a word about you to me before."

Kimberly coughed on the chocolate cake she was swallowing, her eyes watering as she choked out a few words. "Mom, it's not important—"

"She came to my shop and told me she was searching for a dragon familiar. I'm afraid it took me a bit longer to agree to the idea than she might have liked, but I'm doing my best to make it up to her."

Heather blinked. "...come again?"

Cormac sipped his coffee, unconcerned with the nonplussed response from Kimberly's mother. "One of her teachers convinced me to give her a chance. I'm not usually inclined to involve myself in the affairs of magi, but your daughter's abilities are a force to be reckoned with. Even so, with me by her side, she'll never have anything to worry about again."

Kimberly shot him a murderous *kindly shut your face now, thanks* look before adding her own hurried explanation before her mother's speechlessness could wear off.

"I can't graduate without a familiar, Mom. He's helping me out so I can get through school and find a better job."

Heather didn't quite appear to have processed what Cormac had said yet, let alone Kimberly's words. "Dr-d-dra-agon?" she stuttered.

"Yes. If you're worried about a repeat of the incident at Central Park, I can assure you it won't happen again. I intend to do nothing more than keep her safe. No one else will try anything with me here to protect her."

Heather shot up to her feet, barking her shin on the coffee table and nearly sending her plate with the cheesecake on the edge tumbling to the floor. Cormac caught it just before it could slide off.

"Is this some kind of joke? Kimberly, what—"

Cormac pressed a hand to Kimberly's knee when it looked like she was about to rise, a silent request for her to stay where she was. His eyes flashed with a hint of blue-white light as he met Heather's gaze.

"No," he said, "it's not a joke. You can relax. I'm not about to sprout scales and horns."

She didn't move, but her eyes narrowed and her stutter disappeared. "That was *you* in Central Park? Was that you making all that ruckus outside the building the other day? You'd better not be thinking about flying off with my daughter, mister, or so help me I'll... I'll..."

Kimberly snorted. "Mom, please. He's not the fly-off-with-the-fair-maiden type of dragon."

"Who says I'm not?"

"Shush, you. C'mon, ma, sit down and finish dessert."

Heather slowly moved back to her spot on the couch, taking a seat on the edge of the worn cushion, never taking her eyes off of Cormac. She didn't touch the food again.

Cormac settled back and sipped at his coffee again, resuming his languid pose. He blinked the fae light out of his eyes and inclined his head. "I'm sorry if I startled you. I'm not always the most subtle of creatures."

"Understatement of the year," Kimberly muttered. With a tremendous sigh, she turned to face her mom, taking her hand. "I need him around for a little while. He's being my bodyguard. Please don't freak out—he's not going to do any magic or shapeshifting in the house."

He pursed his lips, not liking those blanket limitations, but when he saw how much that appeared to ease Heather's worries he decided against protesting. It was apparent she still wasn't pleased, but she wasn't about to forbid him from seeing her daughter, either.

Instead, he said, "If you would be more comfortable with me keeping watch from the rooftops, I don't have to stay here."

That surprised a sound out of Kimberly. "I thought..."

Heather closed her eyes, gritting her teeth. "I'm not even going to ask why you need a bodyguard. I'm not sure I want to know. But I do want you safe. Mr. Hunter—Cormac—dragon... person. I appreciate you offering to protect my daughter—but I want you to know that if you do a thing to hurt my little girl, I don't care what you are. I will hunt you down."

Kimberly just put her head in her hands.

Cormac, on the other hand, lowered his head, leaning forward on the couch and pressing a hand over his heart. "I swear to you that hurting her is the very last thing on my mind. You have nothing to fear from me."

Heather wasn't entirely appeased, but she did ease up the throttle on her patented Parental Glare of Doom. "Good. You can stay here as long as that's true. No need to catch a chill on the rooftops."

With a nod, he let a small smile slip. He wasn't about to point out that it wasn't physically possible for him to catch a chill save in the deepest winter frost. "Thank you. I appreciate that."

"You'll understand that I am going to kick you out in the morning when I leave for work. You two are not getting alone time in this apartment. She might be old enough to do what she wants with a man... or... or a dragon... but not under my roof."

Kimberly scrubbed a hand down her face. Though his expression was grave, she recognized the underlying tone of amusement, and sorely hoped her mother didn't pick up on it as well.

"Madam, I wouldn't dream of disrespecting you or your daughter in any way. You have my word, while I am here, I will make every effort to be a gentleman."

Heather said nothing, sipping her coffee and watching with narrowed eyes, her expression making it clear that she was possibly the most lethal thing in Cormac's life at that moment.

Biting her tongue, Kimberly got up and began gathering the empty dishes to take into the kitchen. Cormac reached out to help but she pushed his hand back and gestured for him to stay where he was. Heather got up as well, following Kimberly into the kitchen.

The moment they were alone, Heather whispered sharply, her tone brooking no arguments. "If I'm not in the room with him, you're not either. Comprende?"

Kimberly grimaced and nodded.

It was going to be a long week.

Chapter Thirty-nine

Kimberly was sleeping sprawled half on Cormac's lap, half on the couch. Heather had grudgingly decided to leave her be when she had passed out next to him on the couch while studying. He had no objections.

Cormac had not moved from his seated position once she had settled into a comfortable lean against him on the couch. She hadn't pulled away when he put his arm around her, which had earned a fierce look from Heather. Kimberly was so preoccupied with her textbook that she didn't notice, and it didn't take long before she was sound asleep anyway considering how exhausted she still was from the ordeal with Viper.

Monster had emerged from the shadows of the bedroom to growl at him once or twice during the night, but otherwise it was uneventful.

The sun was just lightening the sky when Heather emerged, hair still damp from the shower, to check in on them. She paused when she spotted those glowing blue eyes focused so intently on her daughter shift to take her in. The glimmer of magic in the shadows faded as he inclined his head.

"Good morning."

"Morning," She responded, tone guarded and flat. "Will you wake Kimberly? I need to leave soon. That means you, too. I assume she'll want to go with you."

As she turned away, Cormac lightly brushed Kimberly's hair back over her ear, his voice remaining low and quiet. "Heather, I know you don't approve of me or what I am, but I am sure you understand that my nature is a jealous one. My wrath may be the thing of legends, but that is because I protect what is mine."

Heather paused, but didn't turn back. "Does that mean her heart, Mr. Hunter? Because from here, I see it breaking. You sent her home in tears once. That was one time too many."

Cormac's expression remained stony, though a few fine lines formed around his eyes as they narrowed.

"I am very aware that I've erred in how I dealt with her. I never intended to hurt her."

"That doesn't mean you didn't. You come from a world more privileged than she has. You might be used to throwing things away when you get tired of them. She's not. Not even remotely."

"I know, Heather. I know what it's like for her."

"No. No, you don't. Don't pretend like you do. You don't have a clue what it feels like, hoping your clothes will make it until the next sale at the thrift store. That maybe that hole in your shoe won't get any bigger. That you'll have enough food to make it until payday without resorting to stealing ketchup packets from the fast food joint down the street to just to make some fucking tomato soup so your kid won't starve. Don't patronize me with your bullshit 'I've been in your shoes' in those thousand dollar loafers. Don't dangle things in front of her she can't really have. You hear me?"

Cormac didn't respond right away. He hadn't realized it was quite that bad for her or her mother. No wonder Kimberly had been so adamant that he help her get her job back. Not to mention that she was so reluctant to let him take care of her.

Heather was right. He couldn't begin to imagine what kind of sacrifices they must have made just to survive.

That didn't mean he had to accept it, or that he had to sit back and let them continue to struggle alone.

"I've lived long enough to know my own mind, Mrs. Wells. It's made up about her. I have every intention of helping her in any way she needs, and I have no intention of going anywhere. Not unless she wants me to."

"Yes, well, throwing your wealth at her—or at me—isn't going to buy forgiveness. I may not have any magic of my own, but believe me when I tell you that if you do hurt my baby again, there is no power on heaven or earth that would stop me from finding you and making you pay for it, and I don't mean from your wallet."

Cormac smiled, showing just a few too many teeth. "A woman after my own heart. Now I see where she gets it from."

Heather glared at him over her shoulder, clearly not convinced, then disappeared back into the bedroom, leaving Cormac to wake her daughter. He eased her up to a sitting position, lightly running his fingertips through her hair.

He had taken a great deal for granted about how he could swoop in and fix everything for her. It pained him to recall all the assumptions and cavalier attitude he'd taken. As reluctant as he might have been to admit it, Heather had a point. He had assumed he could write a check to fix Kimberly's immediate problems with money. That he could *make* her choose him to be her familiar and muscle a path for her into the coven of her choosing. Not once had he thought about letting her do any of the work herself.

Somehow he would make it up to her. He had no idea how yet, but he would.

With a little urging on his part, Kimberly woke up with a fierce ache in her neck. After a few moments spent helping her rub the twinge out, she gave in to his suggestion to take her to breakfast at the Black Star Café.

While she was getting ready, he pulled out the new cell phone he had one of his assistants pick up for him the day after he destroyed the other one, and tapped out a text message.

It didn't take long until she was ready and they were facing the day, stepping arm and arm out into the sun. Cormac didn't bother suggesting a cab or the subway. It wasn't a short walk by any means, but the sky was clear and the opportunity to spend time together without the pressure of anything more than deciding what to have for breakfast hanging over them was a welcome relief to them both.

Once they were seated in the Black Star, safely surrounded by the scent of fresh baked pastries and fae-infused coffee, Cormac did his best not to bristle at all of the attention Kimberly was garnering from the few Others also out for a bite to eat. Some were so blatant in their staring that Kimberly had resorted to hiding behind the menu Rieva dropped off when she bustled over to their table, pausing just long enough to give Kimberly a grin and a slug on the arm.

"Up and about already? You're made of tougher stuff than I thought. Try the vanilla bean pancakes with apple compote or a slice of the amaretto cream cheese coffee cake. Or both. Get something that will put a little meat on those bones, girl. I'll be back in a minute for your order."

Rieva gave a terse nod to Cormac, plopping a menu from the stack in her arm in front of him, then hustled off to the next table.

"The brown sugar, bacon and brie crescent rolls are better," Cormac said, earning a sharp look from Rieva. "On a different note, I have a couple of things I would like to discuss with you this morning."

"Oh, jeez. Please don't start up about the familiar thing again. At least let me have some coffee before we start arguing."

A smile twitched the corner of his lips. "As you wish. Actually, the first thing I wanted to talk about was what your plan is to get that job you want at The Circle. You'll have some difficulties walking in the front door to apply considering you're a sorcerer rather than a mage. Eleanor—your Professor Reed—may not have told you that they are not terribly forgiving of sorcerers treading on their turf and they'll have some brutal defensive spells triggered if you should come too close to their seat of power. Unfortunately, it would be just as dangerous for me, if not more so, should I try to step foot in their territory. You're not the only one with designs on a dragon familiar."

"Really?" Kimberly peeked over the top of her menu. "I would think you could toast anybody who tried anything you didn't like, seeing how you can go all scaly and whatnot."

"Very funny. That wouldn't help when I'm limited to this form and might end up inadvertently walking into somebody's binding circle with no room to shift."

"We can only hope," Rieva said, giving one of the spikes of hair at the nape of his neck a tug before she settled into a seat at the table with them. "Might teach you some humility, eh? Don't worry, Kimberly. I've got a mundane friend or two who might be willing to pay them a visit on your behalf."

"Thank you so much, Ms. Ke'rin!"

"Oh, please. Rieva, if anything. Or Rie, if you like. Nobody calls me Ms. Ke'rin unless they're selling me something."

Kimberly grinned. "Thanks, Rie. I thought about your offer. I'd like to take you up on it."

Cormac frowned, but didn't object, much as he wanted to. Rieva gave him a look that said she was daring him to speak up. After a few moments of tense silence, she shrugged and returned her attention to Kimberly as though nothing had happened.

"Excellent. I've got another offer to make as well. I heard through the grapevine that your mother is a waitress. I'm in a tight spot and could use another set of experienced hands around here. Do you think she'd be interested?"

Kimberly shot a look at Cormac. He cleared his throat and studiously turned his attention to his menu. Staring hard at him, Kimberly gritted out an answer through her teeth. "I can't imagine who you might have heard *that* from, but... well, I don't know. I can ask."

Rieva pulled a small sheaf of papers from the stack of menus and tossed them in front of Kimberly with a grin. "Thanks, chica. You'll be doing me a solid if you get her to apply in the next couple of days. I have an immediate opening for the right person. Now, tell me what I can get you. Let me guess—pancakes for the lady, crescent rolls for the gentleman."

While Rieva headed to the kitchen to get their food, Kimberly scanned the application and attached job description. Her eyes bugged at the hourly figure listed under the salary, wondering if it was a typo.

After a quick glance at some of the prices on the menu, she realized no, it couldn't be.

The Others were just about going to kill her with their kindness. Assuming her mother didn't first.

Once Rieva brought them their coffees, Kimberly thanked her yet again.

"Don't worry about it. That reminds me..." Rieva dug around in the pockets of her white slacks. With a jingle of metal, she withdrew a silver cross on a matching chain. It looked just like the one the changeling wore; the only visible jewelry aside from the metal collar. Tiny runes were aglow with dark blue light on the cross, sparking briefly, then fading into the metal to leave nothing but a smooth, silver surface. "This is your Get Out of Jail Free card. Wear this and you won't need him to be your babysitter when you want to pay a visit to the Black Star."

Kimberly nodded, going still as the changeling moved behind her to place the necklace around her neck, then moving to take a seat at the table with them again.

"It's keyed to you, and only you, so don't try fooling around and letting any friends borrow it. I'll know, and they'll be toast. Got it?"

"Got it," Kimberly said. "Will my mom need one?"

"If she's a mundane like Cormac tells me, then no. She might need you to show her the way since you can't exactly trust things like Urban Spoon or Google Maps to find us, but aside from that, she'll be fine."

"You think of everything, don't you?"

"Most of the time. Not always. If I were perfect, Viper wouldn't have had his shot at you." Rieva frowned, her icy blue eyes narrowing as she looked away. "He's still alive. He'll try again. As much as I like the idea of partnering with you for temporary familiar services, you'll be better off once you find a permanent solution."

It was Kimberly's turn to frown. "Did Cormac put you up to saying that?"

He snorted, fingertips drumming an impatient rhythm against the table. "Of course not. I don't need to resort to using Rieva to act as my messenger. Besides, I've told you myself that I would be your best option."

"You have, but I'm not entirely ready to trust you again. Not yet. After I graduate, then we can talk about it again."

Rieva held up a finger. "If I might be so bold as to interject, as much as this giant snake in the grass gets under my skin sometimes, he's still far and away better for you than Viper. He's one of the few of us in the Tri-State Area who has the strength to deal with him."

"I'll be okay. I know how he found me before. He won't be able to pull that trick on me anymore."

"Don't underestimate him. Sorcery might be a hardier type of magic than they tell you in that mage school of yours, but it isn't infallible, and Viper has more tricks up his sleeve than most." Rieva's icy blue eyes flared with fae light, much like Cormac's had the night before. As Kimberly recoiled, the changeling shook her head, though her expression was still full of annoyance. "I'm not angry with you. Or him, really. He chose what he thought was his best option, even if it wasn't what was best for anyone else. What pisses me off is that you're in a position I'm very familiar with. It's no wonder the few of you left were too afraid to so much as show your faces for the last few centuries. If the magi hadn't been so dead set on hunting down all the sorcerers, you might have spent these last few years learning how to use what you have to protect yourself instead of how to pretend to pass as something you're not."

Cormac growled, the sound driving a few of those seated nearby to scoot their chairs back or hide behind their menus. Kimberly gave him a pointed look. He stopped growling, but his tone was still sharp.

"Viper's desperation to follow that misguided quest of his will never work. And there's no need to scare her with stories of the past. They wouldn't have her in that mage school if they were still carrying out that witch hunt for sorcerers."

"Tell that to the one who died in that vampire's restaurant a few months ago. I heard The Circle had a hand in that."

"Wait, what?" Kimberly said, her tone flat with disbelief.

"Yeah, well, he signed his own death warrant when he started summoning demons."

Kimberly made a choking sound, her eyes bugging. As Cormac lightly thumped her on the back, she waved him off. "De-demons? D-d-did you say... demons?"

"Yes. Don't tell me they don't teach you the basic differences between sorcerer and magi powers—oh, for heaven's sake." Rieva threw her hands up, eyes rolling heavenward once she saw Kimberly's expression. "What in the hell do they think they're doing, calling that place a school when they don't even teach you your own history? I doubt you'll be figuring out how to manage it on your own, but that's what drove magi to hunt down and kill sorcerers in the past. Your kind has a talent for it that they don't. Not that they should be throwing stones, considering what they summon for familiars, but that's a subject for a different day."

Cormac's thumps on Kimberly's back shifted to soothing stroking up and down her spine as she slumped forward. "This is another reason you'd be better off with me as your familiar, Kimberly. That is a road I never want to see you walk, and I can help you learn more about how to use *your* powers instead of what the teachers at Blackhollow *think* your powers should be."

Kimberly rested her elbows on the table and put her head in her hands. Rieva *tsked*, pushing her seat back and rising with a lazy stretch that caused her white silk shirt to ride up and gave a brief glimpse of the slashes of scars on her pale skin.

"Stop pressuring the girl," Rieva said, nudging the chair back into place with her foot. She started toward the kitchen, calling over her shoulder, "Do what you feel is right, Kimberly. Don't let him—or anyone else—walk all over you. No matter what path you choose, remember, ultimately you're the one who has to live with the consequences of those choices."

Kimberly couldn't find it in herself to reply.

Chapter Forty

Though Kimberly wasn't thrilled to have Cormac tagging along for her study date with Xander, she preferred to have him by her side. After hearing that Viper was still after her and that The Circle had a hand in killing one of her kind, she couldn't help but feel nervous.

One lone sorcerer against an entire coven didn't sound like good odds. Even with a dragon protecting her, she wasn't sure about her chances. The Circle's power was legendary.

How foolish she had been for thinking they might accept her into their ranks. Even if she could join them, she was no longer entirely certain that was what she wanted. Much about what she had wanted had been called into question by the things she had learned since her first meeting with Cormac Hunter.

He moved beside her like a great prowling jungle cat, strides long, smooth, and hinting at his predacious nature. His pale blue eyes were constantly roving, taking in his surroundings, one hand pressed to the small of her back as they walked. Though she had planned to take the subway to get to Xander's neighborhood, Cormac had insisted on taking a cab instead. Though she argued that it would no doubt cost a small fortune, he had said that he would sooner walk into The Circle to be bound by the first mage to come along than be stuck with a bunch of humans in close quarters in a stinking, sticky, moving metal tube underground.

Considering his tone, Kimberly thought it best not to argue the point.

Xander's house was in Bellaire, part of Queens Village. Kimberly wasn't familiar with the area, but between the cabbie's cheerful banter and Cormac's sense of direction, they found it without too much trouble.

It turned out to be a lovely cream-colored Dutch colonial-style building with white trim and slate-colored shingled roof, punctuated by a pair of shed dormers on the second story. It immediately put Kimberly in mind of the country. The front yard was small but neatly manicured, a wrought iron fence surrounding the property and leading up to the small, gabled porch.

Xander was hanging out on the front steps when they arrived, rising with a wave when he spotted Kimberly. His easy smile faltered when he saw Cormac. Or, rather, when he saw the fierce gleam in the dragon's eyes.

"Hey, hope you don't mind I brought a friend," Kimberly said, giving Cormac a nudge in the ribs with an elbow to give him the hint to settle down. He blinked the glow out of his eyes and frowned down at her. "Xander, I know you guys weren't really introduced before. I'd like you to meet Cormac. Cormac, this is my study partner, Xander."

"Hey, no problem," Xander said, extending his hand. "Nice to meet you. Any friend of Kimberly's is a friend of mine."

Cormac cocked his head, eyes narrowing, then slowly extended his own to shake the offered hand. "Ah, yes. I remember you. Trying to drive off the wyvern with some kind of fire-based shield right in front of the museum. Foolish, but very brave. You have my thanks for keeping her safe."

Xander blinked. "You saw that?"

"I imagine anybody with Sight for a good distance near the museum did that day. Not subtle, by any means, but you've got a powerful spark."

The way Xander's chest puffed with pride had Kimberly rolling her eyes. "You're not one to talk about subtlety, mister."

"Perhaps not where you're concerned. You do seem to bring out the worst in me."

At Xander's look of confusion, Kimberly coughed. "Remember the whole dragon incident?" She hooked a thumb at Cormac and gave Xander a weak grin. "Surprise."

His eyes bugged in shock. His mouth moved, but not a sound escaped.

Cormac snorted, folding his arms. "I go for centuries with only a handful of people learning what I am but in a matter of days within meeting you it feels as though half the city knows."

"Well, if you'd stop giving off those *rawr* vibes and, say, *not shapeshift in the middle of Central Park,* for goodness's sake..."

"Yes, yes," he replied testily, "but I believe I was understandably upset—"

"Sure, fine," Kimberly replied, just as testy, "but we don't have time for this right now. Xander, can we get started? We've got a lot of ground to cover."

Though he was still a trifle shell-shocked, Xander nodded, swallowing hard a few times before leading them inside. He had already set out a pile of school books on the kitchen table in preparation for Kimberly's arrival. "Mr. Cormac, I hope you don't mind my saying, but it is *so freaking awesome* that you are going to be her familiar. I mean, a *dragon.* So cool!"

Cormac grinned, while Kimberly muttered something darkly under her breath.

"Would it be too much to ask to be introduced to any dragon friends you have? You know, anybody else in the market to be a familiar?"

Kimberly glared lasers at Xander, who was utterly oblivious. He only had eyes for Cormac at that moment, who was chuckling. "I'll be sure to tell any I meet where to find you."

"So. Freaking. *Awesome.*"

"Yes. Awesome. Hurray. Homework?"

Xander cleared his throat and turned his attention to the books. "Yes. Homework. Enchantments or summoning first?"

"Enchantments. I have the feeling summoning is going to be a lost cause for me."

Cormac watched on with interest as the two pored over their texts together. Kimberly quizzed Xander on some of the basics but it wasn't until she scanned his sample sketches of runic enchantments before she could pinpoint where he was having difficulty. It wasn't a problem with the theory. He had confused some of the ones that shared common symbols and tangled up their meanings, which naturally led to a confusion on which runes to use in which situation and a fizzled enchantment or one that ended up with far different results than he intended.

It took some time to sort out which symbols he didn't fully understand. With Cormac's watchful eye on them both, Xander was clearly embarrassed and having some difficulty concentrating on his work at first. The arrival of Xander's father's familiar, a jet black raven that flew in through the open kitchen window to land on a perch near the table, didn't help. The raven gave one look at Cormac before braining itself on the wall behind it in its haste to escape the room.

The dragon picked up the limp form of the bird. He moved to the living room, leaving the two students to study in peace, lightly stroking the bird's feathers and focusing on calming the dazed creature in his hands.

With something to keep the dragon's attention off of him, Xander managed to relax and made a greater effort to pay attention to what Kimberly was trying to show him in the textbooks.

Once they found the missing basics he needed, it was a cinch to fill in the gaps. Xander was soon rattling off the proper names and uses of the runes on the pages as Kimberly pointed them out. There were also a few things he hadn't quite grasped the theory of until Kimberly showed him an example by sketching out some of the runes herself and explaining under what circumstances she had used them.

With a little coaching on her part, Xander was soon able to rattle off a number of his own examples of how he could use each rune. It took longer than either of them expected, but his obvious relief and newfound confidence made it all worth it to Kimberly.

"So... summoning?"

Kimberly shook her head, slapping the textbook in front of her shut. "I'm not going to bother. Rieva made a good point. I've been trying to force myself to fit into the mold the school made for me instead of learning how to hone the skills I *do* have. Summoning isn't my area of expertise, now or ever. I've learned as much as I can about being a mage. It's time for me to start learning how to be the sorcerer I am."

Xander's brown eyes went wide. "That was *you?* I mean, I knew you were having some trouble but I didn't realize..."

"Oh, God, I forgot. Professor Reed said the school was sending letters to all the parents that there was a sorcerer at Blackhollow. You heard?"

"Yeah, my parents freaked out and almost pulled me out of school. If it wasn't so close to the end of the year, they might have. You sure don't act like any sorcerer I ever heard of."

One brow arched sardonically. "How many do you know?"

He chuckled. "Sorry, that did sound pretty bad. You're the first I've met. How come you're in school? I thought no sorcerers were allowed anywhere near magi."

Kimberly reddened, turning away. "My mom didn't know. Heck, *I* didn't know until Professor Reed took me aside after class in my first year and ran some tests. Dean Morrell had a talk with me after that, told me to do my best but to see Professor Reed if I had problems in any of the classes. I've been doing my best to fit in, but that's my problem—my magic isn't the same as a mage's, and it's been driving me around the bend attempting to force it. I don't regret going to school. I learned a lot. Having my diploma will help, too."

"Why?"

That gave her pause. Seeing Kimberly's look of confusion at such a seemingly simple question, Xander tapped the schoolbook in front of him.

"What makes you think having a piece of paper is going to make any of this worth your while? There can't be many covens who would welcome a sorcerer, no matter where you graduate from or who writes a letter of recommendation. Especially after what happened a few months ago. I mean, all I ever heard before was how they use nothing but blood magic and black enchants."

Kimberly frowned at him. "It legitimizes me. It shows I play by the rules. Don't lump me in with that one crazy guy. That's like saying all Muslims are violent terrorist extremists or everyone from the South is an ignorant racist or all women become crazed PMS machines during their periods or something. Jeez."

"Don't you?" he asked, eyes innocently wide. She laughed and gave him a sock in the arm. "Okay, okay! Sorry, I didn't mean it. You're right, that was a thoughtless thing to say. Doesn't mean you won't have trouble, though."

"I know. If all else fails, I'm sure Rieva or Cormac will help me find a job."

"Yes, I will," Cormac said, now leaning casually against the doorframe with the raven perched on his shoulder. Its beady eyes were locked on him, raptly attentive. "Are you about done here?"

Kimberly glanced up, giving Cormac a nod. She turned a smile on Xander. "No matter how things turn out, whether I graduate or not, we're still friends. Let me know if you ever need a hand brushing up on enchantments."

He grinned. "Sure thing. Think maybe we could celebrate graduation at the Black Star?"

Cormac shrugged at Kimberly's questioning look, making the bird on his shoulder flap its wings and squawk in annoyance. "I don't see why not. I'll make arrangements."

Xander's cheer made both of them laugh.

Cormac set the bird back on its perch and everyone said their goodbyes.

They enjoyed a few more minutes of chatting and planning the upcoming graduation party at the end of the week until the taxi Cormac called for them arrived. Xander followed them out, thanking them both profusely the whole way.

"You're both awesome. Kimberly, I'll see you at school tomorrow. Mr. Cormac, thanks again so much."

"Save your thanks until after you've met Rieva. You may not think it's such a great favor after that."

Kimberly decided not to add anything to Cormac's assessment. She knew Rieva wouldn't like having magi in her café, but she hoped between her and Cormac they could convince the changeling that Xander wasn't a threat.

A little ambitious and eager to meet a potential familiar, maybe, but not a threat.

Truth be told, she was still feeling a measure of surprise with herself over admitting out loud that she wasn't a mage and that she was ready to learn more about what she was truly capable of doing with her powers. An ember of excitement was burning, deep down, at the thought of accepting Cormac to be her teacher in the sorcerous arts.

None of her textbooks covered sorcery. The closest she had ever come were the classes on defense *against* sorcery and other arts considered black magic, and those had primarily covered minor alterations on counterspells, runic spells, and enchantments she'd already learned in other classes.

Sorcery couldn't possibly be all bad. There was no way the source of her power had anything to do with blood magic and black enchants and dealing with demons. The rumors of sorcery having no uses but to those involving forbidden arts were wrong. She had already learned a great deal about how to cast numerous harmless spells and utilize her power for defensive reasons on the fly. To have a tutor who was knowledgeable and—more importantly—*ethical* in their use of her type of magic meant so much more to her than a piece of paper that *might* help her get a job working for other magic users who were nothing like her.

They didn't have licenses for magic like hers. Not really.

If the covens wouldn't make room for her then she would carve out a place in their world for herself and prove along the way that not all sorcerers were creatures of pure evil. With a dragon by her side, she could blaze a new trail—not just for herself, but for future sorcerers, too.

Chapter Forty-one

Monday arrived too quickly for Kimberly. Much to her mother's relief, she slept in her own bed while Cormac kept watch from the living room couch, a copy of one of Kimberly's textbooks on summoning keeping him occupied in his time alone during the—in his opinion—interminably slow creep of night hours. Monster growled at him for a good portion of those hours from the safety of the hallway.

Heather surprised Kimberly by immediately agreeing to meet with Rieva to interview for a position at the Black Star. When Kimberly explained as best she could that it was a place frequented by supernatural creatures, her mother shrugged.

"They have to eat too, don't they?"

And that was that. Kimberly promised to show her the way to the Black Star after Heather got home from work later that night.

Kimberly and Cormac left before Heather, leaving her still getting ready for work as the pair made their way to Blackhollow Academy.

The sun had only been out for an hour but it was already warming up to the point Kimberly was regretting putting on a light jacket over her t-shirt and jeans. Cormac seemed unaffected in one of his usual anachronistic getups he must have magicked up for himself; a double-breasted navy vest over a plain white long-sleeved shirt paired with charcoal trousers and oxfords polished until they gleamed. She privately thought he looked like he was ready to either walk into work in 19th century Wall Street or attend a steampunk convention.

They made good time. Enough that Cormac convinced Kimberly to stop for a bite to eat on the way. At his urging, despite the butterflies staging an epic battle for dominance in her stomach, she choked down a muffin and coffee. He did attempt to get her to eat something more substantial, but that was the best she could do.

Not long after they reached the Gate entrance on 77th and Columbus, Eddie the centaur joined them.

Cormac made what he thought was a heroic effort not to scowl. Kimberly nudged him with her elbow before turning a tremulous smile on Eddie.

"Thank you again for this," she said. "I really appreciate it."

Eddie gave a terse nod, his gaze locked on Cormac. Despite the centaur's easy stance, neither sorcerer nor dragon missed the slight tremble in his knees or tremor in his arms. No doubt his fingers would have been shaking as well had he not had them buried deep in the pockets of his cargos.

"We owe you a deep debt," Eddie said, his voice low enough to hide the tremor in the words. "I consider this an honor."

Cormac gave a razor smile. "As you should."

Kimberly frowned at him, nudging him with her elbow again. "Don't be like that. He's doing me a huge favor."

"It's not too late to change your mind. I can take his place."

Eddie's sun-bleached brows rose nearly to his hairline as she got on tiptoe and tugged Cormac down enough for her to place a peck on his cheek.

"You will. After my exams. I'll see you this afternoon, all right?"

He turned burning blue eyes down to her, his smile softening. "Until then. I'll be keeping watch nearby. If you need me, come to this Gate. I'll see you."

They exchanged one more sweet, lingering kiss. The centaur looked anywhere but at them, clearing his throat in obvious discomfort.

Cormac headed back in the direction of the coffee shop while Kimberly took Eddie's hand and pulled him through the shadowed Gate between the trees lining the street. He did his best not to gape at the great bone beasts on display as they emerged into the entrance of Blackhollow, soon trailed by a number of other students on their way to class.

She was scheduled to take the familiar binding test during her second period class with Professor Lim leading Conjuration. Professor Cohen had already approved her binding circles and with Xander's help, her circle needed nothing more than a few finishing touches—and Eddie in the middle—to do her test.

Her first class of the day was Counterspells with Professor Towers. As they made their way toward his classroom a few doors down, many students stared at Kimberly and her new companion, whispering to each other behind their hands. Though she had her misgivings about parading Eddie through the halls, he gave no sign of nervousness she could detect. He kept his head high and followed her lead, his gait slow and steady.

They were almost there when Aiden spotted her from across the hall and came at her with purpose, his lip curling in a sneer. Kimberly halted in her tracks, Eddie stopping just behind her, one steadying hand on her shoulder. She didn't dare tear her gaze away from the fierce flash of hatred in Aiden's eyes.

"So," he hissed, coming to a halt uncomfortably close to her so he could use his height and frame to advantage and tower over her and block her way into the classroom. "Still think you're one of us, *sorcerer?*"

The way he said the word make her sound like some filthy thing he'd found stuck to the bottom of his shoe. Though fine lines appeared around her eyes, Kimberly didn't give any other outward sign of how much his tone bothered her.

"Get out of the way, Aidan. I have to get to class."

"You're dead when school is out. You shouldn't even be here, freak."

Eddie stepped around Kimberly to go chest-to-chest with Aiden, the centaur's abrupt show of aggression causing the young mage to stumble back. "Show some respect, boy. You're a mage, for Chiron's sake. Comport yourself like one."

Aiden looked the centaur up and down, his sneer returning. "Wow. Guess you're trading down, huh, Kim? Wyvern wouldn't have you, huh?"

260

Eddie leaned in, making Aiden flinch back. "At least she's worthy of someone willingly choosing to serve her over being forced."

With that, the centaur bodily stepped forward until Aiden was forced to get out of his way, leaving room for Eddie to open the door and wave her into the classroom. Just before it fell closed behind them, Aiden called out one last time.

"First order of business when I get accepted to a coven is to hunt your ass down, sorcerer. Watch your back."

Kimberly picked up an empty chair from a desk at the back of the classroom, though Eddie pulled it out of her hands before she took more than two steps with it. She led him to her desk, where he settled beside her to wait. He looked around with some interest, taking in the charts showing diagrams of opposing elements, a poster with a list of do's and don't's when casting counterspells on the fly, and a long, thin banner over the chalkboard at the head of the room that said, "Disruption Is How You Pass This Class."

Professor Orlando Towers entered the classroom just ahead of the first bell, humming something distractedly under his breath as he scanned the papers in his hand. He plopped the suitcase in the other down on his chair before paying a glance to the students filing in and then those in their seats, noticing for the first time that they had a visitor in their midst.

"Somebody's taking my teaching philosophy to heart, I see. Anyone care to explain the centaur? Bueller?"

Kimberly grimaced and spoke up. "Sorry, Professor T. He's with me."

The professor grinned, a flash of white against his dark skin, before he ran a hand through his graying curls. "Ms. Wells, I should have known. I'll need him to wait by my desk or outside until after you complete your test. Do you mind, Mr...?"

The centaur got to his feet, lifting the chair to set it beside the teacher's desk as ordered. "Just call me Eddie, sir. I'll wait here."

Professor Towers gave him an approving nod, and the other students watched with interest as he settled into his seat, facing the class; more specifically, Kimberly.

Aside from the centaur's eyes focused on her, she shrank down in her seat as some of the other students shot questioning looks in her direction. The professor made no fuss about Eddie's presence as the second bell rang, taking a quick roll call before passing out the written final exam for the class. Kimberly breathed a sigh of relief and threw herself into the test with a gusto, barely taking the time to read the questions before scribbling her answers.

Time simultaneously sped and crawled by for Kimberly. Fidgeting in her seat the entire time, she finished with almost 20 minutes left, and took the opportunity to skim over her work. Which was good, because she had made some truly boneheaded mistakes in the first few questions thanks to her haste. She had to resist the urge to slap her forehead every time she spotted another one.

When the bell rang, the professor shouted above the din of chatter that immediately sprang up. "Pens and pencils down, people! Turn in your test in the basket on my desk. Don't forget to bring your compact mirrors and a change of clothes for tomorrow's practical portion of the finals. In the basket, not the middle of the desk, Jones. I saw that."

Eddie followed Kimberly when she dropped off her test. He gave her a smile and put a comforting hand on her shoulder.

"I'm sure you did great. Don't worry."

She mustered a smile of her own. "Thanks. Are you sure *you're* okay? Conjuration is next."

His smile faded into a grimace. "No, but I'll survive."

His nervous chuckle prompted a little laugh out of her. She took his hand and gave it a reassuring squeeze. Some of the tension in his shoulders eased, though sensing the tiny tremors and how cold and sweaty his fingers were in hers, she pulled him into a quick hug.

"It'll be okay," she whispered.

He didn't respond, other than to return the hug, so tight she could barely breathe. It didn't take long for him to release her, red-faced and muttering an apology as he backed away. She grabbed his hand again and gave it another squeeze, waiting until he lifted his gaze from the floor. It took him a moment to let out his breath, shoulders falling as he nodded in response to her questioning gaze. He was ready.

They made their way in companionable silence to her next class, hand in hand.

Professor Lim didn't even look up from his desk as they walked into the stadium-sized summoning chamber, just snapping his fingers and pointing to her circle in the long line of those waiting for the students to claim the ones they etched with chalk last week.

Eddie took his place in the center without being asked. Kimberly moved the box of components somebody had set before her circle back against the wall and sat down behind her circle, cross-legged and facing the professor's desk.

Other students filed in, chattering with each other, their excitement and anticipation charging the air. Four years of intense study and preparation had brought them to this crucial moment.

The professor didn't budge at the second bell, still scribbling notes at his desk. Several minutes ticked by. A few whispers started up—soon silenced by the sharp *clack* of the pen being slammed on the desk.

"All right. I hear we have something different this year. Show of hands. Who is binding an earthbound familiar instead of summoning?"

It sounded more like an accusation than a question. Kimberly tentatively raised her hand; the only one in the class.

The professor gave her a sharp nod. "You'll be the quickest, then. Get to it." His voice rose, carrying to the rest of the class. "Everybody else, set up your summoning components. Points are deducted for incorrect placement."

He picked up a clipboard and strode over to Kimberly, standing uncomfortably close to observe as she got to her feet and took her position in front of the circle. She knew he was watching her with his Sight, keeping track of how she was casting and whether or not she had control over both the circle and the binding. Eddie shot her a quick smile of encouragement, which she returned with a wan one of her own.

This was it. This was the defining moment of her four torturous years at Blackhollow.

She closed her eyes and took a breath. Let it out.

The circle flared to brilliant, blinding life, a white light shooting from the symbols inside as Kimberly willed her power into them. They soon died down to dim embers, then faded entirely, though the hairs on her arms were standing on end and some of the hair on her head was lifting as if from static electricity. The circle was active; she could feel everything. Eddie's accelerated heartbeat, the sharpness of his breath, the growing panic he hoped wasn't visible to her or the professor, and his overwhelming awe of this den of magi that was so much more than he had imagined. His need to be near his herd, his desperate love and desire for Damaris, his fear that this would hurt, or that he might never see them again.

Kimberly hadn't known that she would see so much. Feel what he was feeling so intensely. His fear of her was so overwhelming that the tears pricking her own eyes from seeing what he envisioned she might do to hurt him barely registered.

How James could have stood by while knowing Sam the naga's thoughts on such a deep and intimate level disgusted her all the more, now that she had a better idea of what the bond was really like.

"Good. Solid circle. Finish the binding, Ms. Wells. We haven't got all day."

For a brief moment, she hated Professor Lim for rushing this process, but she did need to finish what she'd started.

She took one more steadying breath, then reached out with her will into the circle, and dug deep into Eddie's mind, tethering him to herself with as light a touch as she could manage.

That might have been a mistake. Something about her power called to his mind instead of his abilities.

A lifetime of memories flashed by, not her own. A warm, cozy cottage by a field. Being kissed goodnight by his mother. Running from the big kid who wanted his lunch money. Sunset in a patch of clover. The first time he rode a bike. Being stung by a bee. The first time he changed. Playing baseball with his father. The first time he ran as more than a human. The heady rush of wind blowing through his hair, on his chest, ruffling his fur and mane. His grandmother's funeral. A younger Damaris with daisies in her hair, smiling in a way that made his blood run hot for the first time.

It was too much. Too intimate.

With a gasp, she pressed deeper, past the memories, finding his source of power and focusing on it instead. It was a deep, still well inside him, calm and collected, unlike the rush of thoughts and emotions above it. That was what she latched on to. What she drew into herself, and made her own, using the connection through earth and air and body and soul the circle granted her. Things she could sense but not control so thoroughly without a circle to enhance her focus and keep the outside from interfering.

"Pass. Well done, Ms. Wells. You can take a free period in the library after you clean up your circle."

The professor must have been able to tell what she had done through his Sight. She herself couldn't say exactly how it changed, but she knew the moment Eddie was completely and utterly her creature. He would come when she called. She would know his every thought and emotion. He would obey her every command.

When Eddie opened his guileless hazel eyes and turned them on her, there was nothing but adoration visible in their depths. A calm acceptance of what he had become.

A deep and endless need to receive and carry out any order she might give him.

It sickened her.

Chapter Forty-two

The rest of the school day passed in a blur for Kimberly. The school had already made preparations for the multitudes of familiars in a tremendous waiting room opposite the summoning hall. As she attended the remainder of her classes, Eddie waited among the perches, pillows and containers set out for insects, birds, lizards, snakes, cats, mice, bats, a couple dogs, and, in one notable case, a fox. Even when Kimberly pressed, he swore that he didn't mind.

She did her best to concentrate on her tests, but it was terribly difficult with the constant tug of thoughts and emotions on the fringe of her consciousness. A constant flutter of butterfly wings seeking a way out.

By the time the last bell rang, he had come back to himself somewhat. He was up and waiting, falling quickly into step a pace behind Kimberly when she came to get him. He kept his head down, not meeting anyone's gaze. Kimberly didn't know how to ease the deep sense of shame she could sense he was feeling outside of letting him go, which she couldn't afford to do yet.

It pained her to think that Cormac *wanted* to be subjected to the same. She couldn't imagine being in his head this way—and was afraid to know what truths and memories she would find there.

When they emerged on the streets above, Cormac was waiting. As soon as he saw the expression on Kimberly's face, he bit off the greeting he was about to extend and instead swept in to wrap her up in his arms. She let out a shuddering sigh and pressed her forehead to his chest, sinking into his embrace and breathing in the scent of him. Dark and spicy, with a hint of dust and old things.

It was only when Eddie's bone-deep fear and distrust of Cormac broke through the pleasant haze of comfort that Kimberly pulled away.

She turned to Eddie, one hand still on Cormac's chest, curled around the silky fabric of his vest like a lifeline to her sanity. "Eddie, I can't thank you enough for this. Please try not to worry. See you tomorrow morning?"

His relief was obvious and intense. It was all she could do not to flinch at the feel of it.

"I'll be here. See you then."

Eddie all but sprinted away, quickly disappearing in the afternoon crowds of kids on their way home from school and the few tourists wandering outside the museum. Cormac watched him go with an undeniably hungry gleam to his eye.

Kimberly sagged with relief herself once he was gone. "Cormac, this is the most horrible thing I've ever done. Did Viper hear everything I was thinking? Does he know everything about me like I do about Eddie?"

Cormac's breath hitched, and he pulled her around to face him again. "What? Are you saying you saw the centaur's memories?"

She nodded. "Is that bad?"

"No," he replied, though he was clearly still surprised by her answer. "No, that's an aspect of sorcery I did not realize you possessed. It's a... a very unusual talent. Though perhaps I should have guessed considering your skill with illusions. That does require intrusion into the minds of the people you're fooling to make them experience what you want them to, so it's only natural you should also have the ability to gain deeper insight into your familiars. It's possible with practice that someday you might become as good at it as Rieva."

Kimberly grimaced. "If that's a roundabout way of telling me you want her to give me mind-reading lessons, I'm going to pretend I didn't hear it. What about Viper? You didn't answer me."

"Viper has enough experience with the binding process that it is likely he saw a great deal about you. Come, we're drawing attention. We shouldn't discuss this somewhere so public."

They made their way back to Kimberly's apartment in relative silence. Cormac kept his arm around her, providing the support she hadn't known she needed until it was there.

When they got back to her building, it seemed unusually quiet. No kids playing. No TVs or radios blasting. No idle chatter drifting through the paper thin drywall. In the stairwell, Cormac tipped his head up, his brow furrowing as he sniffed the air.

Once they made it to her floor, Kimberly stopped in her tracks. The track lighting was flickering, revealing a furry lump in the middle of the hall. A new reddish stain beneath it added to the myriad collection of blemishes on the worn carpet.

After the shock passed, she rushed over, picking up the limp ball of blood-matted fur. Monster gave a weak growl, one paw swatting at her face and leaving a red streak on her cheek.

"Stupid cat," she mumbled, voice thick. "What happened to you? What the heck are you doing out here, huh?"

She carried him the rest of the way, then came to a dead stop at her door, going pale.

A message had been burned into the peeling white paint.

> I HAVE YOUR MOTHER.
> YOU KNOW WHERE TO FIND ME.
> V

Kimberly sank to her knees, gaping up at the message, too shocked to make a sound. Cormac stopped behind her. His knuckles cracked as he clenched his fists, a low growl rumbling in his throat.

She took a hitching breath. Another. Monster made a low sound of protest when her grip on him tightened.

"He'll kill her, Cormac. He'll kill her as soon as he realizes I already have a familiar. Oh, god."

Cormac knelt down beside her, one hand on her shoulder as he bowed his head. "Don't panic. Give me a moment to think."

She stared up at the door, tears trickling down her cheeks as she squeezed Monster to her chest.

"Don't. It's *my* mom he took. *My* life he's screwing up. I'll get him for this. I'll make it right."

"He's too strong for you, love. I'll fix this for you."

"*No,*" she said, and he turned a sharp gaze on her for the fierceness of her tone. "I'm not going to hide behind you. He'll just find a way to come back and do something else to hurt me or my mom if I don't face him myself. Even if he doesn't, anyone else who hears about it will think I'm a pushover and take advantage of me. This is my fight. I could really use your help, but you can fight him with me, not instead of me."

A slight smile twitched at the corner of his lips. "As you wish. Have I told you yet that your bravery is one of the things I admire most about you?"

She rolled her eyes heavenward, then turned her head and swiped at the wet trail on her cheek with her shoulder. Monster made a protesting sound at being jarred. She couldn't help but cough out a short, tear-choked laugh. "Could you pick a worse time to say things like that? There's nothing brave about this. I'm scared half to death, but I have to do something."

He reached for the cat, who growled at him and flattened his ears, then leaned in to kiss her temple. They went into the apartment together, Monster growling the entire time. As soon as they reached the living room, he squirmed his way out of Cormac's arms and rushed off to hide in the bedroom.

Cormac turned back to face Kimberly, who was pacing back and forth in front of the couch.

"You are braver than you know. You're stronger than you give yourself credit for."

She shook her head and continued pacing, her shoulders hunched and eyes glued to the carpet. The fingers of her right hand absently rubbed at the cool metal oval stamped with Blackhollow's symbol, tracing the circular ouroboros. So much for being whole and protected.

"Being brave doesn't mean I'm being smart. I need to think. I don't know how much Viper knows about me, if he can see through my illusions, anything. If you have any super secret wyvern handshakes I should know about, now is the time to tell me."

He snorted, then reached out to snag her arm and pull her against him. She was wound tight as a wire, even in his arms. Placing a kiss on top of her bowed head, he held her close.

"I won't pretty the situation with lies. Viper is both vicious and cunning. He has reason to want to hurt you after what I did to him. If he sees me with you, there's no telling how he'll lash out—but he'll still expect me to be with you."

What little color was left in her face trickled away. He put a finger under her chin to tilt her head up.

"I am going to tell you some things about how sorcery works. Tricks you can use against him. Things they would never teach you at Blackhollow."

She swallowed hard a few times before managing to get out a few words. "You—you're not talking about black enchants, are you?"

"No, of course not. There isn't going to be much time for you to practice, but there are things you can do that he and I cannot. I know the theory because, like him, I have a limited grasp of sorcery as well as magecraft. If you're willing, and if you can concentrate enough to focus on what I have to teach you, it's possible—not likely, but *possible*—that we can get your mother back without bloodshed."

She nodded, then whispered in reply. "I will... I'll try."

"Good. Don't give up yet." He gave her a fierce grin, eyes lit with blue fire. "We'll do the unexpected. I have a plan..."

Chapter Forty-three

The sun was dipping toward the horizon by the time Kimberly arrived at Central Park. It was too warm for a jacket, but she was still wearing one. The same jacket Viper had curled his lip at when she had asked for his help. She clutched the edges of it tight around herself as she trudged along the path that led to Sheep's Meadow.

At this time of day, there were few people gathered on the open field. A small group of joggers cutting across the grass, a handful of kids playing a late game of Frisbee, and Viper, out of place in his trench coat, standing with his hands pocketed in his jeans as he squinted toward the sun. Kimberly didn't see her mother anywhere, and a light touch to the ley lines told her nothing; Viper was distorting the flow of energy so badly she couldn't tell what he'd done. There were traps laid, and not just for her.

The area where Cormac and Viper had torn up the green had since been filled in, and fresh sod laid down. It was greener than the rest, easier to tell when she passed it by, sending a shiver rolling up her spine. There were still some white patches on the grass where some plaster had been left behind, probably from police or zoological casts taken of the dragon and wyvern prints. Viper turned when she stopped a few yards from where he waited.

Kimberly suppressed a flinch at the sight of thick scars, still raw and healing, ringing his neck. Consider how badly Cormac had torn him up in the fight, she could only imagine what the rest of him looked like under the trench coat and jeans.

"All alone, ducks? Thought you'd have that bleedin' killjoy with you again," he said, eyes glinting with a feral golden light.

"Don't play games with me. Where's my mom? What did you do with her?"

"Nothing that can't be undone. Here's the rub. You have something I need, and I'm not going away until I get it. If you come along, no fuss, it'll stay that way."

Kimberly glared at the wyvern, squaring her shoulders and tilting her chin up. "Here's the deal, you big snake. You give me back my mom and I'll let *you* go. I'm not playing around this time."

Viper threw his head back and laughed, an unabashed guffaw that had the few other pedestrians wandering nearby looking their way. It took a few moments for him to get his breath back enough to speak again.

"Oh, you *are* a love," he said, "but enough taking the piss. You know what happens when you say no, but never let it be said I don't give you a choice. What'll it be?"

Kimberly shrugged, then tossed her nearly empty baggie of table salt at his head, closing the circle she'd drawn around him while the illusion of herself that had been keeping him preoccupied disappeared. He whirled with a snarl and slammed his fists against the invisible wall of power that confined him.

"You conniving, lippy little cow! Let me out!"

She shook her head, folding her arms and rocking back on her heels. "Not the way to win the way to a girl's heart. I didn't expect you to be this easy to fool, Viper. Are you going to tell me where to find my mom, or am I going to have to dig it out of your skull along with however many other dirty secrets are hiding in there?"

He scoffed and stepped back, throwing a punch that sent shockwaves through the circle and made her jump. "Rieva teaching you her tricks, is she? Never you fear, pet. I'm going to teach you a few of my own as soon as I get out of here."

Kimberly tapped her foot. "The sooner you tell me where I can find my mom, the sooner you can come out."

"Oh, no," he purred, yellow eyes locked intently on her own. "Night's falling. This place belongs to the werewolves at night. Doubt they'll be pleased to find a spark on their turf."

"Funny thing about that," she replied. "Turns out they like doing business with Cormac, and continuing to do so hinges on them letting me hang around as long as I need to in order to get some answers out of you. We have all night. Then you get to explain to the Moonwalkers why you're messing around with the ley lines on their turf. Some nasty spells you were cooking up for Cormac there, by the way. You have a permit for those black enchants?"

He snarled a litany of things that made Kimberly blush. With a growl, he put his hand on the circle wall and shut his eyes.

"Enough of these games," he said. Kimberly skittered back with a gasp as he shoved his hand through her circle. "I'm going to burn the spark right out of you for that, you little bitch."

Kimberly scrambled back as Viper clawed his way out of the impromptu salt circle. His glowing eyes never left her as he stalked her, each stride slow and deliberate, moving with serpentine grace around the various hidden magical traps he'd laid for both Kimberly and Cormac.

Reaching into her jacket, she pulled out a handful of the enchanted stone runes her mother had dumped out of her purse and into the kitchen junk drawer. She only slowed down long enough to use her Sight to make sure she wasn't about to stumble into one of the traps Viper had laid for her. Scattering the runes in her path, everything from walls of flame, to blocks of ice, to thick tendrils of creeping vines writhing in search of limbs to wrap around, erupted all around her. Distant screams from startled pedestrians were drowned out by the roar of flames and crack of ice.

The ones that really scared her were the ones with no such visible reaction to the re-enchanted runes she'd keyed to trigger any spells designed to seek her out. Thanks to Cormac's help, she'd figured out how to adapt a runic enchantment to match her aura so that any spells Viper had designed to seek hers in particular would zero in on the stones, tricked into thinking it was her.

Viper had laid an impressive number of traps. If she wasn't running for her life, she might have been flattered he thought he needed to lay such a labyrinth of pitfalls for her.

Then she didn't have time to think of anything, except for how much it hurt to have your ankle yanked out from under you mid-step.

She threw out her hands to catch herself. A yelp of pain escaped her as the thorny vine cut into her skin and dragged her along a sheet of ice, bringing her to a skidding stop inches from Viper's feet.

He set a thick-soled, steel-toed combat boot on her stomach, pinning her in place, and gave her a razor smile. "Well, that was a lovely bit of distraction. Let's get down to business, shall we?"

She opened her mouth, but his boot dug in, driving the air out of her lungs. He knelt down, putting his weight into her until her ribs squeaked and she gave a breathy cry of pain.

"If only," he said, voice a low purr, "you weren't such a handful. The last one wasn't like you. Grateful, she was, to be safe. To have purpose."

He leaned in, his fingers curling around her throat, choking off what little breath she was able to gasp in around the pressure on her ribs. His eyes glinted in the light of the setting sun with avaricious intent as blood trickled from the pricks left in her skin by his talon-like fingernails, unmoved by her thrashing as she struggled for air.

"When I'm done with you," he whispered, "you'll wonder why you ever fought. You'll hurt first, of course. No getting around that. But I'll see what makes you tick this time."

As her flailing weakened, her eyes glazing with impending unconsciousness, his grip on her throat lessened and he eased his weight back to his knee instead of leaning on her stomach. His fingertips brushed over the blood, smearing crimson lines over her windpipe as she panted, chest heaving and fingers twitching as her arms fell limp at her sides.

"No escaping it, I promise that."

After sucking in a few lungfuls of air, she mouthed something inaudible. Viper placed a bloody finger on her cheek, turning her head to face him so he could look into her eyes.

"Speak up, ducks. Let's hear it. Begging for mercy, is it? It won't save you, but I don't mind hearing it. Go on."

Kimberly tried again, her voice little more than a throaty whisper. "You talk too much."

He grinned, humorless, showing his teeth all the way to the gums. "What can I say? I like the sound of my own voice. We'll have more time for that later. Breathe deep, lovely. Don't want you passing out on me mid-flight."

Kimberly glared up at him, both hands wrapping around his leg—to keep him from pulling away. "We're not going anywhere. My turn, asshole."

She took the darkest, most painful memories she had been able to pluck from him in the short time he'd been stuck in her circle and shoved them to the forefront of his mind. There were some things hidden by mental "walls" he'd erected. She didn't know how to get around those. But there were enough recent memories near the surface for her to work with. Moments of terror, such as his first, awkward, painful flight, when he was forced into the air by dragon hunters before his wings had fully developed. Moments of agony, like Cormac's talons rending his wings into tatters. Muscles burning, skin pierced, scales ripped from his skin—any memory of fear or pain she could find she made him relive, over and over again, holding him tight so he couldn't writhe out of her grasp.

He did get in a few good kicks that knocked the air out of her again though.

When he fell back, the vines wrapped around her ankles withering with his failing concentration, she let him go, crab-walking back a few paces to get some distance between them. He lay where he'd fallen, gasping for air and clutching at his chest.

"You will *never* touch me or my family again, or I will make what I just did feel like a holiday. You understand me?"

Viper didn't respond, still gasping like a landed fish. Kimberly slowly rose to her feet. She folded her arms, both in an attempt to add weight to her scolding look, and to hide how badly her hands were shaking.

"Answer me, or I'll do it again until it sinks in. Do. You. Understand?"

"Yes," he choked out, so pitifully that she almost apologized then and there. It was only knowing what he had done to her mom and her cat that kept her from offering him a hand up.

With that in mind, she backed up another couple of paces in case he got it into his head to shift and exact immediate, fiery revenge.

The wyvern slowly rolled to his stomach, pushing himself up to his hands and knees. He didn't look at her right away.

"You're going to clean up the mess you made here," she ordered. "Right now. You're not leaving this park until every trace of magic mischief you planted is gone."

He gave a short nod, then got to his feet. When he looked at her, there was murder gleaming in the depths of those yellow pits of fire in his irises.

"One more thing," she said, pointing directly above their heads. "I don't think you've had the pleasure of meeting my familiar. He would have joined us, but he was a bit busy picking up my mom."

On cue, Cormac let out a deep, reverberating roar that shook the trees surrounding the meadow. Viper flinched and crouched down, his gaze turning to the circling serpent in the sky as distant screams and sirens followed Cormac's arrival.

Kimberly suppressed a sigh of relief when she saw the figure dangling from the dragon's claws.

The one part of Cormac's plan she hadn't been certain about was whether he could find and save her mother while also being able to teleport to the park in time if Viper got his hands on her. Originally she was supposed to lure the wyvern away from the traps he'd laid for them both so Cormac could have a clear path to fly to the rescue if she wasn't able to stop Viper with what she'd learned.

Kimberly lowered her voice, going deadly serious in an instant. "You caught me unprepared the first time. I will never make that mistake around you again. I promise you, what Cormac did was a love tap compared to what I'll do if you ever try to mess with me or my family again."

Viper nodded and hissed a few words. "I heard you the first time. Gods willing, this will be the last time our paths will cross."

"Good. I'll be watching."

He took a few unsteady steps back and began the process of shifting into his true form. Tendons creaked and popped, muscles expanding, bones twisting into new shapes. In the light of the setting sun, the wyvern's golden scales shone like bright sepia toned mirrors. As he stretched his wings, while mostly healed, they still looked tattered and oddly ridged in places where the scar tissue grew thick.

With a string of rumbled Words, the few spells he'd laid that had not been triggered by her runic stones were disarmed. A sharp gesture with a ribbed wing dispelled the evidence of the ones she'd triggered.

He spared her one last look with a slitted, reptilian eye, gleaming amber in the light of dusk. It didn't require words to know that he was thinking something murderous. She returned his look in kind, making her best effort not to quake under his fierce stare.

A rumbling growl and a flick of his barbed tail later, and he was aloft, drifting into the clouds. The rattling clack of Cormac's teeth snapping together followed the wyvern's retreat.

Followed by the panicked shriek of Kimberly's mom.

Chapter Forty-four

By Wednesday night, Kimberly was fairly certain she was going to lose her mind. After Cormac had saved her mother, Heather was convinced there was a monster waiting around every corner. It took a great deal of coaxing and hand-holding to get her to meet with Rieva.

That meeting was the only thing that went well. Cormac's lessons made it harder than ever for her to pretend like what she had learned over the last four years applied to her the way it did to the other students. While she was capable of mimicking a number of spells and some aspects of their arts, it had never been so clear to her that she had her own path to walk, which made focusing on the remainder of her finals a herculean task.

It was only a word from Professor Reed in the hallway on Wednesday afternoon that reminded her she needed to attend some meeting in the dean's office that night.

She was tempted to blow it off, but she needed to stick around to use the summoning hall to remove the bond she had with Eddie and replace it with a bond to Cormac. Tricking Viper into thinking Cormac was her familiar was likely the only thing that had bought her time in the Other community to prevent the wyvern or another like him from attempting to mess with her. The only reason she hadn't done it sooner was because she needed to take the time to redraw a full binding circle and figure out how to sneak Cormac in without sending a panic through the school.

She thought having the legitimate excuse to be in the school after hours would make things easy. If only.

At the end of the school day, once most of the students, save for the few who also had meetings in the dean's office, were gone, she went out to the street and led Cormac and Eddie through the portal.

It wasn't her imagination that the portal had seemed reluctant to let the dragon through, taking longer than usual to deposit them on the other side, even with her hand on Cormac to act as a temporary key to let him pass. Once they reached the other side of the gate, the runes around it were tinted an angry red, and a dull, pulsing alarm was ringing through the halls.

Eddie nearly smothered Kimberly when he threw his arms around her, looking every which way for the source of the danger. Cormac's growl drove Eddie to thrust her behind him instead, lifting his fists in a valiant—albeit misguided—attempt to protect her.

Cormac's reassurances that they would all be fine was the only thing that kept Kimberly from hyperventilating and rushing straight to the dean's office to apologize. She was too frazzled to notice the fine lines appearing around his eyes as he spotted the dragon skeleton on display only a few yards from where they stood. Assuming his low, rumbling growl was due to Eddie's overprotectiveness, she straightened and tried to put on a brave face.

Only to slump again as Professor Lim rushed into the gate room to investigate the alarm. The look he shot Kimberly made her shrink into herself, biting her lip, which had the centaur bristling and stepping forward aggressively.

Cormac ushered her aside as the professor, ignoring the centaur's posturing, stalked up to the gate. He examined it briefly before laying a hand on one of the runes to deactivate the alarm.

He then turned on the trio, demanding to know who Cormac was and what he was doing there. It took a great deal of convincing to get the professor to believe that the dragon was there for her meeting with the dean that night. It was only after telling him to check with Professor Reed that Professor Lim backed off, but with the promise to have her head in a basket if he found out that she was only there to cause mischief.

Once the professor left, Kimberly was shaking so badly that Eddie stepped in to support her as they headed to the summoning room. That drew another irritated growl from Cormac, which made Eddie tilt his head up and go tense, his arms tightening around Kimberly until she squeaked for air.

As soon as Eddie let her go, Cormac stepped in to wrap his arms around her instead, glaring at the centaur over her head. Eddie's nostrils flared and his eyes went wide, putting Kimberly in mind of a horse preparing to charge.

Between their posturing and aggressive behavior, she didn't need to worry about the magi killing her. These two would give her a heart attack first.

It was only her sharp, "Knock it off!" that got them to stop glaring daggers at each other long enough for her to shrug off their hands and take the lead, stomping her way to the summoning room.

With all of the stress and worry destroying her concentration, the spell to release the bond with Eddie backfired. Cormac had to step in and walk her through how to get the backlash giving her a screaming headache under control.

Half an hour later, Eddie was free and saying his goodbyes, Cormac was doing his best to rush the centaur out the door, and Kimberly was trying to keep her head in one piece with nothing but her hands and a handful of aspirin.

Cormac had to coax her through the steps of starting the binding spell, verbally walking her through the process until instinct kicked in and she powered the circle on her own.

When his thoughts and memories swirled through her head, she burst into tears. That sent him into a panic, thinking something was going wrong with the spell. It took her several minutes to get herself together enough to choke out that nothing was wrong.

Seeing how much he loved her, how sorry he was for everything he'd done to hurt her, and how badly he wanted her to be safe and happy had been the straw that broke her composure. Hearing the words was one thing. Feeling what he felt, knowing for the first time in weeks with certainty just how much he wanted her, and how much of a struggle it had been for him to step aside for her to make her own choices instead of acting like the possessive beast he was born to be, filled her with such a combination of love and relief, it was all she could do to finish the spell.

The immense rush of power when she completed the binding made her black out, which had Cormac in a panic all over again. As soon as the circle disintegrated, the dragon dashed forward, scooping her up in his arms and checking her over for injuries.

She flinched and opened her eyes with a gasp as he shoved even *more* power into her in an effort to heal whatever was wrong. With a flail and a wheezed "Stop!" he did.

"Oh, god, my head," she groaned.

"Are you okay?"

"No. I will never be okay. All the Tylenol in the world will never make this okay."

He snorted, running his fingers through her hair. "You gave me a scare. I thought something was misfiring on the spell."

"Yeah. Me. Owwww."

"I would ask what you saw, but I think that will have to wait. What time did you say you needed to be at that meeting?"

Her gaze went to the oversized clock hanging on the wall. With a strangled sound, she shot to her feet and pulled on his arm, dragging him with her. He snagged her bag for her on their way out.

When they reached the front office, the dean's secretary put down the scrying stone she was staring at and frowned at the two. "Kimberly Wells? You're late. Go on in, everyone is waiting."

Cormac held the door for her. She paused, fiddling with the hem of her shirt as the attention of Dean Colin Morrell, Professor Reed, Arnold Moore, and a woman Kimberly didn't know, was focused with keen intent upon her. The newcomer had steel gray hair done in a severe bun, green eyes sharp enough to cut glass, and a pinstripe suit that immediately put her in mind of old gangster movies.

Dean Morrell waved Kimberly in, though his brows shot up near his receding hairline as he noted her pallor and the man trailing behind her. Cormac briefly inclined his head in greeting to everyone, though his lips thinned when he spotted the woman in the suit. He took a deliberate protective stance behind Kimberly when she sat in the chair the dean indicated.

"Well, Ms. Wells," the dean said, "it seems you've survived the trials and tribulations of receiving an education at Blackhollow with enough distinction that you've garnered some intense interest from a very prestigious coven. You know Mr. Moore and Professor Reed, of course. Let me introduce you to Alexandra Peterson, CEO and coven leader of The Circle. And is this...?"

Cormac's eyes narrowed; the only visible sign of the discomfiture Kimberly could feel was twisting his stomach in knots. His voice, though deeper in timbre than usual, was steady. "Her familiar."

The dean rose from his seat, sketching a formal bow with his hand over his heart. "We are deeply honored by your presence, wise one." The other magi followed suit, murmuring their own greetings.

"Mr. Hunter, it's been too long," Alexandra said, nodding to him briefly before turning to Kimberly. She leaned over to extend her hand, which Kimberly shook in a daze. She wasn't sure yet if it was how upset Cormac was or the presence of the leader of The Circle that had her so out of sorts. Maybe both. "How do you do. I have heard a great deal about you from Mrs. Reed and Mr. Moore. They speak very highly of you."

"I... oh, I... uh..."

Arnold clapped Kimberly on the back, making her jump and Cormac glare at him. "She's good people. No security threat to us."

"Yes. Aside from all her other qualities I was telling you about, Mr. Hunter tells me she's got a knack for making unusual allies," added Professor Reed.

Kimberly twisted around to give Cormac a questioning look. He stared hard at Professor Reed instead of meeting her gaze.

"What do you say, Ms. Wells?" Alexandra asked.

Kimberly stared blankly, unable to process what was being asked of her around the headache pulsing at her temples.

The dean cleared his throat. "It is quite an honor for one of our students to be accepted to such an esteemed coven directly out of the academy."

Kimberly shook her head and stood up, backing toward the door. "Thank you, but I wasn't prepared—this is too much—"

Professor Reed stepped in, her no nonsense tone cutting through any building arguments. "Of course it is. We couldn't formally extend the invitation until you finished your finals, so of course you had no reason to think you would be accepted into a coven so soon."

Alexandra added, "I've had Colin and Eleanor here keep a close eye on you ever since I heard we had a sorcerer in our midst. There is a great deal I would like to discuss with you, young lady. It's quite possible that this coven's intervention is the reason you are alive at this moment, with your magic intact. If nothing else, I want you to understand how much your contributions to The Circle would mean, not only to you, but to future sorcerers who wish to train at Blackhollow."

Kimberly bit her lip, glancing first at Professor Reed, who nodded and folded her arms, making the polished school charm at her wrist—teacher's gold instead of student silver—wink in the light. Then Kimberly shifted her gaze to the dean.

His thin lips quirked briefly in a smile. There was no humor in it. "You're very lucky, Kimberly. I'm not sure if anyone has told you just how lucky you are that Professor Reed figured it out before the rest of us. She's been your silent supporter for longer than you've known."

Alexandra continued before Kimberly could fully process that statement.

"You will have the rest of the week to have the opportunity to meet with the other local covens, naturally, but—and I am speaking from experience, my dear—The Circle provides more stability, opportunity, and protection than any other coven on the eastern seaboard."

"Plus the pay can't be beat," Arnold added.

Alexandra smiled. It reminded Kimberly of a shark; it never reached her eyes. "We would like to work with you, Ms. Wells. The potential power in blending sorcery and magecraft could bring a great deal of benefit to this city."

"I'm not sure if I'm ready for a coven. Not after what I've been learning these last few weeks."

"Ms. Wells," Alexandra said, "you're not the first sorcerer to be offered a place at The Circle. We could use someone with your gift in Other relations in our outreach programs for obtaining familiar volunteers. You would be very well compensated. Think it over and let us know."

Kimberly bowed her head and wrapped her hand over the stamped coin on her wrist. It took every ounce of concentration she had to avoid flinching at the influx of Cormac's angry emotions roiling beneath the impassive surface. Flashes of his thoughts about the skeletons in the entrance of the school, Rieva's scars, and both friends and enemies lost to servitude to magi, made her stomach take a sick plunge.

When she had learned what the covens were, and about The Circle, it had been her dream to be offered a job working for them. It had been everything she thought she wanted.

Now she knew they wanted to buy her knowledge and contacts to draw more earthbound familiars into their web, to become pawns to the magi who worked there. The thought of seeing Rieva or Eddie go through that special hell of emotional trauma because of her was enough to remind her of the choice she'd made days ago. Not that it was any easier to get the words out.

This. This is what Professor Reed was talking about, she thought, her hand tightening over the school symbol until the wire band of the bracelet cut into her palm. *Growing as a person. Taking my place in the social order. But maybe that doesn't mean fitting someone else's idea of what makes me whole anymore.*

When she looked up, Professor Reed's normally impassive features were more closed than usual, her lips a thin white slash. Whatever she thought about the situation, by the growing collection of fine lines around her eyes, Kimberly guessed it wasn't anything good. Whatever her opinions, she was keeping them to herself.

Sensing Kimberly's trepidation, Cormac placed his hand on her shoulder, and she let go of the bracelet to lightly touch her fingers to his in a silent show of appreciation. Despite his feelings—so strong she couldn't possibly ignore them—he stayed quiet, leaving the decision in her hands. Though it frightened her enormously to know what she was about to do, she knew Cormac would be behind her, no matter her choice.

"Thank you. All of you. Very much."

She bit her lip, then continued in a rush, knowing there was danger here.

It was time to grow up.

"I'm afraid I can't accept your offer. I've already made plans to act as a business partner and consultant with Rieva Ke'rin. However"—she had to speak up to be heard over the gasps and sputtering—"however, I would be happy to act as a consultant to The Circle in matters of sorcery. We can discuss arrangements for my services after I finish school and officially open for business."

Cormac gave her a light squeeze, pride radiating through the simple touch. Kimberly drew strength from it, and smiled because she knew that—no matter what—she was ready to face anything as long as he had her back.

Epilogue

"I still can't believe you turned The Circle down," Xander exclaimed, his eyes aglow from all the energy rushing through his veins after his first taste of Black Star Café coffee. It had cheered him up enormously after his girlfriend had not showed up for their little graduation party. "The Circle! What I wouldn't give to have a job there."

Rieva snorted, pointing her forkful of brown sugar cheesecake at him before shoving it in her mouth. "You, little man, have a lot to learn about your own people if you're still surprised at her decision."

Xander rubbed the back of his neck, then looked around the café again, taking in the occupants for the umpteenth time since Cormac and Kimberly had brought him. Most of them didn't appear to mind his scrutiny, save for a woman with skin as white as snow and hair dark as a raven's wing who kept hiding behind her paperback every time she noticed he was looking in her direction. It only served to make him more curious about her, though at the nudge on his foot from Kimberly's sneaker he was soon brought back to the conversation at hand.

"Hey, don't sweat it. I know it probably seems crazy now, but if you ever get to feel what it's like having a fae familiar's thoughts in your head, you'll understand why I turned it down."

Cormac huffed, his hand settling over hers. "Don't tell me you're still regretting—"

"Not you, silly. Never you."

As they leaned in for a kiss, Heather lightly flicked her napkin at her daughter, though her steely gaze of disapproval was mostly for Cormac. "That's quite enough PDA, you two. Mom is watching."

Rieva smirked, her eyes gleaming with amusement. "It's best not to come between a dragon and his treasure, Heather. You'll learn these things on the job."

Heather shook her head, her eyes rolling heavenward. "What am I doing working around dragons and unicorns and what have you? I must be mad."

"Not mad, Mom. Wasn't it you who said that supernatural creatures have to eat, too?"

Rieva barked out a laugh as Heather nodded. Cormac grinned as he took another bite of cheesecake, wisely saying nothing.

Rieva turned to Xander. "Speaking of jobs, what is it you plan to do? You graduated as well, yes?"

He nodded. "I did. I'm still trying to figure that out. I took a pile of applications for covens home with me to fill out, but after hearing Kimberly's plan, I'm not sure if that's the right path for me either. I might try striking out on my own, too."

The changeling nodded sagely, as if he had said the wisest thing she had ever heard.

"Not a bad choice. You have some raw power and potential as a freelancer," Cormac said.

"You really think so?"

At Cormac's nod, Xander beamed, the pride radiating from him at the dragon's approval making everyone else smile and laugh.

"So, Kimberly," Rieva said a moment later, reaching over her plate of cheesecake to grab her mug of fae-infused coffee and lift it, "I think we have a few things to toast, don't you? To new partnerships."

Xander reached for his. "To graduating."

Heather smiled and lifted her mug. "New jobs."

Cormac lifted his mug. "New beginnings."

Kimberly reached for her mug, then paused. She looked around at her gathered friends and family. To Rieva, whose respect she finally felt she had earned. Xander, who held no other expectations than those of friendship. Her mom who, for the first time she could recall, no longer had dark circles under her eyes. Cormac, whose blue eyes were aglow with love and need for her.

With a smile, she lifted her mug, and toasted.

"To the things that matter most. The people we love, and who love us in return."

And to that, they drank, and laughed, and took the first steps toward a happy, prosperous future—together.

THANK YOU FOR READING!

To all you wonderful readers out there, I hope you enjoyed this book. Even if you didn't, please consider leaving an honest review on Amazon, Goodreads, Barnes & Noble, your blog, or wherever you prefer to leave your bookish thoughts online.

If you want to stay updated about when the next book is coming, please visit my website www.JessHaines.com and sign up for my newsletter. I promise I don't spam too often.

You can also follow me on the web:

@Jess_Haines on Twitter

https://www.facebook.com/JessHainesAuthor/

http://www.goodreads.com/author/show/3149825.Jess_Haines

https://authorjesshaines.tumblr.com/

ALSO BY JESS HAINES:

H&W Investigations Series
Hunted by the Others
Taken by the Others
Deceived by the Others
Stalking the Others
Forsaken by the Others
Enslaved by the Others

Blackhollow Academy Series
Smoke & Mirrors
Candle & Horn (Coming Soon)

Anthologies
Nocturnal
The Real Werewives of Vampire County

Standalone Novels
Silent Cravings (Coming Soon)